J.A. KERLEY

Her Last Scream

HARPER

Harper
An imprint of HarperCollins*Publishers*
77–85 Fulham Palace Road, London W6 8JB

www.harpercollins.co.uk

A paperback original

1

First published in Great Britain by
Harper, an imprint of HarperCollins*Publishers* 2011

Copyright © Jack Kerley 2011

Jack Kerley asserts the moral right to
be identified as the author of this work

A catalogue record for this book
is available from the British Library

ISBN 978-0-00-738434-1

Set in Sabon by Palimpsest Book Production Ltd, Falkirk, Stirlingshire

Printed in Great Britain by
Clays Limited, St Ives plc

MIX
Paper from
responsible sources
FSC® **C007454**
FSC
www.fsc.org

FSC is a non-profit international organization established
to promote the responsible management of the world's forests.
Products carrying the FSC label are independently certified
to assure consumers that they come from forests that are managed
to meet the social, economic and ecological needs
of present and future generations.

Find out more about HarperCollins and the environment at
www.harpercollins.co.uk/green

HER LAST SCREAM

J.A. Kerley worked in advertising and teaching before becoming a full-time novelist. He lives in Newport, Kentucky, but also spends a good deal of time in Southern Alabama, the setting for his Carson Ryder series, starting with *The Hundredth Man*. He is married with two children.

Also by J.A. Kerley

To the amazing Miz Linda Lou and
the deliciously evil Nurse Jane
(here insert the author's wicked laughter)

As always, I thank the folks at the
Aaron M. Priest Literary Agency and
HarperCollins, UK, who take my words
and make them better.

1

Treeka Flood counted the Beef-a-Roni cans in her shopping buggy for the third time, *one, two, three*. She rounded an aisle without noticing, busy counting jars of tamales, *one, two, three*. Boxes of macaroni, *one, two* –

Treeka froze. Counted again, *one, two* . . .

Treeka saw the final macaroni box under the packs of tortillas – *three!* – and sighed with relief. The macaroni was Mueller's Large Elbows, the only kind Tommy would eat, saying smaller sizes felt "wormy" in his mouth. Count the tortillas again to be safe: *One, two, three*. There had to be three of everything: One for the meal, one for the back-up in the pantry, at least one more for the food cache in the basement. If Tommy saw something missing, she'd have to wear the big sunglasses.

Checking her list, Treeka absent-mindedly wheeled to the next aisle. Sardines in mustard sauce. *One, two, three.* Bumble Bee Tuna in oil . . .

Last month Treeka had forgotten to buy more canned hams after Tommy used two on a fishing trip. He'd noticed the open shelf space – he looked for infractions – and Treeka had to wear the big sunglasses for a week to hide her blackened eyes.

At the end of the aisle Treeka saw chubby, red-haired Brenda Mallory chattering with a supermarket employee. Treeka froze and angled her face away, becoming an anonymous shopper checking a label. Mallory was Treeka's apartment-building neighbor from two years back, before Treeka'd gotten married and moved from Denver to the ranch near Estes Park, Colorado.

Mallory pushed her buggy toward the checkout lanes and Treeka relaxed. Talking to Brenda would only cause trouble. And what could Treeka possibly say when Brenda asked about Treeka's new life?

Treeka counted every item again, then backpedaled one aisle, expecting to see Tommy. The only inhabitants of the corridor were a college kid with a six-pack of Red Bull and a tall and white-haired elderly lady pushing a buggy.

No Tommy.

Panic slammed Treeka's heart and she yanked the buggy back another aisle. Tommy wasn't there, either. How had she gotten so far ahead?

Oh Jesus, please no . . . where is he?

There! Tommy jogged past the far end of the aisle, eyes knifing down the lane, his hands bunched into fists. He glowered up at the aisle number: Six. Tommy must have been back in five when Treeka somehow wandered ahead to aisle eight.

Oh shit oh shit oh shit . . .

Tommy strode to Treeka, the metal plates on his cowboy boots ticking like a bomb. They were alone in the aisle and he grabbed Treeka's arm. "Where were you?" he hissed, pushing back his gray Stetson, cold green eyes daring Treeka to lie. "Where did you go?"

Treeka let her mouth droop open, trying to appear puzzled. Dumb was the best place to hide.

"I've been right here, hon," she said, lifting a box of crackers like she'd been in aisle six all the time. "Didn't you see me? I got my shoppin' dress on." Tommy made Treeka shop in a bright yellow dress because it made her easier to see in a crowd.

Tommy slapped the crackers to the floor. "I goddamn asked where you were," he repeated. "You too stupid to understand English, or what?"

Treeka laughed like Tommy was making a joke. "I been here all the time, babe," she said, stooping to retrieve the crackers. "You must have been going around an end same time I was and we crossed past each other."

Tommy studied the items in Treeka's buggy, then did something to run blades of ice down Treeka's spine: He smiled. It was the same smile Treeka had fallen in love with twenty-six months ago, wide and thin-lipped and brimming with teeth. But now Tommy's smile terrified her; it meant the snakes in his head were heated up and moving.

"What's this?" he asked, reaching into the buggy and tapping a can of tuna. Treeka instinctively started counting tuna cans. *One, two* . . . Then she saw what was wrong.

Oh Jesus no. Oh shit.

"Tommy . . ." Treeka whispered. "I didn't mean to –"

"It's tuna, Treek. From aisle eight, right? How many numbers is five from eight?"

"I got ahead of myself, Tommy," Treeka explained as her breath ran out. "I thought you w-was right behind me."

"I asked how many numbers from five to eight, Treek?"

"Th-three." Treeka felt her heart pounding in her chest.

"How close do I tell you to stay to me?"

"One aisle, Tommy. But I thought you were right behind me. An' I got on my shopping dress."

Tommy's eyes tightened into slits. "You thinking about running off, Treek? Finding some lesbian to live with? I saw one over by the produce."

Treeka shook her bright, artificial curls. Keeping her hair looking like Taylor Swift's bouncy 'do took an hour a day, but it was the style Tommy demanded. "Jeez, Tommy. I dunno where you get this stuff. I just got ahead of myself. Gimme kiss, babe."

Treeka puckered. Tommy stared. "You lied to me, Treek. But the tuna told the truth."

Treeka tried another smile. "You're so smart, sweets.

Like a detective. But I wasn't lying, I forgot where I was."

Tommy grunted as an elderly woman entered the aisle, pushing her buggy toward them. Up close the woman didn't look so old, mid-sixties maybe, dressed in a blue sweat suit and pink running shoes, smooth in her motions, like she really did run. The pair fell silent as the woman walked by, shooting a look their way. When she was past, Tommy's hand lashed out to the soft skin beneath Treeka's breast, pinching it between thumb and forefinger.

"N-no, Tommy. Please . . ."

He squeezed hard, a hot burst of instant agony. Treeka clenched her teeth. If she made a sound he'd pinch again. If she stayed quiet, one would be all she'd have to endure. After several seconds Tommy's hand fell away and Treeka let out a gasp.

A surprise voice from the side. "Excuse me, miss. Are you all right?"

The older woman had seen or heard something.

"I'm fine as I can be, ma'am." Treeka forced a smile, thinking *Please go away, lady. You'll only make things worse.* "My dear hubby and me is jus' talking."

The woman gave Tommy a flinty appraisal. "You don't sound fine, miss," she said. "You sound like you're about to cry."

"Oh no, ma'am," Treeka said. "That's how my voice always is."

Tommy got tired of the woman. "Get the fuck out of

here, you old dyke," he snarled. "This here's private bidness between a man and his woman."

The woman nodded to herself like a judgment had been confirmed. "I'm going to find the manager," she said, looking at Tommy like something a dog had left on the floor. "I know what you are, mister. I know exactly what you are."

The woman left her buggy in the aisle and strode toward the store's office. Tommy grabbed Treeka's forearm and yanked her toward the exit. "Look what you've done to me this time," he whispered as they crossed the parking lot. "Now I gotta teach you a real lesson."

2

Spring in coastal Alabama is a violent time, weather-wise. Two inches of tumultuous, lightning-driven rain an hour is not unusual, nor is it rare for blue to rule the sky minutes thereafter, as if all has been forgiven. Gulls return to the air and the whitecaps on Mobile Bay settle into a mild green chop beneath warm breezes built for sailing.

I drove to work from my beachfront home on Dauphin Island, thirty miles south of Mobile, still stuck in the first movement of the meteorological symphony, purple-black clouds laced with bolts of jagged lightning and rain sweeping down in roiling sheets. Smarter drivers took shelter in coffee shops and donut joints. I was doing fifteen miles an hour, squinting through my windshield and trying to recall when the wiper blades were last replaced.

Three years ago? Four?

A semi raced in the opposite direction, sloshing another gallon of water over my windshield. I peered into rippling gray and slowed to ten miles an hour. My cell phone rang and I pulled it from my jacket pocket, the word HARRY on the screen. Harry Nautilus was my best friend and detective partner in the homicide division of the Mobile, Alabama, Police Department. Harry kept me grounded in reality and I kept him . . . I'm not sure, but it'll come to me.

"I'm at the morgue, Carson," Harry said. "There's a situation here."

I was ticking my head side to side like a metronome, trying to see through the split second of clear behind the wiper blade. "What is it?" I asked. "The situation."

"Just get your ass over here, pronto."

"My wipers are shot, Harry. I'm stopping."

"You and that damned ancient truck. Where you at?"

My truck was old but not ancient, perhaps suggesting antiquity by being the color of the pyramids, roller-coated with gray ship's paint. Say what you will about aesthetics, I've never been bothered by rust or barnacles.

I said, "I'm just off the DI Parkway near the city limits sign. I'm pulling into the fish shack."

"Hang tight and I'll send the cavalry."

"The what?"

Harry hung up. There was a coffee shop past the fish restaurant, but getting there meant crossing twenty feet of open pavement. Lightning exploded above and I sank lower in the seat.

A minute passed and I heard a howling. I thought it was the wind, until it turned into a siren, followed by lights flashing blue and white in my mirror. I sat up as a Mobile police cruiser pulled alongside. I wiped condensation from the window with my sleeve and saw a face on the driver's side, a hand gesturing me to lower my window.

Rain whipped in and a pretty young black woman in a patrol cap and uniform yelled, "Stay on my bumper. But not too close, right?"

I was perplexed for a three-count, then saw the plan. The cruiser whipped away and I pasted myself fifty feet off its bumper. When we hit the highway another set of flashers slid in fifty feet behind me. I was bookmarked by light and sound and we blasted toward the morgue at perilous speed, though I can't say how high exactly, never taking my eyes from the leading cruiser, my sole point of navigation.

Fifteen white-knuckled minutes later our impromptu caravan rolled to the entrance of the morgue, more correctly the pathology department of the Alabama Bureau of Forensics, Mobile office, a squat brick building by the University of South Alabama. I spent a fair amount of time in the morgue for two reasons; one was its ongoing collection of murdered humans, the other being the director, the brilliant and lovely Dr Clair Peltier, was my friend. Take that as you wish, you can't go wrong.

I pulled beneath the portico and parked beside the nearest NO PARKING sign. The cruiser protecting my flank sped away, leaving only the vehicle driven by the young officer. I waved thanks as she stopped on the far side of the portico, rain drumming across her cruiser.

The driver's-side window rolled down and the pretty face frowned at my trusty gray steed. "You really ought to get rid of that truck, Carson," the woman called through the downpour. "You've had it for what – eight years?"

Her familiarity took me aback. "Almost nine," I said. "How did you know how many –"

"Carson Ryder . . ." she said, tapping her lips with a slender finger. "Started in uniform at age twenty-six, made detective at twenty-nine – a record. Paired with Detective Harry Nautilus from the beginning, first as mentor, then as detective partner. An avid swimmer, kayaker, angler."

I smiled at the recitation, common knowledge in the department.

"A man whose intuition often battles his logic," she continued. "At times a problem, but usually working out for the best."

"Pardon me?" I said.

"Some might call you a womanizer," she added, a puckish twinkle in her eyes. "But that's too harsh. Better to say you're a lover of beauty and a secret fan of poetry, mainly Cummings, Dickey, and Roethke."

My mouth was now open so wide that in the rain I might have drowned. I was sure I'd never seen the face before. And she was too pretty to forget.

"We've met?" I said, flummoxed by the surreal exchange.

"Don't you remember holding me in your arms, Carson? Or the time we kissed?"

"Uh . . ."

Her radio crackled with a dispatcher's voice. She canted her head to listen, then looked at me with a sigh. "Lightning blasted out traffic lights along Airport Road," she said. "Time to go. But I expect I'll see you soon enough."

Her window rolled up and she disappeared into the gray. I stared into the rain before recalling the building at my back and the reason for the wild ride that had started my day.

I'm at the morgue, Harry had said. *There's a situation . . .*

Giving a final glance to the space where the woman's cruiser had resided, as if the drenched asphalt held a clue to her identity, I turned and pushed through the door to the morgue, finding – as always – a dry and cold atmosphere spun through with molecules of violent death and human despair.

3

Most folks checked in at the morgue, but I was such a frequent visitor the receptionist signed for me. A rubber stamp with my name would have been even easier. I continued to the main autopsy suite, seeing Harry in a corner beside forensics chief Wayne Hembree, a moon-faced black man with the build of a scarecrow beneath his limp white lab coat. Clair was leaning against the wall with a phone to her lovely cheek, talking about DNA. She looked up, winked one of the arctic-blue eyes, and returned to her conversation.

Hembree tossed a sheaf of pages on a lab table and walked to the center of the room, Harry on his heels. My partner was subdued, fashion-wise, his pink linen jacket riding an aloha shirt of hula girls strumming ukuleles. His pants were something between puce and plum; pluce, perhaps.

We met at a gleaming autopsy table holding a woman's body, slender and well proportioned and with the tightness of youth, mid-to-late twenties or so. Her hair was dark and her skin olive, an impression of Filipino perhaps, or Hispanic. There were abrasions on the legs and arms, probably rope burns. The hands were dirty and bruised and I saw fingerprint ink on the digits. The breasts looked odd, purpled and akilter. Someone had laid a white towel over her face.

"Thanks for sending the escort," I told Harry.

He nodded toward the body. "It's gonna be one of those days."

"Who am I looking at?" I asked.

"Right now it's Jane Doe," Hembree said. "I'm running prints through the standard databases. Nothing so far."

Clair dropped the cell into the pocket of her green scrubs, the only woman I knew who could make the formless garment resemble a Versace gown. She stepped to the table and slipped the towel away. The woman's head was bald, but I stared at the face.

"No eyes," I said, realizing it was a ridiculous thing to say.

"Probably removed with a scooping tool," Clair said, her voice devoid of emotion. "Could be something as simple as a spoon."

"What happened to the breasts?" I asked.

"Contusions. They appear to have been singled out for punishment."

"Tell me about the hair," I said. "Why is she bald?"

"I found a few small nicks. Not a razor; electric clippers, maybe."

Hembree said, "A skinhead, maybe?"

"No tats on the back?" I asked Clair. "No tramp stamp?" A tramp stamp was street slang for a tattoo across a woman's lower back, generally but not always associated with women of low stature, either as perceived by themselves or others.

Clair shook her head. "One postage-stamp-sized tat on her shoulder blade, a butterfly." Hembree and Clair rolled the shoulder up and I saw the tat, a blue-and-orange butterfly that could have hidden beneath a quarter. The artwork was bright and delicate, the style and positioning of tat consistent with those seeking the current hipness of body art without going for the full Winehouse.

"With skinheads it's skulls, swastikas, the usual Aryan-supremacy garbage," I said, nodding that I'd seen all I needed. "Not Lepidoptera."

"I also found a horizontal band of mucilage twenty-one centimeters below her navel," Clair said. "Maybe the killer tried taping her to the chair and went to rope when the tape didn't hold."

"Where was she found?"

Hembree said, "The city dump, sitting at the edge of a sea of garbage. The body was tied upright in a chair, like staring out into the dump."

The information made a surreal picture in my head. "Killed there, you think?"

14

"Dead at least a day when she was bound to the chair, Carson. But the ligature marks on her wrists and ankles are scabbed over in places."

"She was held prisoner."

Clair nodded. "For at least two days before being killed."

I stared at the body, seemingly in good health and attractive, if you ignored the red hollows below her brows and the contused breasts. "Who caught the call?" I asked.

Harry said, "Tate and Bryson. But . . ."

"But Piss-it has ownership now," I said, not happy with the thought. Harry and I were members of a special unit named PSIT, the Psychopathological and Sociopathological Investigative Team, *Piss-it* for short. We were the sole members, calling in specialists as needed. Murders appearing the work of severely damaged psyches landed on our desks.

We retreated to Clair's office to wait out the postmortem. On her desk was a floral vase the size of a half-bushel basket, dwarfed beneath botanical pyrotechnics: roses white and pink, sprigs of dogwood and azalea, camellias, sunflowers the diameter of saucers. Clair's hobby was gardening. I figured since she spent her days with death, coaxing life from the ground was another aspect of her exquisite balance.

Harry and I opened briefcases to review other cases and drink first-rate French roast coffee with chicory. Clair paid the difference between primo coffee and the budget brands of most official venues. Since divorcing old-money

15

Zane Peltier years ago, Clair was fixed for life. She worked because she loved her profession.

I was into my second cup of coffee when I noticed Harry studying me.

I held up my hand. "Only death will keep me from attending your family reunion on Saturday. I'll do it even though we're not related, I'll know almost no one there, and it's way the hell over in Mississip—"

I was interrupted by Clair, stepping into her office and scowling at my shoes on her desk. I looked at my feet with *how-did-they-get-there?* surprise before dropping them to the floor.

"Did you determine when the eyes were removed?" I asked.

"Three to four days back." She paused. "It's the same timeline I'd put on the breast damage."

I considered what Clair's words meant. "Kept as a prisoner for five to seven days, beaten, her eyes removed, then left alive for two or three days. Is that it, Clair?" I kept my voice even, forcing down the rage at what human beings could do to one another.

"Don't think about it, Carson," Clair said quietly, her hand coming to rest on my shoulder. "Like I'm trying to do."

4

Treeka lay in bed holding a bag of frozen peas to her nose and right eye, the malleable packages conforming to a bruised face better than ice cubes. Tommy had beaten her yesterday after the scene in the grocery, her torso mostly, where the marks didn't show. But this morning, when he'd started goading her, calling her a lesbian, she'd screamed out, *Why do women scare you so goddamn much?*

He'd lost it completely and started punching her face, howling he'd kill her. She'd done like usual, curling into herself until the storm passed, grateful to have again made it through alive.

Treeka stared one-eyed at the ceiling, feeling melt-water mingle with her tears. She watched her shameful history parade across the ceiling like a low-budget documentary: molested by her uncle from age nine until he died drunk in a car crash when she was thirteen. Her first high-school crush, Carl, slapping her when she looked at other guys, Treeka the one to apologize. She'd won a two-year nursing scholarship, her then-boyfriend, Lane, forbidding her to attend school, Treeka agreeing, terrified of losing Lane's angry love. She lost it anyway when Lane ran off with Treeka's best friend, but by then the educational opportunity had passed and Lane had drugged away all the money she'd saved cleaning rooms at a local motel.

She'd vowed to never go out with men again. Never, ever, no-way. But after two years, Tommy appeared, and Treeka figured she could be forgiven for thinking he'd been sent by God. They'd met at church, a Pentecostal outpost in a trailer north of Estes Park, Tommy a thirty-four-year-old deacon, Treeka twenty-five and the guest of a friend from the Wal-Mart where they worked as cashiers.

Tommy'd been kind and gentle through the three-month courtship, shy even. It had been his idea that they not be intimate until after the wedding. The newlyweds went to Branson for the honeymoon, renting a cabin in the Ozark Mountains. They'd got tickets for a show at Presley's Country Jubilee, and Treeka had proudly put on a new dress: scarlet red, scoop-necked, and three inches shorter in the hem than she usually wore – it was a honeymoon, after all.

"No," Tommy said, scowling like she was selling herself under a light on a city street corner. "You get something else on, now."

It was a command, the first of many.

The movie in Treeka's head fast-forwarded to yesterday's beating and she shut off the projector. Flipping the bag of peas, she replaced it on her swollen eye; another day for the big sunglasses. She figured Tommy made her put them on so he didn't have to look at what he did, not that he'd see anyway, passed out in the hammock out back and snoring.

He'd wake up soon enough. He always woke up.

But Saturday was coming, and since it was a fishing day Treeka would get hours of blessed relief. Several times a month Tommy joined buddies from Estes Park and they'd fish a lake by Silverthorne, over fifty miles away. The earliest he'd ever gotten back was nine at night. Even better, the mountains blocked cell reception and he couldn't call and check on her. This time, with the fishing trip falling on a Saturday, Tommy would be staying out even later.

Treeka planned to hop a bus and head to Boulder, to that place by the University of Colorado. She seen it when she'd snuck into Boulder three weeks back, a plain brown house on a block populated by student housing, a store selling earth-friendly sandals, a bike shop, and a dark-windowed bar.

It was the sign that had riveted her attention:

WOMEN'S CRISIS CENTER OF BOULDER

Treeka had walked around the block five times before

finally screwing up the courage to walk to the door. Reaching for the door knob, her breath had stopped in her throat and she backed away, looking side to side, knowing it had been a trick and she'd see Tommy's big loud truck roaring up, him knowing about the trips to Boulder and waiting for her to make her move.

"I see every thing you do, Treek. You can't get away from me . . ."

But that night, when Tommy stumbled back to the ranch past midnight mumbling about a cooler full of fish that needed cleaning, it seemed he hadn't seen a thing.

A center for women? Treeka wondered, holding the peas to her face. What could it mean? What did they do?

5

Harry and I spent the next few days working the Jane-Doe-from-the-dump case – we'd started calling her Butterfly Lady – but the body remained unidentified. Though we'd put out a description via the news media, the only calls had been from earnest folks wanting to help but having little to add, and cranks convinced it was the work of space aliens or terrorists.

We did get three confessions from men who were at the department within hours of the first broadcast. Sad, fidgety men who showed up whenever a woman died violently and we were seeking suspects. Their confessions were made with angry eyes and hands clenching and unclenching as they described their victim's last minutes.

"*I killed her, Detective Ryder. She was a conniving, castrating bitch and had to die.*"

"*How did you kill her, Randy?*"

"*I used a knife. A hunting knife with a serrated blade. I told the slut she'd never be able to spit on me again and I stuck that knife in her filthy heart.*"

"*How many women have you confessed to killing in the past decade, Randy? Eight? Ten?*"

"*I really killed this one, Detective Ryder, I swear I did. She was too dirty to live.*"

I never understood what made these men confess, except they seemed desperate to explain evil things women had done to them and describe the killings in lavish, though incorrect, detail. They made Harry angry and they made me sick, but there was nothing to do but listen until assured it was the usual situation, then show these babbling and broken machines the door, gone until the next grisly murder of a woman.

Saturday arrived: Harry's family reunion. We drove to a church nestled in the pines in backwoods Mississippi. Beside the white church was a picnic area on gently rolling land, folding tables set in the sun-dappled shade of live oaks and sycamores. A line of slash pines ran to a distant grove.

I got crushed in the iron-hard hug of Harry's older sister, Molly, a big-boned woman with a yodel for a laugh and a way of making you feel like her day wasn't complete until you stepped into it. Like Harry, Molly went for color, her dress resembling a canvas from one of Jackson Pollock's happier days. We joked around until Molly went to yodel and hug some new arrivals into submission. I leant against the church to sip a cup of overly sweet lemonade and cast an eye over the laughing, backslapping throng, the loose-limbed gaits of relaxation, eyes-wide joy at meeting others in the clan. The children were happy and polite, the families tight, everyone exuding an air of comfort in their skins which, taken as a whole, seemed prosperity in its richest form.

"Hello, Detective Ryder. I heard I'd see you here."

I spun to see the young cop who had led me across Mobile like I was welded to her rear bumper. The uniform had been traded for white hiking shorts and a safari-style blouse with bright mother-of-pearl buttons. Long café au lait legs ran to sleek pink-and-red cross-trainers. Atop her short natural was a blue ball cap stating *MPD Police Academy*. My mind raced to place the face, again drawing a fat blank. After our bizarre meeting I'd figured on looking up my preternaturally informed rescuer, but the savaged woman from the dump had stolen my time.

"You're sure we've met?" I said. "Before the race to the morgue?"

"Positive."

"You made mention of us, uh, kissing," I said. "You were making that up, I take it?"

"We kissed and hugged," she proclaimed. "It was lovely."

I stared, feeling like I'd been pasted in a Dalí painting. A strand of handholding children raced past, stretched out like a line, and it hit me that a family reunion was a string that led into the past. I studied my companion, searched my memory, and finally saw mayhem centered around a pin-the-tail game taped to a wall.

"A party on Baywell Avenue," I laughed, relieved at finding the answer. "Two dozen screaming kids running in circles and wearing party hats. You wore a princess-model topper, a pink cone and veil."

She grinned. "You kissed my hand, gave me a hug, and said I was the prettiest princess ever."

"Forgive me if I don't recall your name, Princess . . .?"

She extended her slender hand. "Reinetta Early. Reinetta Nautilus Early. It was my twelfth birthday party. Uncle Harry stopped by and brought you along. You were in uniform and couldn't stay because you had to get back to work."

"Now it's making sense," I said. "The other stuff you mentioned . . ."

Intuition v. logic. Poetry. The ladies.

She smiled. "Must have been overheard at the Police Academy. Or elsewhere."

"Like good ol' Uncle Harry?" I suggested.

She did the lip-zip motion.

"Harry never mentioned a niece in the department," I said.

"He was respecting my wishes. Our family connection might lead to me getting special treatment."

It took me aback. Most recruits with kin in the department would have used the connection like a backstage pass. I was getting to like this kid when the object of our conversation walked up, slapped a hand on my

24

shoulder, and presented me with a can in a foam insulator bearing the logo of the New Orleans Saints. Beer, bless my mind-reading partner.

"I discovered your secret, Harry," I said, aiming the can toward Reinetta Early. "An empire of Nautilae is usurping the MPD."

"You had to find out sometime," Harry said, sotto voce. "Just keep our kinship under your hat. Rein's afraid it'll –"

A chubby, jolly woman by the picnic tables yelled "*Rein!*" and beaconed our comrade to view a photo in one of the many albums scattered across the white tables.

Reinetta Early touched my hand, said, "See you gentlemen later." She winked and spun away.

"You could have told me," I said to Harry, "that you had a niece enrolled at the Police Academy."

Harry looked into the trees, shaking his head.

"I probably would have, Carson. If I'd known about it myself."

6

It was Saturday, sneaking-into-Boulder-day. Treeka crouched in a stand of trees beside the two-lane highway until she saw the bus cresting the hill in the distance before jumping out and waving it to a stop.

The door closed and Treeka made a fast check of the passengers, though she had scant fear of recognition: the only people Tommy allowed Treeka to befriend were bible-thumpers from their church. Boulder had stores that sold marijuana, restaurants that didn't believe in meat, and couples of the same sex kissing right out on the street. Everyone at the Parch Creek Pentecostal Church held that the Devil had poked his finger up through his roof one day and it broke through at Boulder. The congregation went to Denver instead, which was bad, but not a vent pipe from Hell.

Treeka made her way to a seat, happy for the locale's

26

wide-ranging public-transportation system. Tommy had sold Treeka's red Corolla one month after the union, saying too many bad things happened to women out on their own. After three months of a straitjacket existence on the eighty-acre ranch, Treeka had steeled up her courage and caught a bus into Boulder, eighteen miles away.

Today would start like usual, Treeka figured. She'd wander Pearl Street, enjoying the happy faces of the tourists and listening to the street musicians playing guitars and trumpets and didgeridoos, long Australian horns with low, sad voices. Or she'd walk up to the Hill, the university area, and watch the faces of young college girls, their eyes bright and hopeful.

It was on the Hill where she'd seen the words on that little white sign outside the brown house:

Women's Crisis Center of Boulder

Can I do it today? Treeka wondered as the trees flowed by the side of the bus. *Can I walk to the door, turn the knob, and step inside?*

"So your very own niece joins the academy, goes through all the training, and becomes a Mobile cop?" I asked Harry. "All without telling you?"

He rolled his eyes. "She was in Oxford, last I'd heard. Going to the University of Mississippi, pre-law. Then I find out she got an address in Mobile to fulfill residency requirements, applied to the academy. Naturally, I discovered all this after she was on the force for two weeks."

"Congratulations. You must have been a helluvan influence."

He grunted. "She's a kid, Carson. She should be in college."

Harry looked across the lawn. I followed his eyes to Reinetta Early. There was something coltish in her motions, gangly but graceful, framed in laughter as she carried a bowl of salad to a table, chattering with the women. But she seemed to appear a lot older to me than she did to Harry.

Harry was summoned by a group of men beside the horseshoe court for arbitration on a leaner. I found a sturdy live oak to rest against, sipping beer and watching women trade photos, pointing at the pictures with bright smiles on their faces as snippets of conversation blew past.

". . . *look how she's grown in just a few short . . .*"

". . . *Teri and Shaun's new house in Memphis has a . . .*"

". . . *so handsome in his graduation gown. Where will he . . .*"

My childhood photos were mainly in my mind, portraits dark with tones of fear. My father was a civil engineer who specialized in building bridges, an irony, since his pathological insecurity and anger cut chasms between everyone in our family. My mother was a mouse of a woman who pretended to a storybook life; when my father began his insane rants she would shuffle to her room to sew wedding dresses, the grinding of the sewing machine obscuring sounds beyond her door.

My brother Jeremy, six years my elder, was my hero, loose-limbed and blond, with a piecing intellect and gentle demeanor behind his blue eyes. But he bore the brunt of our father's savagery and, at age sixteen lured the man into a nearby woods and tore him apart with a knife. Jeremy escaped detection and went to college, but was later implicated in the horrific murders of five women. Judged insane, he had been institutionalized, escaping under mysterious circumstances three years ago.

I was mulling dark thoughts when a voice arrived at my shoulder, Reinetta Early.

"I suppose Harry's been telling you what a screw-up I am, moving to Mobile and joining the police force instead of continuing with school."

I took the diplomatic route, smiling and saying nothing.

"He thinks I'd have graduated college, spent two years as a female Clarence Darrow, then ascended to the Supreme Court. The truth is I'd be sitting at a desk surrounded by a gaggle of other lawyers."

"Gaggle?" I asked. "Is that the collective?"

She stuck a finger toward the back of her throat. "*Gag*-gle."

"Studying law's not for you?"

"When I was growing up Harry told me a hundred stories about being a cop. It was like watching heroic movies in my head: good guys and bad guys, the good guys not always winning. Starting eight or so years back, you co-starred in the movies. After seeing you guys in my mind for so long, everything else seemed tame."

"The money's better in lawyering," I said.

She laughed. "Then I'll be a cop a few years, write a book, become the next Joseph Wambaugh." The laugh faded, turned serious. "I don't think you know my history, Carson. If you did, you'd realize I have a lot to pay back. Being a damn good cop – like Harry – is the best way I can think of to return all I've been given."

I had no cogent reply. Reinetta Early's smile returned. "So whatever Harry thinks of my decision, it's done and he'll adjust. I just don't want to become known in the department as Harry's niece, *that Nautilus girl*." She gave me a lifted eyebrow. "Can I trust you'll be discreet about my secret?"

"Mum's the word," I said, zipping my lips, thinking *Is this a bad decision?*

7

The reunion ended two hours later, wrapped and bagged for another year. I said my farewells and found Harry in the driver's seat of the Volvo, leaning forward, head on the steering wheel. He didn't look up when I opened the door.

"Moping?" I asked.

"I'm tired," he said, pushing from the wheel. "You drive."

I retraced our path back to Mobile. Harry stared out the window, not even tuning on his stereo system. I saw a deserted filling station at a lonesome crossroads, a corroded Hadacol sign hanging from the sun-bleached wood. I pulled in beside the rusted pumps, keeping the engine running for the AC. It was ninety-five outside, the sun a white ball in the corner of the sky.

"What's here?" Harry asked.

"The story."

"What story?"

"Rein said she owed a lot to people and I didn't know the story. Tell me a story, bro."

Harry dry-washed his face in his palms, looked out the window for a long time, like arranging things in his head. "Reinetta lost her parents seventeen years ago," he finally said. "Her parents, Johanna and Bayliss, were on a small boat that went down in a storm on Lake Michigan. A freak thing, blew in out of nowhere. They were visiting friends in Muskegon, Rein staying back with her granny in Greeneville."

"Jesus," I whispered. "How old was –"

"Ten. Granny was getting feeble, so the family met to decide who would raise the girl. Everyone wanted to step in, so a committee was created to vet the choices. It came up with a half-dozen possible couples."

"Who was Rein staying with at the time?"

A pause. "My sister, Molly. I was around a lot, too. It was for six months, to give Rein some stability. She went through tough days, but was resilient. Her parents were spiritual, passed their faith on. Rein didn't see them as gone forever, so that helped."

"The couples?"

"The question was put to Rein, who did she want to live with? She said, 'Can I live with all of them?' So Rein lived with a bunch of folks over the years. A high school coach whose wife is a chemist. My cousin and her husband in Raleigh. He's an attorney, she's an

32

accomplished regional actress. Then with relatives in Chicago – you met them, James and Twyla . . ."

I nodded. "The trumpeter and dance instructor."

"Rein lived with musicians, businesspeople, athletes, science types. They're all part of her world."

"Talk about raised by the village."

"She went on to study law and law enforcement at Old Miss. Great grades. Played on the lacrosse team. Acted in plays, musicals, everything . . . a reflection of everyone she lived with."

"But Rein didn't become an actress or a chemist or a lawyer or a dancer, Harry," I said. "She became a cop."

Harry closed his eyes and blew out a breath. "When Rein was a kid she carried a plastic gun and badge and arrested people. Called herself Harriet Nautilus, girl detective. I never figured she'd get stuck that way."

"You're talking like Rein's got an affliction."

"She was on a good, safe road, Carson. College, law school . . ."

"I was on a good safe road myself ten years ago. Studying to be a psychologist." I patted my mouth in a yawning motion.

"It was different for you. You were older and a . . ." he paused.

"A guy?"

"That's not it," Harry snapped. "Not it at all."

"It's Rein's life, Harry," I said quietly. "She's a grown woman."

Harry stared at me like I was speaking Mandarin.

"You know the kind of people out there on the streets. It's just too damned dangerous."

I started to re-state my position, realized it would be like talking into a hurricane. I pulled out of the station, rolled through the crossroads and aimed toward Mobile. Harry was silent on the return trip, staring out the window and watching the phone poles blow by like measurements of time and space.

Treeka had changed from the regional bus to a Boulder local and was now heading toward the women's center. She felt her stomach go hollow and her heart start to race. *Can I do it?*

She exited the bus and angled toward the center, veering away at the last moment, circling the block instead. Again in front of the center, she made herself stop where the center's walk met the sidewalk. *Turn!* her mind screamed and she turned toward the building. *Walk!* her mind yelled. She walked to the door. Heart beating like it was about to tear from its hinges, she willed her hand to clasp the doorknob.

The door opened and Treeka stepped inside. It was a tiny space, darker than outside, and Treeka's eyes adjusted slowly, seeing chairs against the wall and a table scattered with magazines. Across the room and behind a desk sat a square-built woman in her forties with red hair and friendly eyes. She was folding blue paper into a shape.

"How can I help you?" the woman asked, paper dancing through her fingers.

Treeka hadn't prepared for questions. "I'm s-sorry . . ." she stammered. "I thought this was s-someplace else." Treeka backed away, hand grabbing wildly behind her for the doorknob.

"What did you think it was, dear?" the woman asked.

Treeka remembered the sandal shop down the block. "I-I thought it was a shoe store."

"Really . . . a shoe store?" the woman said, head canted in mock puzzlement. "Even though there are no windows displaying shoes, and the sign by the door makes no mention of footwear?"

"I, uh, yes . . . I mean, no. I'm sorry, I have to be go—"

"I think you know exactly where you are, dear," the woman said, setting a little blue bird on her desk beside a paper giraffe, swan, and grasshopper. "Let's talk."

8

Over the next couple days Harry and I tracked down and busted a guy who'd shot a store clerk dead before grabbing seventy bucks from the register. The arrest – combined with two other nasty folks we'd nailed the preceding week – gave us more hours to put against Butterfly Lady, both of us tired of seeing her mutilated, eyeless face in our dreams. I was tapping my pencil on my desk, trying to find an angle into the case when the phone rang. Sally Hargreaves downstairs in Missing Persons.

"How about you and Harry pay me a visit soon?" she said. "Now would be a good time."

Sal was in her cubicle when we arrived, staring at her monitor and twirling a lock of auburn hair. She was a few years older than me, a liquid mix of tomboy and femininity, tough, but always probing for the best in people. She carried a few extra pounds with grace and had a girl-next-door prettiness that tugged at my heart.

"I've got a missing person's request from the Denver area," Sal said. "City workers found a woman's body. Looks late twenties, early thirties, Caucasian."

"And?" Harry said.

"The woman's head was bald, her breasts had been beaten . . ." Sal looked at me to fill in the blank.

"No eyes," I whispered.

Sal nodded. "Just like here."

My heart accelerated its cadence. "Where was the corpse found?" I asked. "The city dump?"

"Floating in a sedimentation tank at the Denver Wastewater Treatment Plant. We're talking about raw sewage." Sal had printed out the report and handed copies to Harry and me. An unknown person or persons had breached the low fence outside the city's wastewater facility and thrown the body into the first-phase settling tank.

"I'd sure like to see –"

"Photos from the scene," Sally completed, pointing to a printer firing out copies about a dozen feet away. "I already talked to the detective in charge – name's Amica Cruz, and she's sending what they have."

"You're the best, Sal," Harry said.

"That would be an understatement," Sally acknowledged.

I grabbed emerging photos as Harry walked over. The Denver photographer had started shooting as he

37

approached. We saw a circular tank forty feet in diameter ringed with a low railing. Then a higher angle, closer, and we saw a steel-mesh catwalk spanning the tank, a dark liquid within. The next shot showed an object in the liquid, a light form against the umber sludge.

For the final shot the photographer had walked out on the catwalk and shot downward. I think Harry and I winced simultaneously at the picture: an eyeless woman's face poking up through human waste, the sockets angled to the sky as if pleading, *Why me?*

I picked up the phone and dialed Dr Alexandra – Alec – Kavanaugh from memory, the psychologist who consulted as the departmental shrink. She walked in an hour later, her smile warm but tentative. Since Doc K was in jeans, ballet-type slippers and a Decembrists T-shirt, I figured she hadn't been with a patient. In her early forties, she had long white hair and quietly piercing dark eyes in a slender face. Kavanaugh moved with a fluid grace, as if not fully tethered to the earth, and reminded me of a lady wizard.

Harry showed the Doc to the meeting room. Sal arrived and we studied photos from the two crimes: the body found at the Mobile dump and the body from Boulder, fifteen hundred miles away. Kavanaugh kept returning to the close-ups of the dead women.

"Any thoughts, Doc?" I prodded as she studied the photos.

"I'm pretty sure we're seeing a symbolic de-feminization. First, their hair was taken away, a major symbol of womanhood in our society. Then the eyes, another symbol of femininity."

"Like breasts," Harry said. "If the breasts weren't exactly removed . . ."

"They were injured, symbolically rendered inert. Hair and eyes removed, breasts attacked. In the killer's eyes, he had de-feminized the women. Then he put them out with the garbage."

"Or sewage," Harry added. "Displayed as what the killer thinks of them."

"One glitch in your theory, Doc," I said. "The primary female sexual symbol is the vagina. There were no injuries to the sex organs in either case. Why didn't the perp negate the vagina?"

Kavanaugh gave me an even gaze. "Because the organ terrifies him."

The room went quiet. I considered Kavanaugh's suppositions. They made sense, given the landscape of a psychopath's mind. I grabbed for the phone.

Because the Denver water-treatment facility was outside the city limits, the case was being handled by the Colorado State Police. The detective in charge of the proceedings was Amica Cruz, who Sal had spoken with earlier.

"You folks down there have an ID?" she asked, hopeful.

"Nothing, sorry. I'm calling about the port-mortem findings."

"I'm in the morgue staring at the deceased. The body

is about to undergo the postmortem. Our pathologist, Dr Leon Lighthorse, is washing up."

"Has Dr Lighthorse completed an external exam?"

"I told your Detective Hargreaves about the battered breasts. We've got ligature marks on ankles and wrists and a few superficial bruises to forearms. There's a pair of moles on her left glute and a dime-sized birthmark at the rear hairline. Or where the rear hairline might normally be."

"How extensively was the body washed?"

I heard the phone covered as Cruz spoke with the pathologist. She lifted her palm. "Very lightly. Enough to remove the, uh, coating."

"Have the doc check the lower belly for traces of gum or mucilage," I said. "He might black-light the area."

"What?"

"Please give it a try, Detective Cruz."

The phone was set aside and I heard voices in the background. A clank of something moved into place. More voices before the phone was picked up.

"Dr Lighthorse found a sticky substance on the lower abdomen, a three-inch line of gum eight centimeters above the pubic bone. He suspects it's residue from tape." A pause. "How in the hell did you know it was there?"

"We've got something similar here in the Mobile morgue. I'll send you everything we have, reports-wise, within the hour. Can I call you later?"

"You damn well better."

I switched the phone off and turned to my colleagues. Kavanaugh leaned back and tented her long fingers.

"I've got a theory on the tape residue."

"Go for it, Doc."

"I'm thinking the perpetrator taped something over the vagina – fabric or paper or whatever. Put the sexual organ out of sight."

"Why?" Harry asked.

"If the vagina couldn't see him, it couldn't exercise its power."

"You mean if he couldn't see it," Harry said.

Kavanaugh shook her head. "My statement stands."

9

Liza Krupnik gathered a dozen academic theses for The Famous Sociologist, some an inch thick and tucked within plastic binders. A review of titles included "A History of Women's Servitude", "Women's Objectification in 20th-Century Art" and "Women as Objects of Torture in the Victorian Novel". Her denim-upholstered derrière bumped into the table behind her as she stood over her desk, the chair rolled aside to provide room, and Liza grumbled to herself. As a doctoral candidate and teaching assistant in the Sociology department at the University of Colorado, Liza thought it would have been nice to have a few more square feet of floor space. It might even allow enough room to nap comfortably on the floor.

At present napping meant rolling the desk chair into the hall, along with the folding chair for visitors, and pushing one of the three-drawer files to the side. Only then could she roll out her yoga mat and grab a few winks in semi-fetal position. Since the miniscule office was Liza's world for a minimum dozen hours a day, catching up on sleep was a necessity, grabbing an hour here and there as time allowed.

An oversize calendar centered the wall above Liza's desk, notes and deadlines scrawled in every daily square. On one side of the calendar was a Rosie the Riveter poster from World War Two, on the other Howard Miller's artistic rendering of a no-nonsense, we're-gonna-win-the-war Rosie rolling up her sleeve as the text bubble above proclaimed *We Can Do It!* On the far wall was a blow-up of Norman Rockwell's heroic *Saturday Evening Post* cover featuring a short-haired, hard-muscled Rosie eating her lunch sandwich atop an I-beam, her clothes and face smeared with the dirt of hard labor and a massive riveting gun across her lap.

A few months back, Liza had brought a date by her office when she'd forgotten to take out the departmental mail. Her date had studied the posters while Liza slid mail into her backpack. "Jeez, Liza," her date had said, "who's the big dyke on the pole?"

The date had ended poorly.

The group of reports now assembled for The Famous Sociologist, she grabbed a pencil from the coffee-mug penholder on her desk, the mug emblazoned with the likeness of the proto-feminist Emma Goldman. Liza leaned to the calendar on the board and checked off the task: *Recent theses to attn of D Sinclair.*

Dr Thalius Benton Sinclair, The Famous Sociologist, would soon be fed for the day. It was Liza's final deadline and she could now go home.

Liza locked her office and turned down the long hall of doors, the majority bannered with names of professors in the department, most doors closed and locked, the day nearing dusk. She shot a glance at a door that was now locked all the time, the office of Dr Judith Bramwell, Dean of Gender Studies. Bramwell was less than two weeks into a six-month sabbatical, wandering Europe and writing. When Dr Bramwell had been here, she'd served as a buffer between Liza and Sinclair. Liza had liked her job a lot better back then.

Only one door stood open, the similarly sized workspace of her colleague, Robert Trotman, another struggling sociology TA, his specialty being statistical analysis. Liza poked her head in the door, resisting the urge to wrinkle her nose: her friend's office always smelled of fast food and the cigarette he snuck every two hours, his body seemingly set to a nicotinic clock.

"S'up, Roberto?"

Trotman's eyes had been riveted to his computer monitor. He startled so hard that his CU ball cap spun to the floor. He became embarrassed by his fright, a shiver of crimson crossing his freckled white neck.

"Whoa," Liza said. "Sorry, Rob. Didn't realize you were in the deep beyond."

Trotman laughed the moment aside and grabbed his cap from the floor, slapping it back over his head, prematurely balding, the front-sweeping comb-over no longer thick enough to lie. He'd had the same affliction with his beard last year, scruffy tufts of hair that seemed more like dirt from a distance. He'd finally given up and shaved it away, his skin now as clear and stubble-free as the typical adolescent.

"No prob, girl," Trotman said. "I thought you did your volunteer stuff tonight and I was the only one here."

"I volunteer tomorrow, I forgot to change the calendar." Liza nodded down the empty hall. "The drones have flown the coop, Rob. It's just us worker bees."

Trotman's eye flickered toward the end of the corridor. "And, uh, of course . . ."

Liza nodded. "Yes. His nibs is here. He's waiting for fresh meat." Liza tapped the stack of theses in the crook of her arm.

"Why do you think he does it?" Trotman asked. "Reads work from across the country?"

"Because one university doesn't generate enough for him to hate," Liza opined.

"Maybe he's making a study of studies," Trotman joked.

"I don't know," Liza said, smiling wickedly. "Because I'm not the . . ."

Trotman slapped his hand over his heart and sprang to his feet as Liza did the same. "The Randall Chair in Sociology," they announced in unison, followed by breaking into laughter. It was their private joke, striking both as a hoot that their feared boss's name was almost never mentioned without addition of the modifier, one of his many academic achievements.

A deep voice from the doorway. "Is everything all right here?"

The pair spun to the door. Framed in the threshold like an age-darkened Rembrandt oil stood the towering figure of Dr Thalius Benton Sinclair. The man frowned darkly, tugging a black beard running from mid-cheek to the second button on his shirt. Sinclair was above average height, barrel-chested, Falstaffian in presence, but not proportion, a man trim at waist and broad in shoulder. Though in his late forties, Liza thought of him as outside of time, like a vampire.

"I saw hands over your hearts," Sinclair rumbled. "I assumed you were having some kind of attack."

The pair stood mute. "Well?" Sinclair prodded, his eyes moving between the pair. "Does anyone here speak the English language?"

"We-uh, were, uh, I mean that, uh . . ." The hapless Trotman could only babble, his mind collapsing into a black hole of terror. Sinclair's eyes moved to Liza. *His eyes have no depth of color*, Liza noted, not for the first time, but surprised nonetheless. They were clear water in an aqua-tinted bottle. And yet, somehow, they were the most opaque eyes she'd ever seen.

Liza's mouth was too dry to speak. She lifted the stack of theses toward Sinclair. *Please don't eat me*, her mind pleaded. *Take this offering instead.* Sinclair's eyes dropped to the stack of paper in her clutch. "Another pile of shit ready for composting?"

"Yes, Professor," Liza managed.

Sinclair tucked the material under his arm, the color-deficient eyes scanning between Liza and Robert. He sighed and turned away, striding toward his spacious corner office, wide windows facing the looming Flatiron Mountains.

"Do you think he heard us making fun of him?" Trotman whispered after Sinclair was far from earshot.

Liza nodded. "He couldn't help it."

Trotman made the sound of a leaking balloon valve and buried his face in his hands.

His academic day now over, Dr Thalius Benton Sinclair stepped from the building with his ancient accordion-fold briefcase in hand and walked briskly toward his home on Thirteenth Street, five blocks from Chautauqua Park. He lived on "The Hill", the University neighborhood, up a modest incline from Boulder's downtown and in the evening shadow of the Flatirons.

Sinclair zigzagged his journey, adding a few blocks to the trip for exercise. After twenty minutes he came to several blocks dense with shops and restaurants and throngs of students. He recognized two hand-holders from one of his classes, Anita Blevins and Terrence Tomville. Blevins was a tattoo-stained dolt obviously given too free a rein by her parents, but Tomville had a spark of intelligence. It would be crushed soon enough if he kept company with the likes of Blevins, Sinclair reckoned.

The two students saw Sinclair approaching and snapped their eyes away as though he were a Gorgon, pretending to study clothes in a shop window. Sinclair moved on for another block, his colorless eyes scanning from the ranks to a shoe store, paraphernalia store, bike shop and a narrow bar named the Beacon, with dark-shaded windows, the only window sign a red neon scrawl proclaiming *Fifty Beers!*

Across the street, tucked behind a pair of trees, sat a small and squat building, a former realtor's office doing its best to be nondescript, brown paint and shingles, pulled shades. The occupant's identity was a small sign beside the door: WOMEN'S CRISIS CENTER OF BOULDER.

They're plotting in there, Sinclair thought, *the devious ones . . .*

Sinclair turned into the bar. The place was less than half full, students mostly, gathered toward the rear and watching a dart game. He caught the attention of a barkeep, a college-aged woman wearing some ridiculous costume he assumed was current fashion.

"Help you?" the woman asked.

"Two shots of Glenlivet, neat."

"Neat?"

Sinclair sighed. Civilization was dying before his eyes. "Neat means by itself. No water, no ice, no nothing."

"I don't think we have . . . what did you call it?"

"Yes, you do. It's on the shelf with the Scotch. Glenlivet." It took effort to keep from spelling it out.

Drink finally in hand, Sinclair went back toward the door and took a table at the corner of the front window. He positioned himself against the wall, hidden

48

from outside view, but able to observe comings and goings across the street just by leaning forward a little.

An hour later, with no activity noted, Sinclair walked the four blocks to his home, a wood and stone two-story hidden behind a wall of hedge and trees. His self-activating porch lamp had burned out two months back and Sinclair hadn't replaced the bulb, finding the dark at his door more soothing than the light.

He entered, further soothed by familiar surroundings: burgundy carpet, brass lamps, solid masculine furniture built of wood and brown leather. Though he had converted a former guest room to a library, the overflow filled an entire wall of the room.

He poured an ounce of Scotch into a snifter and added a splash of soda. From a small box on the mantel, teak inlaid with silver and jade, he removed a tin that had formerly held breath mints, spearmint, *A Burst of Fresh in Every Bite!* He opened the tin and produced a spiraling tube of Purple Thai marijuana.

Sinclair climbed the stairs to his second-floor office, boxes and files and rows of books stacked vertically and horizontally on shelves. The disarray sometimes irritated him – he hated disorder – yet could it be called disorder if he knew where everything was?

He slid his laptop from his briefcase and set it on the desk, pushing it to the side as he booted the big-screen iMac into action. He logged on to a regularly visited site, pausing at the jokes section to see if anything new had been added.

Q: What do you tell a woman with two black eyes?
A: Nothing. Somebody already told her twice.

Q: What do you call a woman with pigtails?
A: A blowjob with handlebars.

Q: What is the difference between a woman and
  a catfish?
A: One is a bottom-feeding scum-sucker and the
  other is a fish.

Old jokes he'd seen a hundred times. Sinclair sighed. Was it impossible for people to invent new material? Be creative? He tapped a few keys, moving to a link that jumped him to another site, one with a woman in chains as its primary graphic. He moved the cursor down the chain dangling from the woman's right wrist, counting off the links of chain. He clicked on the fifth link, a hidden link within the link. He'd spent a month online before someone had trusted him enough to provide the entrance link.

A sound of thunder and heavy metal music. A scream. Crackling flames wiped away the graphic to leave only a gray screen and the low lub-dub of heartbeat sound effects. During the day and early evening, there could be a dozen or more people online, but now, at the bottom of the right-hand corner, were the words 1 Member online.

Someone was in the secret chat room, alone, waiting to have a conversation. Sinclair tapped his handle into the white box.

PROMALE

Sinclair poised his finger above the keys, recalling his day of interacting with dolts and cattle as the Scotch and dope buffered his jangled synapses.

I hate women, Sinclair wrote, the text black against white. I want to wipe them off the planet.

Seconds passed as someone that could be as near as the next block or as far as half a world away entered text. Sinclair hoped HPDrifter would be here tonight, but then, Drifter was here most nights, the most ubiquitous presence on the board and its de facto leader; very bright, but cagey, tight with references to himself, controlling the board with a strange mixture of a fierce and sadistic hatred of women, wry humor, and odd moments of obsequiousness.

Sinclair saw Drifter's handle appear before his words. He slapped his desk in delight: A kindred spirit was in the chat room.

HPDRIFTER: Explain, PROMALE. Tell me about your hate.

PROMALE: Earlier today a woman under my control told me a lie as if I was too stupid to tell the difference. She and another had been mocking me. I have to live with it every day.

HPDRIFTER: Bitch, slut. I'd drag the whore out to the middle of the street and do the doggy on it.

And, of course, make her pay me for the attention.

PROMALE: That's funny, Drifter. But I'm being crushed under the lies.

HPDRIFTER: Lies are all the whores know. The more "educated" they are, the more they lie.

PROMALE: Right on, Drifter. In this situation the taliban have the right idea: keep the X-chromes out of school. It just fucks up their thinking.

Another entity entered the chat room, RAISEHELL.

3 Members online

RAISEHELL: Hey guys, what's going on?

HPDRIFTER: A filthy bitch has shit on brother Promale's day, Raisehell. I'm trying to cheer him up.

RAISEHELL: 2 bad for U Promale. What's X-chrome?

HPDRIFTER: Our brother Promale is noting that men have an X and Y chromosome, women only Xs. It's why men are Y-ser ;)

RAISEHELL: LOL! U R 2 smart for me, Promale and Drifter. Your always saying things like that. Promale. What kind of work do U do?

HPDRIFTER: !!! Remember the rules for the

room, Raise. No questions about identities.

RAISEHELL: I Forgot . . . my bad. Sorry.

HPDRIFTER: There are those who would use
knowledge of our identities against us . . . to
take our jobs, our livelihoods. We must be ever
vigilant.

PROMALE: The FemiNazis hate us for wishing to
regain our destinies.

HPDRIFTER: Well said, brother.

4 Members online

The member named MAVERICK entered the conversation. Like HPDRIFTER, MAVERICK was a regular.

MAVERICK: It will take more than talk to get our
manhood back.

HPDRIFTER: Excellent point, Maverick. But there
are those who work tirelessly on our behalf.
Look to the west for the dawn.

PROMALE: *??*

RAISEHELL: Yes . . . what do you mean, Drifter?

HPDRIFTER: That's enough for now. But we
should all be ready to band together.

PROMALE: I am sick of what the X-chromes have
done to my country. It's time they were stopped.
I am ready . . .

10

I entered the Homicide department at eight a.m., a convenience-store cup of coffee in one hand and a half-eaten apple in the other. My hand had first reached for a glazed pastry the size of a catcher's mitt, but I'd reluctantly snagged the fruit. Across the wide room I saw Harry and Sal in our cubicle. They looked excited.

"You've got something," I said, walking up.

"The Colorado cops ID'd their Jane Doe," Sal said. "Name's Lainie Devon Krebbs. They found out early this morning, got the ID from an arrest seven years back – the lady was caught trying to sneak a few joints into a Jimmy Buffet concert."

"Any ties to the Mobile area?"

Sal flicked the page with a scarlet fingernail. "She lived her whole life here."

If the kick I'd gotten from the discovery of a body

paralleling our crime was a three on a scale of one to ten, the identification rang up a six.

I said, "Was she –"

"Married?" Sal answered, always a step ahead. "Why yes, Carson. Her hubby is one Lawrence Krebbs of west Mobile. And before you ask, the missus filed charges against the mister. One count of abuse filed eight months back, later dropped. Three police calls to the residence, domestic beefs, the lady throwing things, the neighbors calling the cops at two a.m. when they saw Mrs Krebbs run out of the house, get tackled and pulled back into the house by her hair. Krebbs went to jail for assault, made bail in an hour, beat the charge on condition of anger-management classes."

"Probably promised to go and sin no more," Harry snorted. "The abuse continued, of course."

"Three months back the lady got a restraining order on Krebbs, saying he was threatening her life. Krebbs violated by banging on the door at midnight, screaming. The wife said he had a knife, but it was never located."

"He go to jail?"

"He got a warning. The jail was probably full that night. It happened again and he did a week in the slammer. Took mandated anger-control classes. You can read between the lines as well as me, Carson: he abuses her, she leaves, finds she can't make it on her own, comes back when he promises to be a good boy . . ."

"And it all starts anew. Anything else?"

"Yeah, a few similar charges, but spread out over

years. Filed by Mrs Krebbses, but all with different first names."

"A serial matrimonialist," Harry snorted. "They always love the ladies, don't they?"

"Sometimes to death," Sal added.

Lawrence Krebbs lived in a small house, the lawn so manicured it looked like baize on a billiard table. The hedges were geometric forms, not a sprig out of place. The crepe myrtles were tamed to resemble outsize bonsai. I rang the doorbell, two muted bell-sounds from within.

A curtain shifted in the window to my right, the fabric diaphanous enough to display a prominent forehead. The face disappeared.

"Someone's home," I said.

Harry knocked again, harder. Thirty seconds passed and the door opened to reveal a powerful-looking man in his mid forties dressed in a red tee and multi-pocketed hiker shorts. He was slender at the waist, big in the shoulders, bespectacled, the former expanse of pink head flesh now hidden under brown. The guy had needed to slap on a hairpiece to answer the door, which said something about his ego. The toupee was decent. There are no good ones.

Harry held up the badge. "You're Lawrence Krebbs?"

The gray eyes studied us. "That's the name." He made no effort to open the door further.

"It's hot out here, Mr Krebbs," Harry said. "How about we come inside so we don't let all your fine air conditioning out into the street?"

The man looked at our feet. "Take off your shoes. I don't want shit tracked on my floor."

"You're wearing shoes," I noted.

"They don't have shit on them."

I slipped off my suede desert boots, Harry toed off his burgundy loafers, and we stepped on to a white carpet. The interior showed all the personality of a clam, jammed with furniture sold as "American Tradition" or "The Heritage Collection", copywriter's gloss for style-deficient crap with fake carving and dark stain masking the green grain of poplar. The AC was bottomed out and the place reeked of pine air freshener, like Krebbs was trying to simulate a vacation on Hudson's Bay.

"So what can I do for you?" Krebbs asked, closing the door.

"We're here about your wife, Mr Krebbs," Harry said as I gave an eyeshot to Krebbs's physique: shoulder-heavy with thick biceps and triceps. But his legs were soft and the tightly belted shorts showed a couple inches of love-handle slopping over the gunnels, a guy who built the showpiece muscles, slacked on ones he could cover with clothing.

"Which wife?" Krebbs said, inching toward us, his toes edging our comfort zone, broad arms crossed to further fatten the guns, showing us it was his home and he was Alpha Dog.

"Lainie D. Krebbs," Harry said quietly, sliding his six-four, two-thirty body two inches closer to Krebbs's chest. Krebbs stepped back a foot, like needing room to think. "That bitch ran off two months back. Nine weeks to be exact. And two days."

"By bitch, I take it you mean your wife?"

"If you take wife to mean a person who cooks decent meals and keeps a house clean, I've never been married."

"Let's use a legal definition, then," Harry said. "You were married to the former Lainie Place for three years."

"I guess. It felt a lot longer."

"You seem fuzzy on wives, sir," I asked. "I take it you were married before?"

"I've been married four times. And don't give me that look. I'm either a sucker or an optimist. I probably should have my head examined."

I left that one alone, said, "You didn't report Mrs Krebbs as missing?"

"You're not hearing me, Officer. She wasn't missing, she ran off. The woman broke her vows."

"You weren't interested in Lainie coming back?" I asked.

"You can tell her or her shyster lawyer that she signed a pre-nup. She's not eligible for a red nickel."

I looked into his eyes. "We don't serve documents for lawyers, Mr Krebbs. We're here to tell you Lainie was found in Denver yesterday. Dead. She'd had her eyes cut out, her breasts wounded, and her body dumped into a tank of sewage at the water-treatment plant."

I'd hit him with a bat, expecting shock. Instead, Krebbs put his hands in his pockets and jingled his change, wandering to the front window. "Shouldn't you be looking for her pimp?" he asked after a few seconds of reflection.

"You think Lainie turned to prostitution?" I said.

Krebbs sighed. "A woman like that runs off, a failure with no brains and no education, how else is she going to live? She's got one natural talent . . . Not that she was any good at that, either."

Somehow I managed to keep from ripping the man's pathetic hairpiece from his head and shooting it. "You don't seem sad, Mr Krebbs," I said instead, "at the death of someone you lived with and, presumably, loved."

Krebbs turned away, like figuring out how he was supposed to look. His face came back about the same. "I'm sorry it all happened. But she never learned respect, never figured it out."

"There was one thing Lainie could figure out, Mr Krebbs," I said. "How to call the police when you were beating her. And file restraining orders, which you twice violated. That was just the last Mrs Krebbs. Seems you have a record of this kind of action with the Krebbs wife corps."

The eyes flashed. "I fall for these, these ridiculous *sensitive* women. Once they settle into the cushy life, they turn on me."

"Seems Lainie was the one who filed the order, not you."

Krebbs's face reddened with anger. "I never *touched* the bitch. I'd yell at her – hell yes, she pissed me off – and she'd gimme this big shit-eating grin and smack her face against the fridge or the microwave, call the cops. You people would show up, see a tiny little scrape on her face, and fucking pull me out of my own home."

Harry held up his notes. "So all these charges should have been filed against your appliances?"

Krebbs spun to my partner, fists balled, the anger-control classes a waste of time. Or maybe they weren't. Krebbs closed his eyes and took a deep breath. I watched his shoulders relax and the hands loosen.

"You think I did it, right?" he said.

"Everyone's a suspect," Harry said. "Until they're not."

Krebbs stared at the floor. "Boy, that slut really got me good."

"Got you how, Mr Krebbs?" I asked.

"When she was alive she gave me a police record. Then she dies and makes me a suspect." He jammed his hands in his pockets and shook his head. "I sure can pick 'em, can't I?"

11

The peaks of the Rocky Mountains rising around her, Treeka snapped one side of Tommy's blue bikini briefs to the clothes rope, grabbed a pin, fixed the other side tight, making a line of blue flags waving in the breeze. Tommy wore briefs because boxers were for fags and niggers. The rest of the line was denim cowboy-style work shirts and skin-tight jeans. Tommy liked his clothes spread wide so sun and breeze could make them smell fresh. Treeka's clothes were bunched at the end of the line, her yellow shopping dress as bright as neon.

Treeka grabbed another pair of damp briefs from the basket and shot a glance toward the doublewide modular at her back. Sided with wood slats to resemble a mountain cabin, it was a pair of trailers in disguise. Tommy had inherited the house from his daddy, a diabetic who ignored medical advice by drinking hard and eating wrong, even as the doctors amputated pieces until he was little more than a torso with an angry head.

Tommy's mother had run off when he was twelve. There one day, gone the next, leaving only a note saying *I cant take it no more.* Both of Tommy's parents disappeared on him, Treeka thought, the old man just took more time to do it.

Though it was a workday, Tommy was inside sleeping. Yesterday had been payday and Tommy never came home before ten p.m., heading straight from cashing his check to his favorite saloon. He'd gotten up and felt like shit and called in sick at the awning factory.

Tommy boasted to strangers that he was a cattle rancher, but of the dozen cattle he'd bought with Treeka's Toyota money – his starter herd, he'd called it – four died of the bloat, three wandered off through the fence he could never keep patched, one died of infection when Tommy thought he could do better than a veterinarian at fixing a cut, and one tumbled into the abandoned mine at the back end of the property. The other four he sold at a loss, since they looked so sickly. For the last year he'd worked at a place that made canvas awnings for mobile homes, named assistant foreman when the company's absentee owner discovered Tommy's ability to browbeat extra work from the mostly undocumented Hispanic labor.

Treeka was holding the briefs tight against the line, clothespins in hand, when her head snapped back so hard she screamed. Tommy had her pulled tight to him by her hair. His other hand grabbed her neck beneath her chin.

"Where have you been?" he hissed into her ear. She smelled whiskey on his breath. He'd already started drinking.

"W-what are you talking about, b-baby?" Treeka said through clenched teeth. "I been r-right here doin' the clothes."

"Other days. You been sneaking out." Tommy's voice was fire against her ear.

"I d-don't know what you're sayin', baby. How could I get anywhere if I d-don't have a car?"

"You got some guy picks you up," he slurred. "Or one a your lesbians."

"I don't know any lesbians. An' there ain't no one picks me up. You're my man, Tommy. It's just us. You and me, forever. Come on, baby, let go my neck. It's hard to breathe."

His hand fell from her throat as he spun her to him, slapping her face with a gunshot sound. She let herself fall to the dirt, hoping for safety on the ground.

"I work my ass off for you and you're fucking around on me," he hissed. "This is the thanks I get."

"Your imagination is running away on you again, baby," Treeka gasped, trying to catch her breath. "I ain't been anywhere but here all day ever' day."

Tommy reached into his shirt pocket, made a flicking motion. A flash of color appeared in the air and a tiny bird fluttered to the ground in front of Treeka. The blue

63

paper bird the lady at the woman center gave Treeka when they were done talking, setting it in Treeka's palm and gently closing her fingers around it like the bird was alive.

"I found it in your special drawer," Tommy said. "In back, hiding."

Treeka felt sick. As soon as she'd returned from the trip to Boulder she'd put the paper bird in her cosmetic drawer until she could find a better hiding place. Tommy had probably gone through her face creams for something he could grease up and whack off with.

"The bird was up b-by the highway, baby," Treeka stammered. "It must have got blown out of someone's car. It was pretty so I kept it, Tommy. That's all. It was a pretty little bird."

"I TOL' YOU NEVER TO GO TO THE HIGHWAY!"

"I was just looking, Tommy. I'm sorry, I won't do it again, baby, I promise I –"

Tommy's boot came down and stomped the blue bird flat. He pulled a pair of his jeans from the line and flung them around Treeka, her head caught in the crotch. He spun them tight and dragged her by the neck into the house.

12

We had nothing on Larry Krebbs. That meant studying him from the periphery, starting with his employer. Allied Technologies was a big green steel box in a warehouse district in south Mobile. A fenced-in compound outside held stake trucks, outsized crates and sections of industrial tubing. Traffic whizzed by, work vehicles and semis hauling goods.

Inside the building it was cool and smelled of plastics. The reception area was a room with a desk and several battered filing cabinets. Behind the desk was a chunky woman in her early forties wearing a purple pantsuit. Her face was big-eyed and button-nose cute, but overly powdered and hard at the eye-corners. The nameplate on her desk said MARGE GLENNY, OFFICE MGR. She finished ticking out something on a keyboard before looking up.

"Help you fellas?"

We showed our credentials and Harry asked to see the boss.

"That's Mr Choy," Miz Glenny said. "Sam Choy. He's our CEO, COO, and C-about everything else. Can I tell him what it's about?"

"Larry Krebbs works here, right?" I asked.

"Not my fault," Miz Glenny said with a frown.

"Excuse me, ma'am?"

"You don't want to talk to me about Larry, because I don't have much to say and not much of it is good."

I felt a thrill run down my spine as Office Mgr Glenny picked up the phone to announce us. We'd fer-sure stop back at her desk.

Choy's office had paneled walls, acoustic ceiling tiles with fluorescent fixtures, a simple desk. In the corner was a drawing table strewn with blueprints. Choy was in his mid forties, compact, with intelligent eyes behind red-framed glasses, wearing khakis and a gray silk shirt rolled to the elbows. His short hair was hipster-spiked and he less resembled a guy who made pipes than a partner in a Silicon Valley start-up.

"Larry's worked with us for three years," Choy said, frowning through the lenses. "Is there a problem?"

We laid out the facts. Choy seemed shaken initially, but gained composure after a few quiet seconds. "Larry rarely talks about his personal life. I only met Mrs Krebbs once. She was very quiet."

Harry leaned in. "Mr Krebbs has something of a

strident personality, Mr Choy. When I think of office accountants I think of quiet people with –"

"With thick glasses and a pocket full of pens and so forth," Choy nodded. "People who let the numbers speak."

"Pretty much. Mr Krebbs seems to enjoy goading people."

Choy looked out the window as a semi rolled past with coils of steel chained to the trailer. He turned back to Harry and me, his voice lowered. "We're a small company that stays alive by underbidding competitors. That means keeping costs low. We don't short-change our people, but we take advantage of economic advantages when it comes to hiring."

It took a beat for me to catch on. "You're saying Krebbs works cheap, Mr Choy?"

"We pay him eighty-two grand a year. Someone with a comparable skill set could get a hundred."

"Because Krebbs's skill set doesn't include people skills, right?"

Choy nodded. "Larry's a bit . . . opinionated. Probably why he had a checkered employment history. But when he applied here, we figured the pairing would work if he stayed in his office and ran numbers."

I wanted to see Krebbs's work environment and nodded down the hall. "Which office is his?"

"There isn't one. Nine months back Larry decided he could do everything from home, e-commute. Given his effect on some of our staff, we thought the arrangement worked out better for everyone."

Except his wife, I thought. The best part of Lainie Krebbs's day probably started the moment hubby walked out the door. Then, nine months ago, Krebbs is home every second of every day, watching, complaining, correcting. Miz K takes several months of it, then books for greener pastures. But somehow, Lainie Krebbs ends up submerged in excrement in Denver's sewage treatment center, her corpse blind and mutilated.

We stopped at Miz Glenny's desk on our way out. When we asked if she felt comfortable talking about Larry Krebbs, her eyes sparkled. "He brought Lainie to an office party, a mousy little thing with no hips but decent tits. She was always shooting Larry the nervous eye like she was being graded on how she did. It was funny at first, then it got sad when I heard things about him."

"Heard from where, Miz Glenny?" I asked.

A smug smile. "Larry's aunt moved in next to one of my best friends. The aunt says Larry's messed up about women. He's got two college degrees, but every woman he dated or married was a high-school dropout. The oldest one he ever married was twenty-nine and he was forty-one. That was Lainie."

Harry said, "Larry is a charmer?"

Glenny cawed. "Think it through. You're a half-pretty bimbo with no education, a string of leech boyfriends, and living hand to mouth in some rathole. One day you meet this big white-collar dude with all his teeth and a barber haircut, a guy with a college degree and a real

68

job. It feels like you hit the lottery . . . until he starts weirding out." Glenny cackled wickedly.

Harry said, "How'd you and Krebbs get along, Miz Glenny?"

"The first week he was hitting on me, wanting to get me out to lunch. Then I was talking one day to a delivery lady – Myrna from FedEx – telling her how I'd left my first husband and got the house. Larry was eavesdropping. When Myrna left he accused me of betraying my husband, stealing from him, saying I should hang my head in shame. Larry was really hot, shaking and everything. I actually felt scared."

"What happened?"

"I told him spying was a chickenshit thing to do and if he said one more word I'd go to Mr Choy and file a complaint."

"What did Larry do?"

"He started wringing his hands like a little kid and hauled ass back to his office, slammed the door. He never spoke to me after that. Of course, we hardly crossed paths either."

"That being about the time Larry switched to working at home?" I ventured, taking a shot in the dark.

"Yep. Just a couple weeks later."

I pictured Krebbs huffing and puffing, then Glenny getting in his face and forcing him to retreat. In the mind of a guy like Krebbs, he'd been defeated, shamed. So he retreated to a situation he could control: Home with the wife.

"Do you know if Lainie Krebbs held a job?" Harry asked.

"Larry said a real wife stayed home to cook and clean and be spread-ready when hubby has the hornies." Glenny paused, as if replaying in her head what she'd been saying. She shook her head.

"What is it, Miz Glenny?" I asked.

"I said I didn't have much good to say about Larry. Guess I don't have anything good to say about him."

When Tommy had rolled in the night before with a case of beer and proceeded to ignore her while he spooled fresh line on to a fishing reel, Treeka had hidden her joy – it meant he and his buddies were blowing off work for a day of angling in the mountains. Twenty minutes after Tommy left, she was on the bus to Boulder, this time alerting the center that she was coming.

Treeka arrived to find the paper-folding woman, Carol, had been joined by three other women. Carol told Treeka to tell all of her story, to leave nothing out, especially the worst stuff. One lady, older and dressed in a business suit, did nothing but take notes while the others asked questions.

"No *children, right?*"

"Tommy hates kids. He faked like he liked them 'til we got married. Then he made me get pills and an IUD. He watches me take the pills. When we get some money ahead he says I have to get my tubes tied."

"*Did you ever call the police?*"

"Tommy hunts and fishes with some county cops, so maybe they wouldn't do anything. And even if the cops put Tommy in jail, when he got out he'd tear me apart and bury my parts in the mountains. He says he can put them where even the coyotes won't find them."

"Do you believe him?"

Treeka thought for several long moments. The women had told her to be completely truthful, it was very important.

"Yes, ma'am," she said. "All the way."

"Do you have anyone close to you? So close you couldn't bear to not see them again?"

"Not any more. All the people I love are gone."

"How often does your husband beat you?"

"Two–three times a week. It's getting worse."

"Does he rape you?"

"I'm his wife and Tommy says a man can –"

"Does he force you to have sex when you don't want it?"

"Yes, ma'am. In a way."

"What do you mean, 'in a way'?"

"A lot of time he can't, I mean, he doesn't . . ."

"We understand. Your black eye . . . from Tommy?"

Treeka nodded. "As soon as one starts to fade, another takes its place."

"Are there other ways he hurts you?"

Treeka lifted her blouse, showing scrapes from punches and skin pinched purple with bruises. The women gave Treeka a cup of tea and went to a back room to talk together. Treeka didn't know what they were talking about, but they were gone a long time. When they returned, Carol sat beside Treeka and took her hand.

"We're going to tell you about an option you might consider, Treeka. But before we tell you, you have to take a vow of secrecy. You can never tell anyone what we're about to discuss . . ."

13

Harry and I spent the next day investigating Krebbs, finding nothing beyond his sorrowful history with women. We found ex-wives two and three: Two was a frightfully heavy woman who slammed the door in our face and said she never wanted to hear "that goddamn name again". The other was a blank-faced woman in a decayed trailer park, her skin and teeth ravaged by Methedrine. She was stoned or tripping and said she'd been married three times since then and "Larry wasn't real bad", though I didn't think she was remembering Krebbs.

I called the Krebbster and said we had a few more questions to ask, hoping to push him into a misstep. When the forensics types figured out a decent time-of-death estimate, we could find out where sweet Larry was at the time of our murders.

Krebbs opened the door with a flourish, the toupee

pasted tight, grinning like man who'd just filled an inside straight. Harry and I pulled off our shoes and stepped inside. I took the lead.

"We've been talking to a few folks, Mr Krebbs, and a few more questions come to mind, all involving your former relationships with women. The unions don't seem real, uh, what's the word I'm looking for, Detective Nautilus?"

"Stable," Harry said. "Or mature, maybe."

I snapped my fingers. "That's it. Like a guy with deep insecurities. I'm thinking troubled adolescent here . . . a guy who needs to elevate himself by –"

"That's all I need to hear," boomed a voice from behind us.

Harry and I spun to see a guy about five-eight, lean and whippy, with cold eyes and tight-pursed lips, a self-important mouth. The face was angular, photogenic and topped with a haircut that probably cost more than any suit in my closet, a face we knew only from the news. T. Nathaniel Bromley was a prosecutor-turned-partner at the law firm of Blackwell, Carrington & Bromley, its clients including some the largest concerns in the region.

"Are you harassing my client?" Bromley snapped.

"Harassing how?" Harry said, trying to hide his amazement. We weren't surprised Krebbs had lawyered up, but had expected one of those attorneys that advertises at bus stops. Plus word had it that Bromley had retired last year at age forty-six. The move had surprised many, but it was what I'd have done in

Bromley's expensive shoes. The man had big money and big connections, socially and politically. Why not relax and live it up?

But this version of Bromley didn't look relaxed.

"You were insulting Mr Krebbs's character," he continued. "Using the death of his wife to mock him. That's disgusting, Detectives. Mr Krebbs's wife was the insecure one, given to flights of drunken fantasy. It's to Mr Krebbs's credit that he put up with such erratic behavior over a period of years and –"

"Did you just call Lainie Krebbs a drunken liar?" I said. "Which one of us did you accuse of character assassination, Nate?"

Bromley pointed to the door. "This farce is over. If you wish to talk rationally to my client about his wife –"

"Not *wife*, Bromley," I said, ignoring Harry's elbow in my ribs, our signal for me to ease up. I've gotten pretty good about heeding the nudge, but Bromley was pushing my buttons. "It's *wives*, plural. Your client goes through sad little girls like most people go through toilet paper."

"Out now," Bromley said. "Expect to hear from your chief."

We left, Harry removing me by my elbow. "Lawd," Harry said as we got in the car. "Not only does Krebbs have Nate Bromley as his mouthpiece, you go and piss Bromley off."

"He pissed me off first."

Harry headed back to the department to regroup. We'd

never encountered Bromley in a courtroom; the criminal cases his firm defended never involved anything as coarse as homicide, leaning more toward embezzlement, stock swindles, and mail fraud. I recalled a recent case in which Bromley had defended a computer-hacking whiz, a bespectacled man-child of twenty-seven who'd danced effortlessly past firewalls and security programs to steal credit-card numbers, buying PlayStations and plasma TVs and anything made by Apple.

Defending credit-card theft was about as deep in the dirt as BC&B got, and I recalled the hacker had skirted prison, Bromley's deal calling for his client to make financial restitution, do fifty hours of community service, and promise to go forth and never hack again. My cop buddies and I had sneered at the deal, thinking the punishment far too light for the charges, but the public seemed unconcerned, several in the courtroom gallery cheering the decision, like Bromley had dragged an innocent man from the gas chamber seconds before the pellets dropped.

The day was waning, the tops of the live oaks along Government Street turned amber by the fading sun. I'd opened the conference-room window and could smell the Mobile River a few hundred yards east. There was a jazz concert in Bienville Square and the joyous music of a Dixieland band danced though the streets. A scattering of gulls wheeled in the air and a ship's horn sounded on the bay.

I turned from the window. Harry sat at the table, his fingers tented beneath his chin. We'd asked Sally Hargreaves if she wanted to sit in and bump thoughts, but she said she had an important meeting which, given personal experience, I took as a date.

"Two victims," I said to Harry, reprising the thoughts I'd been mulling at the window. "Same killer. One vic in –"

"Same methodology," Harry corrected. "Not the same killer. Not yet."

"I'm making the assumption for brainstorm purposes."

"Are you assuming Krebbs is the killer?" Harry asked.

I nodded. "When forensics tightens the time of death we're gonna put Krebbs in Colorado. A plane ticket, gas receipt, won't take much."

"How you figure Krebbs knew his wife ran to Colorado?"

"My money's on a private investigator," I said, making the money-whisk with my fingertips. "Larry-boy's got the money. He finds the missus is hiding around Denver, races up and abducts her, finds a torture site. I've been in the region before. One direction is miles of open desert, the other is mountains. Everywhere is a hiding place. Krebbs lets his psycho side bloom, then makes a final statement by dumping the body in the sewage tank."

"What about our Jane Doe here in Mobile? Butterfly Lady."

I smiled and gave it a few seconds to build the drama, wishing I had a drum-roll machine. "I think she'll turn out to be Krebbs's first wife, Harry. There are a shitload of details to fill in, but Wife One is the Ur-bitch, where it all started for Larry-boy."

"The first wife? You sure?" Harry leaned forward, trying to keep his voice noncommittal, but I was hooking him.

"I can feel it, bro. Wife One and Butterfly Lady are the same. They're bookend murders. By killing the first wife and the last wife, Krebbs symbolically murders all the women in between."

"Bookend?"

"I just made that up. Pretty cool, right?"

14

The next morning Harry and I figured we'd find who Krebbs had selected as his first wife and match her to the body in the morgue. We were waiting for the records department in City Hall to open and give us the case-breaking news. At five to nine the intercom on our desk was buzzed by Lieutenant Tom Mason, our supervisor, amigo, protector, and saint without portfolio. Tom stayed out of our way and let us work, the supreme compliment.

"You've got a visitor downstairs, guys," Tom said in a country drawl as slow and rich as sorghum molasses. "T. Nathaniel Bromley in the flesh, asking if you were in. I'm bringing him up. You boys working on some kind of corporate acquisition, maybe merging with Goldman-Sachs?"

"Bromley's repping a guy in the Krebbs case – the husband."

A surprised pause. "Didn't you say the suspect was an accountant at a factory? How the hell did a guy like Krebbs get Bromley as his lawyer?"

"I dunno, but it wasn't charm."

We flicked off the phone. Tom hadn't said anything about the Chief being contacted, so Bromley must have had second thoughts after we'd left. I was surprised, actually; people like Bromley enjoy throwing their weight around.

Harry looked at me. "What do you suppose has brought such a potent force in lawyerism to our humble digs?"

I grinned. "I do believe Mister Bromley wants to kick-start a plea bargain for his guilty-as-sin client."

Tom walked Bromley up to the department. We led the lawyer to a conference room, drawing glances as we crossed the detectives' office space with one of Mobile's legal elite. Bromley wore full attorney regalia: a black suit with pinstripes, pink shirt, rep tie. He was carrying a sleek briefcase made of gray animal hide, seal maybe, or vulture. He studied the gray metal chair before he sat, like he hadn't seen anything so quaint since his DA's-office days.

"We got off on the wrong foot yesterday, Mr Bromley," I said, making nice since Bromley was about to raise the white flag. "We were just trying to rattle your client. You know how it goes."

Bromley nodded. "Back in the day I used to push cops to get anything they could on a suspect. We were both doing our jobs, Detective Ryder. Speaking of which . . ." He dug in his briefcase and pulled out a sheaf of papers, setting them in front of Harry and me.

"A confession?" I asked.

Bromley's face was noncommittal. "Mrs Krebbs was murdered sometime between the fifteenth and twentieth of last month, right?"

"How do you know the time of death, sir?" I asked. Last I'd heard, the date was still being considered by the Denver forensics types.

A quiet smile. "My former firm keeps a condo in Aspen. I've met people in Colorado law enforcement over the years, skiing with the governor now and then. The folks in forensics up there were happy to provide the most recent discoveries in the case."

I'd not received that information, but then I didn't schuss with the governor of Colorado. I picked up the papers Bromley had brought, seeing credit-card receipts, phone records, bills of sale, a grab-bag of numbers and dates.

"What is all this?" I asked.

The lawyer's eyes began to sparkle. "During the entire period encompassing Lainie Krebbs's estimated time of death Lawrence T. Krebbs was working from a cottage on Cudjoe Key in the Florida Keys. You're holding receipts from local restaurants and grocery stores, bait shops, a fishing-charter service, barber shop, moped rental . . . and, of course, phone records of calls from Mr Krebbs that originated in the Keys."

I looked at the big pile of alibi while hearing a low hissing in the back of my head: the sound of a case slipping from my fingertips.

Bromley said, "Larry may not suit your standards for matrimonial conduct, Detective, but he had nothing to do with the woman's death. You can now turn your attention – and taxpayer dollars – to a more fruitful avenue of investigation."

"Not yet, Nate," I said, staring him in the eye. "There's the little matter of his missing first wife. I think your client –"

Bromley chuckled openly, shaking his head like he was talking to a child. "You're talking about Angie? She lives in Vermont. I'll email you her particulars. She won't have a lot of good to say about my client, but that's what divorces do to relationships."

Harry clapped his palms to keep me from commenting on Krebbs's wife-collection abilities. We stood, Harry putting his hand behind my neck so I couldn't retreat to my desk, making me walk Bromley to the door like we were all buddies.

"I thought you retired from law, Mr Bromley," Harry said as we crossed the floor.

"I retired from working seventy hours a week, Detective Nautilus. Now I pick and choose my clients and work a few hours a week. It's closer to a hobby than a job."

"Couldn't you have arranged to work a day or two at BC&B? It seems they'd do anything to have your expertise, Mr Bromley, even if only for –"

"I'm done with them," Bromley said curtly. "And a helluva lot happier for it."

He nodded a brisk farewell and was gone.

"Looks like we mark Krebbs off our suspect list," Harry sighed as we shambled back to our cubicle. "A pity. I loved the term 'bookend killings'."

My reply wasn't polite, conjoining Krebbs and Bromley in a position that would have done the Kama Sutra proud.

A throat cleared behind us and we turned to Sally Hargreaves. Sal wore a pink blouse, knee-high green skirt and dark stockings. Her shoes were blue running models over anklet athletic socks, a good choice since she rarely sat but paced the perimeter of the second floor like a track, thinking about cases, darting into her cube only when she needed to make a note or check her computer. I figured Sally completed a marathon about every two weeks.

Sally said, "I was at my meeting last night."

"Meeting?" I smiled. "So that's what you're calling a date these days?"

"How about we retreat to the conference room?" she said.

Once inside, Sal glanced through the windows into the department, jumped up to close the door, like she was worried about eavesdropping. She sat for a three-count, then bounced up to close the blinds.

"Should I activate the cone of silence?" I said.

Sal ignored me, re-sitting and leaning across the table

so her whisper would reach Harry's and my ears. "I know how Lainie Krebbs got to Denver, guys. It'll probably never be verified. At least, I hope not in the press."

"Cryptic, Sal," I said. "How'd she make the escape?"

"Lainie Krebbs took a train."

"We checked trains, Sal," I said. "There aren't any routes between Mobile and Denver."

"I'm not talking about a railroad you can see, guys. I'm talking about one you can't."

Harry looked at me, I looked at him. Then we both stared at Sal, waiting for her to make sense.

15

"An underground railroad?" Harry said, after Sal's brief overview. "You mean like Harriet Tubman created? A secret network of safe houses to help slaves escape their owners?"

"A updated version, Harry. A system that helps women like Lainie Krebbs escape abusive relationships."

I frowned. "This network is reached through the Mobile Women's Services Center?"

"Most women's centers offer safety, temporary shelter, education, counseling, even legal services. A select few go further, becoming nodes in a secret transportation system."

"Spiriting women away for ever?"

"When a woman's life is in immediate and extreme danger. When there's no other choice."

"Calling the cops?" Harry said. "Is that a choice?"

"For a woman in this situation, a call to the cops can

be like stepping on to her own personal death row, except the executioner will be the man in her life."

Sal had hit on a major problem in law enforcement: a woman reports her significant other is threatening or hurting her. He says she's lying. Even if the cops slap the asshole in jail, he gets out ravenous for revenge. It's a Catch-22 situation: the only way to protect a woman is to put her abuser away for years. The only way to do that is if he injures or kills her.

"We can't help you right now, ma'am . . . come back when you're dead."

Harry said, "It seems a tough task, Sal, making someone gone for good."

"Think of an amateur-run Witness Protection Program, Harry. Secrecy, safe houses, transfers at night . . . A woman escapes a step at a time, a hundred miles here, two hundred there. Until she's where she needs to be."

"Who determines the destination?" I asked, fascinated.

"Sometimes the woman will have a friend or relative in an area, someone unknown to the abuser. Often the area is chosen just because it's far away. When the escaping woman arrives, a support system helps with a legal name change – the first step in identity re-creation. Employment is next. And so forth, until the woman has a new life."

"What about children? Seems like a lot of room for legal problems. A woman leaving with a babe in arms . . . the product of her and hubby?"

Sal shook her head. "The folks at the centers work

hard to mediate such situations. To keep the union together without violence. Sometimes it works, sometimes it goes horribly awry."

We didn't have to look far for an example. Last fall a Mobile's man's wife had filed for divorce. Distraught and angry, he barricaded himself in his house with wife and four kids, murdering them before committing suicide. Then there was the man living with his girlfriend and baby in Dothan, Alabama. When she decided to get her GED, he set fire to the house with girlfriend and baby inside.

Some people don't take to mediation.

Harry pushed his chair away from the table. "Let's have a tête-à-tête with the folks at the center. You explained we'd be around, right, Sal?"

Sal cleared her throat. "No one wants to talk to the cops, Harry. They're afraid of what might happen."

"There's a possibility someone in the system was killed," I said. "They have to open up."

"Lemme give you a look inside before you jump," Sally interrupted. "The folks at the center gave me the name of someone who went through the system, coming here from Boise, Idaho, two months back. Let's call her Gail for our purposes. Gail's agreed to tell her story if we commit to total silence. It'll be as close to seeing inside as there is."

"Who would we tell?" Harry asked.

"Not the point," Sal said. "Everyone in and around the system is conditioned to secrecy."

"Harry and I won't put anything in the reports," I promised. "We'll classify 'Gail' as a Confidential Informant. That cool?"

Sal nodded. "That should work. I'll let everyone concerned know."

Harry and I traded glances. We'd still have to speak with people at the center. But listening to Gail would give us better questions to ask.

Sal said, "I set the interview up for tonight at Doc Kavanaugh's place, the Doc talking to Gail, the rest of us watching on monitor. I spoke to Gail and promised she'd be safe."

"Safe?" Harry said, looking puzzled. "Then why not meet here, in a cop shop?"

Sal gave Harry a sad smile. "Cop shops enforce the restraining orders against angry boyfriends and husbands, right? How's that been working out?"

At five p.m. we drove together to Kavanaugh's home in Daphne, on the eastern shore of Mobile Bay. Her office was attached to the architectural anomaly of her single-story house, a modernist brick and wood creation à la Wright. Tucked back in the pines and oaks, it looked like part of the natural plan, "organic" being the term du jour. Our petite Merlin had conjured curried chicken salad on fresh-baked baguettes, a tomato-basil-linguine salad and, of course, beer and wine choices.

"Gail" arrived at six and Kavanaugh went to escort her to the office. No one else would meet Gail.

Kavanaugh had traded her usual contact lenses for glasses, freed her white hair to fall to the middle of her back, and wore a black tee over faded blue jeans and battered sandals. She looked like someone you could trust with your story.

The camera in the office was piped to Kavanaugh's living-room television, a flat-screen the size of my dining-room table. Sal, Harry and I turned our chairs to the screen, ready to watch the show. We found ourselves speaking in whispers, though Gail was fifty feet and two walls away.

On the television Gail cautiously entered the room and took a padded, comfortable chair. She was dark-haired, medium height and weight, pretty in a vague, non-sophisticated way. She wore a white ruffled blouse tucked into black Levis cinched with a wide Concho belt with a silver and turquoise buckle. Black middies heels. She was a smoker and Kavanaugh had provided a crystal ashtray and lighter. Gail lit up as soon as she sat. The image on the monitor was so realistic I could smell the smoke.

Kavanaugh went to a small bar in the corner. "I'm gonna have a glass of white wine, Gail. Want one?"

"I'd love it."

Kavanaugh held high a bottle from one of those new California wineries expressing hipness via wine names like Blind Toad Hill, Red Chicken, Velvet Moon and so forth. Kavanaugh's selection was named Crazy Ladies. When Gail saw the label she broke out laughing. *You go, girl*, my mind whispered to Kavanaugh. Her little gag had broken the ice with Gail in five seconds. I figured the Doc had checked every label in the wine shop to find the perfect one.

Kavanaugh poured with a heavy hand. They tapped glasses. "To crazy ladies everywhere," Kavanaugh said, adding, "Thank you for talking about your experiences, Gail."

"Officer Hargreaves said it might help find a killer. If I was dead I'd want someone to do the same for me."

"Let's start with what brought you to the women's center."

"I went there five times," Gail said, her voice a husky contralto. "The first two times for short stays until my boyfriend, James, cooled down. Then, as my boyfriend went from yelling to physical abuse, longer stays."

"Did he know you were being sheltered by the center?"

"James thought I was with friends. It got pretty bad because he terrorized them all looking for me."

"But you went back to him," Kavanaugh said quietly, nonjudgmental. "Several times."

Gail nodded as if it was something she'd considered a lot. "I didn't have a high school diploma. Or a real friend. My family only gave a shit about me when I was working some crummy job and they could borrow money I never saw again. I was fat and pimply and nearly puked when I saw myself in a mirror."

When Gail paused to light another smoke, Sal turned to Harry and me.

"Self-esteem issues. Gail was probably a typical-looking girl, but could only see her life and appearance and prospects as failure in every direction. Women who allow themselves to be abused often think they deserve it, giving subconscious assent to the treatment."

"Things got worse between you and James," Kavanaugh said, pulling our eyes back to the television.

Gail downed a healthy tot of Crazy Lady. "After he knocked out two of my teeth I went to the center in Boise. They helped me see my relationship wasn't normal, that James had a sickness. When he started threatening my life, I got a restraining order."

"How long did it take James to violate the order?"

Not *did he*, but *how long*, I noted.

"Two days. James said the order was just a piece of paper and did I believe a piece of paper could stop a knife from slicing my throat? He had been getting worse and worse, but taking out the legal order turned him crazy. He started driving past my apartment and screaming, calling my phone every two minutes. That's when I knew I had to get away, to become another person. The people at the center almost got mean."

"Mean how?"

"Saying I'd be with James forever. That I'd never change. That I wanted to commit suicide by boyfriend . . ."

I looked to Sal to protest treatment seeming cruel, or at least tasteless, but she held up a hand and nodded to the television, *Wait and listen.*

Gail said, "I broke down and started crying. 'You're

WRONG!' I started yelling 'YOU'RE WRONG, YOU'RE WRONG. I WANT TO LIVE. I'LL DO ANYTHING TO LIVE!'"

Kavanaugh nodded calmly. "That's when you were accepted for the underground railroad."

"I had to pass a test at the center. To make sure I wouldn't run back to James and tell him everything. He would have thrown gasoline into the center and burned it to the ground."

Kavanaugh stood to refill the glasses. Harry figured it out: "The abused woman has to show total commitment to the idea of No Turning Back. To make the decision that will change her life for ever."

Sal nodded. "It helps protect the center from violence. If the woman is gone, the only thing left for the abuser to attack is the system itself. More than a few men would see the system as a thief . . . personify it as a being that stole from them."

"Women stealing women from men," I said. "The misogynist's worse nightmare."

Harry nodded at the television, the interview set to resume. The Doc leaned toward Gail, her voice low. "Tell me what it was like in the system, Gail. Your experiences."

"I felt like a package, but a very important package. The first night I was picked up in an alley. A woman who called herself Alicia drove to Boise from Jackson, Wyoming, to get me. I'm not sure that was her real name – some people use fake ones. I stayed at Alicia's place – slept on the couch – two nights before being picked up by –"

"Excuse me, Gail, picked up how?"

"Alicia left me at a bridge. It was midnight. We stopped on the bridge and way up ahead we saw headlights blink. I got out and Alicia drove away. It was my first transfer and I was standing there with my suitcase – you get one that you can carry – scared to death. A minute later a van picked me up. A woman, Kate, drove for two hours until we came to a house. The highways signs said we were near Fort Collins, Colorado."

"Who owned the home?"

"Two women lived there, Bert and Lolly. They were careful about giving me space, but talking when I wanted to. Lolly always had a phone in her pocket. It rang one night and a half-hour later I'm in the back seat of a car under a blanket. We drove for hours. When I sat up I was in a park, told to go behind some trees and wait for a horn to honk three times. It was a truck with a woman at the wheel. Kathy took me to a tiny apartment above a garage. I had no idea where I was until, looking out the window, I saw a couple of service trucks with Omaha as the address of the company. I stayed there three days."

"You saw no one?"

"Only Kathy. She lived with her husband."

The first man had entered the story. "Husband?" Kavanaugh asked. "You're sure?"

"Kathy had a wedding ring."

"Did you have any interaction with the husband?"

"I only saw him the one time. He was mowing the lawn."

"From there . . .?"

"The same thing eight times. Then I was in a house in Daphne, my final destination. I stayed a week while we made plans to get me a new identity, find a job." Gail rapped her knuckles on the wood trim on the chair. "So far I've been safe."

"Were you around any men besides the husband in Omaha?"

"The fourth hand-over was to a man named Rick. I stayed in a room in his house, out in the country. He said I didn't have to talk if I didn't feel like it, I could stay in the room and read or watch television. The room had its own bathroom to the side and I could live in there."

"Tell me about Rick."

"The first couple of nights I stayed in the room with the door locked tight." She managed a self-deprecating smile. "I was pretty freaked by everything that was going on. The third night, I just wanted to be around someone, to talk about the weather and normal things. I came out of the room and Rick was on the couch laughing at *Will and Grace* re-runs. He seemed so . . . harmless. Like a puppy."

"Rick didn't frighten you?"

"I think he was gay and when I figured he wouldn't be attracted to me in . . . in that way, I relaxed. He was funny and a great cook, vegetarian things. He kept telling me I had beautiful eyes. He took pictures of them."

I shot Harry a glance. We both leaned closer to the screen.

"Your eyes?" Kavanaugh said.

"It wasn't weird or anything. Just a few pictures."

"Rick say anything while taking pictures?"

"The usual stuff . . . smile, don't blink, say cheese. It wasn't a big deal and it wasn't my face or anything."

"You're sure?"

"He showed me the pictures on the camera. Just a dozen pictures of my eyes."

Gail turned away to blow her nose. Sal shot us a glance. *Eyes.* Gail turned back and the Doc continued her gentle probing.

"How long were you there, Gail? Rick's place."

"That was the longest stay. It was a week."

"Why so long?"

"He said we had to wait for someone to make time to take me, that summer was toughest because of vacations. One afternoon he told me to pack my suitcase because it was time. We drove to a truck stop in the middle of nowhere. Another car was waiting, tucked between trailers. Rick said my life would be beautiful one day and he hoped I'd keep him in my heart forever. He kissed my forehead and I walked to the other car. When I turned around he was gone."

"You have no idea where Rick lived. Even after a week?"

"No. We were in a big old wood house in the country, almost no traffic on the road. The satellite TV didn't carry local stations. I'd figure it was in the South. The weather was warm and humid and I saw flowers blooming in Rick's back yard."

"You never asked your location?"

"He said we were somewhere in America, and it would be best if that was all I knew."

"You didn't question him?"

"Rick put his life on the line for me. No, I didn't."

"You really think he put his life on the line?"

"If James somehow managed to find me in Rick's house, he would have killed us both." She snapped her fingers. "Just like that."

The Doc leaned close to Gail. "Do you think James is still looking for you?"

Gail nodded without hesitation. "If he's alive, he'll never stop. He'll kill me in the worst way he can think up."

"Because you left him?"

Gail thought a moment and turned sad eyes to Kavanaugh.

"No. Because I embarrassed him."

Interview over. Kavanaugh and Gail stood, hugged, left the room. Sally, Harry and I waited until Doc K saw Gail to the door.

"Great job, Doc," I said.

"Rick creeps me out. Taking pictures of eyes."

"Spooked us too." I turned to Sal. "The week-long stay at a single safe house – is that normal?"

"Longer than usual. But Rick was right: the runner might be in a place where only three other folks are positioned to take her without driving three hundred miles. These people aren't like firefighters, poised to spring into action. They're ordinary folks with ordinary lives, except two or three times a year they do something extraordinary for someone they've never met and will never see again."

"Isn't the secrecy over the top?" Harry asked.

Sal said, "It was more casual a couple years back, Harry. Everyone along the chain knew in advance when someone was coming, who she'd stay with, where she went next. One day a woman went through four exchanges, made it about halfway to her destination. Turns out her husband was a sociopathic planning machine who followed her every step through the system, living in his car, watching and waiting."

I felt a chill run down my spine. "Jesus. What happened?"

"Remember the husband-and-wife academics in Durham? The home-invasion murder that was never solved? At least in the press."

I recalled the grisly crime. And how it had disappeared from view.

"The killer was the sociopathic husband?" I asked.

"The academic couple ran a safe house, Carson. Few know that. But crazy hubby missed a hand-over – pure luck for the abused wife. She was on the road again when her husband appeared at her former safe house. Finding he'd missed his wife, the husband decompensated and butchered the couple over a two-hour reign of horror, making them name the folks who'd picked up his wife. He was preparing to go after them. Luckily, a neighbor heard screams from the house, called the cops."

I recalled the ending. "The psycho blew his head off with a .45."

Sal nodded. "The law-enforcement people didn't see how publicizing the network would achieve anything. Perhaps because the prosecutor and deputy chief of police were women. The system was revamped, anonymous ever since. No passing off travelers at homes, only places where people can look over their shoulders, head home when assured of not being tailed."

"What keeps everything running?"

"A computer network, from what I hear. Someone gets on the computer and says they have a traveler near Dubuque trying to move east and caregivers east of Dubuque post their availability. Arrangements are made via throwaway cell phones, no home numbers."

"The people at the two safe houses don't meet?"

"Never. Everything's compartmentalized."

"Like spy cells," I noted. "No one knows what's going on except in their own link of the chain. It's the perfect way to keep the freaks out of the railroad. Or . . ." I raised an eyebrow at Harry, knowing he'd already gotten to the bottom line.

"Or give them a private carriage that's completely off the radar," he said.

"Jesus," Sally whispered, seeing the other side of the coin. "And no one's the wiser."

I nodded grimly. "It's a killer's dream universe, Sal. From first touch to last scream, the perp has total anonymity."

16

I called Detective Amica Cruz of the Colorado State Police. It was an hour earlier there, seven o'clock Mountain Time. She sounded tired, like it had been a long day.

"Ms Cruz, is there a Women's Crisis Center in Denver?"

I heard her stifle a yawn. "Yes. Why?"

I told her what we'd discovered from Gail. And that she might want to speak with local women's services centers. "It's a long shot," I added. "But . . ."

"I'm going to make a call or two, Detective Ryder," Cruz said, her voice suddenly all business. Don't go far."

Harry took his chair across from me, Sal pulled up another. My phone rang fifteen minutes later: Cruz. She said, "No woman of that description entered the local node."

I tried to recall if I'd used the word *node* in my explanation. If I hadn't, Cruz had somehow selected the terminology used within the system. "Did you know

99

of the existence of the railroad before this?" I asked.

No response. It was odd, a simple yes or no was all I was after.

"Detective Cruz? Are you there?"

Sal said, "Give me the phone, Carson. You and Harry take a hike for a few, right."

I shot Harry the eye and passed the phone to Sal. We walked out of earshot until waved back by Sally. She gave me the phone.

"Yes," Cruz admitted. "I'm familiar with the center. And a supporter, in most cases."

"But our victim down here didn't go into the system there?" I said.

"The only women put in the system in the last two months are a black woman in her late twenties, a thirtyish Hispanic under five-foot-three and a thirtyish Caucasian woman . . ."

"That's what we've got, dammit! I said she was –"

". . . with heavy tattoos over her neck and upper torso."

"Oh."

"I actually listened when you talked, Detective Ryder. You might extend me the same courtesy."

I apologized and hung up. I looked to Sal. "What did you say to Cruz to get her to open up?"

"I know folks at the center here. And that I consider the center an entity that does a lot of good, but occasionally operates in a legal limbo. Detective Cruz feels the same way. She was worried about negative publicity if you started flailing in all directions."

"Publicity? Flailing?"

"Telling the press your suspicions, making it appear the center had been negligent in protecting a woman. This could become a Missing-Blonde story, Carson. That's what's worrying Cruz."

The world was ablaze with economic uncertainty, nascent wars, regional massacres, and here and there the uplifting saga of hope. But the relentless maw of the twenty-four-hour news cycle seemed fixated on stories of missing young women, often blonde coeds; news organizations turning sad stories into national spectacles, an endless parade of talking-head experts analyzing and decrying every sordid aspect three times an hour. If the story stepped into the news eye, every women's center in the country would be besieged by cameras and reporters.

"Are you part of the women's underground railroad system?"

"What do you do when battered women show up here?"

"Aren't you afraid of angry husbands or boyfriends bombing your center?

The truth about the case would out, I figured. But better when all the facts were known, the lurid aspects muted by reality. Now would only be speculation and sensationalism, good for no one but the voyeuristic parasites who reveled in tragedy.

"So what did you tell Miz Cruz?" I asked Sal.

"That you and Harry were on the side of the angels. You'd keep everything under your hats. I was right, wasn't I?"

17

Q: What do your wife and a condom have in common?

A: They both spend 99% of their time in your wallet

Professor Thalius Sinclair had left his office at the university three hours earlier, had a light supper and a Scotch. He'd been to several men-only chat rooms – picking up conversations from last night – but had shifted to his favorite. He had certain special information to convey, but only if conditions were right.

Sinclair took another hit on the joint and glanced at the clock on the wall: 11.13 p.m. There would be few folks online, maybe just the ever-present HPDrifter.

1 member online

Sinclair typed in his password.

2 members online

PROMALE: Anyone home?

HPDRIFTER: Welcome, brother. You're up late.

PROMALE: I was upset by reading a report explaining why women don't want macho men. Masculine men. REAL MEN!

HPDRIFTER: I read the shit. Lesbian propaganda. You can bet none of the sad little bitches interviewed ever met a real man . . . just pussy-licking eunuchs. That's what it's come to, Promale. The FemiNazis have reduced the average American male to a groveling toadie, his lips wet with female slime.

PROMALE: Amen, brother.

HPDRIFTER: Change is coming, Promale. A hard light's set to shine on the so-called "Women's Movement". Take heart: the REAL MAN is about to return.

PROMALE: You operate this chat room, don't you Drifter? Wait . . . I'm sorry. Don't answer.

HPDRIFTER: No one knows who does what. Secrecy is our salvation. Why do you ask?

PROMALE: I want to bring up a concern. A major concern.

3 members online

MAVERICK: Hey brothers!

HPDRIFTER: Good to hear from you, Maverick. Where you been?

MAVERICK: Shift change. Been working nights,
 but I'm off. You see that magazine shit about
 bitches who hate men with balls?
PROMALE: I've got to grab some sleep, brothers.
 TTYL . . .
2 members online

Sinclair sighed and turned off his desktop computer. He reached down the desk and shut off his laptop as well. It was critical that he talk to Drifter, but alone. He'd try again in the near future.

18

Our bizarre case took a one-day sidetrack to a court action that kept Harry and me in suits and running to the stand in between objections and ploys by the defense. We did good and I was glad the opposing team was sloppy, nothing near the defense a Nathaniel Bromley might have mounted. The case went to the jury late the second morning, getting us out of the municipal courthouse near eleven, just in time to get a nervous call from Kavanaugh.

"Carson, Harry, I just heard from the Pensacola police. There's a body in the morgue they want me to look at."

Pensacola was an hour's drive down the coast. "Why you?" I asked.

"The woman had my business card in her purse. Her name is Rhonda Doakes. I'm sure I've never known anyone by that name. This whole thing is spooky."

"Maybe she had the card for the address," I ventured, my cop's mind generating solutions. "How about your gardeners? Other part-time employees?"

"They'd probably have my business cards," she said, mentally reviewing companies that kept her home and business running smoothly. "I've got a gardening service, housecleaning service, maintenance for my heating and AC, computer-system types, folks who keep the koi pond running smoothly, the place that services my car . . ." She paused in surprise. "I must hand out twenty cards a year to non-patients."

"You may never have seen this person, Doc," I counseled.

"I'm not sure if that helps, Carson. But thanks."

Kavanaugh's work didn't usually involve looking at dead bodies; tough for the first dozen or so. Harry and I volunteered to accompany Kavanaugh on her journey, part out of friendship, part detectively interest.

We made Pensacola in under an hour, entering the cooler room to see a round mound of gowned pathologist sitting and sipping coffee, and a slender black guy in a tan suit leaning a wall and reading the paper. The detective who'd caught the case, I figured. He was young, late twenties or so, meaning he was either good or connected. They rarely went together.

The pathologist was Leo Bates, morbidly obese, mid-forties, a six-foot egg with pumpkin head and a Van-dyke beard. Bates had started his career in Mobile fifteen years back, working with Clair. When it became clear she was the new Leonardo on the forensic pathology scene – or Newton, or Einstein; name your genius – Leo booked for Pensacola, where his two-hundred watts wouldn't be outshone by Clair's thousand.

Bates had done well, but harbored an infantile resentment of Clair for being better and brighter, and since I was a friend of Clair, he didn't care for me either, expressing himself via finely honed passive-aggressivity.

"Well, well, the infamous Piss-it duo," Bates said, making drama out of leaning to study my feet as I approached.

"I got something on my shoe, Leo?" I asked.

He straightened, wheezing from the effort. "Just seeing if your feet ever touch mortal ground."

"You should see how they walk across water," I said, too busy to be bothered by ego games. "You know Harry Nautilus. This is Doctor Nancy Kavanaugh. Your forensics folks found the Doc's number in the vic's purse."

The guy against the wall snapped the paper shut and walked over. "Actually," he said, "it was me who found the business card. I'm Detective Honus Clayton, Pensacola Homicide."

"Honus is an upcoming star here in Pennsy," Bates offered, licking his lips. "Had his name in the paper a half-dozen times this year, Pensacola's own version of Carson Ryder."

Clayton was studying a tray of implements. He selected one and held it in his closed hand. "We super law enforcement types have to talk, Leo," he said. "Why don't you take a restroom break and we'll call you when we need you."

Clayton flipped a shiny object to Bates, who made a clumsy catch. He puzzled at a pair of tweezers in his fat fingers.

"What the hell are these for, Clayton?"

"You got to find that thing, don't you?"

Bates snarl-whined something nasty we were supposed to infer and not hear. He padded plumply away and Clayton moved into Alpha position, waving us to follow him to the bank of coolers. "We haven't found anyone who knows the victim well, since she just moved into the neighborhood," he said, checking a pocket notepad. "She and the next-door lady got on real good, both interested in gardening. Oddly enough, the vic had told the neighbor if she dropped out of sight to call the police."

"Never good," Harry said.

Clayton nodded. "After two days of not seeing Miz Doakes, the neighbor called. It was the day the body appeared, so everything went together fast."

"Where was the body found?" I asked.

"Floating in the river and fouled in mangroves. It was discovered by kayakers."

"Left in the water?"

"We found a shallow grave-sized hole fifty paces into the mangroves. We figured the body got dumped, sand shoveled over it. There's a road and bridge two hundred feet upstream. The perp probably parked there, carried the body into the vegetation. They didn't figure on high tide floating the body free and into the channel. But the same tide obliterated any footprints."

"Cause of death?" Harry asked.

"Bates is a creepy twelve-year-old at heart, but he knows his stuff. He says Miz Doakes was beaten with fists, probably in weighted gloves." He looked to Kavanaugh. "I'm sorry, ma'am, but she's not a pretty sight."

"You don't know much yet?" Harry asked.

"We're finding a lot of dead ends. Things she appeared to be, but wasn't."

"I'm ready," Kavanaugh said, meaning she wasn't, but was as ready as she was going to get. Clayton grabbed the handle on the cooler door, rolled the body out. The face was covered with a drape. He pulled back the fabric and Kavanaugh looked down.

"Oh shit," Kavanaugh whispered, the first time I'd ever heard her curse.

My eyes went to the face of the dead woman and I felt the hard shock of recognition, despite the purple, busted-bone damage to the face. It was the woman we'd known, albeit briefly, as Gail.

The woman who'd made it through the tunnel to a brand-new life.

Kavanaugh's place was closer on the return trip, so we regrouped at Casa Kavanaugh, pushing through her front door at five p.m.

"Doakes was in the system four months back," I

argued after Doc K had brought bottles of Pete's Wicked Ale. "It's the same killer."

"Not so fast," Harry said. "Gail – I mean Doakes's eyes and hair were intact, her breasts were undamaged. She was chucked into a swamp, not set in a tableau of garbage and filth. It's a different killer, Carson."

"Maybe it only looks different to throw suspicion somewhere else."

Harry looked to Kavanaugh, sipping white vino and watching the tennis match of theories. "Doc? How about some refereeing here."

I looked expectantly toward the Doc, but she came down in the other court, handing the set to Harry. "The person who savaged Lainie Krebbs and Butterfly Lady was driven to hurt women and display them as trash and sewage. Rhonda Doakes's death was horrible, but lacking symbolic attacks on her womanhood."

"Bottom line?" I asked.

"Doakes's murderer was killing one woman. The other murderer was killing all women."

19

We called Sal and told her we were brainstorming and drinking good stuff and did she want in? Sal lived in Spanish Fort and Kavanaugh's place was nearby. She arrived at half past six and Harry revisited our conclusions.

"There is one tie to all of them," Sal said, "same killer or not. The underground railroad. Three dead women, each thinking she'd escaped an abusive relationship."

"Unfortunately," Harry said, "the underground railroad is a big and anonymous place."

"Got a US map?" I asked Kavanaugh. She scooted away, back seconds later with an atlas. I turned to the continental states and set the book on the floor, crouching and using my finger as a pointer.

"Here's a Boulder to Mobile line, moving southeast. This would be an approximation of the line an escaping woman would travel."

"A very rough approximation," Sal said. "The true route would be more zigzaggy."

"Still, the result is the same. Now extend the line past Boulder and toward the northwest . . ." I moved my finger about five hundred miles and into Idaho.

Harry knelt beside me to see the cities. "Boise is on the line," he said.

"We've got probabilities of a woman who went from the Floribama coast to Boulder, one running from Boulder to the Floribama coast, and another who escaped from Boise to here."

"Damn," Sal said. "They crossed the same geographical region."

"Somewhere between Boulder and Mobile they were identified, either pulled from the system at that time, or followed."

Everyone went silent, studying the map. It was a huge swath of territory.

"There's only one way to deal with this," Sal said after a minute. "And we're all thinking it right now."

"Put eyes in the system," Harry said.

"Exactly. Have someone pinball through, node to node, see who looks weird or dangerous. Our person's got to be undercover all the way, since the killer could be anywhere."

"It won't be easy finding the right cop," Harry said. "Who've we got?"

"Me," Sal said, like it was a done deal. "We'll invent a history and I'll ride the subterranean choo-choo."

I held up my hand. "Sal, you're a Missing Persons genius, but . . ."

"Don't *Missing Persons* me, Carson. I spent three years in Vice, remember? Half of 'em undercover with some of the nastiest vermin to slither through Mobile. I got the instincts, the radar, the acting chops. You want a terrified wife running from a head-case hubby?" Sal's eyes watered, her voice went quivery. "H-he's gonna kill me, I know he is. I can't spend another week there, he said he'd g-gut me like a deer. You've got to help me get away . . ."

Sally tucked her face in her hands and began weeping.

"Jesus," Harry whispered.

Sal's face and voice snapped back to normal. "How was that?"

"Heart-rending," I said, impressed. "But it's a crap-shoot. You might never pass through the section where the killer's lurking."

"I'll shift my final destination around. How many places did Gail stay . . . eight? I'll see if I can wangle at least a dozen, staying close to the corridor she might have taken, You guys can stay nearby. If anyone suspicious appears, waltz in and check 'em out."

I looked at Harry, figuring he too was thinking this the quickest way to force an answer from the system. But Kavanaugh held up her hand, stepping into the Devil's Advocate role.

"It assumes too much, Sally. You'll be in a blind tunnel connected to nothing but other blind tunnels. You might not see the perp coming."

"A freak like that, Doc? He'll stand out. And anyway, what's Plan B?"

Kavanaugh thought a moment. "I don't have one."

Harry shrugged. "Then this seems our best shot."

"You'll help sell this to the brass, Doc?" Sal asked Kavanaugh. An operation of this scope needed permission from above. Kavanaugh was a renowned shrink who donated expensive time to the department. The brass respected her and listened to her input.

"I'm too worn to think," Kavanaugh said, stretching and yawning. "Let's regroup in the morning."

A shiny blue truck crept past a darkened house four blocks from the University of Colorado, the moon shining over the truck's surface, as clean and bright as polished glass. Treeka parked in the shadows between streetlamps, exited, limping, looking over her shoulder, as if fearful of ambush from the closed shoe store or hole-in-the-wall bar across the street. Shooting a glance at the second floor of the tavern, she saw only darkened windows. She crept to the hatch and removed a bulging suitcase holding everything she owned at this precise moment.

She paused on the sidewalk, turning to the vehicle, resisting the urge to spit on its mirror-bright hood. She limped to the door and knocked three times. The square woman named Carol reached out for Treeka's arm and almost jerked her off her feet to get her inside.

There were three serious-faced women in the center.

The clock on the desk changed from 9:35 to 9:36. Treeka saw a newspaper on a chair, folded open to another story about the dead lady from the water plant. Treeka had seen the news on TV, but not much. The reporters said the cops didn't have a lot to go on.

"You sure you weren't followed?" the square woman said, poking her head out the door and checking from side to side.

"It's Tommy's poker night," Treeka said. "He never gets in before three."

"Whose truck?"

"His," Treeka said. "He an' a buddy take turns drivin' to save gas. They play poker over in Platteville. I never drove his truck before. I ain't driven anything in almost two years." Treeka thought a moment, said, "I forgot an' left something in the truck."

"Get it fast."

The ladies looked less worried, knowing Treeka's husband was forty miles away. She slipped outside and pretended to grab something from the passenger seat. She closed the door, pulled out the key and bent low. Holding the key tight, she scrawled deep into the paint below the window:

I cant take it no more

She started to turn away, stopped, returned to the truck and scratched letters under the previous words that spanned the width of the door panel:

Treeka limped back to the center. It was a done deal: using those words and injuring Tommy's beloved truck would mean he'd kill her for sure. There was no return, Treeka knew; the intimidation, the prison-like scrutiny, that damned yellow dress, the chokings, the three of every-fucking-thing, the relieving herself with the door open so Tommy could watch . . . She would escape or die trying.

"Get the truck out of here," the square woman snapped at a tall skinny black lady with round glasses that made her face look like an owl. "Drive it to Denver and leave it in long-term parking at the airport. Wear gloves and remember there are cameras all over –"

"Christ, Carol," the skinny woman said. "We've done this before. Calm down."

The square-faced woman closed her eyes. "I'm sorry. You guys know the drill."

Both other women disappeared into the night. That left Treeka and Carol. "When you called, you said he'd hurt you again," Carol said. "That's why you're limping?"

"He punched and kicked me. It hurts but I can walk. I'll run fast enough for the Olympics if it gets me free."

"That's the spirit, Treeka," the woman said. "Are you scared of the path you're about to take?"

"Down to my toes."

"Stay that way," the woman said. "It could keep you

alive. And by the way, from now on your name is Darleen."

Darleen. Treeka tasted her escape name on her tongue. It tasted fine.

"Before we get you started on your trip," Carol asked, "is there anything else you need from us?"

"Yes, ma'am," Treeka/Darleen said. "Could you please make me another of those blue birds?"

20

Kavanaugh was at the department when Harry and I arrived in the morning, sitting in Tom Mason's office drinking coffee. We regrouped in the conference room, Tom wanting to hear our plans. Sal ran up from Missing Persons.

"I gave the operation a lot of thought," Kavanaugh said. "I suspect the perp feels completely protected by the anonymous nature of the system. A dozen more women might be killed before he makes a mistake. I'll put my imprimatur on the idea."

"I've already packed my bag," Sal said. "Two pairs of shoes, four pairs of panties, and one nine millimeter."

Harry and I chuckled. Kavanaugh cleared her throat. "There's a drawback or two to the plan, Sally. You're known by the staff of the WCC in Mobile."

"So what? No one in the system will know me."

"We know nothing about how the killer selects his prey,

or where. The undercover plant has to be fully anonymous."

The Doc had an excellent point: We couldn't assume anyone's innocence. But Sal had an immediate counter-move.

"I'll fly to Boulder and get in the system, move south. That's even better because it'll bring me through the same selection of handlers, especially if I ping-pong my destinations. That handle your objections, Doc?"

I figured it would. But Kavanaugh had done a lot of thinking. "There's no time to be delicate, Sally," she said. "You're what, thirty-nine?"

Sally scowled. "Thirty-eight. For two more weeks."

"The other women were in their late twenties, early thirties. Plus they were both, uh, more on the slender side. If we're going to put a target in front of the killer, we should pick a type we know attracts him. Carson, Harry – you've dealt with this sort of monster before – am I right?"

"If we're setting out a meal to entice the perp," I admitted, "it's best to cook what we know he likes."

"Lousy metaphor, Carson," Tom Mason said. "But I have to agree."

"I may not be the perfect meal," Sal said. "But at least I'm food. Who else around here fits the bill?"

Kavanaugh reached into her bag and retrieved a folder. "I found one more candidate." She stood and stuck her head out the door and gestured. Footsteps approached the door until a woman in uniform stood at the threshold.

"This officer is new to the force," Kavanaugh said. "Meet Reinetta Early."

21

"No way," Harry said. "Not a chance. None, nada, nyet. Officer Early is young, unproven and without any experience."

We surrounded the conference table, the Doc and Reinetta on one side, Harry and me on the other. Tom was at the head, quiet, weighing the presentation. Tom had no idea Rein and Harry were related, Kavanaugh equally in the dark. I was starting to regret my pledge of silence.

The Doc said, "Let's listen to what Officer Early has to say. She has –"

"She has three months' experience," Harry interrupted. "It's not an assignment for on-the-job training." He started the *none, nada* chorus again.

"I agree there are experience considerations," Kavanaugh said. "Detective Nautilus, it sounds like you think she's way too green for the job."

"She's not even green yet. She's, she's . . ." Harry sputtered, trying to think of a pre-green color.

"Excuse me," Rein said quietly. "While I'm not fully familiar with everyone in this room, I am aware of their achievements, since successes are taught at the academy." She raised an eyebrow at Harry, tapping a finger on her cheek as if recalling something from a textbook.

"Tell me, Detective Nautilus . . . Didn't you once pull a suicidal man's wife from a burning house as he shot at you? Were you not wounded while doing so?"

Harry waved it off. "A flesh wound," he said, referring to the slug that had blown through one thigh to lodge in the other. "Nothing important."

"Nevertheless, did you not achieve this as a raw rookie, only sixty-seven days on the force?"

"I don't recall how long I'd been a cop, but –"

The warm browns shifted to me. "Detective Ryder, didn't you, while in uniform and new to the force, risk your life to apprehend the insane killer Joel Adrian, saving one child for certain, and many others had Adrian continued his spree?"

"Future killings are a matter of speculation," I said.

"Did you do it, Detective? As I basically detailed?"

"Basically like that, yes."

Rein appeared to think deeply about the answers elicited from Harry and me, giving the perfect four-beat dramatic pause before continuing.

"So it appears training at the MPD Academy is on an extremely high professional level. A level that enables graduates to handle themselves with distinction from the moment they hit the street. Is that not the clear lesson here, detectives?"

You would have been a helluva lawyer, girl, I thought, unable to counter her argument without dissing myself, Harry, or the Police Academy. I looked at Harry, jaw clenched, equally unable to object.

"A compelling point, Officer," Tom Mason said. "Please continue to present your qualifications."

"I received top grades at the academy, Lieutenant. I was in the uppermost percentile physically. My shooting scores were in the top five per cent. I also understand that the assignment requires acting ability. My experience there includes –"

"*Oklahoma* doesn't count," Harry interrupted.

"Oh?" Rein said, shifting her gaze to Harry. "How about *My Fair Lady*?"

"Not that either," Harry grumbled.

Rein did the cheek-tap reminiscence again. "Didn't you once go into jail undercover, Detective Nautilus? Gaining the confidence of an infamous drug kingpin within a week and thereby solving two murders? And weren't you selected for the assignment because you were so new to the force he wouldn't have known you?"

She recited as if recalling an academy text, but I suspected she'd heard the story at Harry's knee. Harry turned away, but had to nod *yes*.

"And what was your acting experience prior to this stellar performance, Detective Nautilus?"

Harry muttered under his breath.

"Pardon me, Detective?" Rein said.

"None. No experience."

"My goodness," Rein said, feigning perplexation. "Not even *My Fair Lady*?"

Tom dismissed Reinetta after her curriculum vitae had been presented and thought for a minute before speaking.

"Ordinarily, I'd put a thumbs down on the idea. But I've looked over Officer Early's records. If anything, she's underplaying her abilities. The idea of putting her undercover scares me, but every time a cop is undercover, it scares me."

"She's too new," Harry protested.

"Her case was well made, Harry. You guys kicked ass coming out of the gate for several reasons: one, you were smart; two, you had gut instincts along with the training; and three, you had mentors giving you inside skinny from day one. You came up under Zip Johnson, right Harry?"

"Zip built me into who I am today."

"And Carson, you had Harry. I want the three of you to spend the next few days together, talk out the assignment. Hit perils more than possibilities. If Early goes in, it'll be you guys handling her. We clear there?"

I looked at Harry. Misery was printed in bold across his face.

"We're clear, Tom," I said.

Tom nodded and stood, knuckles rapping the table

like a gavel. "I'll call Early's commander and get her assigned to Homicide for the next few weeks. Get that girl up to speed, guys. Teach her every trick, because I'm holding you responsible for keeping her safe."

22

"You missed the target entirely!" Harry roared as Rein stood from the floor, the firing range echoing with the sound of her rounds. It was the second of what Harry had turned into sixteen-hour workdays. "What kind of shooting was that?"

I shouldered off the wall and stepped in. "Uh, Harry . . ."

Rein held up her hand to cut me off. "It was lousy shooting, Carson. My fault. I'll try again."

Harry shook his head in disgust and reset the protective headset on his ears. "From the beginning!" he yelled, moving to the target-control button, zipping the outline of a human torso thirty yards down the range. "You've got a perp running at you and firing. You're on the ground with no cover for miles, only one chance in the world, hit him while you're rolling. Here he comes."

Harry pressed the button, the target racing toward us. "Go!"

Rein dove to the floor rolling and firing, an almost-impossible piece of marksmanship, trying to keep the target in her sights while tumbling across a dozen feet of floor.

The target zipped up. Harry rolled his eyes. "One hit," he said. "You hit him in the love-handle, Officer Early. He's still shooting and you're dead." He turned to me, bellowed, "Carson!"

I rolled my eyes. "What now?"

"Can you show Officer Early how it's done?"

"I think it's time we took a break and –"

"She needs to learn this."

I took a deep breath. "Look straight up at the ceiling, Rein," I said. "Point your weapon at that light up there. What I do is lock my shoulders, elbows and wrists into a solid unit and roll mainly with my hips and legs. The top of my body out to my weapon – the firing unit – is stable. Keep your head in the same position as you roll. Fire when you hit your belly, roll away."

She aimed at the light, did as told. "Like this?"

I didn't have time to answer, Harry sending the target down range.

"Here comes your killer," he yelled. The target flew toward us at ten miles an hour. I hit the floor, my body a straight line to the gun sight, cranking off four shots during five rolls. The target zipped to a stop as I stood. One hit in the kill zone, one on the line, two close enough to have done damage in a real-life situation.

"Wow," Rein said.

"OK, but not great," Harry sniffed. "Officer Early, your turn."

Rein stepped into position as Harry reset the target, brought it racing to us at top speed.

"Go, dammit!"

Rein hit the ground rolling and firing. The target was within reach within five seconds, Harry leaning close. "Two hits outside the zone," he snarled. "You're dead again. Set up for another."

"I have to reload," Rein said. She walked to a nearby bench and opened a new box of bullets. I pulled my cap from my back pocket and snapped it on my head.

"Where you going?" Harry said.

"Out for something to eat. You guys coming?"

"You're kidding, right? We're gonna stay until she gets it right."

I stared at him, shaking my head.

"What?" he said.

"Stop being an asshole," I said, turning toward the door. "It doesn't look good on you."

Treeka lay on a single bed in the guest room of a woman named Marge, her first stop on the railroad. Marge had left for work, saying she was sorry she couldn't stay with Treeka.

"I'm just happy there are people like you," Treeka had said.

The night before last, Meelia, the black woman with

the owl glasses, had driven Treeka west for an hour. She was funny, making Treeka laugh and mostly forget that Tommy would go crazy when he saw Treeka had run away. Meelia volunteered at the center to pay back for what everyone there did for her when her boyfriend would smoke crack and kick her around their apartment. She said the people at the center saved her life. Treeka heard the woman's serious voice, the one that was glad to be alive and proud to be part of a system that saved others.

The scariest part came when Meelia pulled into a truck stop at one a.m., the air smelling of diesel fuel and fried food. Treeka was to walk from the car side of the rest stop across to the truck side and stand beside the phone booth, waiting for two rings on the phone, which meant *Get ready to move fast.*

"Won't it look weird," Treeka asked, "me carrying a suitcase?"

"It's a truck stop at one in the morning," Meelia laughed. "Everything's supposed to be weird."

Treeka stood in the hard light beside the phone watching a tractor-trailer rig being fueled, a bearded, bear-sized driver beside the cab in stained overalls and shooting over-the-shoulder glances at Treeka. The driver wiped his windshield and disappeared into the huge black cab. Treeka jumped as the phone rang . . .

Once, twice.

She picked up the suitcase and held it tight with both hands. A rumbling diesel roar and the truck swept from the fueling bay to turn directly toward Treeka. It squealed to a stop at the curb, the passenger-side door swinging open.

"Climb up," the driver said. "Quick."

Her heart in her throat – *was this how it was supposed to work?* – Treeka pushed the suitcase up until the man pulled it inside the cab. Treeka followed, setting herself into the seat.

"Don't be afraid, miss," the driver said as he turned back to the steering wheel, his voice soft and tender, like talking to a lost child. "Sit back and relax and in a couple hours my wife, name's Marge, will fill you with sausage and eggs and tuck you into bed. We've got a nice place for you."

And away they had run.

I ate supper at a po' boy joint, buying an extra shrimp-stuffed model and a six-pack. Harry called two hours later, wanting to meet on the Causeway, a slender strip of dirt and concrete binding Mobile to the eastern shore of Mobile Bay.

He arrived after fifteen minutes. I was leaning against my truck and watching the jewel-like running lights of small craft as they crossed the dark water. Low waves pressed into the shoreline reeds and, though many months had passed since the disaster, I could smell oil, but a lot of times I knew it was in my head.

Harry walked over and leaned beside me, taking his turn studying the boats.

"You eat anything?" I asked.

"My stomach's been knotted last couple days."

I reached in the window for the spare po' boy, handed it to him alongside a can of beer.

"You think I'm being too tough on Rein, right?" he said.

"You're trying to squeeze a quarter-century of experience into a few days' training. How much time did you spend teaching her to shoot while rolling?"

"I keep seeing her outside without cover, the perp running at her shooting as he –"

"How much?"

"Counting the hour after you left, maybe three. We quit when she got dizzy and puked. Thing is, I close my eyes see every psycho we ever faced, Carson. I want Rein ready to stop them all."

"We've got two days till Boulder. It won't happen."

"I can try," he said.

I watched the dark shape of a freighter slip from the river into the bay, preparing to cross the vast waters. I turned to Harry. "Would you act like this if the person going into the system wasn't your niece?"

"I'm tired of all this talking," he said, turning to watch the ship.

23

Our training days passed in what felt like minutes, Harry trying to jam experiences and responses and procedures into Rein's head, me trying to add insight into the psychology of misogynist killers. There was a fair body of literature on these sad boyos, not exactly a rare species.

Tom Mason called Harry, Sal and me into his office the final morning. "The Chief and I talked to the Colorado State Police . . ." He riffled a sheaf of reports. "It's a joint operation and we're good to go."

"How's Amica Cruz fit in?" I asked.

"Detective Cruz is your primary contact. She said she was 'down with the situation'." Tom puzzled a moment and looked at Harry. "That's a good thing, right, being *down* with something?"

Tom was old school, amazed the word "text" had

turned into a verb and "killer apps" were desired features on cell phones. Harry was only five years younger than Tom, but had become the Lieutenant's contemporary linguistics advisor because, being black, Harry was supposed to know hip things.

Harry nodded. "Down is currently up, Tom."

Sal said, "How do I fit into this?"

"I want you digging into the cases from every angle. Putting Officer Early into the system is a crapshoot, and if it doesn't pan out we'll have to crack this nut from the outside."

Sal nodded, miffed at being replaced as the undercover operative, but knowing it was the right play. "I'm gonna ride Krebbs. Check out every piece of his alibi."

"Do it carefully. I don't need Nate Bromley howling at me for harassment. Where's our undercover girl?"

"With Doc Kavanaugh," I said. "Getting some last-minute grounding in anti-fem types."

"Best get Officer Early back here," Tom said, looking at his watch. "You're leaving in two hours."

From an approaching jet, Denver airport looks like Salvador Dalí's idea of a circus tent. I suppose the white multi-pronged pinnacles were symbolic of snowy mountaintops, but all I saw was a weird tent. Then we were down and watching bags ride the carousel. Amica Cruz had wondered about holding a sign, but I'd told her to look for a big square black guy bookended by a lovely light-complected black woman and a six-foot, dark-haired Caucasian guy with a limp.

We were grabbing the final bag when intersected by a petite Latina with shoulder-length auburn hair and brown eyes the size of saucers. She wore a white blouse over khaki pants and looked as fit as a gymnast.

She said, "I take it you're the –"

"The Early Show," I affirmed. "One star, two supporting players."

We did formal introductions. Cruz looked at me and nodded toward the door. "I'm parked right outside, you won't have to walk very far."

"I'm good," I said, slinging my bag over my shoulder as we started for the door. Cruz frowned at my suddenly normal stride.

"You're not . . ."

"It was possible for another trio to look like us," I said, "but I figured the odds of one of them limping were astronomical."

Cruz shot a look at my companions. Rein giggled, Harry sighed.

"Maybe you'll get used to it, Detective Cruz," he said. "I haven't."

Boulder was a half-hour's drive, crossing brown and rolling desert, the magnificent Front Range of the Rocky Mountains in the distance. A wide-eyed Rein pointed at a skeletal orb of brush rolling across the highway.

"Is that a real tumbleweed?"

"Welcome to the Wild West, Officer Early," Cruz said

into the rear-view mirror. "Of course, some days it's wilder than others."

Cruz pulled into Boulder, crossing Pearl Street, a draw for tourists and townies alike. "Anyone hungry?" she asked.

We headed to one of Cruz's favorite lunch joints, happy to move cramped legs. Boulderites spent a lot of time outdoors, every third vehicle boating a rack: bike, kayak, ski or multi-tasking. Bicyclists were everywhere, from students on Wal-Mart cheapies to full-spandex Lance Armstrong wannabees on featherweight road machines. I watched someone's great-grandfather blow past on a recumbent bike, grinning like a madman as wind parted his white beard.

"Everyone looks like they just stepped out of a vitamin catalog," Rein noted with a smile of approval.

Cruz said, "Boulder's the fittest town in the country as determined by weight, hours of exercise a week, time spent outdoors and so forth."

"You look like you spend a goodly amount of time exercising, Detective Cruz," I said. "Part of the culture?"

A rueful smile. "I grew up in Denver, where my aunt owns a popular taquería. Thanks to her cooking I used to weigh twenty pounds more. When I got assigned to the Boulder post I wanted to break all my mirrors. Then I bought a bike. I'm baselining at two hundred miles a week."

"Two hundred lovely miles," I amended.

Harry shot me a look. "This is all real nice, but how 'bout we grab some chow and get working. I want to go over everything with Rein one more time."

134

"Huh-uh," Cruz said. "You had your turn, now it's mine. I need to fill everyone in on what we know, and where we're going with this thing."

After we'd eaten, Cruz drove us to our lodging. We'd hoped to stay near the Boulder women's center, and Cruz had reserved a cabin in Chautauqua Park, a community of cabins on a hill angling up to the Flatiron Mountains, which resembled the back of a gigantic stegosaurus pushing up through the earth.

"Can we take a peek at the women's center?" Rein asked. "It's close, isn't it?"

We passed the center on our way to the cabin, a nondescript house in a business-residential zoning, a bar across the way, a shoe store down the street. The University of Colorado was centered a few blocks distant and students wandered the street, some looking hip, some looking studious, others looking lost.

"There it is," Cruz said to Rein. "Your door to the unknown."

"There's still time to change your mind, girl," Harry said quietly. "Say the word."

Rein either didn't hear Harry or pretended not to, watching the small brown house as if dissecting its secret intentions, turning her head to study it even as the house fell away into the distance.

"What do you think, Rein?" Harry prodded, an undertone in his voice saying, *You can still bag the assignment.*

Rein said, "This is all so cool."

24

Liza Krupnik entered the scarlet-carpeted, high-ceilinged room at seven-fifteen p.m. The bar had opened at six-thirty, perhaps a hundred people in attendance, more entering every minute. It was one of several such gatherings during the year, an opportunity for the social sciences departments to display collegial conviviality and monetary benefactors to be fêted. "The contributors need to feel a connection to the U," someone had once explained to Liza. "They like to be recognized and patted on the head. It helps loosen their wallets and pay our salaries."

"Salaries?" Liza said.

Liza smoothed down her black dress and ambled to the bar table, grabbing a glass of wine, something better than the usual U-whine, as she and Robert termed the boxed swill normally set beside the platters of cheese, crudités, chips and salsa. She bantered with colleagues for several minutes, keeping an eye on the door for her colleague.

Or Sinclair.

She looked up to see Robert crossing the floor, one side of his shirt tucked, the other fluffing halfway out. He finger-pushed his glasses up the bridge of his long nose and his eyes found Liza, mouth arching into a smile. He pointed to the bar, meaning he was going to pick up a drink. *You?* he mouthed, and Liza lifted her full glass to indicate she was fine. He nodded and angled toward the bar.

Robert had been gone for a few days, something he did every couple of months, heading to Montana to care for family. Liza had missed her colleague during his absence. Robert Trotman had become her only confidant in the department, perhaps owing to the proximity of their cubbyholes, or maybe being in disparate sociological fields. Academia offered far fewer jobs than there were applicants, turning teaching assistants into fierce competitors.

Though the soft-spoken Trotman wasn't much of a conversationalist, he was a good listener, interested in Liza's latest musical purchases and her volunteer efforts, and a more-than-willing helper when Liza's unruly civic-volunteer schedule conflicted with academic duties. Recently receiving an award for her work at a local agency, Liza had tried unsuccessfully to get Robert to hang the plaque in his office, since she felt it equally his. Trotman's help even went so far as keeping a copy of her calendar in his office, prepared to step in should a conflict arise, usually in the guise of Professor Sinclair.

"*Roberto? Uh, his nibs just said he needs a hundred handouts copied by . . .*"

"*You've got a staff meeting in an hour, Lize. I see it on the calendar. Go to your meeting, girl. I'll put everything together for His Highness.*"

"*You're a lifesaver, Roberto. It's a training meeting and I have to –*"

"*You can tell me everything in wondrous detail tomorrow. Go!*"

There was another aspect to their relationship: Despite the time the pair spent together, Robert Trotman had never hit on Liza. At first she'd thought him gay, then decided he wasn't, then decided she didn't give a shit either way: he was her friend . . . disheveled, prone to poutery, a bit paranoiac about perceived slights – usually from Sinclair – but bright as a whip, interested in her life, and always ready to step in and lend a hand.

Liza had tried to encourage her anxiety-prone amigo to ask Sinclair for a regular schedule so he could actually plan ahead, but Robert had gone white at the prospect of confronting the Famous Sociologist. Liza felt irritation at Trotman's lack of backbone, and then realized she hadn't set a regular vacation schedule either; both slaves to the professor.

Robert appeared a minute later, a can of beer in hand. With his beardless complexion and languid eyes, he looked almost feminine, and closer to a sophomore than a grad student.

"How was your vacation?" Liza asked.

Trotman pushed a comma of black hair from his forehead. "I only had nightmares of Professor Sinclair twice in four nights. So pretty good. How was your volunteers' meeting? Monday, right? Did the committee change anything?"

"Nope. As figured. The training sessions are still once a month, Wednesdays and Thursdays. Carol's still in charge, but she's been training Charlotte to run things."

"Training the trainers," Trotman nodded absent-mindedly, his eyes searching the room. "Is the king here, Lize?"

Liza shook her head. "His Majesty always arrives late and leaves early. He's not social. He's only here because someone has to represent the department with Dr Bramwell gone."

"When's Bramwell back from her sabbatical?" Trotman asked, his tone hopeful.

Liza chuckled. "Would you stop asking me that! Dr Bramwell's been gone less than –"

"Think we could write and beg her to come home and save us?"

"Where would we send the letter? She's in constant motion."

"Hiding from Sinclair," Trotman said. "A happy woman."

Liza pointed across the room. "There's his nibs coming in the door."

"He looks angry," Trotman said. "Let's move across the room."

"We have to greet him, Robert. You know the protocol."

Sinclair was talking to Robert Morgenthall, the head of the Psychology department, and Liza inched to Sinclair's side as Morgenthall nodded and turned away. "Fuck behaviorism," Sinclair said instead of goodbye, Morgenthall waving farewell over his shoulder.

"Hello, Doctor," Liza said, stepping in front of the Great Sociologist and fighting her feeling that she needed to bow.

"Liza Krupnik," Sinclair said, as if reading a name from a Rolodex. "Tell me, Miss Krupnik, do you feel the desperation?"

"Pardon me, sir?"

Sinclair waved his hand, meaning the crowd, everyone in the room and maybe beyond. "Desperate souls jockeying for position near someone noteworthy, the frozen smiles of false bonhomie, the sharpening of knives awaiting unsuspecting backs?"

"I guess I'm too busy enjoying the free food, sir," Liza offered.

"Good evening, Dr Sinclair," Trotman said from the side. Sinclair turned as if expecting something interesting, face falling at finding the jittering Trotman.

"Oh, Robert, you're here."

"Y-yes sir. I got back from Montana just a couple days—"

140

Sinclair turned to the sound of his name trilled across the room. Liza looked over her shoulder to see Dorothy Balfours, a slender and stately woman she and Trotman had named the Dowager Fundraiser. In her early sixties, Balfours was the widow of the infamous "Timber" Bert Ellison, a man who'd made his money in logging businesses from the sixties into the eighties. She'd spent her early life accompanying her husband from logging camp to logging camp, a quiet woman who walked her husband's footsteps like a shadow.

"The Dowager Fundraiser crooks her finger and he runs to her," Trotman whispered as Sinclair turned and crossed the floor. "I'll bet the Famous Sociologist hates being a woman's wind-up toy."

Liza watched Sinclair greet Balfours, barking out a greeting. The Dowager's timber-baron husband had been cut down twenty-three years ago while poaching virgin timber from government land. He'd been standing atop a donkey engine and cursing his workers when a dragline snapped, a recoiling cable slicing Timber Bert in half as neatly as a buzz saw, one side falling east of the engine, the other dropping west. Sierra-Club types – and folks who'd had the misfortune to work for Ellison and get shorted on a paycheck – dubbed the incident "The Revenge of the Trees".

Ellison died childless and intestate, the bulk of his money invested in strip joints and legal brothels in Nevada – the swaggering lumberman bragging that "pussy was where the money was". To the surprise of everyone, and as if a yoke had been thrown off, the quiet wife somehow found her voice and – with the help of a feisty lawyer – blunted efforts to buy her off for pennies on the dollar, standing defiant until standing atop one-point-six million dollars.

As if in penance for her husband's often-illegal denuding of forested mountainsides, Dorothy Balfours – reverting to her maiden name a month after her husband's demise – began studying investments in the future, green technologies that were at the time barely pencilings on engineer's desks.

Avoiding more fantastical concepts, Balfours invested in structural advances: improved home insulation, less toxic coolants, energy-efficient electrical motors. As the ideas and inventions of the non-glamorous companies in her portfolio quietly become mainstream technology, Balfours found her net worth increasing to what many whispered was a fortune surpassing forty million dollars.

Nonetheless, her mountainside home in northeast Boulder was modest by local-wealth standards, a half-hidden assemblage of local stone and glass and solar panels, nestling like a bashful gem in the magnificent setting of the Front Range.

"Oh God," Trotman said, looking across the room, face drained of color and his voice weak as wet paper.

"What, Robert?"

"Sinclair yelled your name. He's waving us over. What'll we do?"

"We go as summoned, Roberto," Liza said, taking her

companion by the arm and pulling him toward their boss. "Whatever you do, don't piss your pants."

They darted around a tipsy, overdressed professor from the theater department who slit his wrists annually – very shallow cuts; the university kept it quiet and waited out the next yelp for attention – who made a flamboyant twirl as they passed, bumping Liza's glass and sending wine splattering across her right breast. She dabbed frantically with Trotman's proffered napkin before arriving in Sinclair and Balfours's company.

Sinclair raised an eyebrow at Liza's dampened breast. "Are you lactating, Liza? I didn't even know you were pregnant."

"No, I mean . . . uh, there was a bit of a spill and –"

Liza caught herself in mid-apology and looked at Sinclair. He was grinning. Was the Famous Sociologist joking with her?

Sinclair nodded toward Dorothy Balfours, dressed in a simple green sheath, natural gray hair piled atop her head like it had been the easiest way to deal with it. *The Dowager Fundraiser looks like a real person,* Liza thought, not like certain pampered-poodle benefactors who needed royalty-level pampering to keep the largesse flowing. Balfours seemed genuine, whatever that meant any more.

"Ms Balfours wanted to see where her money is going," Sinclair said, "so I'm humoring her." He nodded toward Liza. "This is one of my most promising apprentices, Liza with a Z. Please don't ask her to sing."

143

Liza extended her hand. "Liza Krupnik."

Balfours's handshake was dry and firm. "Pleased to meet you, Ms Krupnik. Anyone who works in the Sociology department has both my respect and condolences."

Sinclair grinned past the barb and nodded to Trotman. "And here's Robert, another toiler in the vineyards. He crunches numbers. Positively massacres them."

Balfours leaned forward. "I'm sorry, what was your last name, Robert?"

"T-Trotman."

"You're a statistician, then?" the woman asked, her head canted as if actually interested. Trotman stared at the graceful woman like he didn't understand the question. Liza bumped Trotman's ribs with an elbow, restarting his brain.

"Y-yes, Statistics. Volumetrics involving consumer choices based on data derived from –"

Sinclair held up a hand. "Please, Robert. We have to stay awake until the soirée is over. Was that enough, Madame Balfours, or should I introduce you to the departmental dog?"

"Do you really have one?" Balfours asked, a wry smile on her face, as though long accustomed to Sinclair's antics.

"Yes, and it's probably the best TA I have." Sinclair looked at the pair and nodded. "Thank you, kiddies. You may now return to anonymity."

25

"You have your action clothes?" I asked as Rein pulled garments from her suitcase. We were kicking off the action tonight, turning Rein into a threatened lady. Normally a woman might make several visits to a center – like Rhonda Doakes – before the threat level made the vanishing act a possibility. Disappearing into the system was a red-alert condition, and we had to get past the ramp-up colors in days, not weeks.

"I'm thinking something spangly." Rein held up a low-cut sleeveless shirt with gold sequins.

"No, dammit," Harry said from the couch, turning a thumbs down on the selection. "You're out of the life, right? That's the role."

Rein took a deep breath. "My character is used to glittery clothes, Harry. I can't go dressed in business casual. It's not what she'd wear."

"It's too revealing," Harry argued.

Rein cocked her hips and rolled her eyes. "It's what people my age wear, Harry. Stop being so old."

Harry froze. Rein realized what she'd said. "You know what I mean," she backtracked. "I'm dressing in a contemporary manner. The top came from Wal-Mart."

"I'm taking a walk," Harry said. The door slammed behind him.

"It's OK, Rein," I said. "He's having a hard time."

"This operation is the kind of thing he's told me about since I was a kid. Putting yourself out there to help others. I'd think he'd be – he'd be . . ."

I saw tears come to her eyes. "What?" I asked.

"Proud of me. I just want him to be . . ."

Her voice failed and she fell into my arms. "He's very proud of you," I said. "But the pride is hidden so deep under his fear he can't find it. It's why he pushes so hard, gets so angry. He's scared."

"It doesn't seem to get to you, Carson," she said. "His moods. Snapping at everything."

I shrugged. "Mostly I find myself studying the power of his feelings."

She looked at me in puzzlement. "Why?"

"It's foreign to me, Rein. No one ever loved me like that."

Treeka slipped from the compact car into the dark country park, pulling her suitcase behind her. The only sounds were the burring of crickets and a growl of semis from the distant interstate. A gibbous moon hung low in the sky.

"The road circles behind the playground," Marge said through the window, pointing past shadowy swings and slides. "Your next helper should be parked behind those trees. Wait for lights to blink three times."

Treeka nodded. Everything about the system – the 'underground railroad' several had called it – was spooky.

"Walk to those trees and wait for lights to blink," Marge said. "Don't dare get close if there's no lights."

They'd been on the road for hours, Treeka's heart in her throat every mile of the way. Though she was sure Tommy couldn't have tracked her, she was still frightened. She reached into her purse and found the blue bird in her wallet, safe. She squeezed her wallet for luck.

The woman beside Treeka said, "Time to go, Darleen. God be with you."

"Bless you," Treeka replied, pushing tears from her eyes and waving a forever farewell to the woman with whom she'd spent three days. Treeka had stayed in a spare bedroom in the woman's home, never venturing outside unless it was night, and only then in the back yard. Marge's husband, the trucker who picked her up at the truck stop, had left the next day, running a load of electronic parts to Detroit.

Treeka crossed the small roadside park, feeling cool grass on her sandaled toes as she passed swings and a slide. She looked into the cluster of maples behind the playground. There, on a pull-off, was a large truck, black in the shadows.

The lights made three brief blinks, like Morse code: *flashflashflash*. Behind her, Treeka heard her temporary savior drive away. The hand-over was made.

Treeka pulled her cardboard suitcase tight and walked to the SUV. "Darleen?" asked the driver, a voice a dozen feet away, behind the wheel. It was a whispered rasp.

"I'm Darleen," Treeka replied.

"Hop in, dear. Toss your stuff in the back seat. Hurry . . . The police patrol the park every half-hour. They're almost due."

Treeka climbed into the front passenger seat as the diesel engine rattled. She aimed a prayer toward the moon and held her breath as the truck roared toward the anonymity of the interstate.

In the low light of the truck's instrumentation, Treeka shot glances at her new protector. A lesbian, almost surely. No trace of make-up, rugged, lined face of someone in her forties who'd seen time outdoors. It was actually a rather handsome face, slender and well proportioned, cheekbones high, nose straight and aquiline, the jaw firm. The brown-toward-blonde hair was close-cropped and mannish, with just a touch of feminine shag and highlighting. The woman wore faded blue denim, shirt and jeans. Cowboy boots below. She drove the truck with a solid authority, blowing past slower traffic, settling into the center lane, the engine at a steady rumble, like a powerful ship cleaving through deep night.

During her pre-flight instructions, as they were laughingly called by the black woman with the owl glasses,

Treeka had been told most of the links in the chain were women. There were some husband-and-wife teams and a few men. Some of the women were gay, as were some of the men, but in the system everyone was sexless, no interest in anything but helping women along the road to freedom. "So if you have anything against gays," her instructor had pointedly told her, "get over it now."

"I don't dislike anyone for being who God made them," Treeka had said. "Except one."

"Are you hungry, dear?" the driver, her new benefactor, asked Treeka when they were fifteen minutes past the exchange.

"No, I'm fine, thanks."

"I've got coffee in a Thermos. Valium, if your nerves are shaky. Or whiskey if you prefer. Hell, my nerves are shaky and I'm not on the run."

"Really, I'm fine. I just need to –"

"I'll stop talking so much, and you just lean back and relax, sleep. We've still got a couple hours to go, but then you'll have a bright new place to live. At least until the next jump."

"I think you folks were sent by Jesus," Treeka said. "Helping people get new lives in new places. I can't wait until I get to –"

The driver jammed her palm into the horn, the blast drowning out Treeka's words. "No," the driver said, releasing the horn. "Don't tell me. Don't tell anyone. That way only one link in the chain knows where you are at any given moment. You don't want *him* finding you, do you?"

"I'm sorry. I was told a dozen times not to say where I was coming from or going."

"Don't worry about it, dear. It's all about keeping you safe."

Treeka looked at the woman's hands. Large and hard, like a rancher's hands. The woman was tanned, too, like she spent a lot of time in the sun. Even her raspy voice sounded sizzled in the hard sun. A lesbian for sure, Treeka thought. It didn't bother her a bit; Treeka figured that, given the hatred Tommy had for lesbians – though he'd probably never knowingly spoken to one – they must be pretty good people.

"Half-past nine," the driver said, breaking into Treeka's thoughts. "We'll be there by midnight. You can get a shower; I'll fix us up a big snack. Tomorrow, well . . . you'll love what I've got planned for you."

The woman started laughing.

26

*Q: What's the first thing a woman does when
she gets back from the battered women's
clinic?*

*A: The god-damned dishes if she knows what's
good for her.*

Setting his briefcase and laptop on the desk, Sinclair fired
up his iMac and hurried to the chat room.

1 Member online

Figuring HPDrifter was lurking silently and waiting
for company, he sipped his single malt, took a toke from
his joint, and entered his password.

2 Members online

PROMALE: Another day surrounded by women. I
had to kiss one on its filthy cheek to display
camaraderie. I'm living a false life, a chain

built from lies, having to interact with these objects, to pretend they're fully sentient humans.

HPDRIFTER: Sorry you had to touch one without getting a blowjob in return. I've been camping alone beside a mountain stream filled with trout. I didn't see a woman all weekend and yet I was a half-hour from a town filled with them, the worst kind: educated (supposedly). More than half the undergraduates in our once-proud universities are women! The goddamn quotas push them through the doors like so many grunting swine.

3 Members online

RAISEHELL: The job I WANTED got handed to a woman. I been working toward it day and night but the goddamn supervisor handed it over to a fucking woman. I been working there ten years, she's been there four.

HPDRIFTER: The time will come when justice will prevail. Mark my words.

RAISEHELL: I'M READY! TELL ME MORE.

HPDRIFTER: A New Time is about to dawn. We're going to undo the sins of the past. I give you my solemn pledge you will see the effect of these words.

RAISEHELL: When is this going down? What is it?

HPDRIFTER: I can't speak freely because the

FemiNazis have castrated the First Amendment. But major changes are in the wind.

RAISEHELL: About fucking time! OH SHIT . . . got to go, dog just puked on the floor.

2 Members online

PROMALE: Now that we're alone, Drifter, I have something I'd like to say.

HPDRIFTER: I remember you were about to say something the other day. Why didn't you?

PROMALE: It concerns one of us . . . a regular visitor to this holy room: RAISEHELL. I worry about him, Drifter.

HPDRIFTER: He's been a solid member of this room for months. Explain yourself.

PROMALE: His grammar is erratic one day, good the next. Sometimes he uses numbers for words, sometimes not. One day he puts exclamation marks everywhere, the next time he barely uses them.

Sinclair leaned back and watched the screen as a minute elapsed.

HPDRIFTER: Conclusion?

PROMALE: There are two RAISEHELLS. At least.

This time three minutes passed. Sinclair relit a dead joint and stared at the screen until lines appeared.

HPDRIFTER: I've considered your thesis and find merit. You suspect RAISEHELL is a fake? A plant?

PROMALE: The FemiNazis gather anything they can get against us. I think we've got a spy in the house, brother.

27

A half-hour later Rein and I parked in front of the center in an eight-year-old Chevy pickup Cruz had borrowed from a colleague. I wore paint-spattered cut-offs and a T-shirt advertising cigarettes, one of those freebies handed out by tobacco companies near high schools and colleges. My role was Accidental Samaritan. Rein was Battered Woman. My job was to set the scene, hers to upstage me and be sheltered by the center tonight.

Harry had another act to add, but that came tomorrow.

I looked across the street at the slender two-story bar, the Beacon, seeing no one at the front window, no one on the small porch upstairs either, just a lonely blue bike. Rickety metal stairs angled down the side of the building. The place recalled an apartment I once rented on the periphery of the University of Alabama, tumbling down the stairs a time or two after nights on the town.

I gave Rein a good-luck hug then reached into my pocket for the vial of fake blood, splashing her blouse as she dabbed drops into her nose. I took her hand and guided her to the front door of the Women's Crisis Center of Boulder.

"Showtime," I whispered, one-arming the door open and pushing through, holding Rein under my arm as if keeping her up. She played fumble-footed, disoriented, like she'd been pulled from a garbage compactor. There were two women talking, one behind a desk, one leaning the wall to the side. The sitting woman was fortyish, square-built, with short red hair and dark eyes. The standing woman was in her mid-thirties, slender and black, with delicate features and round, Elton John-sized glasses. Their eyes went wide at our entrance.

"What is it?" the square woman said, jumping up. I swung Rein around to drop her into one of the chairs in the tiny room, barely space for a desk and four mismatched chairs. She flopped forward and tucked into herself, a portrait in misery.

"She's my neighbor," I said. "Y'all got to do something. She told, uh, this guy she wanted to leave him. He went crazy and started pounding on her."

"Is he nearby?" the square-built woman asked, jumping to the front door and throwing the lock.

"No. He beat and booked."

The square-built woman knelt beside Rein and took her hand. "What's your name, dear?"

Rein wiped her face with the back of her hand, wet,

she'd made herself cry real tears. "S -Sondra, Sondra Jakes."

"My name is Carol," the square woman said. "That's Meelia over there. Are you all right, Sondra? Is your nose broken?"

Rein started sniffling, like trying to grab hold of herself but not there yet. I leaned in again. "I had medical training in the Army, ma'am. Nothing's broken and I got the bleeding stopped on the way over."

Carol looked at me and nodded. I'd jumped from unknown quantity to someone with the intelligence to understand first aid. We wanted to make Rein look hurt, but didn't want paramedics called.

"Do you know the signs of concussion?" the woman asked me.

"I've made three pupillary checks and she's OK. I stopped at a gas station and told her to pee and look at it. No blood."

I'm not sure what all that meant, but it added to my cred. "You don't think she's injured enough to call an ambulance?" Carol asked.

I waved it off. "The guy wanted to scare her bad, but not break anything."

A frown from the lady in the owl glasses. "No one called the police?"

"The guy had a gun, ma'am, the grip hanging outta his pocket. I never seen so many doors close so fast."

"But couldn't someone make an anonymous call to –"

I motioned the woman named Meelia to follow me to

the corner. Carol sensed I was about to say something important to the situation and followed.

"She called the guy her boyfriend," I whispered. "But he's really her, uh, pimp. Everyone on the street's scared of him because he's a psycho. I heard rumors about him, nasty stuff."

"Like what?" Meelia asked.

"Two women that worked for him disappeared. There one day, gone the next. Tee Bull – that's his street name – laughing about them being where no one would find them. He didn't mean California."

Both shot a look at Rein, then at each other. I said, "Sondra's a really good person, lady. I think she got jammed up, had to do what she had to do. We live in a rough neighborhood."

"She's on drugs, though. Right?" Meelia asked.

Most hookers are on drugs. Some get hooked before they enter the life, selling themselves to pay for the habit. Then it becomes the only way to get through the days and nights. An addicted woman wasn't allowed into the system, the addiction making her erratic and a threat to everyone concerned. But we had cooked up a story that brought Rein in clean and, even better, made her a candidate for redemption.

"She was on dope once," I said, setting up the story. "You could tell by talking to her. But for the past couple months she's been off the shit – you can tell that, too. I thought she'd stopped doing that, uh, other thing. Hooking. Until he showed up."

The women went back to Rein, taking a chair to each side.

Carol said, "Sondra? Are you using? We don't judge anyone here at the center, but we need you to tell the truth. Truth is how we help you."

Rein unfolded from herself, her face a mix of fear and determination.

"I quit drugs, every one. I been to that twelve-step over on Riser Avenue. I did it all in secret and on my own. I been clean of dope for two months and the thought of ever doing that stuff again makes me sick. I even quit smoking and drinking, everything. My baby sister goes to high school and I been borrowing her books so I can get my diploma. I took the practice test two weeks ago. The teacher said I'd nail the real test. All I got left to do is get away from Tee Bull and I can have a real life."

"What's that mean to you, Sondra?" Carol asked. "Real life?"

"I wanna go to school and be a nurse. I did my own study of the job market and there's a real shortage, so I can get a job right away when I get certified. I wanna work at a doctor's office, a pediatrician. I wanna get married to a guy who likes to laugh and tell stories. I wanna family and a house with grass in the yard. I can do it, too. I know I can."

Rein's delivery was brilliant: street rough with the incidental polish of someone driven to read, to grab the bootstraps and pull. I gestured the lady named Carol to the side.

"Can you help her?" I begged. "Can you hide her?"

"We can give her a place to stay for a night or two."

I shook my head like the offer was totally inadequate. "Lady, if you saw Tee Bull, you'd know she needs to be locked away in a Brink's truck."

I left Rein at the center, a one-woman show whose opening-night performance had to convince the women that she was in dire need of a disappearance in days, not weeks. Returning to the truck, I felt hairs prickle on the back of my neck and checked behind me, to the sides, seeing only darkness and the interior lights of the bar across the street, its second-floor windows dark and curtained.

From this point on, everyone was suspect.

28

We met with Cruz the next morning. Perhaps knowing our Southern systems wouldn't take well to tofu smoothies or whatever fuels the bodies of Boulderites in the a.m., she took us to a buffet joint where we could have eggs and bacon while Cruz nibbled prosciutto-girdled melon.

"When Officer Early comes home, so to speak, we have a special suitcase for her. It has a powerful GPS device built into a false bottom. The satellites keep track and you watch on an enabled phone or laptop. You'll be living out of the vehicle hours, maybe days at a time."

Cruz was dead-on about living in the car: Staying close to Rein meant staying in motion. If she got to a safe house and it had a low threat index, we might be able to get a motel room if one was close, but everything would be dictated by circumstance.

"How do you see this going down?" Harry asked after

Cruz had filled us in on other planned aspects of the operation.

"Officer Early should return from the center's safe house in a day or two. She'll have to do the act a few more times, bring the threat home to the folks at the center. You're on stage tonight, right, Detective Nautilus?"

"So I'm told."

"Break a leg," Cruz said.

"This looks ridiculous, Carson," Harry said, staring into the full-length mirror. Ten hours had passed since breakfast with Cruz and we'd re-played our roles a dozen times. My partner was wearing a purple pinstriped suit with extra padding in the shoulders. We'd found the improbable getup at a costume store, maybe created for XX-size Dick Tracy wannabes or Sky Masterson impersonators. Harry was born with shoulders you could set pumpkins on, the outsize pads making his profile Frankenstinian. His silk shirt was silver lamé, open to the third button. The chains around his neck were fake gold, but we didn't think anyone would get close enough for an appraisal. Ditto the rings on Harry's sausage-thick fingers; dime-store crap, but they sparkled like the first ten seconds of cheap champagne.

"Stop whining," I said, standing behind him like a tailor, picking lint from his collar. I reached to the box at my back and revealed a black fedora with scarlet band, size 7 $7/_8$. When I'd tried it on, the chapeau had fallen to the bridge of my nose. I set it atop Harry's noggin, a perfect fit.

"Your crown, sire," I proclaimed. "Thou royal pimpness is complete."

Tonight's performance involved shortening the length of time it took for a potential runner to be accepted by the center. We'd established Rein as smart enough to get off drugs and make something of herself, and lacking family in the area to either turn to or keep her anchored. My concerned-neighbor scenario had established a viable threat to Rein's safety via her procurer. She was, in short, a candidate for the underground railroad.

Now it was time for the final straw, ratcheting up the threat index. Harry was in costume, Amica Cruz had supplied the wheels, a ride confiscated from a fer-real pimp in Denver a month back: a chartreuse Hummer with twenty-four-inch spinning rims and two month's worth of Zimbabwe's chromium exports. The upholstery was fake leopard. There was a wet bar in the rear. The buggy sat outside our door where it seemed an attractant for a group of nameplate-wearing conventioneers from Cincinnati, and I had to twice shoo them away and wipe sweaty fingerprints from the smoked windows.

I reached into a bag on the nightstand and picked up the final piece of subterfuge. "Hey, bro," I said, tossing a small package to Harry. "Catch."

He stared into his hand. "Grillz?"

Grillz were metal jewelry worn over the teeth; like pants worn around the thighs, medallions the size of pies, and side-facing ball caps, they were another fine gift from the hip-hop culture. Harry slipped the monstrosity over his teeth, turned to me and stretched back his lips, showing a row of silver fangs studded with diamelles. The effect was freakish, a grillz-wearer's metallic grin as unsettling as a person with no irises, just white.

"Well?" Harry asked.

"You look like a piranha."

He thought about the simile. "Seems to fit."

Time to boogie. I went to the window, the parking lot now dark, the conventioneers off to steaks and a strip club. Harry snapped his lapels, canted the hat to a menacing angle, and checked the mirror one more time.

"You got my back?" he asked.

"I'll be at the bar across the street."

Harry had to walk a fine line: menacing without being call-the-cops threatening. The last thing we wanted was for the folks at the center to bellow for the constabulary, resulting in our outing. I'd be nearby in case we had to explain the charade.

Harry slipped to the Hummer and rumbled away. I pulled on a University of Colorado ball cap and followed, blowing past Harry a minute later at a stoplight, not honking nor waving. I knew my partner was generating the imperious attitude copped by whore-sellers since creating the World's Oldest Profession. I figured glittery-eyed pimps had crawled like flies through the camps housing the builders of the pyramids, offering human wares to masters and slaves alike.

Within minutes I was inside the Beacon, a narrow bar

with a slender visage on the street, its sole sign announcing *Fifty Beers!* We'd scoped it out yesterday, finding a quiet neighborhood bar built around local brews. I'd figured I could grab one of the two front-window tables and keep an eye on the women's center a hundred paces across the street. Even better would have been the second-floor balcony, but given the bicycle slung up there, it was someone's apartment, student housing being ubiquitous in the university area.

Most of the Beacon's action was in back, folks dividing their attention between a pool game and two darts matches. Behind the bar was a door to a side room. Some kind of meeting was in progress, a dozen middle-aged people at pushed-together tables. Someone was talking about making posters and sponsoring an awareness-raising dance. Yesterday the folks in the room had been younger and the topic was an arts festival. A bulletin board beside the door was plastered with info about a charity car wash, a block party and so forth. I figured the Beacon was the de facto neighborhood center.

I noted an older guy at one of the front tables, late forties or early fifties, big and fit-looking and heavily bearded, in a dark suit and open-neck white shirt. He had an old-school briefcase at his knee and was nursing a whiskey and scowling into the night. He sat where I wanted to and I cursed his presence under my breath, ambling toward the bar weighing my options.

"Mind if I sit here?" I chirped, walking to him. As if the answer was already *Yes*, I set my foamy green

Grasshopper on the table, not one but two cocktail umbrellas rising from the rim, along with the heady vapors of crème de menthe. The dark eyes turned the scowl from the window to me. He nodded at the adjoining wooden circle. "There's another table over there."

I brushed hair from my eyes with my fingers, venting my gayest persona, stolen from the Georgia Peach hisself, Little Richard. "You look lak a pro-fes-sor," I tremoloed. "Do you work at the universiteee?"

He looked away. "Not interested."

"Just talk?"

"Get the fuck away from me."

I sat at the table two feet over and threw one leg over the other. "This is such a nice place," I said. "Are y'all a reg'lar?"

He vacated the bar a moment later, muttering as he went past. I traded the candied froth for a bourbon and slipped into Mr Professor's still-warm chair, checking my watch. Two minutes later the big Hummer rolled to a stop across the street. I whispered *Good luck, bro,* and leaned back into the shadows.

Hearing the door, Carol Madrone looked up from folding her birds. She saw what had crossed the threshold and loomed above. She swallowed hard, hoping her terror didn't show. *Where was Meelia?* She'd been here a second ago. "Meelia . . ." she called to the door at her back. Meelia Reston was a dozen feet away, one door down the hall in the file room.

"What is it, Carol?" Reston called.

"Could you come here, please?"

Madrone pasted a tight smile on her face and looked at the arrival, a black man approximately the size of a refrigerator crate, his garb leaving no doubt as to his occupation. Madrone glanced at the phone, estimating the time it would take to call 911.

"Can I help you?" she asked.

The hulking monster said nothing, studying the surroundings like an appraiser. He went to the window and parted the curtains, peeking outside as if checking the safety of his vehicle. Madrone saw an outlandishly green Hummer outlined in the dim streetlight, mirror-bright reflections from chrome and polish.

Madrone cleared her throat. "Excuse me," she repeated, trying to keep the fear from her voice. "May I help you with something?"

The man turned from the window as if seeing the woman for the first time. His eyes were like twin drills boring into her soul. "I'm looking for a friend. There's a chance she might have come here."

When he spoke, his teeth were like flashes of silver lightning and his voice was a cross between a rumble and a hiss, the most frightening voice Madrone had ever heard.

"What's your friend's name?" she asked. Three numbers and the police would be on the way. *How long would it take them to get here?*

The man seemed to consider the question carefully.

"Her name's Sondra, but she don't go by that all the time. She's a fine-looking sister: mid twenties, real light skin, five-nine. Big eyes, long legs, short hair. She got a pretty little mouth, too. Her lips look like candy tastes."

The two women shot each other a glance. "We've never heard of anyone with that name," Madrone said.

"Or description," Reston hurriedly added. "Why would you think she'd be here?"

The hulking monster thought about the question for several seconds. "She gets confused," he said quietly, eyes roaming the walls, posters, windows. "About who she is and what she needs. It's been a problem." The man nodded toward the hall at the rear of Madrone's desk. "Who's back there?"

"It's just an empty room and a door to the outside," Reston said. "Check if you wish, but there's no one here but us."

Madrone took a deep breath and stood. "I don't mean to be rude, but we'd prefer that you leave. This is a place for –"

The man stepped to the desk with motions as smooth as quicksilver over glass. He picked up the paper crane from Madrone's desk, grinning with his fierce metal teeth.

"Pretty birdie."

"Take it," Madrone whispered. "My gift to you. Your gift to me is leaving, like I just asked you to. Please leave before there's a . . ." Madrone's voice failed.

"Before there's a what?"

Madrone steeled the courage to let her hand rest on the phone, an implied threat to call the police. "Before there's a problem."

The man looked between Madrone and the phone. "I got no problems with you fine ladies," he said. "My problem is with Sondra. She owes me money. All I'm looking for is what I'm owed." He paused, twirling the white bird in his black fingers. "If my friend shows up here, I want you to tell her something."

"What's that?"

Nautilus cocked the hat, lifting his arm enough to open his jacket, giving the women a glimpse of the holstered nine-millimeter. "Work starts tomorrow. Same time, same place. If she ain't there, she ain't nowhere no more, get my drift?"

He squeezed the bird into a broken clump and let it drop to Madrone's desk, grinned the metal teeth, and slid out the door, leaving it open as he walked down the drive like a man without a care in the world. He slid into the Hummer, stared for a long moment toward the women at the center, and was gone.

"Holy shit," Reston whispered, leaning back against the wall, sweat beaded on her forehead. "What the fuck just happened?"

"I'm getting everyone together for a decision," Madrone said. "This is an emergency."

29

Professor Thalius Sinclair was still muttering as he arrived home, having walked for a half-hour to vent his anger at being cruised by some preposterous gay. Probably should have lifted the flit like a sack of feathers and pitched him from the bar, and maybe would have, except there was something odd about the guy – something in the fluidity of his walk, maybe – that said he wouldn't go that easy. Something had felt off in the exchange, but what? Sinclair was a good reader of people and thought maybe he'd held his fire because there was something – *threatening? was that the word?* – about the gay guy.

Sinclair shook off his thoughts, rolled a joint, and sat at his computer. He steered to the familiar website, five users online. He watched the conversation for several minutes until all had signed off save for Drifter.

PROMALE: I've been lurking. Checking for RAISE-HELL.

HPDRIFTER: Raisehell hasn't been on since you told me your misgivings. Now that you've told me what to look for, I saw the anomalies. You have superior perception, Promale. I salute you.

PROMALE: I suspect he is a she, Drifter.

HPDRIFTER: Like you noted, the FemiNazis are always trying to storm the gate. Cunts! They're about to get a fierce comeuppance, and right where they live.

PROMALE: Where is that, Drifter?

HPDRIFTER: I'm not at liberty to say. Not because I don't trust you, because I trust no one. RAISE-HELL shows us why.

PROMALE: But the women say whatever they want.

HPDRIFTER: We have no free speech. You know where the oppression is the worst? The universities. Try to put together a course called Men's Studies. You'll be excoriated. But every university in the country indulges in something called WOMEN'S STUDIES. The whores have whole departments, grants, symposia. What do we get? Goddamn nothing!

PROMALE: One could put the history of females into a two-hour survey course: ten minutes of history, an hour and fifty minutes for them to whine about everything you left out.

171

HPDRIFTER: LOL Nicely put.

PROMALE: Women are mentally and physically inferior to men and built for one purpose. There are dozens of studies proving it, all suppressed before they can get to publication. I myself have just authored such a piece, a breakthrough: a pure scholastic dissertation without shackles.

HPDRIFTER: Surely you know there are many such works on the net. Most are simplistic echoes of one another.

PROMALE: I don't echo, Drifter. I pioneer.

HPDRIFTER: Given your exposure of RAISEHELL, I'm interested in how your mind works, Promale. Here's a gmail addy. Send me your works, but soon, as I get a new addy every week.

Sinclair's phone rang. He reached to shut it off – no one important ever called this late at night – but instead pulled it up and saw the caller's coded name. His fingers ran back to the computer keyboard.

PROMALE: A cautious man . . . very good, Drifter. We're of like minds. I'll send the piece later tonight.

Sinclair logged off and re-dialed the phone to the last caller. Heard it picked up on the other end. He felt sweat prickle on his forehead.

"Do we have one?" he asked.

*   *   *

I waited in the Beacon until Harry drove away. The meeting in the side room broke up, spilling laughing people out into the street, their mirth late counterpoint to the menace Harry projected as he left the center. When I arrived at the motel Harry was stripping off the costumery like it burned his skin. The fedora was upside-down on the bed, the grillz inside, still shiny with saliva.

"How'd it go?" I asked.

"There were two women in the center, a stout lady doing origami, and a skinny lady with big glasses. I said I was looking for a friend who might have gotten confused."

"They were scared?" I asked.

"The lady at the desk kept her hand on the phone. I was afraid she'd freak and call in an air strike. But she stayed cool."

"I'll go in again tomorrow, say you're out on the streets threatening everyone, trying to get Rein back."

"Will I go in again?" Harry asked.

I shrugged. "We'll see how it goes. Hopefully it'll just take a couple–three days to convince them this is a get-Rein-gone situation. We'll fix her up with the electronics and start following."

I heard Harry tossing through the night. This was a guy who could sleep standing up, like a horse. *Rein's safe somewhere only blocks from us,* I thought, hearing the springs complain beneath him. *What's he going to be like when she's undercover and on the road?*

30

"Sondra?" a voice said. "Sondra, wake up."

Rein blinked her waking eyes toward the window to see a sky still dark, the bedside clock indicating four a.m. Shapes at the foot of her bed resolved into Carol and Meelia. They'd brought her to the safe house last night, a garage apartment only blocks from the center.

"You had a visitor this evening," Carol said. "At the center."

"Tee Bull?" Rein knew she'd hear about Harry Nautilus's visit, but didn't expect to hear so early. "A big man with . . . things on his teeth?"

Carol's voice got hard. Inquisitorial. "Did you tell him where you were? You did, right?"

Rein snapped up in bed, eyes wide for surprise, hand on heart for sincerity. A quiver in the voice for fear. "I've never mentioned anything about this place, ever. But other women Tee Bull knows . . . they've gone to shelters to hide. That must have been it."

Meelia stepped forward. "This – this monster wanted you to get back to the same place. What did that mean? The truth, Sondra."

Rein looked away, shame. "You know what Tee Bull is?" she whispered.

Meelia nodded. "We're not stupid, Sondra. He's your pimp."

"Then you know what he wants from me."

"But isn't that where you want to be, Sondra? You're here taking a vacation, right? A few days off to show Tee Bull how much he needs you. When you go back, he'll have the crack pipe waiting and you'll happily suck every –"

"I don't do that shit no more," Rein hissed. "I hate drugs, they steal me away from me."

Rein knew this was part of the process, a hard-edged interrogation. It was like banging a hammer on a ship to make sure the hull was resistant to leaks.

"Off drugs one day, on the next," Meelia sneered. "You're like a light switch, girl, on, off, on, off. Getting clean for a while makes the dope that much nicer, right?"

"I told you, I don't do that now," Rein said. "Why are you being so mean?"

Meelia made her mouth into an O and performed air fellatio. "How many cocks you suck a day for Tee Bull, girl? Fifty? A hundred? I bet you especially like the ones that haven't been washed in a week."

Rein puffed out her cheeks, made gagging sounds and put her hand to her mouth, pushing past the two women and into the bathroom. She slammed the door and knelt beside the toilet, making vomiting noises.

A knocking at the door. "Sondra," Carol asked tentatively. "Sondra, are you all right?"

"I-I'm OK," Rein said. "I need to wash my face."

Rein opened the door to hugs from the women, explaining their cruelty had been necessary. "We had to know you really want out of that life," Carol said. "That you'll do anything to escape."

"All I want is freedom."

"We're gonna get you out of the area, out of the region," Meelia said. "We're going to put you into a system that will aim you toward a new life. It may take a week, it may take three, but you'll be free and far away."

"Tee Bull has eyes everywhere. He'll track me down."

"He can't have eyes in the system, Sondra. It's a chain made of black holes. No one can see in."

Rein let her Sondra character consider the words, then washed joy over her face. "Thank you," she said. "Thank you so much."

"You have anywhere to go?" Carol asked. "A place Tee Bull will never look?"

"Don't tell us where it is," Meelia cautioned. "Just if there is one. And where it is from here: east, west . . .?"

"Down south on the Gulf," Rein said. "I have a couple aunts near Mobile, wonderful people. I was always too ashamed to go there."

"Tee Bull doesn't know?"

"I never wanted a person like that to know my true past, y'know? I always told Tee I'd grown up in Detroit, left when my husband started drinking and beating on me. It was true, but not Detroit."

The women looked between one another, communicating with glances. Something was going on, Rein knew. A decision was being made. But if they'd already decided to put her in the system, what was now being decided?

Within seconds, she had her answer.

"We've cleared things with people," Carol said. "It's never done this fast, but having a monster like Tee Bull after you makes you a special case. You're leaving in a half an hour."

Rein fought to control her surprise, thinking, *The suitcase. I have to get the GPS suitcase. And my gun.*

"I need to run to my apartment," Rein said. "I've got some money there. Clothes."

Carol shook her head. "We've dug into our clothing stores and made you up a traveling kit with everything you need – clothes, hygiene items, some money. People at the other end will help you build a new life."

"I just need a few minutes," Rein pressed. "I'll come right back and –"

Meelia stepped in. "You just said Tee Bull has eyes everywhere, Sondra. Going back is way too dangerous."

Carole looked at her watch. "Best get showered and dressed, dear. You're on the road in twenty minutes."

31

Nine a.m. and I stared at my phone in disbelief. Harry was snoring in his small room, a fitful sleep overtaking him in the early hours. I called Amica Cruz with the news.

"It worked," she said quietly. "But I never expected them to hit the launch button so fast."

Gritting my teeth, I opened Harry's door and jostled his shoulder. "Get up, bro. We overplayed the threats."

He grunted to an elbow, looked up with blinking eyes. "What are you talking about?"

"Rein's in the system. They put her on the railroad."

Harry sat bolt upright in the bed.

"What?"

"She just sent me a text."

Harry grabbed the phone from my hand, squinted at the screen:

Srprs! In trnst. Wll cll w/chnc. HGTWYWH

I said, "It translates to, 'Surprise! I'm in transit and will call when I get a chance.'"

Harry stared. "She has nothing with her. Gun, the suitcase with the –"

"I know," I said.

Harry stared at the message again, maybe hoping she'd texted *April Fools'* in the interim. "What's that gobbledygook at the end?" he asked.

"She says she's having a great time and wishes we were there."

Harry glared at me. "That's not funny, Carson. That's not funny at all."

"I'm not the one saying it."

I was actually buoyed by Rein's flip sign-off – staying cool – but kept it to myself, Harry was clearly not in the mood for glass-half-full optimism.

He was pulling on his pants as Cruz entered, shaking her head. "I've never heard of someone put on a train so fast. Usually there's a meeting of the top brass. It takes days." She raised an eyebrow at Harry. "What did you do last night?"

"You're blaming me?"

"Blame? Whatever you did must have been Oscar quality."

Harry met Cruz's words with a look of disgust. "We've got to get Rein her piece and the suitcase with the GPS."

"You might get close enough to pass her a weapon,

though it'd be hard as hell, but how to explain a different suitcase?"

"Unless the case is passed over when Rein's between caretakers," I said. "Caretaker number two has never seen the case."

Cruz frowned. "That's a tiny damn window, and anything suspicious cancels the hand-over. By suspicious, I'm referring to one of you guys crouching in the shadows with a suitcase."

"Shut the operation down," Harry declared. "Tell Rein to come home."

"Whoa, cowboy," Cruz said. "My people put a lot of thought into this op. Let's think things through before we start freaking out."

"Freaking out? Listen, lady, that girl out there is –"

"A professional," Cruz said. "Your Lieutenant called her the cream's cream of your Police Academy."

"She's out there with nothing to protect her," Harry shot back.

"She's got brains and training," Cruz said. "And you know fuck-ups are part of the undercover biz. If this officer is as resourceful as everyone keeps saying, we'll get things figured out."

"This is insane," Harry said, throwing his hands high and storming outside. Cruz looked at me, perplexed.

"Uh, just between you and me," I said, "Officer Early is Detective Nautilus's niece."

Disbelief. It took a few seconds for Cruz to recover.

"Personal involvement is against every rule in the

freakin' book, Ryder. How the hell did Nautilus get assigned to a case with a family member involved?"

I tried a smile. "Seems no one knows about the relationship."

Cruz met the smile with a scowl. "Apparently *someone* in this room did. If Nautilus blows up the operation, we'll have to start from scratch. That won't sit well with my people."

My cell rang. I looked at the caller name: Reinetta. "Get Harry in here now," I said, hearing the crackling of a drifting connection.

"Rein?" I said. "You there, Rein?"

A buzz of interference as I pressed the speakerphone button, Rein's words filling the room. "Gotta talk fast here, guys. I'm at a rest stop by Castle Rock. They got me up at four, in transit by five. What did you do last night, Harry . . . strangle someone? A woman drove me south to a rest stop. Two minutes later my new carrier was a nice lady named Lena. Grandmotherly type, but a lotta backbone. No killer here. She's taking me to her home – whereabouts unknown– for a day or two."

"You don't have a weapon or your tracking device," Harry said, as if explaining something to a kid.

"You can use my cell phone, right?" Rein said, calm as always. "To get a fix?"

"It's only approximate to the nearest cell tower," Cruz said. "Do you have a charger?"

"No, and my battery's low. I'll call when I've got something to report. Phones are a major no-no, so don't

– repeat, don't – call. I'm afraid it'll make a sound. It's gonna be hidden anyway. I'll call you when –"

Harry grabbed the phone from my palm. "I don't want you out there alone, Rein. I swear I'll –"

"I'll be fine, Harry. Even my caution has caution."

"I want you out, Rein. At least until we can get you the –"

"Carson," Rein said, overriding Harry's words. "Help me out here, willya? Gotta go."

Rein wanted to stay in the system. Cruz wanted her there, too. So did I. Only Harry was trying to haul her out. "Rein, wait!" Harry bellowed into the dead connection in his palm. "Rein!"

I looked across the room and saw Cruz staring at me, her eyes saying, *How long you gonna let this go on?*

I managed to calm Harry by assuring him we could get Rein her .32 and the suitcase. Cruz was dubious, but played along. "If she can figure when the next switch happens," Cruz speculated, "we can try and cross paths. It'll take luck and timing."

Harry snapped his fingers. "Wait . . . we don't need to get Rein the suitcase, we can pass over a smaller GPS. Like the ones they put on dog collars."

"Something to consider," Cruz said without conviction, nodding at the battered yellow case intended for Rein. "But our suitcase has a built-in battery stash. The case transmits for a couple weeks at least. A tiny tracker holds a tiny battery. It works for a bit, then craps out."

"Usually when you need it most," I muttered, having

dealt with the things before. Nothing ever worked like in the spy movies.

"Let's get the suitcase packed with everything Rein needs," Harry said. "A spare phone and charger, her weapon and a few speed-loaders, maybe a spare GPS locator, a survival knife –"

"An inflatable raft," Cruz said, rolling her eyes. "A parachute . . ."

"Here's how we run it," I interrupted, grabbing a map of Colorado. "If Rein was by Castle Rock, she's heading south. Let's bust ass toward Colorado Springs. Maybe between Rein and us we can dope out where she'll make the next transfer. It's usually a truck stop or a park, right?"

"Do you know how many parks are in this state?" Cruz said.

"Got a better idea?" I asked.

The Colorado State Police had readied us a surveillance van. It looked like a retired couples vacation-in-a-box but held several communication options, a tiny refrigerator and microwave oven, and a bit of room to stretch out when needed. I'd worked from similar units before and, while not the Ritz, it beat bagging out in the backseat of a VW Beetle.

We'd put a hundred miles under our wheels when my phone rang: Sally Hargreaves.

"We have another killing," she said. "Last week a group of hikers were using an outhouse near Arches National Park in east Utah. One of them looked down and screamed."

"A body," I said.

"Female, Hispanic. Eyes removed and head shaved bald. One breast badly damaged, the other jabbed with something sharp. Vic is Tomasina Herdez, age twenty-seven, former address is Pittsburgh. Her sister filed a missing-persons report five weeks ago. The body was ID'd by dentition yesterday, the report hit the national logs an hour ago. I've been on the phone to Utah. The local pathologist estimates the corpse was in the muck for three days."

"Our corpses were put on display, Sal. At the dump and in a wide-open settling tank. You sure this one belongs?"

"When the body got yanked from the shit stew, there were half-moons of closed-cell foam taped under her armpits. Get the picture?"

"No."

"Think of life vests."

I thought a moment, saw the physics. "She was supposed to float," I said. "Face up."

"Her head and shoulders were out of the muck, Carson, her face looking up as people urinated and defecated on it."

"Jesus. Any evidence still on the body?"

"That strange mucilage on the belly – waterproof – and the ligature marks again. The Utah ME's dating of the wounds as recent parallels the other cases."

"You're saying Herdez was held captive?"

"By her killer. There were older wounds and scars

as well. Miz Herdez was an ongoing victim of domestic abuse in Pittsburgh. Busted nose, broken fingers, cracked cheekbone. Miz Herdez put the boyfriend in jail for the last beating. He was three days from completing a six-month sentence when she disappeared. I figure he was gunning for her and she had to get gone fast."

"So Miz Herdez dropped into the women's underground?"

"Confirmed by the Pittsburgh cops. There's a women's center in Pittsburgh and Miz Herdez was on the railroad. No one knows where she was going, of course. But the sister who reported her missing lives in Baja California."

I studied a map of the continental US in my head. "A rough center line of a Pennsylvania to Baja trip crosses the Boulder to Mobile line, Sal."

"Exactly. It looks like Miz Herdez crossed into the perp's territory and got killed."

I rubbed my eyes. "Where you going with this?"

"I'll stay in touch with the Pittsburgh cops and keep digging down here. You guys being careful with Rein?"

"Trying our best," I said. "Gotta go."

I relayed the ugly news to Cruz. Harry and I drove in silence, both thinking of the kind of mind that would float a woman in a latrine. My phone beeped.

"Text from Rein," I said. "Plnes ovrhd. Sgn: Devine 5."

Harry veered to the side of the road, Cruz ran up and I showed her the message. "Planes overhead," Cruz

185

translated. "And a sign reading 'Five miles to Devine'. That would be under the approach to the Pueblo airport. We're maybe forty-five miles north of Devine, just east of Pueblo."

Cruz took the point with siren and flashers, pulling forty-plus miles under our tires in a half-hour. My phone tinged the arrival of another text. I tossed the phone to Harry.

"It says, 'Styng sf h nr Rck Frd.'"

"She's going to a safe house near something. Call Cruz. Put it on speaker."

Harry relayed the message. I watched her on the phone in my rear-view; not hard, she was fifty feet from my bumper.

"Rocky Ford, ahead about twenty miles. I dunno about a hand-over at a truck stop or park on this one, guys."

"Why?" Harry said.

"Any back road would work as a transfer site. In case you haven't noticed, we're in the middle of the desert."

Reinetta Early ran to the Hyundai Sonata from behind a tumble of rocks and sagebrush, her phone in her underwear. They were in a flatland nowhere, baked dirt with scruffy undergrowth, rocky mounds, and the occasional house. The roads were signless, barely roads to begin with.

"Better, dear?" the woman at the wheel asked.

"Yes, thank you, Lena," Rein said, pulling her seat belt back on. "I guess it's the tension. My insides are kind of acting up."

"We're near my house," Lena said. "I'll get some Imodium in you. Then we'll have an easy-on-the-digestion supper and you can relax."

"There's a Rocky Ford near where I'm from, Lena," Rein lied, never having heard of a Rocky Ford until now. "Very green, and surrounded by hills and meadows."

Lena chuckled. "That's not mine. All I see looking out the window is desert and sky. And that damned cell tower."

Rein laughed, improvising as fast as possible. "A friend of mine had a house on the beach with a beautiful sunrise view. Then a cell tower went up. Now the sun throws a shadow of the tower into his yard."

"I fought the blamed tower," Lena said. "But there it is today, eight hundred feet away."

"Not in your sun, I hope."

"Off to the west. Something to be thankful for, I suppose."

"I hope there are some trees or hills between you and the tower, Lena. So you don't just see the thing."

The woman sighed. "Nothing. Just my little white ranch house and that big blinking tower."

Rein made a grunting noise and put her hand over her belly. "Uh, Lena . . ."

"Sure, dear, I'll pull over just ahead. See? There's a little place behind the sagebrush where you can relieve yourself."

Two minutes later a message appeared on Carson Ryder's phone:

```
Whte rnch hse 800' SE cll twr otsd RF.
Lve 32, smll stff @ ct crnr CR bndna mrk
```

"I gotta learn this stuff," Harry said. "What's she saying?"

"She's at or will be at a white ranch house eight hundred feet southeast of a cell tower outside of Rocky Ford," I translated, going silent to read ahead. I said, "Holy shit, Harry . . ."

"What? What's it say?"

"She wants us to leave her .32 and any small stuff we might have at a corner of the cell tower and to mark it with one of my bandanas."

I laughed. I couldn't help it. Rein had not only sent along her position, she had arranged a drop. I felt like pulling the van over and dancing: the girl had magic.

32

Cruz called the cell company for tower locations – one in the area, thankfully – and pulled some weight. Ninety minutes later Harry and I were in a Southwest Communications truck and raising dust. In Harry's pocket was a double-zip bag holding Rein's gun, extra rounds, charger to fit her phone and a tiny GPS locator that would do until we could work out how to get the suitcase to her.

We came in from the north, not passing the house, pulling down the slender dirt road running to the communications tower and building. The base and building stood inside a square barricade of hurricane fence.

Figuring Rein didn't want to be seen grubbing in the dirt from the house – and would know I'd surmise the same – I knelt at a back corner of the fence and dug a small hole in the pebbled dirt. I wrapped the baggie in a red bandana and buried it, leaving a corner of cloth exposed, a tiny bright pennant yelling *Look here!* Our "work" over, we drove away, passing by the house where Rein was hiding.

"She's a hundred feet away," Harry whispered, so low I could barely make it out. "All we do is knock on the door and pull her out of this."

I pressed down the accelerator.

"I'm stepping outside for a bit, Lena," Rein called over her shoulder, watching from the window as the work vehicle left the tower. She would have loved to have texted Harry and Carson – *Hot out there guys?* – but her dwindling battery couldn't afford flippancy.

Rein started toward the cell tower, two dozen feet gone when the door opened at her back. "You can't go out there, dear," Lena called. "It's too open."

Rein turned, pressing her hand to her belly. "I think a walk would do me good. Get my guts back in order."

"We can't take the chance."

"Please, Lena? It would really make me –"

The woman was out the door, taking Rein's hand and leading her back to the house. "Let's not argue, Marla," Lena said, using the name Rein had been assigned. "You were told to always listen to the caretakers, right? We know how to keep you safe. Walking in a big open area isn't smart."

The evening passed slowly, Rein taking refuge in the provided bedroom as she figured most women would do.

Now and then she glanced through the window at the tower, a vertical line bejeweled with red lights and crowned with a pulsing white strobe.

At ten p.m. Lena knocked tentatively at Rein's door. "I'm preparing for bed, dear. Is there anything you need?"

For you to go to sleep, Rein thought. She could get to the tower and back in a half-hour. Tiptoe for fifty silent feet, then walk quickly to the tower over flat hardpan. The moon would light the way.

"No thanks, Lena. I'm fine."

If Rein got caught she'd say she felt sad and wanted to be alone to cry, afraid of disturbing Lena. Since it was dark, it was safe to be outside, surely? Rein could improvise something.

"That's good, dear," Lena said. "If you're up in the night, I've set out some herbal teas on the kitchen counter. Don't worry about waking me, I sleep like a log."

Yes! Rein thought. *Sleep on, girlfriend.*

"Thanks again, Lena. You're very brave to help people like me."

"You're the brave one, dear. Oh, and if you do get up, don't open the doors or windows, please."

"Why's that, Lena?"

"Since I'm out here all by my lonesome, I've got alarms. Touch a door or window and the alarm howls like a banshee and the system dials the police. Can't be too careful these days."

*　　*　　*

191

I stared at the line of text from our undercover operative:

```
Fk! Cldnt gt 2 ct. Tght cntrl. Wll try
agn ltr
```

"Fuck! Couldn't get to cell tower. Tight control. Will try again later."

I rendered the translation to Harry and Cruz and watched Harry frown at Rein's expletive. We'd parked behind a rocky uplift a mile from the house. The sky was grapeshot with stars, the brightest originating atop the distant tower where we'd stashed Rein's necessaries.

"What does tight control mean?" Harry said.

"I expect it means her caretaker ordered Officer Early to stay inside," Cruz said, stretching her arms in the back seat and yawning. She nodded toward her cruiser, a dark shadow beside us. "I'm heading to that crummy little motel back on the outskirts. I need my beauty sleep. You guys checking in?"

I was about to agree to a real bed when Harry shook his head. "We're staying here," he said, staring at the blinking tower in the distance. "All night."

I looked at Cruz and shrugged.

2 Members online
PROMALE: Who's there?
HPDRIFTER: Good timing, I was just checking in and hoping to see you. I received and read the abstract of your article.

192

PROMALE: I thought I'd send the abstract first. I didn't want to send you the whole freaking piece if it sounded boring to you. The full piece is 345 pages.

HPDRIFTER: It's in manuscript form?

PROMALE: Yes. Would you like me to send it along?

HPDRIFTER: 'The Women's Movement as a History of Lies?' The title alone makes me NEED to read it.

PROMALE: On its way when I get a chance.

Sinclair turned off his desktop computer and leaned back in his chair, thinking, *Manuscript form?*

33

This must be what an alien abduction feels like, Treeka Flood thought, staring at the saucer-shaped shadow looming ten stories above, red lights glinting from its edges. She clutched her suitcase tighter.

The shape was a municipal water tower and Treeka stood beside the pumping station, a brick building with cables running inside. The road was a hundred feet away, a dark country lane leading to the tower. The red tail-lights of her former rescuer had disappeared a minute ago. The night sizzled with the sound of insects and Treeka felt sweat dripping from beneath her arms in the humid night. She spun to the sound of motion through dry grass, seeing nothing. From the other side of the building came a clattering of rock, feet racing over gravel. There and gone.

I'm imagining things, Treeka thought. *It's bugs.*

The growling began, a low and guttural rumble. Treeka gasped at alien eyes in the black, twin disks of green light, there and gone. A flicker of motion caught Treeka's eyes and horror gripped her heart.

A pack of feral dogs had encircled her, the smallest a beagle, the largest a German Shepherd. They stank like rotting meat. The Shepherd was the pack leader, head low, moving closer. Her heart now in her throat, Treeka pulled her suitcase between her and the slavering beast, backing up until stopped by the pump house. A smaller dog leapt in and snapped at her suitcase.

"Go away!" Treeka yelled, kicking at the dog. It retreated several feet and began snarling and circling. The Shepherd slashed in and seized the suitcase with a flash of teeth, retreating with strips of fabric in its mouth. It crouched and prepared a second leap, strands of foam falling from its jaws.

The night was torn by a flash of white light, like the water tower was beaming Treeka inside, the beam emitting a blast of noise that froze the building, the dogs, the suitcase . . .

The noise stopped, replaced by the words, "Get inside!" Treeka turned to see a compact car beside her. She jumped into the vehicle as dogs barked at the window, teeth snapping inches from her face. The car moved to the road faster than the dogs could run.

"That was close," the driver said, checking the rearview mirror. A man. "The wild dogs are bad this year

– the drought. They've been known to take down sheep, cows . . ."

"Thank you so much," Treeka said. "But I was waiting for someone. I should probably –"

"Go back? You won't stand much of a chance with those critters, ma'am." A smile came to the man's lips, visible in the lights of the car's instrumentation. "Anyway, I figure I'm who you were waiting for." The man held out his hand. "My name's Rick. Who are you today?"

Rein was floating somewhere between her dreams and the soft sunrise light streaming through the window when a voice snapped her head from the pillow.

"Wake up, dear," Lena was saying, knocking on the door. "I've got good news . . . It's your lucky day."

Rein pushed aside the bedclothes and wriggled to her elbow. "Come in, Lena." Rein shot a glance at the window, saw the tower. *Maybe today. Convince Lena to drive to town and get me some special medicine. Asthma? A cold? In daylight I can sprint to the tower. Just give me a few minutes alone, Lena.*

Lena was dressed in slacks and a western-style denim blouse embroidered with roses, mother-of-pearl buttons, her white hair bound back in a red bow.

"How are you feeling this morning, dear?" Lena asked.

"My head's congested," Rein said, pushing her speech through her mouth, like her breathing passages were clogged. "I can't breathe."

"We'll get something at a drugstore, dear. Hurry and get dressed."

Rein stared. Lena smiled. "Like I said, it's your lucky day. Your next caretaker is ready. Usually there's much more of a wait. It's the asterisk."

"Asterisk?"

Lena sat on the bed as Rein pulled on her clothes. "There's a computer site where information is entered – very hush-hush. No details, just when a traveler is in one area and the basic direction she's heading, nothing more than points on the compass. People in the next-step destination area post their availability. If the woman appears to be in severe danger, an asterisk goes beside her position and everyone is encouraged to drop everything to help. The asterisk is like a fire alarm."

"And I was an . . ."

"An asterisk, dear. I've had nine years of doing this and you're the first asterisk I've ever seen. I can't begin to imagine the danger you were in." Lena stood and checked her watch. "Best hurry. I'm taking you to a transfer point a few hours away and the clock is ticking. We'll grab something to eat along the way."

34

Gd mrng! Dprt this am.

"Leaving?" Harry said. "Already?"

"Rein also wishes us a Good Morning." I stepped outside the Hummer to push kinks from my back. Sleeping in a car – even a big-ass SUV – was like sleeping in a coffin, except a coffin let you stretch out. Plus I've never understood how a desert could be so hot in the day and so goddamn cold at night. I opened the hatch and scrabbled through my bag for toothpaste and brush.

"We have to excavate the stuff we left for Rein," I said. "At the tower."

"No time. She leaves, we lose her."

"We can't leave a loaded .32 an inch below the dirt. What if some kid finds it?"

"You're arguing some million-to-one shot when Rein might be pulling away right now?"

Maybe my imagination gets away from me, but I saw a kid walking a dog, the dog sniffing the corner of a bandana . . .

"I'm not leaving until we grab the gun."

Harry sighed, thought a second. "Get in, we can do both." He backtracked down a side road, the departure route toward the main highway.

"The gun?" I said.

"I'll follow Rein. You grab the buried stuff and have Cruz pick you up. We'll meet up the road."

I looked the thousand or so yards to the tower, sand and rock and spiny brush. The sun was barely off the horizon, a shimmering red ball. Vultures were already floating in the sky, waiting for something to die.

"If I don't get eaten by scorpions," I grumbled.

"Eat them first," Harry advised.

I called Cruz with the plan, exited and began trotting toward the tower, a ten-minute lope over dirt as hard as asphalt. Cruz picked me up at the tower fifteen minutes later, looking fresh and rested and smelling like citrus. She'd grabbed coffee and power bars in town. I ate a Clif's Crunchy Peanut Butter bar for breakfast, a Luna Iced Oatmeal Raisin bar for dessert, then called my partner.

"We're on the road," I said. "Where are you?"

He told us the mile marker, twenty-seven miles ahead. "The old girl has a pretty heavy foot."

"Two previous speeding tickets," Cruz said. She'd run an info search on the owner of the house: Audrey Townsend, sixty-nine years of age, a retired social worker. One arrest in 1969 for disturbing the peace at an antiwar rally in Grand Junction, Colorado, another arrest in 1974 for chaining herself to a piece of equipment at an anti-logging protest. Though feisty in her youth, there didn't appear to be a lot of homicidal maniac in Ms Townsend.

When we hit the main highway Cruz flicked on the flashers in the grille, fired up the siren, and nailed the cruiser at ninety-five. I stayed in contact with Harry until we'd bridged the distance in a town called Lamar, spotting the brown Hyundai ahead a quarter mile or so. Halfway between was Harry. We sped up, so did he, until a hundred feet behind the Hyundai. The brown car moved to a lane veering toward Interstate 385 South, Harry following and gaining on the Hyundai.

"He's getting too close," Cruz said.

I picked up the phone. "Harry, get back. You'll make the driver suspicious."

"I want to let Rein know we're near. She might think we're lost somewhere."

"She freakin' knows, Nautilus!" Cruz yelled. "Trust her!"

Harry backed off the gas, more space opening up between him and the Hyundai. Turn signals blinked on the Hyundai as it aimed for the ramp. Harry kept a couple hundred feet behind until we'd switched highways, then closed in again.

"He's going around them," I said, mouth wide.

"I can't believe this," Cruz whispered. The high-powered binoculars put me twenty feet from Harry's bumper. I watched him pass the Hyundai.

"He's actually looking at them," Cruz said, the motion visible even to her eyes. "A full-face shot toward the target car."

And then Harry was past. I knew Rein was wondering what was going on. We were five hundred feet back, but she turned and made us. She spun forward again, probably as confused as me.

I called Harry again, trying to stay calm. "What was that about?"

"I wanted Rein to know we had her back."

Cruz grabbed my phone. "Dammit, Nautilus, are you a cop or a babysitter? This is an operation for professionals and if you can't . . ." She stopped and stared at the phone in disbelief. "He hung up on me."

"It seems to be over," I said, seeing Harry a hundred yards past the Hyundai and pulling away.

"A brilliant move," Cruz said. "He's going to follow them from up front."

We dropped back to the quarter-mile distance. Traffic thinned as people exited for offices and factories. Cruz studied me.

"How did you two ever become partners?" she asked. "You seem sane and Nautilus seems loopier than hell."

"That's the first time anyone ever put it in that order," I said.

*　　*　　*

Harry stayed a mile ahead of the Hyundai, Cruz and I the same behind. There was nothing between Lamar and the Oklahoma Panhandle. Or as close to nothing as a landscape could offer. I thought of the Dust Bowl drought of the 1930s and figured this was where they got the dust.

We made one bathroom and fuel stop along the way, me freshening up at a sink, Cruz in the distance with her phone to her ear, an intense conversation. The land began to green up and Cruz noted we'd entered the Comanche National Grassland, next stop Oklahoma.

"My people spoke to the Oklahoma staties and we're anticipated," she said. "The OSP offered help if necessary, but will otherwise stay away. We often stretch jurisdictions out here, no big deal."

"How long can you hang in here?" I asked, knowing Cruz hadn't signed on for the surveillance, her role to work the Boulder investigation while Harry and I tailed Rein.

"Yesterday," she said.

"Sorry."

"It's a joint operation, right? We've got a dead body at our end that needs a killer's name attached. That's everyone's goal. And with Nautilus as a partner, you need all the help you can get."

There was more truth in her words than I wanted to acknowledge. Harry had let the personal eclipse the professional and I was concerned about his judgment.

Cruz's cell went off and she slapped it to her face, her

tone businesslike, official. "Where are you? OK. We're just above Highway 160. Um-hmm? No, no idea yet. No, haven't heard if contact was made, still being discussed I expect – tactics. Listen, uh, things could get . . . unusual."

She snapped her phone shut. I'm a detective, and I detected her conversation was purposefully cryptic. "Anything going on?" I asked, recalling her pacing and being dead serious into the phone earlier at the fuel stop.

"Just making sure everything keeps running clear and easy."

I was about to ask what that meant when Harry checked in. "Target pulling into a Flying-V truck stop. I'm circling to follow."

"Don't get seen," Cruz barked. "Keep your head."

"I've got the suitcase," Harry said." I might get it to her."

"Don't try," Cruz said. "It's broad-fucking-daylight."

I had an uneasy feeling as we pulled into the truck stop, a zillion acres of parking lot centered by a sprawling complex holding fast-food eateries, a convenience mart and a souvenir shop. All that seemed lacking was a bowling alley. A dozen trucks were filling up at the fuel bays on the truck side of the complex.

"Rein's out of the car," Harry said. "She hugged the driver. It's the transfer."

"Stay in your vehicle, Nautilus," Cruz said, dodging lumbering semis as we wove toward the main building.

Harry said, "She's got her suitcase and heading into

the main restaurant. The new driver must be on the far side of the building, that's how it happened with Gail."

"There's no pattern to a transfer," Cruz yelled. "Stay in the goddamn car."

"I can get the suitcase to her when she's inside."

Cruz whipped toward the structure, eyes flashing with anger. "There he is," she said, pointing across the lot. "Pulling up to the restaurant."

Harry parked beside the building as Rein was entering, legs scissoring quickly in loose jeans, a black tee, suitcase in hand. I used the binocs to scan the restaurant windows: Truckers at tables shoveling down eggs and bacon, guys at the cashier paying for snacks and petrol, more truckers trading jokes with the lottery-ticket cashier.

And one lone woman with her face behind a newspaper, a bright red hat perched on her head. She seemed to be hiding behind the paper, peeking past the edge as newcomers entered. And the red hat . . . a visual ID for Rein?

"Oh Jesus," Cruz moaned, "Nautilus is getting out with the suitcase."

"Get in front of him," I said to Cruz, my heart pounding. "Cut him off."

Cruz swooped the cruiser at Harry. He jumped back to keep his feet and legs clear. I bailed out and ran to Harry, grabbing the suitcase from his hands. He snatched it back.

"What the hell are you doing?" he snapped. "I've got to –"

"The transfer's inside, bro. It's going down now."

"What?"

"Turn to the building like we're talking. See the woman with the red hat about eight tables down? What's she doing?"

When Harry looked I saw his shoulders droop, heard the chest-deep groan. "She's standing and shaking hands with Rein."

Cruz walked up. She looked through the window and saw Reinetta wrap the red-hat lady in a hug. Had Harry made it inside the whole operation could have crumbled.

"I've had about all I can take of this," Cruz said.

Harry looked disoriented by his misjudgment and I pulled him to the car. We had to get back on Rein's tail. I took the wheel and we drove over to the truck side, expecting that was where she'd emerge. But she wasn't in sight.

"I don't see her," Harry said, looking side to side.

"Bathroom break, maybe?" Cruz radioed. "Freshening up?"

We circled the building, Cruz doing the same "You see anything?" she called over the radio.

"No," Harry said. His voice was getting tight again.

"Uh-oh," Cruz said. "I'm on the back side. There's another door for the fast-food joints . . ."

"We lost her," I said. "We've got to fuel the cars and us, and wait for Rein to communicate. Want to meet us inside, Detective Cruz?"

"I'm gonna eat in my car," she said. "I'm not in a socializing mood."

*　　*　　*

Rein watched the truck stop recede in the side-view mirror of a brand-new electric-red Cadillac Escalade, wondering how Harry was holding up. She knew her assignment was hard on him, her uncle never quite adjusting to her maturation. Rein recalled the time he took her camping. She had just started wearing a bra, barely necessary. Rein remembered how he kept stealing glances at her bosom, like it couldn't be true, something was terribly wrong. It seemed to Rein that Harry had largely chosen to continue that thinking, not consciously, of course, but deep in a secret chamber of his heart.

The big Caddy motor gave a jet-engine whoosh as the driver passed a stream of slower-moving vehicles, folks only doing eighty. The driver was Victoria, a slim, fortyish woman in a burgundy dress, medium-length black hair lacquered in place, big purple-blue eyes with long lashes and dark mascara. Her lips were full and scarlet and with her creamy skin the woman reminded Rein of that movie star from a long time ago, Elizabeth Taylor. Victoria held the steering wheel wide, like a ship's wheel, a half-dozen gaudy bracelets on her wrists jangling with her movements. Every other finger held a ring, semi-precious stones in silver and gold. Baubles dangled from her ears like Christmas-tree ornaments.

Victoria saw Rein studying her. "Nothin' matches an' I can't he'p it," the woman chuckled in a textbook Texas twang. "Ah'm addicted to the Home Shopping Channel."

"I was thinking you must be what an angel looks like," Rein said, settling into her role. "Thank you for helping me."

"I got a little twitchy back at the truck stop. I saw a black guy looking at you when you was steppin' inside, some huge ol' boy totin' a yella suitcase, of all things. I had half a mind to stay hid, but then he started talkin' to a couple of people outside the door – one was some weird guy wearing binoculars like a birdwatcher – and I figured it wasn't connected to you."

Rein stared straight ahead, said, "No, thank God."

"I wasn't plannin' on being in the area. Usually I'm available onct or twice a year cuz a my bidness schedule. But then I saw the sign by your dot on the website."

"The asterisk?"

"Two other folks on the website could move you to the southeast, but couldn't get to you for another day. I figured, given the danger, you wanted to put a lot of gone between you and wherever you're from."

"Bless you," Rein said.

The woman waved it away. "I'm a sales rep for a medical-equipment company, bouncin' from hospital to hospital across the southwest. I just bent my route a bit north, and now we'll bend south. Ever been in Texas, Marla?"

"Only Texarkana," Rein lied, hoping to exact information a *No* answer wouldn't get. "I'm lost in the rest of Texas."

"Texarkana's way over on the other side a the state, hon. I'll be takin' you to Amarillo for a couple days. The next link will show up from there."

Amarillo, Rein thought. One piece of the puzzle filled.

The next trick was getting to her phone. Several miles of barren desert blew by as she pictured her plan, then began taking little whistling gasps.

The driver looked at Rein. "Goodness. Are you all right, Marla?"

"A touch of asthma," Rein said. "Nerves, I guess. My inhaler's in my case."

"We'll get things handled right now," Victoria said, the caddy veering to the berm. Rein ran to the open trunk. Hidden by the lid, she fired off a message, jammed the phone back in her pants and stepped into mirror view, hands cupping her mouth like holding an inhaler. She pretended to return the device to the suitcase and closed the trunk lid.

"Better now?" Victoria asked as Rein climbed into the Escalade.

"Much, thank you."

35

Professor Sinclair stared down the hall. Music came from Krupnik's rathole, she was in there assembling whatever, or preparing for a class. Trotman was still out, thankfully, though he'd called yesterday as though his absence was a big deal. One of Bramwell's addled Gender Studies TAs had pestered Sinclair with questions all morning, Sinclair finally telling the mindless dweeb to learn to use a library. Another of Bramwell's robots arrived wanting to send her a fax about class schedules. He informed the automaton that sabbaticals were how academics escaped from academia and faxes.

Having finally found silence, almost – what was bubbling from Krupnik's hole, the Dixie Chicks? Jesus! – he sat in front of his computer and traveled to the special site, logged on.

PROMALE: Who's there?

HPDRIFTER: Good timing, I was just checking in and hoping to see you.

PROMALE: Nice to be appreciated.

HPDRIFTER: More than you know. I read "The Women's Movement as a History of Lies", Promale. I stand in awe of your scholarship. You take an ax to the FemiNazi shibboleths, no . . . an atomic bomb! You have the potential to be a great intellectual leader if presented to the right crowd. Your time is about to come.

PROMALE: May I ask what you mean, Drifter?

HPDRIFTER: The Great Upheaval is close at hand. We need your ideas and your scholarship.

PROMALE: I humbly beg for any assignment I might receive.

3 Members online

RAISEHELL: Fucking A, dudes. What's shaking? Damn, the bitches are wearing me out at work. I'm about to chop some serious cunt throat. What assignment is this? What's a Great Upheaval???

HPDRIFTER: We can no longer meet in this room, Promale. There are safer places.

PROMALE: I agree. Dynamite the bridge.

RAISEHELL: What you talking about, no longer meet here?

HPDRIFTER: The return addy on your piece of genius, Promale . . . still operable?

PROMALE: Use it to contact me. We'll make new arrangements.

RAISEHELL: What's going on?

HPDRIFTER: Hey, Raisehell . . .

RAISEHELL: What?

HPDRIFTER: FUCK YOU, SPY BITCH!!!!!!!!!!!!!!!!!!!!!!!!!!!!!

PROMALE: Well put, Drifter. Later.

HPDRIFTER: We have much to discuss . . . my brother.

1 Member online

"S 87 2 Amllo MS 1103."

I read the message to Cruz, its brevity indicating it was sent in haste. Harry and I were standing from our table where I had polished off two cheeseburgers and Harry had nibbled an ounce off one pork chop. I studied the vast plain of asphalt and trucks knowing Cruz was out there somewhere. I felt bad she had to eat alone, but she wanted nothing to do with Harry. It was like all his needles had locked in red and he couldn't dial them back.

"South on Highway 87 to Amarillo," Cruz translated.

"I figure the rest is the tag number. Officer Early is one savvy lady. I'll find out who owns the vehicle."

"Where from here?" I asked.

"Go out the east side of the truck stop, that's 87. I'll put myself behind you."

Harry went to pay the bill. I wandered outside where the din of diesel engines was close to deafening, the smell of fuel and exhaust soupy in the desert heat. I still had the binocs swinging around my neck. They'd drawn weird looks inside the restaurant – was I a food inspector? How did field glasses fit in the equation? – and I'd diddled with them like I was performing some form of repair.

I lifted the binoculars to my eyes, looking for Cruz. I saw her vehicle about three hundred yards away at the end of a line of parked trucks, drivers catching up on rest. I waited for the cruiser to move, then adjusted the optics into tighter focus and saw the vehicle was unmanned.

Where was Cruz?

I scanned the area: trucks and more trucks. A Kenworth loaded with a refrigerated silver trailer roared between the cruiser and me. When the truck passed I fixed on the motion of a black Yukon with windows tinted equally dark, a CB-style whip antennae on its bumper. Shifting back I saw Cruz stepping into her vehicle, heat rising from the asphalt making her appear to ripple.

Where had she been?

"How long have you been doing this?" Rein asked

Victoria, barren brown land stretching for miles on either side of the vehicle, the sky endless blue. Rein had become fascinated by the people in the system.

"It's my second year." A pause. "I do it for my sister, Nina. Nina was abused by her husband."

Rein said, "I'm sorry. Can I ask what happened?"

"My two sisters and I thought Nina had a perfect marriage. She had a beautiful home, her husband was a dentist who volunteered his time to coach baseball after school, gave big to charities. He wanted to get involved with local politics, be a town commissioner. But Nina was living in hell: abused, mocked, stripped of every bit of self-esteem."

"I understand," Rein said, feeling shame at her lie.

"He was sick and depraved and used my baby sister in filthy ways, sexually. Somethin' might have clicked with us, except she lived in Macon, Georgia, and the rest of us live in Texas and New Mexico, so we only got together every year or so."

Victoria looked at Rein with apology in the vivid eyes. "Sorry. Talkin' about this is prob'ly too close to what you're tryin' to get away from."

"I asked you, Victoria," Rein said gently. "Remember?"

"Then I'll tell the story to the end. A psychologist living down the street from Nina saw certain signs in my sister, got the full story. She finally convinced my sister to leave him after . . . her husband – I cain't bring myself to say his name – burned her with a cigar in places. Private places. *Inside* the private places."

Rein could only shake her head.

"Nina up and left him. A week later he came crawling and crying about how he loved her and missed her and how he'd changed completely. You can prob'ly guess what happened."

Rein closed her eyes as if that would blunt the horror. "Nina went back to him."

"Things started right back the way they were. I . . . I uh, have a hard time with the next part."

"That's all right, Victoria," Rein said. "You don't have to go on."

"I do, I got to get it out. My sweet, tortured baby sister went down in the basement one day and hanged herself from the plumbing. She couldn't leave that life, she couldn't stay in that life, so she left life itself."

Rein closed her eyes, wondering, *How do these monsters gain such power?*

"You know what the legal system did to him?" Victoria continued. "Nothing. Even though my sister left a note tellin' all that went on, he got his lawyer to keep it out of evidence at the trial."

"But wasn't the suicide note . . ."

Earrings jangled as the driver shook her head. "The reason for the trial in the first place. He was a slick one, that lawyer. Slick like pond scum. Between Nina's husband and his lawyer, they made Nina the crazy one. They said she was blackmailing him, threatening to hurt herself and claim he'd done it unless he gave her more money. They said Nina had burned herself . . . claimed she needed pain to have pleasure. They made up lie after lie after lie, turning my baby sister into a sick money-grubber who was the one threatening *him*. Nina was dead and they still poisoned her, poisoned how people thought of her."

Victoria wiped tears from her eyes. Rein said, "I can't imagine what you must feel about –"

"Wait," Victoria said. "The story ain't done yet. My older sister, Jenna, she's got a temper. She confronted Nina's husband after the trial, packed along a pistol. She stood on his front porch and called him ever' name in the book. He grinned and said she'd feel better if they went inside and had a nice hot fuck."

"My God," Rein whispered.

"Jenna tried to shoot his balls off but only nicked the bastard's thigh." Victoria let a long breath escape. "Long story short, Marla: I've got one sister dead, another with four more years to do in prison."

"What about the husband?" Rein asked. "The dentist? What happened to him?"

A mile of sun-baked prairie passed by before Reinetta got her answer. "He got elected to the city council in his town. And he's married again. With a kid this time."

"I'm so sorry."

Rein saw Victoria's multi-ringed fingers tighten on the wheel. "You asked why I do this, Marla. Maybe I can keep one family safe from what mine went through."

For the first time Rein felt visceral anger, *personal* anger, at the killer. She also felt proud to sit beside a woman who had turned bereavement into salvation by offering her help to people she didn't know. Suddenly Rein understood the depths of madness and depravity that made the underground railroad not just important to women, but essential.

Reinetta Early looked out the window, aiming her mind out over the boundless landscape, trying to will her thoughts into the mind of the killer, wherever in the system he was lurking. *Find me, you bastard*, she thought, *Find me . . .*

If you dare.

36

"Got a make on the plates," Cruz said on the speaker. "Vehicle owner and presumed driver is one Victoria Miles, 1153 Bluebonnet Way, Amarillo. Ms Miles is forty-four years old, no police record – at least, nothing beyond the usual speeding tix, but it's west Texas, no one drives below ninety unless it's a funeral cortège. They usually stick in the eighty-five range."

"Get the dead buried then grab some beer and barbecue," I said. Harry glanced into the mirror and I could tell he didn't think it was the time or place for humor.

Cruz chuckled. "Like I said, it's Texas. We're about two hours out of Amarillo, so see you there. We've got things to discuss."

"Like what?"

"First, let's make sure our carrier's home is where

Officer Early is safe-housed. We'll find a place you can stick close to her, then we'll have a little heart-to-heart."

Cruz clicked off. Harry frowned. "What's she talking about, Carson?"

"Got me," I said.

I felt my elation at having a handle on Rein's whereabouts dissolving. I'd had a slightly uneasy feeling about Cruz's cryptic phone conversation in the car earlier, amplified by her odd absence from her cruiser at the truck stop. Now she wanted to have a 'heart to heart'. Something was happening, but what?

As soon as Harry clicked off the connection, I felt my cell buzzing in my pocket. I fished it out and saw the caller's name: SALLY.

"I have confirmation that our body in Utah, Miz Herdez, entered the underground railroad way over in Pittsburgh twenty-seven days back. The timing reinforces that the perp is keeping them somewhere for several days. Any ideas why?"

"He needs time alone with them, Sal. To show off. To bask in masculine superiority. I imagine it's the highlight of this boyo's life."

"Jesus. I want to bounce Herdez's death off Krebbs, see how he acts when I tell him a third woman is dead. If I can get to Krebbs, that is."

"What are you talking about?"

"Remember Krebbs's asshole mouthpiece, our old buddy T. Nathaniel Bromley? Guess what the Bromster

218

did about an hour ago? Here's a hint: Krebbs has suddenly turned into a grieving widower."

"Grieving widower?" Then I understood and whispered, "It can't be."

"It is," Sally sighed. "Bromley's gonna sue the Mobile women's center on behalf of Lawrence Krebbs, claiming they brainwashed his beloved wife into leaving him and sending her into a dangerous system that resulted in her death. The people at the center think this could paralyze the entire underground railroad, stop it in its tracks."

"Has Bromley's action hit the news? How are they dealing with it?"

"It's low key so far," Sal said. "Bromley's subpoenaed the center's records. I only got word because the center called and filled me in. Nothing's hit the media because no major paperwork has been filed."

"But the bomb has been set in place," I said, picturing the coming newscast: Bromley before a bank of microphones outside the Mobile women's center with a grieving and downcast Krebbs at his side, the attorney bloviating about the women's organization plucking a confused Lainie Krebbs from her loving hubby's side and forcing her into an anonymous system fraught with peril. Spoon-fed with Bromlinian sound bites, the media would lap up his words like starved Dobermans. The Missing Blonde story was about to get a new permutation: the Deadly Women's Centers.

"What do you think Bromley's waiting for?" I said. "Why isn't he on the news right now?"

"The news down here is consumed with that last round of actions on the oil spill. But the cases head into arbitration next week."

"You think Bromley's waiting . . ."

"Until he's got center stage to himself. It's gonna be a helluva show."

I hung up, shaking my head, and called Cruz. She listened in silence as I laid out the details, finally asking, "Who is this fucking Bromley character, Ryder? No – *who* makes it a human. *What* is he?"

"A guy with a huge ego and no boundaries."

A long pause before she came back, anger hard in her voice. "The Boulder center will surely be named a co-conspirator and, by extension, all centers engaged in relocating endangered women. When this Bromley asshole goes public, no more women are going to enter the tunnel. Maybe forever."

"Jesus," I whispered, realizing she was right.

"It's a banner day for women's abusers, Ryder," Cruz said, bitterness in her voice. "They're gonna be dancing in the streets."

We hit Amarillo at four in the afternoon. At three we'd received a message from Rein giving us the Bluebonnet address previously supplied by Cruz. I figured Rein had sent the info from the home's bathroom, operating like a seasoned professional, not missing a step.

Cruz had a line on a nearby motel. Harry wasn't interested in lodging, and we did a drive-by of the tidy

Spanish ranch in a new community of similar homes. "There's an uncompleted cul-de-sac around the corner," Harry said, eyes scoping out the neighborhood. "We can stay there tonight. Tell the local police we're there, so if –"

"There's motel a half-mile down the road," I interrupted. "Beds. Hot water. Toilets. Remember such things?"

"A half-mile?" Harry said, like a half-mile was halfway to Borneo.

"Do what you want," I said. "But tonight I need a shower above and a bed below."

The motel was clean and bright and I was happy to toss my bag in the air and watch it land on a mattress. Fifteen minutes later I exited the shower to a ringing phone. I dripped to the bedside table to take a call from Lieutenant Tom Mason, our boss back in Mobile.

"Howdy, Tom," I said, prepared to give the usual *nothing's-happening-everything's-cool-talk-to-you-later* report.

"I need the truth, Carson," Tom said, his voice tight, not the usual relaxed drawl. "Is Harry fucking up?"

It was a punch to the gut. "What?"

"I heard he nearly blew a tail by trying to wave at Officer Early from the surveillance vehicle. I also heard he tried to contact Officer Early in the restaurant where she was making the transfer to her next handler."

I sighed. "He's protective about Officer Early, Lieutenant. Maybe overly."

"Didn't you work this out in advance?"

"I thought so, Lieutenant, but Harry hasn't quite –"

"I've received an ultimatum from the Colorado State Police, Carson. They want Harry off the case. Or should I just shut the operation down from this end?"

I saw the body in the morgue on day one of the case, a woman abducted and tortured by a mind so far off the rails there was no name for the location where it landed. I pictured a dead woman in a sewage-treatment facility, just another piece of waste. I saw a woman's face bobbing below the hole in a Utah park latrine.

"An undercover operative is our only way in, Lieutenant. The chances are slim that Officer Early will cross paths with the killer, but it's all we have. She's doing a helluva job so far."

"I'm calling Harry back to Mobile. He won't be happy, but I'm not real happy either. You're in charge, Carson. Find the killer and keep Officer Early safe."

I pulled on clean hiking shorts and a tee advertising fishing gear, added a ball cap, and stepped into battered running shoes. I walked outside; Cruz's room was two doors down. I cringed at the blast of Texas summer and paused to let my eyes adjust to the light. Three parking slots down from Cruz's cruiser was a black Yukon with a whip antennae on the bumper, a dead ringer for the vehicle I'd seen at the truck stop.

I walked to Cruz's door and knocked. She was there seconds later, wet hair rolled into a white towel above her head, a pink robe around her slender body, bare feet. She smelled like mint and lilacs.

I jabbed a thumb toward the Yukon. "Is that yours?" I said, meaning the Colorado State Police.

The brown eyes narrowed. "I'm not sure I like your tone."

"Harry's getting yanked off the case. That was your doing, right?"

She stared at me. "Nautilus should never have been on the case. Failing that, he should have been pulled the day Officer Early went into the system. I got nothing to feel bad about, Ryder. How you doing?"

She closed the door. There was nothing to do but wait until Harry got the news from Lieutenant Mason.

Harry roared into the motel lot fourteen minutes later, the van braking hard, leaving trails of burnt tire across the pavement. He jumped out, hands clasping like needing a throat.

"You didn't strangle her?" Harry spun toward her unit, banging on the casement.

"I'm not discussing it," Cruz yelled through the door. "You're gone, Nautilus. Accept it and act like a professional."

"Open this goddamn door or I swear I'll kick it down."

The door opened and Cruz stood on the threshold. Behind her were two big Colorado cops. I figured they were called over for the day, Cruz fearing Harry might fly off the handle. The staties looked ready to move on my partner but Cruz motioned them back and stepped outside.

"Why did you blow me up, Cruz?" Harry demanded.

"You were being overly protective. Not keeping it real."

"Do you know how long it takes to remove someone's eyes?" Harry said. "Is that real enough? How about a minimum of three mutilated corpses. All killed by the guy we're setting Rein in front of. How's that for reality?"

Cruz looked at Harry like he was babbling nonsense. "The game plan isn't protecting her, Nautilus. It's putting Early out there like cheese at a rat convention. We *want* the perp to notice her."

"We've got to keep her covered."

"Covered doesn't mean you follow her around with a parasol."

"I want her safe," Harry said.

"I want a killer," Cruz responded.

This would go nowhere. For the deal to go down, we had to give Rein a fair amount of rope and trust she knew when to pull it. Then, and only then, would we appear.

"You never discussed any of this with me," Harry told Cruz.

"I warned you that you were going off the reservation, Nautilus. You went off farther. I said not to pass the target vehicle, you drove by doing everything but blowing kisses. When I complained, you hung up the phone. Then you went traipsing into the goddamn restaurant lugging a suitcase."

"I'm protecting my niece. You put your nose in my private business."

Cruz looked behind her and pulled the door tight, leaning toward Harry with lowered voice. "I never mentioned you're the officer's uncle. I only said you were being overly protective of the undercover operative. Taking an assignment with a relative is stupid beyond belief, but maybe you've never worked an undercover op before. Are we done here, Detective Nautilus? I've got reports to file."

Harry seemed unable to find words. The door closed.

37

In the too-early morning I drove a sullen Harry to Amarillo Airport to catch a pre-dawn flight on a regional airline. When I returned the temperature was already pushing past a sultry eighty degrees. Cruz was lounging beside the motel pool in a loose blue-and-red Hawaiian shirt and green calf-length pants that seemed made of overlapping pockets. The ensemble was topped by a broad-brimmed straw hat. I'd stopped on the way and picked up coffees at a Starbucks. I set a cup on the table beside Cruz, took a seat. She nodded thanks.

We sat in silence and studied the tangled morning traffic on the highway. A service road was on the far side, lined with a laundromat, pawnshop, gas station, junk store, accountants' office and a couple of restaurants.

"I had no other choice," Cruz finally said, staring across the street.

"I know," I said, also looking forward, like we could address the subject if we didn't look at one another, a phone conversation sans phones.

"Is he a good cop," she asked, "Nautilus? I mean, usually?"

"The best there is."

"Why'd he take an assignment with his niece as killer bait?"

"It just happened."

We stopped talking as an ambulance wove through the traffic, its siren so piercingly loud I couldn't arrange my thoughts. I imagined Harry trying to work the case with that kind of noise in his head, couldn't.

Cruz said, "I'm finding it hard to believe Nautilus is a pro when he's not an emotional wreck."

"There's a barbecue joint across the highway," I said, pointing to a red barn-shaped building with smoke rising from a brick pit to the side. "I need real food."

"Barbecue for breakfast?"

"Sometimes it's necessary."

"You gonna tell me tales of derring-do?" Cruz said. "Is that the plan?"

"Yep."

"Think we can look at one another over there?"

Harry Nautilus landed in Mobile at eight-fifteen and was standing in front of Lieutenant Tom Mason a half-hour later, explaining he'd been worried owing to the youth and the slender experience of Officer Reinetta Early.

Nautilus knew Mason was a sucker for contrition, especially with an explanation.

"I allowed emotion to overwhelm judgment, Lieutenant," Nautilus said, "recalling a couple times when I was nearly killed because of one bad split-second decision in a day where I made fifty good ones. I couldn't get the mistakes out of my head."

The lanky lieutenant thought about it, tipping back the ubiquitous Stetson. "You and Carson worked with her. How did she do there?"

"The kid was first-rate," Nautilus had to admit.

"And you were still worried?"

Nautilus looked at his feet as if embarrassed. He also knew Tom Mason was old-school Southern. It didn't mean thinking of women as less than men, but a certain protectiveness was rooted in the culture and still powerful among men of a certain age, about that of Lieutenant Mason.

"I, uh, maybe . . ." Nautilus stammered.

"Maybe what, Harry?"

"Maybe I shouldn't say it, given the times and all."

Mason nodded toward the closed door. "It's just you and me and the wallpaper. Out with it, Harry."

"Maybe it would have been different if Officer Early was a guy, sir. I know it sounds sexist or whatever, but . . ."

Mason sighed. "Yeah, Harry. I can understand that, even if I'm not supposed to. Jeez, women cops on the front of the front lines . . . I can't imagine how I'd feel if it was one of my daughters. Anyway, the case'll be

228

over soon enough, right? Either Officer Early will spot a breach in the system or not."

Nautilus cleared his throat. "I know I got too close up there, Tom. But in Mobile it's all standard police work, shoe leather and analysis."

"You're saying?"

"I want Sally and me to work hard from this end. Carson thinks squeezing down here might pop rivets in the underground tunnel."

It was an exaggeration, but it got Mason's Stetson bobbing.

"I can go along with that, Harry. Nail the bastard."

A half-hour later, Nautilus and Sally Hargreaves were cruising through Larry Krebbs's neighborhood, a slice of middle-class suburbia. They saw a large silver Beamer in Krebbs's driveway, the vanity plate stating BRMLY1.

"Looks like Bromley's having a consultation with his client," Hargreaves said.

Nautilus pulled in behind the BMW and the pair exited. The knock was answered by Krebbs, wearing khakis and a polo shirt and polishing the head of a putter. A bag of clubs rested against the wall, ready for a round.

"What now?" he said.

"Where's your lawyer, Mr Krebbs?" Nautilus asked, hoping maybe the mouthpiece had just choked to death on some foreign substance – Truth, perhaps.

"He's watching stock quotes on the Bloomberg channel. Nathaniel!" Krebbs barked over his shoulder.

"It's one of those cops, the black one." Krebbs looked through Hargreaves like she was too lowly to mention.

"I heard about the upcoming suit, Mr Krebbs," Nautilus said. "You're now missing Lainie? You didn't seem concerned the last time we talked."

"Because you were harassing me. I miss her more than anything." Krebbs shot a look behind him, yelled "Nathaniel!"

"Harassing you, Mr Krebbs? How did –"

"You and that other moron, acting like goddamn storm troopers and –"

"That's enough, Lawrence." Bromley said, appearing beside his client, Tweedledee to Krebbs's golfing Tweedledum: burgundy slacks, striped golf shirt: ready to tee up. Both men were wearing street shoes and Nautilus realized all Krebbs's crap about keeping the carpet clean had been an exercise in control.

Bromley studied Hargreaves. "Well, well . . . what's this?"

"A thing is a what, Mr Bromley," Hargreaves replied evenly. "A person is a who. Who I am is Detective Sally Hargreaves, Missing Persons."

Bromley raised an amused eyebrow. "Who's lost?"

"I am, Mister Bromley," Nautilus said. "Last I was here, Mr Krebbs was happy his wife had left him. In keeping with that spirit, you were referring to Lainie Krebbs as a drunk and a woman who –"

Bromley waved the words away. "Larry was overwhelmed by emotions that day. He had problems with his wife and made a couple bad decisions owing to his fear she would leave him. But the Krebbses were very much in love and working out their problems."

"They were seeing a counselor, then?" Nautilus said. "You have a name?"

"I'm not at liberty to discuss personal matters, Detective. Then Mrs Krebbs – a confused woman, perhaps even clinically bipolar – got ensnared in the anti-male propaganda espoused by the hardcore radical feminists down at the women's center."

Hargreaves jaw dropped. "Hardcore radical . . ."

"They brainwashed Lainie Krebbs into thinking she was endangered and put her into an uncontrolled system that led to her violent death. Whatever these women are doing in the dark needs more oversight and scrutiny –"

"Are you nuts, Bromley?" Hargreaves snapped. "That's exactly what will kill it."

". . . before any more women are destroyed by this secret society, this sisterhood of death."

"What the hell do you mean by sisterhood of –"

Nautilus edged Hargreaves back, shooting her a *shut-up* glance. She stormed toward the cruiser. Bromley watched with a satisfied smile.

"Is there any reason for you to be here, outside of harassing my client, Detective?"

"I wanted to tell you another body turned up. At a park in Utah. There are some similarities with Ms Krebbs's murder and the one in Denver."

"When did this death occur?"

"Several days ago, nothing exact."

"More proof my client has no – repeat, no – involvement in these matters. Thanks for bringing that to my attention. Is there anything else?"

"No."

Krebbs pushed to the fore and angled his head toward Sally Hargreaves, now simmering in the cruiser. "Is that your new partner?"

"Why?"

Krebbs winked. "Best carry some heavy-duty tampons in the car, Detective. She seems permanently on the rag."

The door closed. Nautilus walked slowly back to the car, head canted at the thinker's angle. The pair drove away. "Something's itching in my head . . ." Nautilus frowned. "Bromley's a hotshot lawyer, mover and shaker, right? Did so well he quit the law firm and now picks and chooses cases. Lives in a hoity-toity neighborhood, from what I hear. He's a star."

"No, Harry, he's an ass-teroid. But go on."

"Larry Krebbs, on the other hand, is an antisocial lump who makes less than he should, lives in a tract house in average-ville, beats on women and is, in general, a failed human being. Why would they be golfing buddies?"

"Maybe they both love golf," Sal said after a few seconds of thought. "I know a guy in the motor pool who can't string together five words without a double negative, and he golfs with bank presidents and the like, all because he's good at smacking that little white ball back and forth."

"I guess that's it," Nautilus said, not sounding convinced.

38

"Hardcore radical feminists, secret society, sisterhood of death?" I repeated after Harry phoned to relay his recent encounter with Bromley and Krebbs. "It's a preview, bro," I told him. "Sound bites he'll use when the case hits the media. Remember when Bromley was defending the hacker who cracked into the credit-card accounts?"

I heard the chair creak as Harry leaned back. "Yeah. He called the little thief a victim of curiosity, a cyber fall guy for societal ills and the sacrificial lamb of conspicuous consumption."

"You remember what happened there, right?" I asked.

"The larcenous little pissant got off with a wrist slap and community service. He probably worked it off teaching PlayStation to kids at community centers."

I found it interesting that Harry recalled the cyber-perp as a kid. The guy was in his mid-twenties, a troubled man-child with a genius for computers. But Bromley had presented the hacker as a wayward teen who had simply taken a misstep, and the image had stuck. Bromley, love him or hate him, was damned good at what he did.

"Take the hacker case," I said, "double it, square it, cube the result. That's what you're gonna see when Bromley pulls the trigger on the women's center suit. I figure this case will summon the national cameras and keep clients rolling in until Nate shuffles off the mortal coil."

"Not a moment too soon," Harry said in lieu of goodbye.

I was wondering how much even Bromley could squeeze from non-profit women's centers when my phone rang. I grabbed it, eyes wide at the name on the screen.

"REIN!"

"Hi, Carson. Only got a minute. I'm at –"

"We know, Victoria Miles. Great job with the tag."

"Miss Miles is outside watering the prickly pears or whatever. I'm on her landline, watching from a second-story window. How's Harry? I swear when he passed by us I nearly –"

"Harry went back to Mobile," I said, as falsely cheerful as a game-show host. "He's gonna work with Sally. Cruz is staying on the case full time and we'll be nearby twenty-four-seven, no lapses in manpower."

A long pause told me Rein saw through my plastic exuberance. "It wasn't voluntary, right? Harry got pulled for being too protective?"

I dropped the smiley voice. "Harry let emotion cloud judgment a couple times, Rein. I've been there myself."

"It's my fault. I should have done more to assure him I could handle myself."

"Doesn't work that way, Miss Early. Anyway, Cruz and I are right down the street from the Hotel Miles."

"Vicky Miles told me a story that had me crying. She's a hero, Carson. All these people are heroes. Want to hear a sad story?"

"Sure." Rein could have recited the phone book and I'd have listened, happy to hear her voice. She told me the tale of Nina and the dentist and the scuzz-bag lawyer, adding, "Miz Miles is no threat unless she made up that story – and it was real and horrible as it could be."

"Don't get cozy, Rein," I cautioned. "For all you know, the killer lives next door and waits for Miles to bring women home. Everything's possible, never forget that."

"I feel lousy about what I'm doing, Carson. Lying to good people. Taking up time that could be used to help real women in trouble."

"Four women are known dead, Rein. You're the most important woman in the system right now."

"Four? When did –"

"A woman jumped into the system in Pittsburgh. She was found dead in east Utah a few days ago. It was our guy, a grim death tableau. We're not sure how long he held her after she'd been grabbed, only that he kept her prisoner before, uh . . ."

"Gotcha. Any reason why Utah?"

"We think the victim was trying to get to Baja California. A line drawn from Pittsburgh to Baja –"

"Cuts across Colorado," Rein finished, as fast in geography as everything else. "Listen . . ." she added.

"What?"

"If I get out of the system and haven't seen anything, I'm going back in. We can change the route a bit, maybe. Go in at Birmingham and say I'm heading to Utah or wherever moves me through the danger zone. That way I can . . . Uh-oh, looks like the watering is over, Carson. Gotta go put on my traveling face. Tell Harry I love him and to stop worrying. I'm gonna be fine."

I passed the news to Harry. He and Sally were in the MPD conference room dedicated to the case, so I jacked my computer into the wall and set my little camera on the table, the pair down south sending vid-feed my way. The MPD conference-room scene had a herky-jerky motion and was tinted orange, as if Harry and Sal were in a citrus fog. The wall behind my colleagues was a collage of case information. Photos of dead bodies centered the wall, the pinions around which all else flowed.

"Nothing on the Butterfly Lady in Mobile?" I asked, showing up on the computer screen in front of my colleagues.

Sal shook her head, or maybe it was the video. "I check national missing-person reports three times a day. No one's missing her, which is odd. Dr Peltier also shifted her age estimate from late twenties to mid-thirties."

"Why the initial discrepancy?"

"The Doc thinks Butterfly Lady was seriously into health and nutrition. A runner or rock climber, triathelete, something like that. The body tone made her appear younger. Listen, Carson, I want to go to the Mobile women's center and show photos of Butterfly Lady."

"With Rein in the system? You'll tip them off to our operation."

"I won't tell them we've got an op going on. I'll play it like shooting in the dark."

"Opinion, Harry?"

He surprised me. "When Rein gets out in a few days, and if she's found nothing, we go to the center and start working from the outside in."

Sal nodded, not happy, but outvoted. "So what's the update on Bromley?" I asked.

"No movement. But the sword is hanging."

"Krebbs?" I asked.

Harry leaned forward. "He was in the Keys when the missus was killed, no way around it. You know he's a big golfing buddy of Bromley?"

"Krebbs?" I pictured the misanthropic, misogynistic simian standing beside the nattily dressed and impeccably coiffed Bromley. I knew a lot of lawyers that repped nasty types, but that didn't mean they socialized with them.

"Odd, right?" Harry said.

"I guess Bromley expects to make a haul off Krebbs's case, wants to keep his golden goose close."

We were reviewing details for about the fortieth time when my phone rang. The ID said VICKY. Victoria Miles's house, Rein on the landline again.

"I'm getting ready to leave," Rein said. "Miz Miles went to pull the hogmobile from the garage. You guys ready to give chase?"

"I'll grab Miz Cruz and we'll be in your tailwind."

"My phone doesn't have enough juice to power a jumping bean. It'll be text from here, but not many." I heard something in Rein's voice, different, less of the detached calm and more of a quiet intensity. It gave me an eerie sense of déjà vu until I realized Rein was using a tone I'd heard in Harry's voice when a case was turning into a crusade.

"Got it," I said. "Any idea where you're going?"

"They never say. But I'm hoping for Casa Rick, the weirdo who takes pictures of eyes. Didn't Gail get to him about mid-point in her journey?"

"He was protector four out of the eight Gail stayed with on her journey to the Gulf." Finding Rick might reveal all we needed. A police record could let us drag him in under suspicion, find out where he'd been the last few weeks. Ricky-boy had smelled bad from the git-go.

"If this trip doesn't pan out, I'm going back inside the system, Carson. Until the perp is nailed. We're cool there, right?"

"Stay safe, Rein," I said, avoiding an answer. "We're a half-step behind you."

Two streets distant and with field glasses to my eyes, I watched the garage door open at the Victoria Miles household. "Here we go," I said to Cruz. "They're out of the driveway and heading east."

Cruz dropped the van in gear and we were back in pursuit. "There are only a couple highways heading east or southeast. Nice to have a fire-engine-red Escalade to track. I swear that thing glows."

"Harry and I once had to follow a silver Corolla from Mobile to Pensacola," I said, setting the glasses in my lap.

"Ouch," Cruz said, knowing how many silver Corollas cruised the road, resembling every other silver compact from a few hundred feet behind.

"Two dimwits rented the car to move a few thousand hits of meth, we dubbed them Beavis and Butthead. B and B stopped at a Mickey D's for food, backed into the spot. Harry was getting tired of picking them out in traffic so he did the drive-through, got a fish sandwich and fifty packs of mustard."

"Fifty?"

"The drive-through lady gives him a look and Harry says, 'Lawd miss, I jus' loves my mustard.' So he gets about a pound of mustard in those little squeezy things. Beavis and Butthead are just getting into their chow. We park beside the Corolla and Harry paints the rear of the

239

trunk with a foot-round smear of yellow mustard. Then he poked eyes and a mouth in the goo."

"A smiley face, oh my God."

"You could see that happy trunk a half-mile away."

Cruz laughed, a high and pretty sound. "My favorite is the time Nautilus got the perp to throw back his Frisbee and snagged the unsuspecting guy's fingerprints. That was classic. How come I never saw that Harry Nautilus?"

"Maybe you can visit us down Mobile way. I have a spare room for guests. Won't cost you a cent to stay at the Carson Hilton."

She didn't say no, a good start. Cruz and I were getting along nicely, considering eighty per cent of our consciousness was focused on giving Rein the right amount of chain.

"They're ramping toward Interstate 40," Cruz said. "We're going back into Oklahoma, thenceforth into Arkansas or Louisiana, I expect. We're stair-stepping toward the Bama coast." She paused, dainty nose sniffing the air. "Do I smell burning rubber?"

A red light began blinking on the dash. A buzzer sounded.

39

His day over, Dr Thalius Sinclair filled his briefcase with papers and closed the door of his office behind him. Dr Bramwell was on sabbatical – nice to walk down the hall and not trip over one of her damn bicycles or listen to her constant cawing laughter. He passed the office of Liza Krupnik, empty. Was she at one of her volunteer activities again? When did she do *his* work?

Sinclair continued to the lair of the hapless Trotman. The lanky grad student was behind a desk buried in pages of figures and a scribble-laden atlas, keyboarding furiously while listening to twanging rock and roll on an iPod, the drums so loud they bled into the air. Sinclair stood in the doorway and cleared his throat. Nothing. He reached forward, grabbed the white cord and pulled twice, as if ringing for a butler. The grad student looked up with anger, blanched when he saw Sinclair. Trotman's lips formed soundless words.

Sinclair waved his hand in front of Trotman. "Hello? Anyone in there?"

"W-what can I do for you, sir?" Trotman finally managed, yanking the cords from his ears.

"Where's Krupnik?"

"She volunteers at a women's center. She's there tonight and in the morning."

Sinclair scowled. "Why does she work there, you got any idea?"

"I never asked. I'm sorry."

"Sorry for what?"

"I . . . don't know."

Sinclair shook his head. "Why are you here? I hoped – or rather I thought you had another symposium to attend."

"I l-leave later today."

Sinclair popped open his briefcase. "I need a few pages copied for a meeting. Is that within range of your capabilities?"

Trotman nodded like his head was in a paint mixer.

"Can you do it now?" Sinclair said. "Then I don't have to worry whether it's going to be done."

Sinclair pulled a sheaf of paper from his briefcase, a thesis titled "Rising Voices: Feminism in the 1960s", handing them to the grad student and following Trotman down the hall to the room holding the copier, a shelf of supplies, and a table for assembling materials. The room did have a window, however, angled west, in the distance the five angled plates of the Flatiron Mountains, the cobalt sky behind them like a luminous gel.

As Trotman set the copier into motion, Sinclair studied the grad student for a long moment, then stepped to the window and nodded toward the green peaks.

"Do you like the mountains, Robert? The Flatirons? The Rockies?"

Trotman nodded as the machine fed pages into his waiting hand. "Very much. They're where I go to get away from all the –" Trotman caught himself in mid-sentence.

"From what?" Sinclair said.

"Uh, nothing."

"From the pressures of work?" Sinclair demanded. "The quotidian demands of your day? That's what you were about to say, right? Something to that effect?"

"I-I didn't mean to imply th-that . . ."

"For Chrissakes, Robert," Sinclair said, "I'm asking simple conversational questions, not interrogating you. Why do you like the mountains? Besides what you were about to say, that you went there to escape your hideous fucking part-time job."

"I . . . like the quiet," Trotman said, looking toward his shoes. "I like it when it's just me and . . . the wind."

Trotman looked supremely embarrassed and Sinclair fixed him with a questioning eye. "Are you talking about the wind as it hisses though the pines, Robert? Like on an early spring morning when a man can smell the pinesap and hear

243

a stream tumbling down a ravine like it's surprised by its own unimaginable joy? Do you like it when moon-bright snow is punched through with the tracks of mule deer and rabbits? Is that what you're trying to tell me, Robert?"

Trotman looked like he was lost in a house of mirrors. "Y-yes, Doctor. That's exactly it."

Still shaking his head, Sinclair jammed the papers in his briefcase. "Christ, Robert. How hard was that to say?"

Sinclair left the building and wove his way home, striding past the Beacon tavern, feet and thirst wanting to turn inside the door for a Scotch, but he had things to do. He glanced across the street at the Women's Crisis Center, the door opening to disgorge a stout woman of military bearing carrying a handful of mail, probably to the box on the corner, though she clutched the envelopes as if conveying secrets to an exiled king.

Carol W. Madrone, Sinclair ruminated. W for Welles, a family name. Forty-four years old, unmarried – never will be. Degrees in Women's Studies and Social Work. Lived at 2657-A Aspen Trace, a two-story duplex with two young lesbians renting the other side. Madrone was built like a bulldog, strode like a colonel, and – *Dear Jesus, what kind of color is that for human hair?* Madrone turned in Sinclair's direction and he spun his head quickly away, hand patting at his hair to hide his face.

Cruz and I stood on the highway berm with traffic blowing by at eighty miles an hour. The beefy guy in the blue work shirt looked up from the steam-trailing engine compartment. His wrecker truck sat behind us, lights flashing.

"It's your coolant hose," he said, wiping his hand on a rag dangling from his belt. "The clamp busted. No big deal."

"How long?"

He nodded to the wrecker. "I got a clamp in the truck I can put on, refill the radiator. Twenty minutes and you're fixed."

I studied the fading daylight and pulled out all the cash in my wallet, waving it at the mechanic. "Do it in ten and it's all yours."

"Early will be on the highway," Cruz said, taking my arm and nodding up the road. "I'll call the staties and get a light-and-sound escort. We'll move at warp speed until we find her."

"Sure," I said. "Piece of cake."

The mechanic slapped the new piece on in seven minutes and made a hundred-thirty bucks. Cruz's people called their Texan contingent and explained how our surveillance had bumped into trouble. Two minutes later an officer sirened up to our taillights, Sergeant Willis Layton. We filled in the details. Layton studied the van through mirror sunglasses.

"That thing go faster than it looks?"

"A hundred for sure," Cruz said. "Maybe one-ten."

Layton nodded toward the bumper of his vehicle, said, "Stay tight."

We highballed until we hit Oklahoma. We'd cut across its panhandle on the road south into Texas, were now hitting the fat part of the state. I always wondered why more states didn't meet as efficiently as Utah, Colorado, Arizona and New Mexico, Pythagorean borders.

"State line coming up," Layton radioed.

Cruz looked at me. "At the speed we've been moving, we would have caught up by now. They turned off somewhere."

We pulled to the side, thanked Layton and pressed eastward into Oklahoma. Day became night and we found a motel in the Midwest City section of Oklahoma City, allowing fast access to major highways once we nailed Rein's location. I paced the floor and stared at a map like it had the answer. Cruz leaned the wall in jeans and a bright aloha shirt, arms crossed.

She said, "How about we call Miles and take the chance she's not involved."

"What if Miles and the killer are in this together?" I argued. "Vicky and Ricky, the Bonnie and Clyde of abduction?"

"After that story Miles told Officer Early?"

"I've known sociopaths who invented stories on a finger snap."

Cruz pulled the band from her hair and shook it loose, a brown swirl. She thought a moment, dark eyes scanning the ceiling. "Didn't Miles say her sister's name was Nina? That she married an abusive, uh –"

"Dentist," I interrupted, seeing where she was going. "And the sister who shot him went to prison."

"Macon, Georgia, right?"

I pulled my laptop, Googled *Dentist, wife, suicide, trial, Macon*. Hits galore. I opened the top link, scanned, and held the screen to Cruz so she could read the archived newspaper headline: *Macon Dentist Cleared in Wife's Suicide*. The subhead said, *Lawyer proclaims client a 'Wronged Man'*

"Miles is for real," Cruz said. "I'm calling." She put her phone on speaker and set it on the desk, taking the chair. I stood at her back as she dialed.

"Miz Miles, my name is Detective Amica Cruz. I'm with the Colorado State Police."

Hesitation. "Yes?"

"You just delivered a woman somewhere along the women's underground railroad. Her name is Reinetta Early and she's an undercover officer investigating the deaths of several women who might have been targeted because they're in the system."

"I'm not sure if I –"

"Please listen, Miz Miles. We were tracking you until our vehicle had problems. The red Escalade. We've been your escort since you retrieved Officer Early at the truck stop in Oklahoma. We need to know where you left Officer Early . . . the transfer point."

Fear. Confusion. "I can't . . . I've been told not to –"

"Officer Early called from your home phone when you were watering your yard. She said you were a hero.

247

She told me about your sister, Nina, and the tragedy in your family. Miz Miles, I hate these people almost as much as you do."

A long pause before Miz Miles spoke.

"I took her to Sayre, Oklahoma. I was to drop her at a crossroads. He'd be nearby."

"He?"

"I've spoken with him before. We did a transfer earlier this year in a city north of Amarillo. Last Fall this gentleman left a parcel – a woman – for me. If you know the system, you know all I hear is a voice. But I left your colleague in Sayre hours ago. She could be anywhere by now."

Sayre was over a hundred-fifty miles away. Cruz and I rolled in at midnight and grabbed a cheap motel room, all that's needed when you're gonna fall across the mattress and crash. We were drowsing on a bed with the lights off and a soundless Weather Channel throwing light across the walls and ceiling. We'd taken showers and changed in the bathroom while the other babysat my cell phone. Food had been a bag of soggy objects from a fast-food joint. Most of it occupied the trashcan.

My phone pulled me from a tattered dream into a swirl of color, the pretty lady on the television gesturing to a brightly hued map of high and low pressure. The clock said 3:34 a.m. I grabbed at the phone, knocked it to the floor. By the time my hand was reaching for the device, Cruz was handing it to me. I flipped the cover, read the message and my shoulders slumped. I held the phone so Cruz could read the screen. The message was simple:

```
w Rick. Sty cls.
```

"With Rick. Stay close," Cruz translated unnecessarily, her voice a dry whisper.

40

Cruz sat cross-legged on the lumpy bed, phone to her ear, pen and paper at the ready. The clock changed from 4:12 to 4:13 a.m. The room was on the highway side and every time a loud motorcycle or truck passed by Cruz stuck her finger in her other ear.

"How's it coming?" I asked. "The cell info?"

"The tech guy keeps saying any minute."

"It's been twenty-seven minutes."

She shrugged. Cruz had set us up with the phone company's tech services people, made the usual nods to privacy rules. The vast computer network of the phone service ensured every call was tracked for billing's sake, and the machines knew the exact routing of every blip of information.

"Yes," she said into the phone. "I'm still here. Ready."

She wrote, frowned, wrote some more. Said, "Thanks," and hung up.

"Where's the tower?"

"Tower 1165-A4. About a dozen miles southwest of Tulsa."

"Not overly far," I said, taking anything hopeful I could get.

"The coverage is a circle. The south side is farmland, spare housing, a couple exurb neighborhoods. North is urban sprawl, about five thousand households."

We tumbled back into the van and were in south Tulsa by eight in the morning. We grabbed another motel room, staying stationary to await information and needing more room to pace than the van allowed. I stood on the second-floor balcony of the motel and studied the cloud-strewn morning sky, psychic antennae bristling, trying to feel Rein's presence.

"She's near, Ryder," Cruz said, patting my hand. "She'll send another text soon. We'll set up camp Nautilus style, right in Rick's side yard."

I grunted and gnawed a power bar, feeling it turn to wood halfway down. My phone rang with a voice message and I grimaced at the screen. I'd hoped to hear from Rein before I heard from Harry. I put the phone on speaker so Cruz could be part of the conversation.

"What's happening?" Harry said. "Everything fine? Where's Rein?"

"We don't know where she is, Harry. We had her in

sight when a clamp on the radiator hose died. We got the cell-tower site from the wireless company, so we're close, just south of Tulsa. It's been a long night."

Five seconds of black silence.

"Why not just call her and –"

"She'll get a message to us, bro, she always does. Calling gains us nothing, not yet."

"Who is she with, Carson?" Harry asked. "Did she get a name?"

Cruz saw my slumping shoulders and stepped in. "It was Rick, Detective Nautilus . . . the eye guy."

I jumped in and explained how we'd made Rick with the call to Miles and confirmed with the text from Rein. I expected an explosion. Instead, Harry's voice came back calm to the point of cold. I was hundreds of miles away, but I swear I could feel him thinking.

"You've got to take the chance there's no involvement on the Colorado end, Carson. Maybe we can sneak up on Rick from the Boulder side."

"You're saying we should contact the Boulder women's center?" Cruz asked, raising an eyebrow at me. "Take the chance someone might know Rick, how to get to him?"

I'm not sure Harry had forgiven Cruz, but Rein's safety superseded anger. "Everyone vows the system is super tight," he said. "A chain of territory-based cells, each its own enclosed world. It's bullshit."

"How's that?" I asked.

"It ignores human nature, Carson. People need to talk,

to gossip. And how do these fucking cells get set up in the first place? By magic?"

Cruz frowned at me. Her eyes said she was starting to see things Harry's way. She leaned toward the phone. "So you think the possibility of getting usable info from Boulder outweighs the potential of tipping off the killer?"

"Everyone pretends the system is anonymous, but people on the inside talk to one another, depend on each other. Someone has to goddamn know something."

"What if they start talking about a plant in the system and it gets to the killer?" I said, replaying the reason we'd stayed quiet from day one.

"Two people have moved through Boulder, then come under the care of Mr Eye Pictures. We know them as Rhonda Doakes and Reinetta Early. One is dead."

I looked at my watch. "Let's figure Rein is watching her back. Give her another couple hours. Let's make it four."

"Four hours?" Harry said, tension rising in his voice.

"Outside of a thing about pictures, we have no solid reason to think Rick's the killer. Plus the perp doesn't kill immediately. I don't know what he does, but he doesn't kill them right away."

"He tortures them, Carson," Harry said. "That's what he does. I don't see what waiting a few more hours buys."

I started my line of reasoning again, but the line was dead.

41

"Good morning. The Women's Crisis Center of Boulder, Liza Krupnik speaking."

"I need to talk to the person in charge," Harry Nautilus said, his eyes wandering the almost-deserted detectives' room. "Is that you?"

"I'm just a staffer. You want Carol or Meelia. Carol's the director and she's here today. May I say who's calling?"

"Tell Carol you've got Tee Bull on the line. That's Tee with two Es."

The phone system clicked as the call transferred. Nautilus heard a long pause, expected as the square-shaped woman with short red hair recalled her visitor.

The phone picked up, the voice making ice seem warm. "We don't know anything about your . . . friend, Mr Bull. We wouldn't tell you if we did."

"May I have your email address, Carol?"

"Why would you –"

"You need to see something."

"I doubt that. But send whatever you feel you need to show me."

Nautilus created an email, attaching an archived photo from an award ceremony a few years back, Carson in it as well. Both men were in uniform, Nautilus stern as he held his certificate, Carson grinning like a freaking jack-o'-lantern.

"It'll be there momentarily." Nautilus hit Send.

A half-minute passed. "You're not a pimp," Carol finally said, confusion in her voice. "You're a policeman."

"A detective, ma'am. With the Mobile, Alabama, Police Department."

"And this man beside you. He was . . ."

"That's my partner, Carson Ryder."

"I'm terribly confused. What is going on here?"

Nautilus laid it all out, taking under five minutes, using graphic detail when he felt necessary.

"I'm sorry, Detective," Carol said. "But I have no idea where your undercover officer could be. We're set up so that –"

"Do you personally know anyone in the system?" Nautilus said. "The folks who handle the transfers and safe houses?" He knew this was tightly protected information, necessarily so.

"Sometimes I enlist people at regional conferences," Carol said, tentative. "Or people volunteer. What I don't know – what I tell volunteers I don't want to know – is their full name and exactly where they live."

"But you sometimes still know, right?"

"Do this work for years and you learn things," Carol said quietly.

"The person I'm looking for goes by Rick," Nautilus said. "Real name or not, I don't know. He's handled two known transfers under that name. One of the women is dead."

"Oh lord."

"You know him?"

"He called a year ago, saying he'd done the same work in the northeast and was moving into our region. It's a big region, Detective. I checked with the center in Seattle, or was it Spokane? They had nothing but praise."

"Do you know his name?"

"Rick. I'm sorry, but it's all I ever asked."

"Can you call Spokane or Seattle for me and put me in touch with whoever recommended him?"

"It could be several hours because of the time change, Detective. But I'll do my best."

Carol took an hour and twenty minutes to get back. The director of the Spokane Center for Women's Health was named Marjorie Kinter.

"Yes, Detective Nautilus," Kinter said. "Carol in Boulder said you'd be calling. A nightmare. I don't understand how it happened. Do you need the name of someone from our vicinity?"

"Someone who moved to Kansas, the Wichita area. Male, probably gay and –"

"Richard. You're talking about Richard."

Nautilus's breath seized in his throat. Time stopped.

"Richard who?"

"Carol doesn't trust anyone, but she seems to trust you. Normally I'd never tell anyone a name."

"I know, ma'am."

"You're looking for Richard Salazano. We were so sorry to see him relocate. He lived by Eugene, Oregon, and if needed would come all the way up here. He'd drive all night to take a woman."

Harry called and told me what he'd done. I held the phone a foot away and stared at it. "You what?" I finally said.

"I made the calls."

I closed my eyes and shook my head. "Jeez, and here I thought we were going to wait and see if Rein checked in. Because if she did we wouldn't have to break cover."

"You know that alarm in my head?"

I looked at Cruz. She shrugged. "It's doesn't matter, Ryder. It's done."

"The lady in Boulder put me on to Spokane," Harry said. "This Rick guy did the same thing in the northwest region for a few years, moved to Oklahoma. You maybe want his full name?"

"Can I . . . ask you a question, Marla?" Rick asked Reinetta, the pair in his living room, spare furniture and framed black-and-white photos on the wall, the brown

257

curtains pulled tight. "It's important to me. A project I'm working on."

On full alert behind her drowsy smile, Rein studied her supposed protector: mid-thirties, slender waist and wide shoulders, a bit taller than average, tousled black hair, brown eyes often called puppy eyes, soft. He wore khaki cargo pants, black T-shirt and an amethyst stud in his earlobe. It was obvious that he was in good physical condition, worked out hard. His voice and mannerisms were shaded toward an effeminate side, a contrast to the powerful body.

"Of course, Rick. Ask me anything."

"May I take some photographs of you?"

Rein had been waiting and wondering if she'd hear the request Rick had asked of Gail – the late Rhonda Doakes – several months back.

"I don't know, Rick," Rein said. "I'm not sure if that's what I'm supposed to –"

"Not your face, Marla. Oh my, never your face. Just your eyes. They're for a special piece I'm putting together. A personal memento."

From the moment Rein arrived at the isolated house in the dead of night – a half-mile from the nearest suburban-style community – she'd memorized everything she saw, planning for a getaway. She hadn't made it upstairs, or seen behind a door on the hall leading to the guest bedroom. Office? A second bedroom? Did it hold the standard accoutrements, or a chamber of horrors?

258

"I guess," Rein said. "Sure."

Rick pointed down the hall. "Let's go to the studio down the hall. I have my gear in there and can set up a stand for an umbrella."

"Umbrella?"

"A kind of reflector to make the light perfect. It'll take ten minutes, about all we've got before you become a goner."

Rein raised an eyebrow as if contemplating the request, in actuality scoping out points of attack on Rick's body: eyes, throat, solar plexus, groin, knees . . .

Get ready, girl.

"I guess it's all right," Rein said, internally replaying moves her uncle had made her perform for hours in the Police Academy gym. Grab his collar, drive your knee through his balls, get to the phone, call in the troops . . .

"I need to get something else." Rick went to the closet behind the front door and retrieved a chrome bar, two feet long, a black knob on one end, a winding of duct tape on the other.

"What's that for?" Rein asked.

"Just a little something to hold the umbrella."

Rick held the pipe loosely to his side and nodded toward the room. Walking down the tight hallway Rein had to maintain an over-her-shoulder conversation with Rick because she had made a rookie mistake, and a very bad one.

Rick had gotten behind her.

42

Richard Salazano's home was on the rural side of the tower's domain, a pink, sixties-style single-level set on a corner of farmland, a farmhouse barely visible in the mile-away distance. Crows pecked beside a fence line in the rear, beyond only fallow land stretching toward the horizon. It was the perfect place to do nasty things, any screams lost in the trees and hiss of summer insects. The Oklahoma sky was a bright blue bowl dappled with cirrus, a happy sky over what might be a very ugly situation.

"I'm going in hardcore," I told Cruz on our second pass-by, the curtains tight, a bright compact import in the driveway. "Watch the back door. There's a side door as well. He might pop out shooting."

"Or he might be innocent. You sure don't want to –"

I was looking at the situation, forming a plan. A cop

might be scary, but the worst nightmare for the transfer and safe house people was an insane hubby or boyfriend who'd breached the system.

"Watch the rear. Give me three minutes. Then come in."

"Three minutes?"

"Cruz . . ."

She cut the engine and we drifted across the dry grass of the front yard. I bailed ten steps from the house and ran to the front door. It was unlocked.

"EVERYONE GET DOWN," I screamed, leaping inside, gun drawn.

Silence. I heard a clock ticking on the mantel. The décor was simple and straightforward and had an artsy inflection, black-and-white photos on the walls, bridges and landscapes and windmills as design elements. The furniture not country but urban: clean-lined chairs and a sofa, bookshelves, small tables, all seemingly from Ikea or a similar outlet. Crouching, I made my way through the dining room and into the kitchen. A teapot sat on the stove and I tapped it with a finger. Warm.

I froze to a murmur from a tight hall, sidled down the wall with the muzzle of my pistol at eye height, waiting. A sniffling sound was coming from a doorway and I entered low, gun first, double-handed. A bedroom, the same simple, direct furniture as the other pieces. A man in red silk boxers and a white tee was on the floor beside the unmade bed, curled into a fetal comma, snuffling, "Don't kill me, please don't kill me."

"Get your hands out to your side. DO IT!"

Shaking hands moved outward, trembling fingers gripping the blue carpet. The man shot me a look, saw the gun. The snuffling turned to crying.

"What did you do with Marla?" I said, using the only name the guy would know Rein by. "Where is she?"

"M-M-Marla's gone. I-I dropped her off over an hour ago."

I pressed the gun against the guy's head. "Bullshit! What did you do with her?"

"I passed her on. She didn't s-stay here long . . . I d-don't know where she is, I'm not s-supposed to."

I cuffed the guy's arms behind his back and ran room to room, yanking open closets. No Rein. Upstairs. No Rein. Basement. No Rein. I thundered back to the bedroom. The guy's eyes were as wide as if he'd touched lightning.

"A-are you her husband?" he said, lower lip trembling. "Her b-boyfriend? I'm sorry you two had problems but I'm j-just a link in a chain. It has nothing to do with you."

I stared at him. "You take pictures of them, don't you, Richard? You need souvenirs."

"How d-do you know about that?"

"I'LL ASK THE QUESTIONS! Tell me about the pictures."

"I-I wanted a memory trail of the women in my care, that's all. They're so b-brave and scared at the same time, it sh-shows in their eyes."

"BULLSHIT!"

"P-please . . . look on the table b-by the couch, the binder."

I dragged a blubbery Richard with me and found the binder alongside books on antiques and birds. My fingers flipped pages of artful black-and-white photographs. Eyes. Eighteen pairs. Some looked sad, others hopeful. All looked alive.

I pushed Rick to the couch and stood absolutely still in the living room, trying to smell what was hanging between the molecules. I'd come to believe madness had its own odor, a pungent dankness. I'd never been able to understand what caused the smell – whether it emanated from psychopaths themselves or was something the universe put around them to make them visible to the senses of the unwary – but I knew that smell like I knew the stink of gas from a leaky stovetop.

I couldn't smell madness, only chamomile tea. Richard was benign. I sighed and tossed the binder to the table, turning to see Cruz standing in the living room, her drawn weapon at her side.

"Your minutes are up," she said.

Richard Salazano stared at Cruz, sensing he wasn't going to die. Not today, anyway. "Who are you?" he asked.

I showed my ID. His head slumped forward in relief.

"Where did you take her?" I asked. "Marla."

"A park just over the Missouri border. I-I usually keep them longer. But it worked out that another protector was in the area. I handed Marla to her."

"There must have been communication with the person on the other side."

"I used a pre-paid phone. The number's on it." Salazano looked between Cruz and me. "What's wrong? Why are you here?"

Cruz stepped forward. "You helped a woman six months back, Richard. Her name was probably Gail. Dark hair, medium build, button nose?"

"I remember Gail." Rick went pale as the worst possible reason for our visitation sunk in. His hands flew to his mouth. "Oh, no, please don't tell me . . ."

"Gail's dead," I said. "And she's not the only one. Someone's using the system as a killing machine and we're trying to find out who."

"Dear Jesus. How can I help?"

"The phone number you used to make the connection . . ."

Rick Salazano ran to a dresser, pulling a cheapie phone from the top drawer. "I was going to clear everything today. But I was thinking about calling back, checking on Marla."

"You usually do that?" Cruz asked.

"I planned on Marla being here a day at least. Probably two or three. It's a sparse part of the country for links in the system. People need time to clear schedules, make long drives."

I looked at Cruz, then back to Rick. "You're saying something felt a little off, out of the ordinary?"

He frowned. "Everything seemed rushed. And two in almost as many days?"

"Two what?" Cruz said.

"Two runners, ma'am. Marla was the second woman in three days. Before her was Darleen."

"Two so close together. Is that unusual?"

He nodded. "Normally I handle four or five a year."

"These two women, Marla and Darleen. Did they go to the same link?"

"Both were headed southeast, but a link in the chain – Astra – called and said she was free immediately. We set it up, made the transfer."

I dialed the number of Astra. No service, dead. Another drugstore cell phone, used for a few vital minutes, thrown into the weeds beside the road.

43

Rein's driver wore a formless tie-dye dress, cowboy boots and beads, an unruly mass of curly brown hair jutting in every direction and falling over most of her face, round, red-lensed wireframe shades on a slender nose, her mouth wide enough to hold both a grin and a brown cigarette in a white holder. Rein had seen the woman on television shows about the history of rock'n'roll. She'd heard her sing on the radio and seen her photo in magazines.

Rein was being chauffeured by Janis Joplin.

"Hop in, girl," Joplin had said at the transfer point, looking over the top of her small round sunglasses, her voice low and gravelly, a smoker's voice. "Or we're gonna be late for your revolution."

It turned out the driver's name wasn't Janis – which would have been too weird for Rein to take – but Astra, which the now non-Janis was happy to explain as she slid from lane to lane down the highway.

". . . birth name was Jane, which I never liked cuz the name was too, well, plain fuckin' Jane. Then, when I was like sixteen, I decided to change it to the month I was born in, called myself January which was cool, but of course everyone shortened it to Jan which was no more than dropping the 'e' from Jane, so I felt I was going backwards. There was a Goth period when I called myself nada – with a lower-case 'n' of course – but dressing in black became so, so dark, you know? A few years back one of my boyfriends – just a casual friend, but an amazing fuck, tantric, went on forever – looked over to me after we'd finished about two hours of ride'n'glide and gasped, 'Dana, you are a star.' I had shifted around the letters in nada to get Dana – capital-D this time – but Dana was getting old and when my sweet fuck-ace called me a star, well . . ."

"'A star' anagrammed into Astra," Rein completed.

"I've had it for six years now," Astra grinned, large soft hands with outsized rings on every other finger spinning the wheel. Rein thought Astra's penchant for make-up and jewlery made even the bangly, jangly Vicky Miles seem sedate. "I think it's here to stay, unlike my ex tantric fuck-muffin, who actually turned out to be a total asshole – ain't that how it goes."

"What sort of work do you do?" Rein asked.

"I have a little restaurant in Springfield, Missouri," Astra trilled, stubbing out a cigarette and lighting another.

"And opening a second one in Branson. I'm lucky to have an absolutely *inspired* chef as a partner – Londell, a TG who cooks the best barbecue you ever –"

"Teegee?"

"Transgendered, dear. A sheep in wolf's clothing, so to speak. He's crossing the line a step at a time. It's *so* expensive."

Rein wondered if her protector was of similar persuasion, but decided against asking, judging the garrulous Astra to be an intelligent if loosely collected human being of a Bohemian nature. Feeling secure, Rein had allowed herself needed sleep, dozing when she felt the van veer sharply, opening her eyes to find the vehicle swooping up an off-ramp into farmland.

"We're almost there," Astra said. "I expect you'll enjoy having a companion to talk to."

"Companion?"

Astra sucked a drag off the cigarette and side-lipped a plume of smoke out the window. "I didn't tell you? You're going to be sharing a safe house with another runner. I picked her up last night, which is why I'm kinda frazzled." Astra grinned and shook her curly mane of unkempt locks. "I didn't even have time to do my hair."

"Is this unusual?" Rein asked. "Two women at once?"

"Safe houses are kinda at a premium out here on the range. If two of you poor girls can take a section of the railroad together, it'll save time. I'm making arrangements to get the next step made, so I expect you'll both be moving toward destinations in a day or two. In the meantime, Londell and me need an espresso machine – *very* expensive. I'm trying to pick up a used one from a defunct coffeehouse in Branson. So much to do, so little time." Astra winked. "Relax, girlfriend, you're in good hands."

Rein didn't relax, but pretended to drowse, head lolling toward the window every few minutes, collecting data: highway signs, locations on billboards, local attractions. She was still stinging from her mistake at Rick's, walking a dozen feet with her back open to a man one step behind and carrying a length of pipe.

Luckily, Rick had turned out to be a gentle man who detested violence against women after growing up with a father who abused his mother. Rick had lived in three disparate places since graduating from Indiana University with a degree in photography and among the first things he did at each place was make himself a part of the underground railroad.

The chrome pipe turned out to be a counterweight for the umbrella he'd mentioned, a white fabric reflector. Rick was serious about his work and had taken some lovely photos, showing her each one after snapping the shutter, assuring her it was just her eyes.

And then it had been time to go, Rick saying someone down the line had called and was heading to a transfer point, a woman. He had held her tight, told her to be strong, and dropped Rein off at a small park. Five minutes later Janis/Astra had arrived.

"Do you know when we'll leave the safe house?" Rein asked. "And will the other woman be leaving with me?"

"It's always a fluid situation. Right now it seems you'll share the next phase of the journey together."

Astra rounded a bend and pointed to a blue two-story farmhouse on a flat carpet of green lawn surrounded by fields. "Here's your latest bed and breakfast, Marla. A perfect little jewel in the middle of nowhere."

"You're sure it's safe?"

"The place is owned by Katka, a local hero in the women's movement. Normally Katka would have stepped in, but she's on vacation – Brazil." Astra switched to a Brit accent à la Monty Python. "Frightful bother, this lack of qualified help."

They pulled up the drive, stopped, the engine running. "What do I do?" Rein asked as she slid from the van.

"The door should be open. Eat, drink, or use anything you find. See you later, girlfriend."

"Wait . . . I, uh . . ."

But Astra was heading down the road. Rein noted the license tag on the van and the address on the mailbox, taking a few seconds to log them in memory. She turned to the house, a light on in a back room. She wondered if she was being watched, saw no silhouette at the window. Rein paused. Things seemed a bit out of pattern, but Astra appeared to be the real deal, a hoot actually. And her backup was somewhere nearby. There was a small motel a few miles back, Carson and Cruz probably there right now, waiting for night to make a drive by. Astra wasn't going to be around for several hours . . .

Rein could finally get the small GPS locator, at least. And her gun.

44

Reinetta pushed the door open, said, "Hello?"

Nothing. She stepped inside, scanning every detail: frayed Oriental rug, solid comfortable-looking furniture, several old sepia-toned photos on the cream-and-red wallpaper. For a split second she detected an off smell, like something had gone bad in a far corner of a refrigerator.

"Hello?" Rein repeated.

An eye peeked around a corner, the kitchen to the rear, a questioning female eye under dark hair pulled back in a ponytail. The accompanying eye appeared, making two green eyes in a round and pretty face. The face was above a petite body in a simple red blouse, faded jeans, and blue running shoes.

"Is this the Oklahoma station on the hot chick railroad?" Rein said.

The woman stepped out, the tentative look on her face replaced by a smile. "I heard I was getting some company," the woman said, crossing the room and holding out her hand. "My name's, uh, Darleen."

"And I'm Marla," Rein said. "Sorta."

The woman smiled even more broadly. "I'm kinda Darleen. Astra split?"

"Branson."

"The restaurant with Lindell or whatever. I swear it's half what she talks about – and does she talk."

The woman laughed with genuine humor and Rein's alarm system backed down a notch. "I take it you've been here a bit, Darleen?"

"Since last night. Astra dropped me here, ran off to get you. She's weird, but she's a whirlwind."

Rein went to a photo on the wall, a stern-faced man and woman in fifties garb before a brick home, between them a smiling little girl of eight or so. Penciled across the bottom of the shot was *Daddy, Mommy, and Katka, Erie, 1958.*

"The owner of the place is named Katka," Darleen said. "She and a friend are on a trip. There are pictures of them in the kitchen. Speaking of that, are you hungry, Marla?"

"Starved."

"There's meat and cheese in the fridge, bread on the table. Let's eat."

Cruz and I were still at Salazano's home. He'd been kind enough to fix us a pitcher of iced tea and set out cheeses

and crackers. He was a seven-year veteran of the underground railroad, thus I was worried by his worry, his
sense that two women passing through his care in four
days was anomalous.

My phone rang. Harry.

"Nothin' on Rein. Right?"

"Not yet. You know I'll call you as soon as –"

"Listen, Carson, I just talked to Detective Honus
Clayton, Pensacola Homicide. They're sure they've got
Rhonda Doakes's killer, Gail's killer."

"Who?"

"Remember James, the boyfriend?"

I heard Gail's hushed words as she'd described James
to Doc Kavanaugh.

*Knocked out two of my teeth . . . did I believe a piece
of paper could stop a knife from slicing my throat? . . .
driving past my apartment and screaming, calling my
phone every two minutes.*

"I remember James," I said, my voice tight.

"Clayton found the place where Doakes was killed, a
fishing shanty up the Pensacola River. Forensics lifted
prints belonging to James Peyton. They were on the
system courtesy of a restraining order taken out against
him some months back."

"By Rhonda Doakes." I nodded. "Where's Peyton
now?"

"In the Boise lockup. Boise was where Doakes began
her journey, Carson."

I closed my eyes and saw a map. Rhonda Doakes had

ridden the railroad from Boise to the Alabama coast, finally thinking she was safe. Finally letting out a breath held for years.

"I remember."

"Detective Clayton flew up to Boise yesterday. James Peyton is talking, Carson."

"How'd Peyton find out where Doakes was living?"

"Get this: Peyton was sitting around his crib one day when the phone rings. Caller asks Peyton what he'd do to Rhonda if she was standing in front of him right then. Peyton says, 'Kick her fuckin' brains in.' Caller says, 'Got a pencil to write an address?'"

"Peyton got the address where Doakes was living?"

"No, Carson. He didn't."

Puzzlement. "What did he get?"

"Directions to the fishing shack."

My puzzlement turned to head-spinning confusion. "Peyton didn't take her there?"

"Peyton swears his caller gave him directions to the shack. He drove straight through, found Rhonda bound with tape, wrapped in a tarp on the floor. Detective Clayton doesn't think the guy's lying."

"Is Peyton our killer? The perp in the system?"

"Clayton says Peyton's not smart enough to light a fart. Clayton went to the Pensacola version of the women's help center, where Doakes came out. Except she almost wasn't Rhonda Doakes any more, she was about to be Randi Doyle."

"Right . . . the new name." I'd forgotten that women's

centers helped women get new names, chopping off the pasts forever.

"Yep. Rhonda was becoming Randi. Just a couple weeks from having the new name legalized, Carson. Then James showed up."

"Doc Kavanaugh was right," I said. "The same perp murdered Lainie Krebbs, Butterfly Lady and Herdez, but it was Peyton who killed Rhonda Doakes, aka Gail. But who the hell kidnapped Doakes and left her in the shack? The system killer?"

"Probably. He had to be in the Mobile area to put Butterfly Lady in the city dump. Unless there's another person out there . . . an accomplice." Harry paused to consider that aspect. "Jesus, it keeps getting worse. Am I on speaker?"

"Yes," Cruz said.

"Nothing against you, Miz Cruz, but I'd like to talk to my partner alone."

"You won't be dissing me, will you?"

"No. I owe you an apology."

Cruz winked at me. "I don't want to hear it. Shut the damn phone off, Ryder."

I took the device off speaker, went outside to the porch and stood in the shade, the summer sun beating down on the fields like a hammer.

"Listen, Carson, I uh . . . spent last evening with Detective Hargreaves."

"By 'evening' do you mean . . .?"

"I mean what I just said. I spilled the news about

Rein, about how I'd nearly fucked up the case by . . . by that damned alarm in my head. Sally had some time alone with Rein before she went off on the assignment, time for girl talk – dammit, I mean women talk. I told her how I could never get the pictures of Rein out of my head, her dressed up as Harriet Nautilus, playing a game. Sally told me Reinetta's a grown-up woman. She knows what she's up against, and she knows what she's doing. Probably a lot better than you or I ever did at that age. I guess what I'm trying to say is . . . I'm no less scared for her, but I'm more sure that she can handle what comes her way. Does that make sense?"

Thank you, Sally, I thought.

"Yes."

"You tried to tell me all that, I think. But Sally knew how to say it so I could understand it better."

"She's like that, bro."

"I've boxed up my scared and Sally's boxed up her scared and we're tearing things apart down here, re-analyzing this madness from every side. You're kind of isolated up there, Carson, hard on the trail of Rein and . . . can we turn the speaker back on now? There's something I want you and Detective Cruz to think about."

"Hang on."

I jogged back inside, waved Cruz over, turned the speaker back on. "You there, Detective Cruz?" Harry asked.

"And as stunning as ever."

"I'm staring at a map with a pin in Mobile and a pin

in Boulder, each for a battered body set in a tableau. I've got another pin in east Utah. Then I study the space between the pins. That's a helluva lot of territory to cover, folks."

"True," Cruz said. "Your point?"

"Carson said the women's underground railroad was the worst thing a misogynist could ever imagine, women stealing women from men."

Cruz nodded. "I'd think it would be the face-slap of all face-slaps."

"What if Krebbs and Peyton aren't isolated cases but part of a group of women-haters?"

"What?" I said.

"I admit it's weird, but it does fit in with your idea, Carson: What if there's a men's version of the underground network, dedicated to shutting the women's system off – an anti-system system?"

I looked at Cruz. She mouthed *Anti-system system?*

45

During their meal at the kitchen table, Rein started crossing Darleen off any threat index. The woman was too open and genuine. Her intelligence was tinged with self-conscious naïveté, saying she'd never gone past high school. Still, Darleen looked through the window into the back yard, naming the trees and plant varieties.

"That's a pretty flower over there," Rein had said, nodding out the window. "The blue one."

"That's an American Bellflower," Darleen said. "Campanula americana." When she heard herself, she reddened. "I don't know why I knew that last part," she apologized. "I wasn't showing off."

Darleen had a habit of walking from room to room and looking out every window, as though seeing the world anew, or maybe for the first time. Rein got the impression of a woman who'd never expected to be in

279

a safe house with nowhere to go but forward, and was liking her prospects for the future.

Rein wrapped the food and put it back in the fridge. The scent she'd noted earlier had come and gone a couple times and she found a tub of what appeared to be forgotten baked beans, mold across the top. She scraped them into the garbage disposal and washed the tub and lid, problem solved. A wall phone hung in the kitchen and Rein listened to the receiver.

"No dial tone," Rein said, puzzlement in her eyes. "The phone's shut off."

Darleen was sitting at the table nibbling from a pack of Oreos. "I guess you can turn off them types of phones when you go on a long fancy vacation, but I wouldn't know. We never had a phone outside of cell phones and Tommy's idea of a vacation was renting a rotting shack in the Rockies, shooting a deer, then spending the rest of the time drunk while I tried to figure out how to cut the thing into pieces and –" Darleen clamped her hand over her mouth, but her eyes glittered with a sly delight. "Whoops! We ain't supposed to talk about real stuff, are we?"

Rein took a chance that the modest intimacy of the moment held promise of a bond. "Wanna tell real names, Darleen? Just between us?"

"We're not supposed to tell anything about us, Marla. They kept saying that and saying that. I swear I hear it in my sleep."

"We're not supposed to tell *them*. We're the *us*. Names can't hurt, can they?"

"OK, but just first names. I still feel like I'm cheating, but . . .

"I'll go first," Rein said, not seeing harm in using her real name. "I'm Reinetta."

"That's a pretty name. I've never heard it before. Is it like –?"

Rein shook her head, having heard the question innumerable times. "Not like the weather. It's a form of the name Regina and means queen." She smiled. "My parents were hopeful, I guess. But friends call me Rein."

"I'm Treeka."

The women shook hands under the bond of truth. "How long you been gone from, uh, your start place?" Rein asked.

"Ten days," Treeka said. "You?"

"Today's my five-day anniversary."

"Anniversary?" Treeka clapped her hands. "We've got to celebrate." She produced a half-bottle of chardonnay from the fridge. "We got permission, right?"

"Pour on, sista," Rein said.

They poured wine and sat in the living room.

"Have you been scared?" Rein asked.

"Until the third night. Then I started to believe that somehow, God willing, I'm gonna get a second chance. Once I began thinking like that, I fell in love with my escape, like it's a movie called Treeka's Big Adventure."

"It's great you can think like that."

"After two years of my husband thumping my head I'm amazed I still have enough brains to think."

Rein took a sip of wine and shifted gears. "Speaking of the journey, did you ever feel there was anything off? Like someone had an interest in you? A man, maybe?"

Treeka's glass paused in front of her lips. "That's a weird question."

Rein waved it away. "I'm paranoid by nature. An over-reactor."

Treeka stood and paced the floor, finger tracing the rim of her glass. "There was only one man along the way – Rick. I think he was gay. Tommy hates gay people, especially lesbians. But Rick was super nice."

"I stayed with Rick for a night. I agree."

The women compared notes on their time in the railroad system and clicked glasses again. Best keep things tight, Rein thought, setting aside the wine. And best zoom this news to Carson and Cruz. They may have known where she was, but they sure wouldn't know anything about Treeka.

Rein went to the bathroom, pulled her cell. The charge was almost past tense. With Astra gone Rein could get Carson to drop the new phone and her weapon – where? She went to the window – out under the roses beside the driveway? He could do it tonight and she'd be resupplied.

Bingo.

Rein tapped out a message, considering what to include. Harry always said communicate everything when you get the chance, even if you think we got it all, cuz we make mistakes. Of course, that was with a full charge on the battery. Still, Rein dutifully added the license tags and what she knew of location, finally having time to do more than jab at the keys and jam the damned phone back into her underpants.

My cell rang and my hand had it out before I'd even directed my hand to move. Cruz was on the balcony and heard the first ring through the window, was inside before the second ring.

I looked down at the screen:

REIN

"Open the message," Cruz said, my nervous fingers fumbling at the phone. "Get it in gear, Ryder."

I tapped the button, saw a long stream of text:

```
wAstra til tmrw nite? @ 11267 Mill rd.
notfar fr Brnsn MO 234EA. Lv thngs undr
rosebsh s side f prch asap. I gt soon! &:
w/2nd UR wmn, Treeka, tgthr nxt stp at
least.
```

Cruz laughed. "The girl's writing a novel."

I grabbed a pen and paper and between us we doped out the meaning in under two minutes. I read from the scribbles and mish-mash.

Cruz said, "OK, as we get it now, the message is '*With Astra until tomorrow night? The address . . .*'"

"It's somewhere around Branson," I said. "We can get closer from the cell tower location."

"She's put in the damn vehicle tag number, Ryder. The lady's a champ! *'Leave things under the rosebush on the south side of the front porch and I'll get them soon!'*"

"Shit, we can't do it."

"Maybe we can, Ryder. It depends on how far away she is. She's fine, that's the big news. She's simply moved another step, now with a woman safekeeper. Finish the translation."

"*'And I'm with a second underground railroad woman, Treeka from Boulder. We're together on the next step at least.'*"

"Seems like she's got a traveling companion," I said.

"I'll run the plates," Cruz said.

"And I'll call the wireless service and get the cell tower location. Get ready to roll."

We looked at each other with a simultaneous sigh of relief. We'd soon have Rein back under our wing. I called Harry, almost giddy at the chance to deliver good news.

"Where are you headed?" Rein asked Treeka. "I don't mean exactly."

"Southeast toward Florida. I want to look out a window and see a life that's all different: no mountains, no snow, no Tommy."

"You got people there?" Rein asked Treeka. "Florida?"

"No, which makes it even better, given the kind of people who make up my people."

Rein nodded. "Gotcha."

"There was a poster I saw in a hippie shop on Pearl

Street in Boulder, saying 'Today is the first day of the rest of your life.' That's how it's gonna be when this is over and I'm standing on a beach and squeezing my toes in the sand and looking out over the ocean. The first day of the rest of my life."

Treeka smiled and leaned back and Rein saw how her companion's face was relaxed and smooth, beatific, as though her vision of the future had momentarily washed her clean of fear.

Then, as swift as if a switch had been thrown, Reinetta watched Treeka's face distort like melting wax, her smile dissolving into the shape of horror.

"Treeka," Rein asked, "are you all right?"

Treeka didn't answer, eyes and mouth wide and unbelieving, staring at something behind Rein's back. Rein's head snapped around. In the doorway stood a slender man in denim jeans and shirt, his brown Stetson tipped back to display eyes glittering like wet coal. There was a ten-inch hunting knife hanging from his belt. He was holding a huge chrome revolver and grinning like a child whose every Christmas wish had been granted.

"Hey, Treeks," he said softly. "How you been, baby?"

The man started laughing.

Blood draining from her face, Rein turned to Treeka. She was crying. And whispering a single name over and over.

Tommy.

46

Rein never had a chance. The man named Tommy made a weeping Treeka tie Rein's wrists behind her back. The knots were clumsy but Tommy kept saying "tighter" until they cut into Rein's flesh. Through the ordeal Treeka kept apologizing to the man.

Tommy went outside, gone five minutes, then Rein heard an approaching engine. The man's vehicle had been hidden nearby, she figured; he'd been fetching it. Tommy entered with a six-pack and walked to Rein, pulling off his hat and touching her hair with the sweat-stained brim.

"You got some nigra in you, don't you?" he said, looking at Rein with a mixture of fascination and disdain.

Rein nodded.

"Damn fuckin' shame," he said. He backpedaled to Treeka, now huddled on the floor. "I wanna show you something, baby," he said. "Look this way."

Tommy walked through the kitchen, opened the back door and pointed to a blue truck, dusty, like it had traveled a long distance over back roads. A silver livestock trailer was hitched behind the truck.

"You can't see through the dust, Treeks," he said. "But someone wrote some real hurtful words on my door."

"I'm so sorry for what I did to your truck, Tommy," Treeka whispered. "It was mean and hurtful and I'm ashamed."

"Guess what it cost to paint my door, baby? Two hunnert an' seven bucks. I can't even see how the new paint looks cuz the truck's all covered with dirt."

"I'll clean it for you, Tommy," Treeka pleaded. "Get me a hose and some soap and rags. I'll shine it so pretty it'll be like new, just you wait and see, hon."

Tommy tipped back his hat and studied the dusty truck for several seconds. He broke into a grin.

Cruz grabbed my computer and keyed in the password for the law-enforcement system. She waited until the information returned, stared at it.

"What?"

"Maybe I made an error . . . no, I typed it in right."

"What's the problem?"

"The license tag for Astra belongs on a 2003 Nissan Pathfinder registered to a Howard Redfeather in Medicine Lodge, Oklahoma. He's eighty-three years old."

"He must be a true believer."

"Mr Redfeather has a driving restriction, daylight hours only. Kinda limits working on the railroad."

"Astra might be his daughter," I said, mulling over possibilities.

"Or maybe wife. You don't look happy, Ryder."

"I want to know exactly who Astra is."

Cruz frowned in thought. "Gimme a couple minutes. Can you grab me a Coke?"

I snatched up the ice bucket and rummaged in my pockets, came up with a couple bills. I jogged down the balcony to the pop machine. When I returned to the room Cruz was looking at notes on her pad. Her eyes were tense.

"What'd you get?" I asked.

"I called Mr Redfeather and said I was a friend of Astra's, trying to get in touch with her. He didn't know who Astra was."

"Astra's a fake name."

"Mr Redfeather has no daughter, and his wife's dead. Here's what it all came down to, Ryder: Mr Redfeather parks in the alley behind his home. I told him I was a cop, asked him to do something for me. It took a minute for him to check his vehicle. The car's there, but . . ."

"But the license tag is gone," I said, feeling the room start to whirl.

Rein lay in the corner, initially hearing wails from outside, but eventually they gave way to just an occasional sob from Treeka, or a threatening murmur from Tommy. She

288

struggled mightily against the bindings, but they hadn't yielded a millimeter.

When the door burst open an hour later, Tommy had a look of insane pleasure in his eyes. He was dragging Treeka across the threshold, the woman's face brown with dirt, the front of her blouse crusted with mud.

"Learnin' to be a woman!" he yelled, shoving Treeka across the floor. She collapsed beside Rein, sending a chair tumbling as her head banged the hardwood, coming to rest two feet from Rein's face. Tommy walked back outside, pausing a second to click kinks from the small of his back.

Treeka moaned and vomited brown foam. It pooled between the two women like a sticky pond. "I think I'm gonna die," Treeka said. Her cheeks ballooned again and she puked a river of brown clots.

"Oh my God," Rein said. "You didn't . . ."

"Tommy made me lick all the dirt off his truck."

Treeka turned her head away, shame closing her eyes. A half-hour later, crows arguing in a nearby tree and yellow sunlight drowsing into blue twilight, Tommy reappeared, a gasoline can in each hand. He ignored the women and poured the liquid over the furniture, sloshing it across the carpet in the next room. He whistled as he worked, the air filling with acrid fumes.

It was over, Rein knew. All she could think of was Harry. How her being burned up would destroy him, how he'd blame himself. Rein knew him so well that sometimes it seemed like she was alive inside his head and he in hers. Harry'd stop being a cop, turn inside himself and never let an hour pass when he didn't tell himself he'd failed his mission and let her die.

You should always be allowed a note, Rein thought, tears in her eyes as she heard the sound of empty gasoline cans flung to the floor. When the Universe flashed alive it made a lot of laws for itself: nothing goes faster than light, objects in motion continue in motion until acted on by another force, and so forth. It should have thought things out better and made one final law: when people are going to die and that death will hurt other people so bad that they'll never be the same, the person about to die should be able to leave a note that sets people straight.

Dearest Uncle Harry,
Stop being an idiot and blaming yourself,
you hear? The choices I made were always
my own . . .

The cell tower was in rural Missouri, a dozen miles above Branson. Cruz took the wheel and I tracked down the chief of the county police force, Larkin Teemont. There seemed a lot of commotion at Teemont's end, a background clamor of voices and equipment, like Teemont was on a construction site.

"Could you repeat that, Detective Ryder?" Teemont said. "Pretty noisy on my end."

"We may have a situation in your county, the

potential of an officer in trouble. Can you do a drive-by of an address, just to take a look, especially at a license plate? We'll fill you in when we get there."

"Might help if you filled me in now, seein' as it's my jurisdiction."

I laid out an edited version of the story, making sure Chief Teemont knew the operation was cleared at state level.

"What was that address again?" Teemont said. "The one you want us to check out?"

I repeated it.

"Detective, Ryder, I'm right now looking at the house at that address. Buddy, there ain't gonna be nothin' left but a hole in the ground when them firefighters leave."

"You're saying it's burning?"

"I'm saying it's about done burning. It was a bad-ass fire."

"Was there anyone . . ." I couldn't complete the sentence.

"Inside? That's not confirmed yet." A pause. "You ever been around a fire where someone was burnt up, Detective?"

"Several times."

"You know that meat smell?"

"Yes."

"I'm smellin' it now."

Cruz and I entered town after dusk. The house was a charred frame lit by the white lights of emergency vehicles, steam rising into the sky, a crew of firefighters kicking through rubble. I caught a whiff of a bad smell, lost it. Told myself it was just stuff in the fridge or freezer cooking down.

I saw one fire truck, one ambulance, two cop cruisers, and a dark blue van marked Coroner's Office. Larkin Teemont was a tall and rangy guy who reminded me of the scarecrow in the *Wizard of Oz*, except he was in a green uniform. We shook hands, I introduced Cruz, and we replayed my story, short and simple.

"I'll git that tag number out on an APB," Teemont said. "You don't know the kind of vehicle?"

"No."

Teemont nodded to the smoldering ruin. "It's just starting to cool enough the fire guys can check inside. You know who did this?"

"We don't," I said, shaking my head. "That's the problem."

"Fire Chief says there was an accelerant," Teemont said. "Gasoline, by the smell. A neighbor saw smoke, called the FD. The house was engulfed when they arrived."

"Body!" someone yelled. "Down in the tornado shelter." My heart froze to see a firefighter at the edge of the foundation pointing a flashlight downward. "No," the man amended as he kicked aside a fallen rafter. "Not *a* body. *Two* bodies."

Cruz and I sprinted over. A pair of local cops tried to jump in front of us, but Teemont yelled, "They're OK, let 'em by."

292

The corpses were in a room below the kitchen, a tornado shelter, brick-lined, the entry not into the house but through a steel trapdoor beside it, a tight hideaway revealed when the floor burned away, embers tumbling into the shelter and turning it into a barbecue pit.

After photos were taken, several firemen dug a corpse free of ash and charred timbers. When the cooked body was on the ground, they turned their attention to the second body, pulling it up and into the pulsing lights.

"Outta the way," a short and bespectacled man in a suit said when both bodies were up; the county coroner. I was staring at the charred forms and shaking like I was freezing. There was something tight around my body: Cruz's arms. I realized she was holding me up.

"Hang on, Carson," she kept saying, the first she'd ever used my given name.

I watched numbly as the coroner used a white towel to brush char from the face of a body, a distorted mask. The smell of rotten meat was overwhelming, the coroner holding a handkerchief to his nose as he worked. It seemed wherever he touched, skin or meat sloughed from the bodies.

"You able to make an ID, Earl?" Teemont said from the far side of the house, staying upwind.

"I'm only sure of two things," he said. "Both bodies are female . . ."

"And the other thing?"

The coroner stood, snapping off latex gloves. "They've

been dead a while. No matter how long you cook meat, you can't cook that rot smell off it."

It took a few beats for his words to gel in my head. I grabbed his arm as he passed. "The bodies were putrefying?"

He nodded. "They might have been there a couple weeks, maybe more. It depends on how cool and dry it was in the shelter."

"It's not her, Carson," Cruz said. "It's not Rein."

47

The medical wagon was backing to the victims when Teemont stepped over, studied the bodies, shaking his head. "One body's slim, the other's hefty. You can tell that even through . . . everything else. I think it's Katka Kassolian – the slim one – and her partner, whatever, Delma Thorne. They've lived out here for years, decades. It's a damn shame."

"Partner? Were they gay?"

"You saw one, you saw the other. I patrol this road a lot. On hot days they'd wave me over and give me a glass of ice tea or lemonade, tell me how much they appreciated us, the force. I had no problems with them two ladies at all."

"They were the sole occupants?"

"Now and then you'd see another woman on the porch or sitting out back. It's sometimes a safe house for women here."

Cruz and I turned to him like synchronized robots. "You *know* that?" I asked.

Teemont leaned against his cruiser and tipped back his hat. "Y'know how some people ain't got enough to do in their lives they gotta sneak around and look at ever'one else's?"

"Too much," I said.

"There used to be this busybody ol' hen down the road, called once to say Miz Katka and Thorne was holding some young girl here, like running a white-slave thing. I came out and Miz Katka introduced me to the woman . . . not a girl, a lady in her middle twenties who was gettin' away from a guy who used her like a punching bag. I guess the ladies did that sort of thing now and again, and I say good for them." Teemont shot another look at the bodies, forlorn shapes against the dry grass. "You people say you're working on something along them lines?"

"I'd appreciate it if you could look long and hard for that license plate," I said.

"You got it, buddy," Teemont said.

"I'm moving toward Dodge City. Everything's cool."

Tommy Flood left his message in the voicemail box, flicked his cell phone shut, and set it atop the dashboard beside the packs of cigarettes and lighters and fast-food wrappers. He cranked the Dwight Yoakum CD up, hard bass and twanging guitar again filling his cab and pouring out the open windows as he shot an eye at the speedometer, careful to keep the rig below the limit and safe from the prowling eyes of the occasional cop. It was ten p.m., the sky like a black blanket pulled flat over everything for a hundred miles. Only occasional flashes of heat lightning shivered under the far edges of the blanket to display scrubby plants of brown and gray.

Tommy was two-thirds of the way through Kansas, more than halfway home, the threads of lightning edging the sky like God telling him he was on the side of the righteous. He'd gotten justice, right? Got back what had been stolen from him?

Tommy lit another cigarette, smiling at his fortune. Hell, he hadn't even known Treeka'd been snatched away by a system of dykes. He'd been looking for her all over the county when the phone call had come in.

"Brother Flood?"

"Who's this?"

"Your wife betrayed you, didn't she? Ran off."

"Who the fuck is this?"

"A friend, Brother Flood. One of many who understand you. We're a band of brothers, Tommy, helping one another. Let me show how we can help you . . . what's the thing you want most in the world right now?"

"My goddamn prop'ty back."

"It's not that hard, Tommy. She's just settled into a house in south Missouri. Would you like the address?"

"You damn bet I do."

"It's yours in return for a few small favors, payback to your brothers . . ."

Everything since had been too good to be true, and

he'd figured there'd have to be some kind of fly in the ointment, somebody asking him for money to give up the place the bitch was hiding.

But everything happened as promised: Treeka was his rightful property and he could do with her as he pleased. All Tommy had to do was burn down the house when he left, and bring a second slut back to Colorado. He was allowed to discipline the whore if she acted poorly – and discipline her hard – but was not allowed to kill her. Someone else, it seems, had that right.

Tommy Flood looked at the clock again. Eight hours and he'd be back on the ranch. There were things that needed doing to keep Treeka in line, plus he was going to pass the other whore to his benefactor.

A busy day coming up, good business all around. Tommy Flood checked his speedometer again and began singing along with Dwight Yoakum, his voice booming out the window and into the desert sky.

Can a man get any happier than this? he wondered.

I called Harry, then Cruz and I returned to the motel. We had no idea which way Rein had gone, everything depending on a license tag attached to an unknown vehicle. Teemont had expanded the APB to surrounding states.

I was pacing the balcony, wanting to jump in the van and join the search. But at this hour it was just headlights in the black. Plus there were four directions I could take, three of them wrong, so I paced and wrung my hands and tried to think of things I had missed.

Meanwhile, Cruz sat on the bed checking every note generated while following Rein, every detail from Boulder to Branson. She'd been working for an hour when I heard a door opening.

"Carson!"

I spun to see Cruz waving me back to the room, her laptop in one arm. "What?" I said, pushing into the cool of the air conditioning, the scent of the fast shower she'd taken.

"I was checking into Victoria Miles, the transport and safe house before Rick, thinking about her story about her sister. We hadn't really read it, just scanned the headlines for verification, right?"

"Something wrong with it?"

"It happened as Miss Miles said: the wife's suicide, the court proceedings, the acquittal, the shooting by the sister. Without the details from Victoria Miles, you get the impression the wife was a psycho sex weirdo who made hubby's life a living hell."

"That was Miles's contention: The lawyer was shameless but talented, turned facts on their heads."

Cruz tapped keys on her laptop and pulled a newspaper headline to the screen: *Dr Conette Acquitted of all Charges*. The subtitle was *Lawyer Paints Wife as "Sad, Sick Woman"*.

"Read this and see if anything jumps out at you." Cruz passed me the laptop and I started reading. Three paragraphs were all it took.

"Holy shit," I whispered.

48

It was almost ten thirty p.m. Mountain Time and Liza was dozing on the floor of her office for the second time in a week. Dr Bramwell was on sabbatical, Robert in and out, Deanna Werly, another TA, was ill with strep throat. Liza had been attending classes during the day, teaching Sinclair's freshman-level courses at night. She planned to rise at four and grade quizzes before Sinclair arrived with his demands.

A sound intruded on her dreams and Liza found herself staring at the leg of her desk. The door of the elevator closed and she figured its opening had roused her. She opened her door a sliver and saw Dr Sinclair walk past. She started to speak, but was on the floor with her hair flat on one side, a drool-wet sleeve, and a sweater as a pillow.

Plus Sinclair was moving like a man on a mission, on

full-mull as Robert called it, deep in thought. Disturb him at your peril.

Liza wiggled forward until peeking into his office. Sinclair was standing with a sheaf of papers in his hand. He set them on his desk, seemed to have second thoughts. He turned a full circle with the papers, as if unsure where to file them, then jammed the pages into a thick textbook on his shelves. He laughed darkly, then sat at his desk with his back to Liza. He tapped at the keyboard for two minutes, shoulders rocking with the motion.

He froze, then leaned toward the screen, as if not believing what he saw.

He whispered, "They're my words."

Liza watched Sinclair jump from the chair, still fixated on the screen.

"You stole my words! YOU SON OF A *BITCH!*"

Liza couldn't tell if Sinclair's voice held anger, confusion, or triumph. Suddenly fearful – though not sure why – Liza slipped her door shut. A minute later she heard Sinclair's steps fade down the hall and disappear into the elevator.

One final *Son of a bitch* and he was gone.

Liza stood shakily, as if Sinclair's voice still roiled the air. *What the freakin' hell was that all about?* There was a cup of cold coffee on her desk and she drank it, part thirst, part to wake her dream-drowsed head. Dr Sinclair had either been too angry – or too jubilant – to remember to pull his door tight; half the time Liza or Trotman had to lock it at night anyway, Sinclair too lofty for such duties.

Liza crept toward the office, eyes on the textbook with Sinclair's sheaf of papers jutting from the book pages. She felt gravity pulling her into his office, across the carpet. The pages seemed to tremble toward her shaking fingers.

Pick me up, Liza, they begged. *Read me.*

"Say again," Harry said, the sleep dissolving from his voice. I'd called his home at six a.m. to share the latest twist in this bizarre whirlwind of a case.

"You heard me, brother. The scumbucket attorney in the Macon case was none other than Nathaniel Bromley." I looked across the room, saw Cruz rolled in a sheet, stripped to her skivvies and starting to stir.

"C'fee," Cruz mumbled.

"What the hell does it mean?" Harry asked.

"Maybe nothing. Maybe Bromley fell into the case by accident, a friend of the dentist passing along the name of a high-level bottom-crawler. As a member of Blackwell, Carrington & Bromley, he would have been law-licensed in Georgia. They have clients in Atlanta."

"The dentist, Krebbs . . ."

"You thought Bromley and Krebbs were an odd pair of golfing buddies. Maybe what's bonding them isn't smacking a little ball but a hatred of women. You said it yourself, brother: what if there's an anti-system system?"

"That golfing stuff never felt right," Harry said. "If Bromley wanted a golf buddy he could probably rent Tiger Woods."

I hung up. Given what Harry'd said about Bromley's comments to Sal and his BFF chuckling with Krebbs, women weren't high on Bromley's list. That alone meant nothing – I knew folks with similar issues, and it made them insecure, but not malevolent – still, it was a connection.

Cruz had slung a robe around her and was assembling a cup of coffee. My phone rang. "Chief Teemont," my caller said, the chief of the county mounties. "We found the license tag from Mr Redfeather's vehicle in the ashes of the burned home. The killer obviously grabbed another. There's nothing to look for."

I cursed beneath my breath as Teemont continued. "Doc Winegartner, the coroner? He reports that both women were lacking eyes, and from what he could tell, their breasts had been slashed. What the hell kind of maniac is out there?"

Sally Hargreaves sat at the desk in Harry Nautilus's home reading archived articles on the trial in Macon. She wore one of his robes, a small pretty head poking from the top of a blue velvet tent. The walls were covered with posters of jazz greats: Miles Davis, Duke Ellington, Charlie Parker. The house smelled of fresh-brewed coffee.

Nautilus leaned down. "Cruz dug this stuff up late last night. Guess this means I got to be nice to her."

"Jesus, Harry, I hated Bromley before, now I gotta get a twin to handle the overflow. Where from here?"

"I asked Bromley why he didn't do any work for his old firm. He got snippy and made a face like smelling dog plop on his shoes."

"Who's the head shyster at Blackwell, Carrington & Bromley?" Sal asked.

"Carrington, I think."

"Lemme make a call. I'll bet they get started early at BCB, more hours to bill."

Hargreaves dialed the firm, asked three questions, rolled her eyes and hung up. "The receptionist over there sounds like she's got a broomstick up her ass, probably part of the job description. We need an appointment to see 'Mistah Carrington'; the earliest he's taking audiences seems to be next week."

"Schedules of the rich and famous."

Hargreaves eyes twinkled. "But broom-butt lady revealed that Mr Carrington is heading to the federal courthouse, something to do with a motion."

Thirty minutes later the pair made their way through the high-ceiling halls of the federal courthouse in Mobile, Nautilus wearing a powder-blue suit with a scarlet shirt, Hargreaves in a dark jacket-skirt ensemble over a maroon blouse. Her artsy lapel pin was a scalloped, silvery disk with six holes toward the outside centered by a smaller hole. It resembled an organic form until closer inspection revealed a cross-section of the cylinder of a revolver.

"It looks like a suit convention," Hargreaves said. "Have you ever smelled so much musk?"

"Not since my springtime visit to the zoo."

Hargreaves pointed to four men in earnest conversation in a corner. "Looky there . . . Arnold Carrington of Blackwell, Carrington & Bromley, Nate's old firm. I got to say hi."

Nautilus started to grab Hargreaves's arm to discuss strategy, but decided to let Sally brace the lawyer on her own. He watched Hargreaves plant herself in front of Carrington like a hungry bulldog.

"Howdy, Mr Carrington. I'm Detective Sally Hargreaves of the MPD. I wanted to say I wish you'd kept Nathaniel Bromley in the firm. It just doesn't seem right that Blackwell, Carrington & Bromley is lacking its Bromley."

Nautilus thought Arnold Carrington looked like an actor who played aging lawyers on TV: a touch of belly roll over the belt, brown hair with gray wings, a blue pinstripe suit without a wrinkle, as if constantly pressed by some internal engine. He was tanned and his teeth were capped and Nautilus figured the man never passed a mirror without snapping it a wink.

Carrington stared at Hargreaves over tortoiseshell reading glasses. "You're behind the curve, Detective. We're now Blackwell, Carrington & Associates. Mr Bromley is history. May I ask why you'd wish him still within the firm?"

"You haven't heard? Your old buddy is preparing to attack the women's center of Mobile. I think the center does important work. Maybe if you'd kept the Natester on the payroll he'd leave women alone."

Carrington shot a heartbeat-long glance at his companions. One of the lawyers studied Hargreaves, the other two looked away, as if wanting no part of the conversation.

Carrington's response was measured and precise. "Whatever Nathaniel Bromley is doing these days, it in no way reflects the views of the firm. He has no part in the firm, none. Bottom line: Blackwell, Carrington & Associates has absolutely no ties to Nathaniel Bromley, business or philosophical. Are we clear there, Detective?"

"Do you know why the Natester might –"

But Carrington and his posse were moving toward the courtroom at escape velocity. Hargreaves returned to Nautilus.

"Jesus, Harry . . . In no way reflects our views, no part of our firm – I was half-expecting Carrington to go all Mafia: 'Nathaniel Bromley is dead to us.' What do you make of that weirdness?"

Nautilus watched the quartet pushing into the courtroom, Carrington shooting a backward glance, his face a mix of curious and troubled.

"Seems the parting wasn't so amicable, Sal. I Wonder what Nate did to make his old buddies take his name off their expensive door?"

"Must have been pretty major. Where could we get the low-down on Bromley?"

Nautilus stared into the distance and grimaced.

"What's the matter, Harry?" Hargreaves said. "You look like a skunk just squirted under your nose."

"Worse. You ever head of D. Preston Walls?"

"That little law office by the bail bondsmen and pawn-shops?"

Nautilus nodded. "You ever meet Walls, Sally?"

"Never had the pleasure. Why?"

"We'll stop on the way and get some Lysol. You'll want to spray yourself when you leave his office."

49

"T. Nathaniel Bromley?" Walls said. "He's outta my league, Harry. I'm just a ham'n'egger who deals with real people with real problems – salt-of-the-earth types."

Preston Walls held his hands palm-up at his sides. He was in his mid forties, five-eight, overweight. His suit was mouse brown with a limp carnation dangling from a lapel. The gray in his thinning, ponytailed hair had been darkened with cheap dye, but the stud in his ear was a flawless ruby and the car at the curb was a high-end Porsche, the tag stating LGLEGL. The pneumatic blonde receptionist was a call girl Nautilus had arrested several times when she was in her thirties and Nautilus was in uniform, twenty years ago. The receptionist had been filing her nails when Nautilus and Hargreaves entered and had pretended they'd never met.

"You know everything about everyone, Walls," Nautilus said. "Lawyers, judges, prosecutors. You sweep dirt into a file and hope some day you can use it to buy a break for one of your scuzzy clients."

Walls shook his head. "Harry, Harry, Harry . . . my clients are good people trapped in bad situations. I'm less a lawyer than a social worker, a champion for the poor and downtrodden."

Nautilus rolled his eyes. He'd been in the office for two minutes and was already craving a shower. "I recall one of the clients, Walls: Ronnie Hill. Didn't poor, downtrodden Hill drive a purple Benz, five-hundred class or whatever?" Nautilus turned to Hargreaves. "The damn thing had a twenty-grand stereo system: whenever Hall cruised the 'hood he'd be followed by falling glass from all the busted windows."

Walls smiled at Hargreaves. "He's a great kidder, Harry is. But the truth is, Ronnie Hill is a product of the system. When society wouldn't give him an outlet for his entrepreneurial instincts in society, he built his own business."

"Moving a half-key of coke a week," Nautilus added.

Walls sighed. "Had the young Ron Hill been given a chance, he might have owned a Coca-Cola distributorship, Harry. We all failed poor Ronnie: the community, the educational system, the –"

"Where's the guy now?" Hargreaves asked.

"Holman prison," Nautilus said. "Every time Hill got busted for moving dope, Mr Walls got him out. Last year poor, downtrodden Ronnie Hill shot at a competitor, missed, hit the guy's twelve-year-old sister instead. She's now a paraplegic."

Walls frowned. "Why are you here, Harry?"

"Bromley, remember? I need to know why Nate's former partners are treating him like a fence-jumper from a leper colony."

"Bromley, Bromley . . ." Walls tapped his fingers on his desk. "Seems I do recall a few sub rosa murmurings around that name. Colorful stuff."

"Colorful how?"

"Listen, Harry, I've got this client, Marcus Flatt . . ."

"Don't do this to me, Walls."

"C'mon, Harry. Marcus is a good smart kid, a striver, a mensch. His case comes before a judge next week, prosecutor is Willis Baines. You know Baines, don't you?"

Nautilus stuck his hands in his pockets to keep them from Walls's neck. "I'll check into the case. Maybe I can wangle a little something if Flatt's not a psycho."

"Marcus is ambitious, Harry. He needed venture capital to open a strip-o-mat and –"

"A what?"

"A combo laundromat and strip club. Great concept, right? Marcus even had matchbooks printed up: *We Take Off Ours While You Wash Yours*. Problem is, Marcus kept getting turned down for loans. Then a few dollars belonging to his employer disappeared and –"

"How many dollars?"

"Twenty grand or so. Maybe thirty."

Nautilus pushed his hands deeper into his pockets.

"I'll check with the DA's folks. See if they can back off on the sentence a bit. No promises. And that's only if you give me enough dish on Bromley."

"Have a seat, Harry. And you too, pretty lady. I'll give the dish I know. It's only a little appetizer, but delicious . . ."

The trailer bounced hard, clattering down what must have been one of the world's most-rutted roads, Rein thought, the back of her head banging the wooden floor. Rein never figured she'd be happy to be jammed into a livestock trailer, its floor covered with hay and manure, its window hatches locked tight and the door slammed shut. But the hay had smelled like salvation after the fumes of gasoline.

She'd heard a crunching of feet over grass, the scrape of a flare dragged across the striker, the whoosh of fire and the run of boots back to the truck. Rein had felt the trailer shudder and grab, creaking as it gained speed. Then, the sound of tires over highway and the twang of country music drifting back from the cab became all Rein heard for hours.

The banging stopped as the trailer angled downward and jolted to a halt. The door squealed open, Tommy outlined against a blue sky with a bag in one arm and jamming a sandwich in his mouth. She saw nothing past her captor but endless brown dirt studded with scrubby brush and rock outcroppings. Tommy pulled himself inside to squat beside the women, peeling back the tape from their mouths.

"Time to piss and shit and eat. You can think about screaming, but the closest people are two miles away and going eighty miles an hour. If you do scream, the next thing that'll happen is you'll be screaming even louder, because it'll be me making you scream."

He waited for the women to nod acceptance, then gave them a drink from a half-liter of Mountain Dew. He loosened Treeka's wrist ropes, waved her to stand. "Come on, baby. Time to get emptied out." He grinned. "Me too."

"Sure, baby," Treeka said, stumbling toward the end of the trailer. "Whatever you want, hon."

Rein heard footsteps grow muted in the distance. The manure in the still trailer was attracting flies and they crawled over her face. The heat was climbing fast and her sweat made the hay stick to her body. She heard grunting in the distance, knew Tommy was raping Treeka.

Ten minutes later they were back, Treeks pulling herself into the trailer. "Come on, woman," Tommy said to Rein, leaning to loosen her ropes. "Your turn."

Rein jumped from the trailer, saw it was parked in a depression behind a looming rock formation. She figured she was to be sexually assaulted, but all Tommy did was lead her to an arroyo and stand a dozen feet distant as she pulled down her pants. She glanced at her panties, feeling the signs of her approaching period.

"Do you have to look at me?" Rein said.

Tommy's face wrinkled in anger. "I'll look right up your pussy if I want."

312

"OK," Rein said, realizing the phone was a no-go, if it even had power left. "Do what you want."

"I want to watch you, bitch, I'll fucking watch you. Shit and git."

Rein kept the phone rolled in her panties and relieved herself. Tommy hustled her to the truck. He upended the bag he'd brought from the cab, littering the trailer floor with convenience-store sandwiches, beef jerky, packs of chips and cans of soda.

"Git to eating or go hungry."

Treeka said something muffled, her head turned away. "I didn't hear you, Treeks," Tommy said. "Talk up when I ask a question . . . 'less you feel like giving this dusty ol' truck another washing."

"I said thank you for the food, Tommy. I was getting hungry."

Tommy was so close to Reinetta she could smell his odor: stale sweat, cheap deodorant and one of those acrid, old-time colognes pushed on television by faded sports stars, probably the same stuff his father had used. He looked at Rein and grinned yellow teeth.

"You know what I think, pretty lady?" he said. "I think if you're gonna break bread with Treeka and me, you should give the holy blessing."

Rein didn't think she'd heard correctly. "What?"

He grinned and stood, pushing back his hat, gnawing on a lunchmeat sandwich, half-moons of dirt beneath his fingernails. "You people s'posed to be so spiritual an' all. Give us one a them nigra prayers to eat to."

313

"I just want to eat."

"Give us a prayer, please, Marla," Treeka said, turning to Rein. Beneath her breath she said, "Don't make him mad or he'll hurt you."

"You lissen to little Treeks. She wants a prayer. Right, Treeks?"

"Yes, Tommy. We should have a blessing before we eat. Please, Marla?" Treeka's eyes were imploring.

"Dear heavenly Father," Rein recited, her voice scarcely past a whisper, "bless this food and thank you for providing it."

"That ain't no kind of prayer," Tommy snarled. "I want a fucking good prayer."

"I'll do it, Tommy," Treeka said. "Let me do the blessing, babe. I ain't said a prayer in a while."

"Yeah, you go ahead then."

Treeka bowed her head. "Bless this food, dear God, and thank you for all the other blessings in my life, like this good and righteous man. Thank you for providing him to me and making him strong and wise and everything I could hope for. I am just a humble woman, dear God, so please help me to see the error of my ways and know that Satan got inside my heart and told me lies. Help me to understand my transgressions and to learn from them and please make me the wife this good man deserves, though he deserves so much more than me. In Jesus' name I pray, Amen."

"Ain't you gonna amen Treeka's prayer?" Tommy said, staring at Rein.

"Amen," she said, thinking, *Give me a chance to kill you*.

"Louder," he snapped.

Rein was hot and worn and aching and angry. She said, "Leave me alone."

"Don't," Treeka whispered.

Tommy Flood's fingers curled into a fist. He glared at Rein. "What did you say to me, slut?"

"I said to leave me alone, you pathetic excuse for whatever you're attempting to be."

The man's eyes widened as if slapped. His hand slashed at Rein's face and knocked her backwards. "I can do what I want, bitch!" Flood screamed. "I'm allowed to do everything but kill you. You got that?"

"What are you talking about?" Rein gasped.

"You ain't mine," he said. "But I got permission to hurt you however I need to keep you in line. You got that?"

Rein nodded and went slack in the hay. Tommy slapped the tape back over the women's mouths, re-set the ropes. "I don't care about you," he snarled to Rein before slamming the door. "I got back what's mine and pretty soon you'll be where you're supposed to be, too."

50

Cruz and I were in the motel. It was mixed-feelings time, both relieved Rein wasn't dead, but knowing it was a matter of time. We knew the women had been held captive for days before being mutilated, then held a bit longer before being killed. Though grim, it was the distant star on which we'd hung our hopes.

My phone rang and Cruz looked up from her reports. I shook my head, the screen said CLAIR.

"Howdy, Clair," I said. "What's up?"

"You wanted me to stay in contact with the forensics people in Utah and Denver, try and figure out what the mucilage is on the bellies of our victims?"

We were hoping Clair might find an esoteric polymer used in a specific industry or process, anything to advance our cause.

"You've got something?"

"Nothing on the glue," she said. "It's a common PSA – pressure-sensitive adhesive."

Another dead end. "Like you thought, duct tape or similar?"

"I'm afraid so."

"Thanks, Clair. Gotta go –"

"Hang on, Carson. I started reviewing uterine findings for rape or object insertion. I didn't find anything like that, but I did note an odd commonality among the victims."

"What's that, Clair?"

"All three uteri were in the early stages of shedding endometrial lining when the process was stopped. By death, of course."

"You're saying that these women were killed . . ."

"Shortly after their periods started, Carson. Could be coincidence, but I figured you should know."

The blonde and thirtyish receptionist at Blackwell, Carrington and Associates not only spoke as if afflicted with an interior broomstick, Nautilus thought, she walked that way too: back straight, nose high, long but formless legs scissoring in choppy strokes. Her dress was white and double-breasted and fit very well.

The pair had cooled heels in the wood-and-brass reception area, Nautilus looking out the windows while Hargreaves seemed entranced by portraits of the legal staff, each with a copywriter-quality bio extolling the virtues and specialties of the practitioner.

"You're very lucky Mr Carrington agreed to see you on such short notice," the receptionist sniffed as she opened the door to a long corridor.

"Maybe we knew the secret word," Hargreaves said. "Y'know, like Open Sesame."

"What does that mean?"

"Never mind."

Thus aimed toward the corner office, Nautilus and Hargreaves wandered at sightseer's pace. At corridor's end a visually resplendent Arnold Carrington appeared, no hand offered, nothing but a flick of a finger to indicate entry into his personal burrow with its Oriental carpet, bronze sculptures of cowboys on horseback, paintings of ships and seascapes in ornate frames. The corner office aimed eastward across the green and blue of the Mobile river delta. Carrington's desk, the size of a single bed, held nothing save for a green-shaded lamp, a computer monitor, and a leather pad. The lawyer closed the door as Hargreaves and Nautilus walked to the trio of chairs semi-circled before the desk.

"No need to sit," Carrington announced. "You won't be here that long."

Hargreaves sat.

Carrington frowned. "I'm not making myself clear, Detective. My statement is simple: This firm's relationship with Nathaniel Bromley is over. Severed. There is nothing more to add."

He turned back to the door and put his hand on the door knob, announcement over.

"How many female lawyers do you have here, Mr Carrington?" Hargreaves said, not moving from the chair.

"Did you see the photographs out front?"

"Indeed I did. Eight out of a legal staff of twenty-seven."

Carrington nodded. "A bit less than one-third. Not bad, and improving."

"The average age of your male staff is about, what? Forty-five or thereabouts? I'm not counting the old guard, I'm talking rank and file."

Carrington narrowed his eyes. "I seem to be missing your point, Detective Hargreaves."

"Of the female staff, most look to be early thirties. When were the ladies hired, Mr Carrington?"

"What are you getting at, Detective?"

Hargreaves stood and faced the lawyer. "The question is so simple I'm going to supply the answer. The majority of the women were hired recently, most fresh from law school. There a reason you didn't hire women in the Bromley years, Mr Carrington?"

"That's ridiculous. We hired several women and –" Carrington froze, realized where he'd been led.

"Where are they today?" Hargreaves asked.

"We're not here from affirmative action, Mr Carrington," Nautilus said, seeing where his partner was going. "Women are dying. We need help and that's why we're here."

Carrington absorbed the words slowly and stared between the two detectives.

"Women dying?"

319

"Not in pretty ways," Hargreaves said.

"Y-you suspect Nathaniel in these . . . these crimes?"

"No suspects, only suppositions," Nautilus said. "You say Bromley's not associated with this firm. Prove it by telling us why you've put the big wall between yourselves and your former star attraction."

Carrington again looked between the pair, as if gauging their resolve. His shoulders slumped and he sighed, taking his place behind the desk, looking suddenly shrunken.

"This is between us?" he asked.

"I have corpses," Nautilus said. "I need answers, not pacts."

Carrington took a deep breath, as if bracing himself for his own words.

"Whenever we'd add an associate, a new hire, Nathaniel always found reasons why women on the short list were wrong for the firm. They were too strident, or too ugly, or too devious."

"Devious?" Hargreaves asked. "Bromley had some meter to judge, what . . . deviosity?"

"Nathaniel claimed the ability to sense that trait and vetoed the candidate."

Hargreaves said, "Judging by the photos, you gave him plenty of latitude."

"We all had veto power, the partners."

"But surely now and then you'd hire a woman? Aren't women a majority of law students?"

"Several times the other partners felt strongly about a female candidate and Nathaniel would give in."

"They just didn't last long," Hargreaves said. "Was that it?"

"Nathaniel seemed to fixate on the women, finding mistakes in their work, haranguing them, spreading rumors they were lesbians. The women eventually left for less-stressful employment options. They always received a generous severance and excellent recommendations."

"How very thoughtful of you," Hargreaves said.

"What was the final straw?" Nautilus asked. There was always a final straw.

Carrington walked to the window, stared out across the flat and spreading delta. "The company party at the end of the fiscal year. Spouses and significant others are invited. It's a grand occasion: bonuses are distributed, champagne flows . . . Nathaniel arrived with a woman, very pretty but . . . not overly educated. He was drinking too much, telling people his date was dumb as a rock but she could, uh . . ." Carrington glanced at Hargreaves, embarrassed.

"Go on, Mr Carrington," she said. "I've heard it all twice."

"He said she could suck the chrome off a trailer hitch. Nathaniel made several remarks in this vein, as if they qualified the woman to be with him."

"And?" Hargreaves asked.

"The woman heard one of his remarks and took offense. They wandered from the general party, squabbling. A few minutes later I was called to a back office, along with two other partners. Nathaniel and the woman were in a back office and she had a bloody nose and mouth. Her dress was torn and she was crying. I wasn't the first person in the room, that was Ted Clark. Ted said when he arrived Nathaniel was lifting the woman's head by the hair and smashing her face into a desk."

"Jesus," Nautilus whispered.

"Long story short: the woman was extremely well compensated. Nathaniel Bromley's relationship with the firm changed inexorably and he was asked to leave."

"Gone the next day?" Nautilus asked.

"I wish it had been that easy. Nathaniel said we were eunuchs for taking the side of a whore. He threatened legal action, obviously."

"Your response?"

"Like most firms with similar client lists, we maintain relationships with several security-oriented firms."

"Private investigators," Nautilus translated.

"Nathaniel had an emotional response to the dissolution of the partnership. A more rational man might have realized where this would lead. Or maybe it was his monumental ego. We enlisted a team of investigators led by Clarence Trump."

"I know Trump," Nautilus said to Hargreaves. "Good and fast. Works out of Birmingham."

"Fast as you say Mr Trump is, Detective, it took his staff three months to unearth the story. It seems Nathaniel was married years ago, something none of us knew.

Nathaniel had so terrorized his young wife that she sought escape. He told her he would destroy her if she left him."

"She got on the train," Hargreaves said.

Carrington looked puzzled. "If you mean she used some kind of women's network to disappear, you're correct."

"Where was, is she?" Nautilus asked. "The wife."

"Somewhere in the Northeast, living a happy life with no wish to ever return." He paused. "That's not what we told Nathaniel."

"You told Bromley she'd come back and tell her story."

"Nathaniel feared damage to his reputation. He relented and our relationship was over."

"And in the end, everything was hushed up," Hargreaves said, doing the dusting-hands motion.

Carrington jutted his considerable chin. "The firm's reputation should not suffer for the actions of a single member of staff."

Hargreaves smile was without humor. "And should the women who were let go discover the reason was solely their gender, they could slam this place with a hefty lawsuit. Is that the way it goes, Mr Carrington?"

"I've been honest with you. I'm trusting your discretion."

Nautilus and Hargreaves retreated from Carrington's office. The plush carpet soaked up their footfalls as they walked the wainscoted hall to the lobby, Hargreaves leaning toward Nautilus.

"Can we stop for that Lysol now, Harry?"

51

Liza Krupnik sat in her one-room rental in a local hostel, looking blankly out the window, her cell in her back pocket, turned off. Her room was small but inexpensive, and the other dozen people living in the hostel were intelligent and kind. Most weren't students but older men and women who cared little about material possessions and lived quiet, often interior lives.

Liza drifted to the common kitchen to make a cup of tea, taking it to the large shared living space, with chairs, couches and a single small television. One of the residents enjoyed caring for plants and had filled the room with ivy and snake plants and philodendron. Liza sat cross-legged in a chair in a shadowed corner and sipped tea.

"Liza?"

She looked up and saw Alice Dreyfuss. Dreyfuss was in her sixties, a tall, white-haired woman who had come to Boulder from Massachusetts to visit her daughter, a student at the university. Dreyfuss had fallen instantly and madly in love with the locale and stayed on after her daughter had graduated and moved to Seattle, eight years ago. Alice spent the bulk of her time outdoors, running, biking, hiking and snowshoeing, working at a local food co-op to finance her life. Her single room held a cabinet of simple clothes and a closet of first-rate outdoor gear. Liza thought Alice Dreyfuss one of the best-balanced human beings she'd ever met.

Liza looked up and managed a smile. "Hi, Alice."

Dreyfuss pulled a wicker chair close and sat. She was wearing a blue sweat suit and crossed long legs ending in pink running shoes.

"Can I ask what's wrong, Liza?"

"What? Nothing. I'm fine."

Dreyfuss inched the chair closer. "We've known one another for, what? Three years now? I know when you've got something troubling you. You've got clouds in your eyes, dear. Want to talk?"

Liza shifted in her seat and cleared her throat. "It's hard to talk about, Alice. But I . . . I found out something about someone I work with. My boss. I don't think he's, he's . . ."

Dreyfuss frowned. "He's what?"

Liza shook her head, unable to find words. "Maybe it's nothing. Maybe I'm missing something. I accidentally happened across something he had written. Something dark."

"Accidentally?"

Liza swallowed heavily. "He was in his office late at night acting real odd. Like guilty of something. He, uh, hid some papers in a book – manuscript pages. He didn't know I was watching."

"You took a look at the pages, I take it."

"This man has incredible power in my field, Alice, he's an institution. If it got out that I'd snooped in his office, read his private writings, I might not only get fired, I might never work in my field. No one would hire me."

"You're positive he wrote . . . whatever this is? There's no other explanation?"

"I've read everything he's ever written academically. There's no doubt it's his writing. And there's something else . . ."

"What?"

"He's done all sorts of sociological studies and cultural studies. Lately he's taken an interest in women's history. Not the full history, but its darker side. Its ugly side."

"Is someone threatened by . . . whatever he wrote?"

Liza considered the question for a full minute. "Not directly, maybe. It's just that the thoughts are so filthy and disgusting."

"Do you have to work with him?" Alice asked.

"His office is two doors from mine." Liza closed her eyes and shook her head. "But now I don't think I should be in the same building with him."

Harry called me from outside Carrington's office. It took five minutes for him to walk Cruz and me through the

326

discoveries. "No wonder Bromley's reveling in the idea of tearing apart the system," I said. "He's probably been planning it for years."

"Maybe killing a few women along the way," Harry said.

"You've got eyes on Bromley?" I asked.

"We're looking for him. His service says he's taking a working vacation, incommunicado. Apparently this is typical before a major action: he rests up for battle."

"The women's center action," Cruz said.

"Bromley can't know we're on to him yet," I said. "He'll put up a smoke-and-mirrors show like you've never seen. We've got to uncover his role in this before he knows we're looking."

"Bromley," Cruz said toward the phone. "How could a walking piece of diarrhea break into a system designed to keep freaks out? Wait . . . this asshole Krebbs, he know anything about computers? The system is run by –"

"Computer," I said, tumbling back in time to another Bromley case. "The computer geek – the hacker Bromley defended a year or so back."

Cruz gave me a puzzled look.

"Some guy was breaking into sophisticated systems and grabbing credit-card info. He was caught red-handed, but Bromley made him into a kind of victim, got him off with a wrist-slap."

"More connections," Cruz said, looking at me. "We're making connections."

"Let me make a couple calls and I'll be right back."

I had followed the hacker case closely, a buddy of mine in the e-crimes unit being the arresting officer. I called Carl Stella.

"Bemis," Carl said. "That's the hacker's name. Chet Bemis."

"I recall the guy seemed like he was fourteen."

"Good ol' Chet, IQ around 160, emotional age around adolescence."

"I need to bust him wide open and fast, Carl. No time for legal niceties – but I don't need him for anything legal, I hope."

"Jesus, Carson. Don't tell me anything else."

"I need a lever to get this guy to spill. Any suggestions?"

"Unless Chet's taken maturity pills recently, he's probably still a horny fourteen-year-old at heart. I figure the guy'd sell his soul – or even his video games – for a night with a woman. He's got a rigid schedule, finds safety in structure, same regimen every day. Maybe if you –"

"Tell anything you think would help to Harry and Sally Hargreaves, Carl. Could you call them soon's I hang up? We're tight on time."

I snapped the phone shut and looked at Cruz. I was terrified for Rein, but the feeling of helplessness was falling away.

We had forward motion.

It was four in the afternoon. Hargreaves entered the bar section of the neighborhood restaurant to see her quarry nursing a beer near the end of the bar, eyes watching a soundless CNN. She and Harry had stopped by the MPD's tech unit, who'd provided recording and transmission hardware. Hargreaves wore a sheer white blouse unbuttoned to show three inches of cleavage and a black skirt ending where the top of her knee commenced. She'd had to tease her hair out at her desk, trying for a trampy take on hip. The purple nail polish had been provided by a twenty-year-old clerk in the Vehicle Theft unit.

"This seat taken?" she asked Chet Bemis, chunky and bespectacled, wearing a SpongeBob SquarePants tee over knee-length shorts and boat shoes sans socks. His Atlanta Braves ball cap was angled slightly to the side, its brim flat.

"Uhm no. Huh-unh."

Hargreaves tossed her spangly purse on the wood. "Can I get a hand here?"

Bemis turned to her, confused. "What?"

"Put out your arm," she said, using it to hoist herself on to the barstool. "They make these damn stools too high. You got to put your foot on the rung, step on to the sitting part. Fine, if you're a guy, but try it in heels like these."

Hargreaves wiggled a black suede high heel, forcing Bemis's eyes down a silky length of leg. Bemis seemed pleased with the view, studying for several seconds before reluctantly turning back to Hargreaves's face.

"I can see how that'd be tough."

Hargreaves squinted at Bemis, leaned back, and studied for another few seconds. Brightened. "I know you."

"You do?"

329

"I saw you on the news last year. You're that computer genius, like Bill Jobs."

A hint of a smile from Bemis. "It's Bill Gates. But Steven Jobs. Gates is Microsoft, Jobs is Apple."

"Which is your favorite?"

"Excuse me?"

"They're competitors, right? Like ball teams. Which do you root for?"

"I like Apple from a design standpoint, but MSDOS is a lot easier to play with."

"Play with?"

"Adapt to specific needs. There's a wider range of juicy things you can do."

Hargreaves gave Bemis a sly smile. "You mean like using your brains and a computer to go where you're not supposed to?"

"Uh, I don't really do that any more."

Hargreaves winked. "C'mon. Just a little?"

"I'm like, totally not allowed. I'd go straight to prison."

Hargreaves sipped her drink, thinking. She checked the deserted bar as if wary of eavesdroppers.

"Can I tell you a secret, Chet? You won't tell anyone?"

"Of course."

"I used to room with a friend who's a cleaning lady. She has keys to people's houses and knows when they're on vacation. Once when she was out of town I got into her keys. They're labeled with addresses and phone numbers and dates when people are out of town . . ."

Bemis's eyes had started to sparkle. "What did you do?"

330

Hargreaves leaned closer. "Two of the keys were to homes where the people were gone. Know what I did, Chet?" Hargreaves put her hand over Bemis's forearm. "I waited until after midnight and went to one of the houses and let myself in."

"Cool," Bemis whispered, sounding on the edge of arousal.

"I walked into each room and just stood there looking around. It was so –"

"How could you see?" Bemis interrupted.

Hargreaves froze for a split second, thinking, *whoops.* She took a sip of her drink to buy time. "Some lights were on those timer things. So a couple rooms were bright, but most were like a cave, all shadowy and spooky. Those were the coolest rooms. It was so exciting to just stand there that I nearly, uh . . ."

"Nearly what?"

She waved Bemis's head toward her, leaned over and cupped his ear, whispering, making sure her lips brushed the flesh.

"Nearly peed my pants."

Bemis looked dizzy. "That's how it is for me when I'm inside a system. Did you, uh, take anything?"

A sly grin from Hargreaves. "I needed something to remember it by. That's like what you did, right, Chet? Go inside places and look around, maybe take a little keepsake."

"What did you take?" The man's voice was a dry rasp.

"You'll laugh," Hargreaves said; thinking, *What did I take?*

"I won't. I promise."

"I took . . . a memory."

"A memory? How?"

"I pulled off all my clothes and laid in the bed in the master bedroom. The sheets were silk. I rolled all over the bed, pressed myself down into the mattress until I, uh . . ." Hargreaves winked.

"Oh yessss," Bemis whispered. "Incredible."

"About once a month I drive by that house and it brings it all back, like a dream, but a big sexy dream."

"I know," Bemis said, a vein pulsing in his neck. "I know."

Hargreaves made her breath shallow, a purr. "You still do that sort of thing, Chet?" she said. "Go where you're not allowed?"

Bemis swallowed hard. "I'm not supposed to."

Hargreaves winked and gave Bemis a sly smile and wiggled her hand, just a shimmy. "But it's like playing with yourself, isn't it?"

Bemis's mouth fell open.

"P-pardon me?"

Hargreaves voice was a warm velvet breeze in Bemis's ear. "When I was a kid my pastor was always saying how bad it was, you know, diddling yourself. How it meant going to hell and all that. So I didn't do it any more . . ." Sal gave it three beats, wiggled the hand again. "Except when I needed to."

52

Nautilus sat in the parking lot beside the restaurant, shaking his head under the headset, figuring it was the first time a woman revealed her masturbatory patterns to Chet Bemis. He pressed the cans tight to his ears as the conversation continued.

"Do you still do it, Chet?" Hargreaves prodded.

"Usually in the morning and always at night. Sometimes at work I lock myself in the bathroom and –"

"I mean computers. Do you still go where you're not supposed to. Just to stand there and look around?"

A long pause. Nautilus held his breath.

"Yesterday I was in PayPal's master computer for hours," Bemis whispered proudly. "I went through a couple firewalls. It wasn't like, inside the house, but more like standing inside the entryway. I could go to prison just for that, but, like you said, I had to do it. It was like . . . you know, with yourself."

"Diddling," Sally said. "Feeling the glow."

Bingo! Nautilus thought.

There was a pregnant silence until Hargreaves returned with a breathy, soulful sigh. "God, you're so young, Chet. Jeez, what are you, twenty-four, -five?"

"Twenty-seven."

"You seem so youthful. But manly at the same time. You work out, right?"

"Uh, sure. A lot."

"God, it's so noisy in here," Sal said. "I get noise at my job all the time and about now in the day I like just quiet and –"

"Want to see my shop?" Bemis said. "It's across the street and real quiet about now, no one there. Sometimes I sleep there when I work late."

"You mean you've got a bed?"

"More like a cot, but –"

"Take me there, Chet," Hargreaves whispered.

Nautilus watched Hargreaves and Bemis walk an access drive to the hundred-foot-long strip center, a beige masonry building holding a laundromat, pizza joint, used vacuum-cleaner shop and Bemis's business, a sign in the window stating *CB Computer Services*. Nautilus gave them a minute while he cued the hand-held recorder, and then casually crossed the pavement to the door, stepping inside as a bell tinkled above.

One wall was taken up with shelved devices, a crayon-lettered sign proclaiming *Used Comps 4 Sale*. Hargreaves and the hacker were behind a counter littered with computer organs: hard drives, memory boards, ventilating fans, loose keys from keyboards. Bemis looked up.

"I'm sorry, we just closed. We open again at –"

"I can't wait that long, Chet. I've got a problem needs dealing with right now."

The hacker frowned at the use of his name. "Do I know you?"

Nautilus pulled his ID, flashed the gold. "I'm Detective Harry Nautilus of the Mobile Police Department. Homicide Division."

Bemis did confused. "What do you want?"

"I'm working on a case, Chet. OK to call you Chet? I only need to ask you a single question. Nathaniel Bromley was your lawyer during your trial. He did a very good job for you, spent a lot of hours, brought in expert witnesses, a psychologist. A jury-selection expert . . ."

Bemis frowned. "That's not a question."

"Very perceptive, Chet. Here's my question . . ." Nautilus looked around at the small shop. "Given that you're not a visibly wealthy man, how did you pay Mr Bromley's bill?"

"W-what does that have to do with –"

Nautilus held up his hand. "I'm a homicide investigator, Chet. That means there's a dead body somewhere. That makes my question extremely important."

"I-I had some money in investments and, uh –"

Nautilus smiled. "If you're going down that road,

please consider that my next request will be the paperwork involved in selling the securities. Oh, and I expect I should let you hear something that has a bearing on things . . ."

Nautilus pulled the recorder from his pocket, set it on the counter and pressed Play.

"*Yesterday I was in PayPal's master computer for hours . . . through a couple firewalls. It wasn't like, inside the house, but more like standing inside the entryway. I could go to prison just for that, but –*"

Bemis turned to Hargreaves with his mouth open. She winked. Bemis stared between the pair.

"Y-you can't u-use that ag-against me, it was –"

Nautilus sighed. "Are you a lawyer Mr Bemis?"

"No."

Harry's huge fist slammed the counter. Computer parts jumped in the air. "THEN DON'T YOU EVER DARE PRESUME TO TELL ME WHAT I CAN DO!"

Bemis turned white. "Well enunciated," Hargreaves said to Nautilus.

"Chet seems to have a hearing problem, Detective Hargreaves."

Hargreaves leaned the wall and buttoned the top of her blouse "You've violated your parole, Chet. I advise you to listen to Detective Nautilus. If there's anyone with your interests in mind, it's him."

"There's a clock ticking on a case I'm working on, Chet," Nautilus said. "Women are dying. What can you tell me about that?"

"Women *dying*? Nothing!"

"See how easy it is?" Nautilus said. "One simple answer and you've cleared yourself of complicity in murder. I accept your statement. But we have to find out what you did to pay off Mr Bromley's legal tab. I expect the bill was excessive."

Bemis's eyes darkened in anger. "My bill was over a hundred and fifty thousand dollars. Bromley said it would be a lot less. There was no way I could pay it off. I'd lose my shop, everything."

"But Bromley said you could work it off, didn't he?"

"There was a website Bromley wanted me to hack. A blind one, closed. A system only available to those with several passwords. Bromley had the level-one entry word but needed me to open the rest of the network."

"What's the name of the site?" Hargreaves asked, now taking notes.

"It's called Tubman. Layers of security – more than a lot of government systems. Took me two weeks. I expected something big, complex. But all those layers of security are protecting a kind of message board, basically. I think it's got something to do with drugs moving by courier. Where they're at."

"Why's that?"

"You can tell where a shipment is in a specific region, but you can't see where it came from. Each region has its own server, its own code. Think of a checkers board. It's like you can see one piece and the ways it might move, but you can't see the whole board, or any history of where pieces have been, or will go in the end."

"But a person could, with computer access, jump in front of a piece and hijack it?"

Bemis nodded. "I never wanted to know anything else."

"What door did the password open?"

"I got in at Boulder, Colorado. I had to hack other doors from there."

Nautilus looked at Hargreaves, mouthed *Boulder.* He turned to the shaking hacker. "Here's how it's going down, Chet. Bromley extorted services from you using your unpaid legal balance as leverage. He didn't set up an alternate payment plan. He simply said, "Break into this system or you'll be living under a bridge until some psychopath slits your throat."

"That's about how it really was. He's a nasty man."

"Ain't that the truth? But in your story there will be no mention of tonight's little drama. It's gone from your head, Chet. We requested your help and you were a good citizen every step of the way. Testify to Bromley using you and I can keep your ass out of prison. Bromley can't, cuz he's gonna wind up there first. So, who's your friend in all this nastiness?"

"You, Detective Nautilus."

They left Bemis the way they had wanted: him shaking their hands and thanking them.

*   *   *

338

The pair returned to headquarters, Nautilus sitting with feet on the desk, Hargreaves taking Ryder's abutting desk. Nautilus stared across the wide room, his face as impassive as stone, yet inside his head wheels were spinning like buzz saws, cutting the case down to discrete packets of data. The chunks of data were transferred to a weighing station, where Nautilus balanced each against each.

"Krebbs's wife went through the system," Nautilus said quietly. "Bromley's wife, too. Both men hate the system for stealing from them."

Hargreaves nodded. "You were right, Harry. Our smiling boys share a lot more than golf."

"I've been thinking about Larry Krebbs's place in the timeline. I've got a call to make." Nautilus checked his notes, dialed his desk phone, spoke for three minutes. He hung up and looked at Hargreaves.

"Sam Choy, Krebbs's boss. He confirms Krebbs is a golfer."

"We kinda knew that," Hargreaves said.

"Krebbs's old office had a poster of St Andrews on the wall. He spent lunch hours putting across the floor. He once referred to a female intern as having a six-iron mind in a one-wood world."

"Whatever that means. You're out ahead of me."

"There aren't many places to golf on the Keys – land's at a premium. Instead, Larry took up . . ." Nautilus reached into his desk and produced the file of receipts provided by Bromley, shaking them on to his desktop, studying several, "kayaking, fishing, snorkeling, riding a moped and jet-skiing. Krebbs wasn't vacationing, he was establishing an airtight alibi."

Hargreaves smiled. "Larry Krebbs was in the Keys when his wife was killed. But he was around when Jane Doe – Butterfly Lady – turned up at the dump. That's what you're getting at?"

Nautilus nodded. "We don't know who the woman is. So no way to establish motive. We don't even know if she was ever in the system. But she was killed exactly the way Krebbs's wife was killed, same tableau death setting. I'm positive it's the same killer, and our boy came down from Colorado."

"Lay it out. I want to hear."

Nautilus tapped his fingers per incident. "Lainie Krebbs was living near Denver when she was abducted. Rhonda Doakes had moved here from Boise, the underground railroad running her through Colorado. Herdez, the Utah body, likely moved through the Colorado region on her path from Pittsburgh to Baja California. Bemis's password got him in at Boulder. It's all Colorado-centric."

"Someone wrapped Rhonda Doakes up and left her for her angry boyfriend. How'd she get found out?"

Nautilus smiled. "I've got something. A little research sparked by a comment from Detective Clayton in Pensacola. Rhonda Doakes was about to become Randi Doyle."

Hargreaves nodded. "Right, women who make it to the other side get their names changed so the old hubby or boyfriend can't . . ." She stopped dead, looked at Nautilus. "A name change is a legal action. A matter of public record."

"And the record includes the old name, name sought, current address – everything. Most people wouldn't know that, but Bromley would. We've got two suspects in the area: Bromley and Krebbs. There's no one else, Sal. It's one or both."

"How do we get inside, Harry? Who's the weak link?"

"Krebbs's Keys getaway was such a perfect alibi it must have been planned by Bromley. You should have seen that sleazebag's eyes when he handed the receipts over to Carson and me – total superiority. Problem is, Bromley has brains deluxe. He's probably prepared a dozen legal escapes from anything we'd throw at him. We can't use the info we got from Bemis, since our approach was a little, uh, beyond bounds."

"You're saying we hit Krebbs? How?"

Nautilus linked his fingers behind his head and stared at the ceiling for a full minute. He nodded at his conclusion.

"We toss everything into the air like a pot of spaghetti and hope Krebbs sees a strand or two that scares the hell outta him."

53

Hours passed in the moving trailer. The pain in Rein's cheek subsided; the blow had been a reminder her captor was not bound by any rules, except those of whoever was directing him.

The truck finally stopped and Tommy opened the door.

"You're back home, Treeks," he grinned. "Place needs a good cleaning."

Fifty feet beyond him Rein saw a modular home slatted with yellow lumber. Behind, tucked into aspens and pine, were a couple broken-down vehicles. The landscape was mostly rock and the sky was a blue fire.

Tommy loosened their leg ropes enough to allow shuffling, stood above Rein and an eyes-down Treeka as they entered the cluttered living room. He stripped the tape from the women's mouths.

"I learned from my mistake, Tommy," Treeka said,

shivering. "I learned how much I love you. It was terrible out there, babe. I'm so happy to be home."

"Sure, hon. Sure you are." Tommy caressed Treeka's face with the back of his hand, then slapped her to the floor. "We're gonna have a long talk about that, Treeks. But we got plenty of time." He looked to Rein. "Guess your man's comin' pretty soon. Then Treeks and I will catch up on things. For now, I gotta run to town and provision up for the party." He re-secured the ropes and left the house, whistling like a man without a care.

Rein turned to Treeka.

"I want you to pull my pants down," she said.

Twenty minutes after leaving headquarters, Nautilus and Hargreaves were looking at an irritated Lawrence Krebbs.

"Come on, Larry," Nautilus said. "We need you downtown for a conversation."

"I'm working. What the fuck are you talking about?"

"The Colorado cops are about to close the case on Lainie," Nautilus lied. "They've got a couple local loonies probably did it. We just need a statement, then we can give back your receipts and stuff. You have to sign."

"Loonies killed Lainie?"

Nautilus shrugged. "Brain-dead crackhead types. The cops are about to get out the *Case Closed* stamp."

A grinning Krebbs followed the pair downtown. When they arrived Hargreaves walked behind as Nautilus and Krebbs passed by Lieutenant Tom Mason. Mason pulled Nautilus to the side, pointing to a door just closed. "He's in there," Mason whispered, loud enough for Krebbs to hear. "The hotshot lawyer. He wants to talk to you or Hargreaves."

Nautilus nodded and shot a thumbs up.

"Who's in there?" Krebbs asked as they continued down the hall. "What hotshot lawyer?"

"No one," Nautilus said too fast. "Another case."

He pointed a suddenly wary Krebbs into a small room with a table and three chairs, a large mirror on the wall. "That's one of those special mirrors, isn't it?" Krebbs complained. "You can see through from the other side."

Hargreaves went to the glass, pulling a lipstick and attending her lips. "It's a cop shop, Larry. Every third room has mirrors."

"Have a seat, Lar," Nautilus said.

"Where are my receipts?"

Nautilus ignored the question, instead leaning the wall with arms crossed. "Larry, Larry, Larry . . ." he said, shaking his head.

"What?"

Hargreaves pressed her lips tight, made a kissing face at the mirror and spun to Krebbs. Her eyes twinkled with delight. "We have an undercover operative in the women's underground railroad, Mr Krebbs. She's been very productive."

Nautilus saw Krebbs freeze, a split second, nothing more. "Underground what-road? The fuck you talking about?"

"The system Lainie was yanked out of and killed," Nautilus said, pulling Krebbs's head his way. "You knew it would happen, right? The trip to the Keys fooled us for a while."

"You just said she was killed by –"

"Musta been another woman named Lainie," Hargreaves said, spinning Krebbs's head back to her. "Sometimes Detective Nautilus gets confused."

"I-I want my lawyer."

Nautilus affected puzzled. "You want Nathaniel Bromley here, Larry? As your lawyer or your co-defendant?"

"Co-defendant?"

"Someone's gonna tell the story," Hargreaves said. "You or Mr Bromley." She paused. "Or your friend up in Colorado."

Krebbs's eyes flickered with fear, covered fast. *Bingo,* Nautilus thought, registering the signals. *Colorado.*

Krebbs said, "I don't know anyone in Colo—"

"Really?" Nautilus said, throwing spaghetti as fast as he could. "Looks to us like Colorado and Mobile were where it all happened. We know about the women's center up there, the computer network Bromley had hacked by Chet Bemis, the –"

"I don't know a GODDAMN THING ABOUT BOULDER!"

Nautilus cocked his head and raised an eyebrow. "I never mentioned a city, Larry. And Lainie was found in Denver. What made you say Boulder?"

Lawrence Krebbs's mouth fell open. Nautilus put his hand on the back of Krebbs's chair and leaned close.

345

"Someone's going to confirm the story, Lawrence. Whoever gets first in line with the truth becomes last in line for the needle."

The blood drained from Krebbs's face. "N-needle?"

Hargreaves said, "It's like a game show called *Talk First and Live*, Mr Krebbs. You like breathing, right? Kind of gotten used to it?"

"I didn't *do* anything." Krebbs was sweating. Nautilus could smell the fear.

"I heard the likely judge for the case is Silas Jaynes," Hargreaves lied. "He's so pro-capital punishment they call him 'Cyanide Silas'." She looked into the mirror and winked. On the far side of the glass Tom Mason pressed the button on his phone's speed-dial.

"One chance to tell the truth, Mr Krebbs," Harry said. "Unless someone gets there ahead of you."

The phone on the wall rang. Krebbs looked wild-eyed. Hargreaves picked up the receiver and pressed it to her ear. "What? He has? Oh, almost." She looked at Krebbs like so much dead meat. "Let me know when it's all done and we can bag it here."

"NO!" Krebbs yelled as Hargreaves hung up the phone. "HE'LL LIE!"

"What are you talking about?" Nautilus asked.

"That was about Bromley, right? Fucker says he'll talk? He'll lie to cover his ass, make you fry mine instead. I'll tell you the real story."

"I don't think so," Hargreaves yawned. "Sounds like someone's cutting a deal."

346

"Nate planned it out," Krebbs said. "Nate ordered me to take the body to the dump. He used me. Please, I'm TELLING THE TRUTH!"

Hargreaves looked at Nautilus and shrugged, like *what do you think?* She squeezed another wink at the mirror. Five seconds later the phone rang again.

"NO!" Krebbs wailed. "You want to hear ME!"

Hargreaves let the phone ring beneath her palm as sweat raced down Larry Krebbs's forehead, veins pulsing in his head. Hargreaves picked up the phone, said, "Let me call you back in a few."

Harry Nautilus made a big deal of adjusting his watch, turned to Hargreaves. "The timer's set for five minutes. If we don't like what we hear from Larry, we'll take the call from, well, whomever." Nautilus eyed Hargreaves. "Why don't you take a break, Sally? Grab a coffee and hang tight."

Hargreaves pretended reluctance at leaving the room to the two men, but closed the door behind her. Nautilus pulled his chair closer to Lawrence Krebbs and put concern in his voice. "I can't bring myself to hate you," Nautilus said. "My first wife left me after a year, the second wife after just three months. I'm still fighting it out with the third. It's been tough, right? An emotional time for you?" Nautilus had been married once.

Krebbs nodded. "Three years down the drain with that bitch, not that she learned a damn thing the whole while, a fucking waste of my time. I tried my best to turn her into something useful, but she was a worthless –"

Nautilus tapped his watch. "Better get talking, Mr Krebbs. A minute's already gone."

Krebbs closed his eyes to collect his thoughts. "I got a call six weeks back, one of those things on the phone that distorts voices. The caller said he knew where Lainie was, did I want to know? I said, Hell yes, lemme know so I can go . . . deal with the bitch. The caller said there was a better way we could handle things."

"The caller used the word *we?*"

"He called us a band of brothers, men who could make sure other bitches didn't stray like mine did. We could start something here that would travel across the country, change things forever. He said it was a legal approach and we should talk through a lawyer."

"The lawyer was, of course . . ."

Krebbs nodded. "Bromley said if we played everything right, we could fuck up all this women center shit and stop the FemiNazi dykes from stealing our women. Nate knew 'em for the grubby whores they really were."

"How did Lainie figure in?"

"Nate said he had a brother in Colorado who thought the same way. He'd been the guy who'd tracked Lainie down. Nate said by all of us working together we could use Lainie. She could make a contribution to the betterment of men everywhere."

"How would that happen, Larry?"

"Lainie was going to, uh, pass away – not by me, I never hurt anyone. I just had to go on a long vacation and make sure it was documented with receipts. Nate

348

said the cops would show up, but it wouldn't matter since I had a perfect alibi."

"What's your alibi for the woman at the Mobile dump?"

"I . . . I did take the skank's body to the dump, set her up like I was told."

"In a chair looking out over garbage?"

"The Colorado brother told Nate the women had to be made into examples. Nate liked the idea too, so that's what I did."

"That's why Lainie was killed, Larry? To be an example?"

"There was more than that. She was a trade, like balancing the ledger. The Colorado brother does Lainie, Bromley does a woman down here."

"There were two women killed down here, Larry. Are you forgetting the one in Pensacola, Rhonda Doakes? She'd escaped here from Boise and was settling into a new life. She had to be punished too, right?"

Krebbs's eyes flickered from side to side, evasion. "I don't know anything about that. Ask Bromley. He did it."

In all likelihood both men had taken Doakes to the fishing camp, Nautilus thought. Either they or the Colorado connection had called James Peyton and told him where he could find his ex-girlfriend. Just as the killer in Colorado had insisted his Southern accomplices share culpability in murder, Bromley would make sure Krebbs was implicated as well. Nautilus loved it when trapped rats began eating one another.

"OK, Larry, the woman you took to the dump. How did she get to Mobile? Who abducted her?"

Krebbs shrugged. "I have to figure it was the Colorado brother. Nate and I drove to Missouri in his big-ass Benz. The woman was in a house in farmland, all tied up and ready to go.

House in farmland, Nautilus thought. Probably the house above Branson. Roughly equidistant between Boulder and Mobile, it was likely the killer's temporary base of operation in the locale . . . after he'd killed the two innocent owners and tossed them in the storm cellar. Was this the monster who now had Rein?

"You never saw who left her there, Larry?" he asked.

"No. Hell, I never even seen her until I got back to Mobile."

Nautilus frowned. "What do you mean, you never saw her?"

Krebbs circled his hands in a wrapping motion. "She was wrapped in a tarp like a mummy. Nate and I dumped her in the trunk and drove like hell back to Mobile."

"Who ended up killing her, Larry?" Nautilus asked quietly.

"She died on her own."

On the far side of the mirror, Hargreaves whispered to Mason, "I think I know what's coming. This is gonna make me sick."

"What killed her, Larry?" Nautilus asked.

Krebbs shrugged. "I dunno. She was pretty beat up and her eyes were gone."

On the far side of the mirror Hargreaves whispered, "God damn you, you bastard."

"No one undid the tarp?" Nautilus said, keeping his voice level, though his stomach was turning. "You didn't know this until . . ."

"Until we unwrapped her in a deep woods just north of the dump. She'd been moaning and shit as far as Vicksburg, but she stopped after we had lunch."

Nautilus shot a glance at the mirror, a split second of disbelief, then turned back to Krebbs. "The guy in Colorado, your 'brother'. Was he down with Bromley's suit against the centers?" Nautilus did the money-whisk with his fingers. "Getting his slice of cake?"

Krebbs shook his head. "From what Nate said, the Colorado brother didn't give a fuck about money, he wanted two things: To show women for the garbage they are, and to kill the system."

"You don't know who he is? Your Colorado brother?"

Krebbs shook his head. "I don't know if Bromley does either. They met in a chat room, safe and secure." Krebbs jutted his chin, his final act of defiance. "Women got safe places to go, so do we."

54

"Come on, Treeka, I need you to pull my pants down. We might get my phone out."

Rein's companion stared at the slatted pinnacle of the ceiling as if hypnotized. The cabin was a box of shadows, the sun low behind the mountains. Somewhere outside, deep in the trees, a coyote yipped, tuning up for the coming night.

"Treeka!" Rein snapped. "Help me, dammit." Her words seemed amplified by the log walls that surrounded them.

Treeka's head rolled like she was waking from a dream. "We can't do anything. Tommy's too strong."

"Everything in him is weak," Rein hissed. "We've got to figure out how to use his weakness against him."

"If he's so weak, how come we're the prisoners? I'm a dumb nobody, but you're smart. And you're right here beside me."

"Listen, Treeka, we've got a chance. We have to try the phone."

"I'm going to make my peace with God before I die."

Treeka turned her head away and began mumbling. Rein stared at the square of fading twilight on the wall and floor and turned back to Treeka. "Now I understand why you stayed with Tommy."

"Yeah?" Treeka sniffed. "Why?"

"Because you're a stupid hick incapable of ever doing anything without a man there to tell you what to do."

A pause. "What?"

Rein forced the sound of a chuckle. "I'll bet when you came out of your mama she looked between her legs and wondered why she'd birthed a punching bag."

"Fuck you," Treeka said.

"No, fuck *you*, you ignorant hillbilly. Today's the first day of the rest of your life?" Rein laughed. "You actually believed that shit?"

"YOU BITCH!" Treeka struggled toward Rein, trying to kick her with bound legs.

"Save your energy, *Treeks*," Rein jeered. "Maybe when Tommy gets back he'll let you wash his truck."

Treeka started to scream a response but her face collapsed into crying. She curled sideways into herself, tears pooling on the pine floor.

"Come on, girl," Rein said gently. "Maybe it won't work, but we'll go out like women, right?"

*   *   *

353

Robert Trotman's face was intense as he tapped his keyboard. He sat in his tiny office with the door nearly closed and the only light coming through the window. Though the sun had dropped below the peaks west of the university, it was light enough to peck at his laptop. He cocked his head, hearing the elevator door open and shut, hard boot heels approaching at march rhythm. He looked up to see Professor Sinclair stride by, a sheaf of pages tight in his hand. He heard the heels stop across the hall, a banging on a door.

"Krupnik, you in there?"

Sinclair was banging on Liza's door, the man's voice a basso roar. "Krupnik?"

Trotman screwed up the courage to address Sinclair. "I haven't seen Liza all day, sir," he called out the door. "It's unusual. She's not even answering her mobile phone."

Trotman heard an electronic key slide into the reader on Liza's door. As departmental heads, Sinclair and the absent Bramwell had passkeys to all teaching-assistant offices. Trotman heard his colleague's door open, followed by pages pushed around, as if Sinclair was scrabbling through materials on Liza's desk and looking for something.

"Trotman!" Sinclair bayed. "Come here, would you?"

"What can I –?"

"Goddamit, don't question me . . . come here."

Trotman shut off his computer and closed the lid. He poked his head out the door to see the outsized Sinclair on Liza's threshold. Heart pounding, he inched his way across the hall.

"What is it, sir?"

Sinclair jabbed his finger at Liza's wall, the two posters of Rosie the Riveter flanking Liza's heavily noted calendar. "What do you make of all this shit, Robert?"

"Sh-shit, sir?"

"These goddamn posters. That woman there . . . does she look like some kind of dyke? She does, doesn't she? Those clothes, that hair? Trying to do a man's job?"

Trotman pushed hair from his eyes. "I . . . guess so. If that's what you think, Doctor."

Sinclair wheeled to Trotman and studied the grad student as if he was a newly emerged form of life. "Don't feed me what you think I want to hear. I need to hear *your* truths. Let's start with Krupnik. Do you like her? Really like her?" Sinclair thought for several seconds, held up a massive palm. "No, wait . . . don't tell me. This is not the venue. I want you to come to my house for dinner this weekend, Robert. We'll drink fine liquor and eat good, honest red meat."

"D-dinner?" Trotman stammered.

Sinclair glanced down the hall as if making sure they were alone. He put his hand on Trotman's shoulder and lowered his voice to a whisper. "This department is eighty per cent female, Robert. And all the other men are goddamn fruitcakes. Emasculated. I'm a lonely man with no one to talk to, Robert."

Trotman looked weak in the knees. "You want to t-talk to m-me?"

Sinclair's voice continued its conspiratorial whisper. "I want to hear what fortunes led you to this university. To this very department. Why we were selected in your university search. I want to hear about your graduate thesis. I want to hear your history, Robert. I've been remiss in my duties and need to talk to a man."

Sinclair slapped his thick chest with his fist, eyes glittering like a man in the throes of a vision. "Things are changing around here, Robert. Evolving. Let us drink brandy and smoke cigars and scratch our balls, as unashamed as simians. Can you come tell me your tales, my young friend?"

Sinclair took Trotman's dropped jaw as assent and wrapped the dazzled Trotman in a hug, the grad student's pale and scrubby face buried in the professor's dense beard. Sinclair released the woozy student, patted his skinny hindquarters like he was a football player who'd just made the big catch, and turned toward the elevator, clapping sonic booms of delight from his palms.

Treeka bit one side of Rein's panties and pulled them down three inches, squirmed to the other side, teeth-tugged the panties lower. The jeans were snap-closed, a piece of luck. Treeka paused, puffing after the effort.

"That's as far as I can get unless I pull your jeans down more."

"Let me try this . . ." Rein called upon moves from

her gymnastics classes, planting heels and head on the floor, bowing upward in an arc. She bounced her feet, heels thumping the floor. Her pounding shook the windowpanes.

A clatter as the small black phone slipped free and skittered on the floor. Rein caught her breath as Treeka wormed to the phone.

"There's a smear of blood on it."

"I'm, uh, starting my –"

"I understand," Treeka said. "What do I do?"

Rein thought through the sequence. "Press Contacts. There are three: AC, CR and HN. Press . . ." It didn't matter who she called, if the message got through, it would get to all of them. But if it got through, Harry needed it the most.

"Press HN," Rein said. "Then press Call, that's it. I'll take it from there."

Treeka pressed at the phone with her face, licked at it. "I can't push the buttons. My nose is too soft, so is my tongue. Let me see if there's anything around here to use."

"Hurry!"

Treeka spotted the bottle cap from Tommy's beer. She flipped it into her mouth with her tongue, wiggled it until tight in her teeth, pecked at the phone.

"It's too short. I can't see what to press." She spit out the cap, rolled across the floor, stopping after each roll to scout the darkened floor. Dust motes sparkled in the blue twilight.

"Fuck! I can't see nothing."

"The fireplace," Rein said. "The wood."

Treeka rolled to the hearth. "I got a piece of kindling," she said, excitement in her voice. She wriggled back to the phone. The stick was the size of a pencil. She held it in her teeth and pressed Contacts.

The screen lit, flickered. Went black. Flickered on again.

"Hit Call," Rein said. Treeka pressed Call. "Push it here," Rein said. Treeka chinned the phone across two foot of floor.

"It's ringing," Treeka said.

There was no time for conversation and Rein had nothing but slender facts to present. Hopefully they would put Harry and Carson on to Tommy Flood.

"Another ring," Treeka said. Rein counted heartbeats. Ten beats passed without a ring. Then another.

Rein heard Harry's voice. "Yes?" he asked, a whisper.

"Held by a Thomas Flood," she said at auctioneer speed. "In Colorado, probably by Boulder. Armed and dangerous and –"

Treeka stared at the phone, looked up. "It's dead, Rein."

"Do you think he ran?" Hargreaves asked, spooning sugar into a cup of coffee. "My buddy Bromley?"

A confused Larry Krebbs was in the Mobile county jail. He'd called a lawyer, not Nathaniel Bromley. Nautilus and Hargreaves had done two checks of Bromley's home, the man had disappeared. After putting a surveillance unit down the block from the lawyer's house, the pair had retreated to the comfort of Nautilus's home, the dining-room table overlaid with copies of files.

Nautilus thought a moment and shook his head. "Bromley thinks the Krebbster is still his good buddy. Less than ten people know Krebbs turned."

"That was scary. Krebbs could have clammed up any moment. I'm surprised he came to the station."

Nautilus laughed darkly. "Larry Krebbs is one-half pure ego, and one-half pure stupid. He really thinks he's gonna get a couple years because he didn't strangle the poor woman with his bare hands."

Hargreaves cradled the mug in both hands and shook her head. "Well, she's just a woman, after all."

Nautilus's phone rang from the table. He lifted and opened it in one move. He said, *Yes?* then said, *Rein? Rein?* He stared at the phone. "It was Rein. Her phone cut out."

"My God. What'd she say?"

Nautilus looked bewildered. "Held by Tah . . ." he said. "Then it went out."

"Tod?" Hargreaves said. "Tom?"

"I'll get the phone techs on the location," Nautilus said, snapping into action and dialing furiously.

55

Harry called with the news that Rein's fading sprinkle of electrons had originated from a cell tower north of Boulder, a last-outpost spire before the Front Range of the Rockies vaulted from the earth. Rein was alive and knew the name of her captor. Her truncated call was either shutting the phone down out of fear of discovery or the battery dying.

Harry and Sally had broken Krebbs, a phenomenal piece of work. Krebbs had implicated Bromley, whereabouts unknown, but by proximity alone ruled out from being Rein's captor. Harry and Sally had put Bromley's vehicle on alert-notify status, meaning if it was spotted, take no action except for notifying Harry.

Cruz and I were in Boulder at nine a.m., courtesy of Hal Lewis, a private-pilot friend of Chief Teemont, an ex-cop making a lot more money running a security firm in Branson. Lewis turned a twelve-hour drive into a four-hour flight. The light of the day was behind the plane and, had I not been so worried, it might have been a beautiful sunrise.

After touching down in Boulder, Cruz detailed events to her overseers and APBs were sent out. Within an hour we had hundreds of eyes searching for Reinetta Early. There was an officer in trouble and jurisdictional boundaries meant nothing. Cruz grabbed a new ride, a blue Crown Vic just like Harry and I had in Mobile.

"First stop is the Boulder women's center," Cruz said, jamming the big car into gear. "Right?"

"Past due," I said.

"The woman who runs the place, Carol Madrone, will be there. I believe you two have met."

"I'm sorry the place is so small," Carol Madrone said when Cruz and I stepped inside the Women's Crisis Center of Boulder. The sun approached the ten a.m. mark and streamed into the window. Meelia Reston was the only other person there. "We could go across the street to the Beacon. They have room to –"

"It's fine, Carol," I said. "Officer Early mentioned being with another woman on the run. They'd crossed paths in the system. Is that common?"

"No. At any given time, we estimate three to five women in the system. That's nationally, with perhaps eighty to a hundred safe houses and handlers."

I leaned against the desk and nodded; slim chances

indeed. "So the other woman didn't come from here?"

"Probably not, though we did put a woman into the system four days prior."

"Treeka?"

Madrone's eyes went wide. "She said her name was Treeka Lane."

I shot a hopeful glance at Cruz. "Was Lane her real last name?"

"A lot of abused women give us false names. We don't discourage it. We're here to help, not identify. We assign a travel name, Darleen was hers."

"Shit," I said. "Layer after layer of deception."

"We've had people in the system killed, Detective," Carol said gently. "Just knowing a name can –"

"I know, I'm sorry. Tell me anything you can about Treeka."

"Treeka lived up north, I think. She came to town on the bus because her husband took her car away. She said she lived . . . on a sad little ranch in the country."

I turned to Cruz. "Bus line any help?"

"If we had a photo we could show it to bus drivers, but getting them together quickly would be problematic."

"Treeka came in on a bus the day she left?" I asked.

"In her husband's truck," Meelia said. "He was away and she took it and came here. Everything was ready and we –"

"The truck . . . did you get the license plate?"

"No. We just, uh . . ." Meelia looked to Madrone.

"I don't care if you blew it up or sunk it in a river," Cruz said. "What happened to the truck?"

"I drove it to Denver Airport," Meelia said. "Long-term parking. Another staffer brought me back to Boulder."

Cruz pulled her phone. "Connect me to Vehicle Theft, please." She hung on the line and waited for the information. Cruz snapped her phone shut. "A Ford F-150 was reported stolen the day after the Treeka woman went underground. The truck was found at Denver Airport and returned to its owner."

"Who is . . .?" My heart was suddenly in my throat.

"Thomas J. Flood."

Tom. My knees almost buckled. "Particulars?"

"You got a computer I could use?" Cruz asked Carol Madrone.

"Let me log on for you."

Carol opened the computer. Cruz pulled up the local law-enforcement database. "Address puts Flood outside of Meeker Park, about eighteen miles north of here, near Estes Park. It would be near a regional bus line, by the way."

"Your SWAT folks up for some action?" I asked.

56

Our caravan rolled down the labrynthine canyon guided by a helicopter fly-by from a distance, transmitting photos of terrain to the SWAT commander, a hulking red-faced guy named Strather. We stopped for a last-minute meeting, Strather and Cruz addressing six men and three women in armored gear, pistols strapped on thighs and assault rifles slung over shoulders.

There'd been discussion of a low-key action, but photos put the house in an open area where an unhappy guy with weaponry could do a lot of damage before being nullified. We all knew the first damage was often to the captives.

Twenty minutes later we were in position, the troopers moving like dancers while bristling with firepower. Even crossing jagged terrain the noise level never overrode the breeze in the pines. When everyone was ready, Strather, crouching behind a boulder the size of a bulldozer, lifted his bullhorn.

"Thomas Flood! This is the Colorado State Police. Come out with your hands high, no weapons."

Nothing.

"We know you have prisoners, Flood. Come out now and no one gets hurt."

A flash of motion behind a window. Then a voice from the cabin.

"She's MINE! Get the fuck away."

"Come on, Flood," Strather called. "Make it easy on yourself."

"Traitor! Eunuch! What did they do to your balls?"

"Come out, Flood. Don't make us have to come in and get you."

"Go away or I'll KILL the bitch."

"Give up, Flood."

"Come closer and she's DEAD!"

Cruz and I were a hundred feet from Strather, tucked behind another boulder, peering around its edge. Flood was using the singular, scaring the hell out of me. And I'd heard that kind of voice before – at the outer edge – when the last strands of wiring melted away and perpetrators began considering martyrdom preferable to their shabby little lives.

"Flood . . ."

"I'LL KILL HER IF YOU DON'T LEAVE!"

I looked toward Strather, saw him lowering the bullhorn while considering his next move. I poked my head around the rock.

"Who fucking cares, Flood?" I yelled.

Strather spun my way, did the throat-chop motion: *Shut up!*

"Who gives a shit, Flood?" I continued, riffing on themes Harry relayed from Krebbs. "She's just a woman. Boy, you sure can pick 'em, can't you?"

"Who the FUCK are YOU?" Flood called.

Strather was glaring daggers until he saw Cruz pointing at me, mouthing *Let him talk.*

"You're gonna die over some whore?" I yelled. "You call that a fair exchange: Thomas J. Flood equals one woman? What the hell's wrong with you, boy – you crazy? You got a whole band of brothers waiting to help you. What's one more damned bitch in the scheme of things?"

Nothing. It was like time froze. "Tom!" I prompted. "Yo, Tom?"

"*What?*"

"Is the slut alive?"

A beat. "Kind of."

I looked at Cruz, breathed out. Took another breath. "Look at it, Tom. Take a long look at the woman. Are you looking, Tom?"

"Yes."

"Look at her carefully."

"I AM!"

"Do the fucking math! Is she – *it* – worth the life of a man?"

Seconds ticked by, the only sound the breeze in the

trees. I saw the door open a crack. A white rag shook in Flood's hand, surrender.

"I'm coming out," he yelled. "I want a good lawyer."

Flood stepped outside with hands on his head and was immediately trussed like a turkey, screaming about knowing his rights. Team members rushed the cabin, Cruz and I on their heels. We saw only one woman on the floor, eyes swollen shut and her mouth a purple bruise. Her blouse was shredded and her torso was beaten and bruised. But it was rising and falling with ragged breaths.

"Treeka?" I said, kneeling beside the woman.

The purple mouth whispered, "Who a-are . . .?"

"The police," I said, taking her hand. "There was a woman with you, right?"

"R-rei-Rein. Sh-she got t-taken away last night."

"Last night?"

"T-Tommy dragged her outside and came back ten minutes later. We n-never saw who got her, only heard him drive up a few minutes later and yell. He sounded real happy."

"What did he say?" A medic rushed in with a gurney. Cruz waved him back, mouthed *Hang on.*

Treeka opened one eye to a slit, her hand tightening on mine. "Rein was going to b-be his best example, his . . . I don't know, he said something weird."

"What?"

"Rein was going to be his PA's restaurants. Something like that."

I frowned in thought. "*Pièce d'résistance?*" I said, inflecting the accent.

She nodded. "Please help her."

Reinetta Early's eyes opened again. They had opened before but her head screamed in pain and she closed them, drifting back into unconsciousness. But the ache had dissipated and she saw shapes of black and yellow and gray, smelled dirt and damp. Her memory was returning: Tommy getting a phone call, eyes on Rein as he spoke, the towel – a makeshift hood – wrapped around Rein's face as Treeka stared in horror. Tommy leading her into the chilly outside as she stumbled for two hundred and five steps as if the counting had mattered.

She'd been tied to a tree, wrists behind the trunk. Tommy's laughter melted away with his footsteps. It had been cold and she'd been gripped with pre-menstrual cramps.

She'd heard the sound of a vehicle creeping close, stopping. Footsteps. A long period of . . . what, appraisal? A freezing cold cloth over her nose and mouth – *chloroform?*

And now . . .

A world of shapes and shadows. Rein took a dozen deep breaths and pushed to sitting, her arms free, her legs still bound. A wave of nausea overtook her and she vomited. The process helped to clear the toxin from her body and she surveyed her surroundings.

She was in a cave. No, a mine . . . dusty beams

supporting the ceiling. It was a tight area, little more than a tunnel. The moving shapes were shadows thrown by a lantern in the corner, glass globe in a metal frame. She could suddenly smell its acrid fumes, as if her senses were rekindling one at a time.

There was an animal in the corner, a small one, like a rat. Not moving. She blinked twice and refocused on the dark shape. Not an animal, a pile of hair.

Her hair. She'd been shaved bald. What did Dr Kavanaugh called it . . . defeminized? Rein fought her pounding heart and listened into the dark beyond the slender range of the lantern light.

Heard footsteps approaching.

57

Cruz and I studied shreds of rope at the base of a fir tree. "Flood staked Rein here until someone came and cut her loose," I said, seeing impressions in the dirt: Rein's footprints. "Took her."

"We've got tire tracks," Cruz said, trying for glass-half-full. "Maybe more. The state's best forensics people are coming."

I stared into the sky, achingly blue. "That and another month might lead somewhere. We have to move to the next lead . . . the password leak from the center."

We arrived at the center an hour later, Carol Madrone out front on her cell. "I've called an emergency staffers meeting," she said. "Like you asked."

"Who's coming?"

"Five volunteer staffers and all five active directors;

six, if you include one who's more of an in-absentia advisor and never attends meetings."

"Five volunteers for the whole center?"

"*Staff* volunteers. We have nineteen phone volunteers who mainly answer the hotline and write call reports. If the caller fits the profile of abuse, we try to get her to talk with a trained staffer or director. Find some way to communicate safely. Our upper-level folks – volunteer staff and directors – are trained in all aspects of domestic abuse, including domestic-violence advocacy in the legal system."

"You're saying hotline volunteers don't know the password?"

She shook her head. "There's no need for them to see files on our clients. Or access the escape system."

"The staffers and directors all know the passwords?"

"As a matter of protocol, yes. But most aren't involved in day-to-day operations. Most are high-profile community leaders who advise and help secure donations."

"Do they have anything to do with the system?" I asked. "The directors?"

"Do I really have to –"

"You have to answer," Cruz said. "We need to know everything. And we'll do our best to protect any information."

Carol nodded. "When a woman seems to be a prospect for, uh, relocation, all the directors are consulted. Everyone has to be in agreement that it's the only step left. Why do you need them here?"

"It seems one of them leaked the password," I said. "Or sold it. Or –"

Carol shook her head. "We change the password once a month at our directors' meeting. Plus it's not a system-wide password, it's –"

"It's an entry point for a hacker," I said. "In this case a very talented fellow who used the foothold to pry open the hood and get at the engine."

Carol looked about to weep.

"When will your people arrive?" I asked.

"In a few minutes. They're all local."

I studied the tiny house. "You can get them all in the center?"

She pointed across the street. "Our meetings are held in a side room in the Beacon. The owner lets neighborhood organizations meet for free. We have planning and training get-togethers there."

"Excuse me?" said a voice at my back. "Are you in charge?"

I turned to a slender woman with blonde hair and intelligent eyes, a blue backpack over one shoulder. I gave her a raised eyebrow, *What?* Cruz turned to listen, sensing something in the young woman's nervous voice.

"I'm Liza Krupnik. I volunteer here, on the staff. Meelia called us, something about attacks on the center?"

"Do you know anything?" Cruz asked.

The woman looked away, her pale face reddening with embarrassment. "I, uh, can't be sure. I'm still trying to process . . ."

"We're in a hurry here."

"I, uh, found a hidden article, angry and full of slurs against women. Ugly, really. I never thought –"

"You have this thing?" Cruz asked.

The woman slung off her backpack and pulled out a sheaf of clipped-together pages. "I made a copy . . . I'm not sure if I should have it."

Cruz began reading aloud. ". . . *Analyze the hierarchy of femicentric organizations and one invariably discovers moronic followers led by a few 'intellectual' lesbians for whom the control of the robo-slut masses fills the void of the missing penis . . .*"

"One of the more rational passages," Krupnik said.

Cruz flipped a page. ". . . *women are by nature id-driven proto-humans clinging to men for food, clothing, shelter, protection (and any baubles they can wring from their bread-winner) in one breath, using the next breath to decry their 'victimization' at the hands of men. This anti-male movement has systematically castrated an entire gender, leaving them wallowing in the shit of self-pity and begging their whore overlords for mercy . . .*"

"My boss hid it in a book in his office," Krupnik said, crimson with embarrassment. "He was acting so strange and I was curious and –"

"What's his name?" Cruz interrupted. "Your boss."

"Sinclair. Doctor Thalius Sinclair. I teach undergrad classes for him, know his work. It's his style, but . . . the words are so ugly."

"Where could we find Sinclair?" I asked.

"He might be in his office, but he doesn't keep a regular schedule and . . ." I saw her eyes move from my face to behind me.

"There he is," she said, eyes wide in amazement, pointing across the street. "Professor Sinclair."

Moving at double-time into the bar was the scowling man whose table I had usurped when Harry did his act and I'd needed to surveil the center.

Had Sinclair been doing the same?

Rein heard a sound at her back, swung her head. A tunnel entering the cavern held the outline of a man, slender. He wore a cowboy hat over his eyes and she saw a holster at his belt, slung low, like in old movies. The other side of his belt held a knife. He wore a flannel shirt and jeans, hiking boots at bottom.

I hear his breathing, Rein registered, her heart pounding. *Fast and shallow: Fear? Anger? Arousal?* "Who are you?" she asked as he walked within a dozen feet, stopped.

"You will never, ever, ask me a question," the man replied. "The next question will be met with pain. Do you understand?"

"Yes," Rein said quietly.

"Ask me a question."

"You just said I couldn't –"

"Please. Ask me a question."

"Where am –"

374

He crossed the room in a heartbeat, slapping her. "Ask me a question," he repeated.

"I don't want to," Rein whispered, hand to her stinging cheek.

"See how it works?" he said.

Rein nodded and started to sit up.

"No," he said. "Lay flat on the floor. Look up at the ceiling, not at me. If you look at me I'll have to discipline you."

Rein did as ordered. Her captor produced three lanterns from the wooden cabinet, lighting them. He sat on the chair and she felt him staring at her for several minutes.

"When will you ripen?" he finally asked. "Soon, right?"

"I don't understand."

He bent and spoke slowly, like Reinetta was a five-year-old. "When . . . will . . . you . . . ripen?"

"I don't understand the question. I'm sorry."

"It doesn't matter," he said, turning and walking away. "I'll smell it."

I unsnapped the restraint strap on my under-jacket weapon as we entered the Beacon's meeting room. Carol was assembling directors and upper-level staff, a half-dozen women and one man in attendance. Carol was gesturing toward the man.

". . . Doctor Thalius Sinclair is with us today. Most won't know him, since he's not directly affiliated with the center – a very busy man – but he's instrumental in our work. Ms Balfours asked that he be included in today's . . ."

Sinclair was big and powerful looking, wearing a light jacket loose enough to conceal an armory. He was studying the floor and scowling. I caught Cruz's eye and nodded toward Sinclair. We slipped to the man's side. Cruz produced the gold badge and tapped his shoulder, provoking a glare.

"Come with us, Professor," she said. "We need to talk."

He glowered at Cruz, not recognizing me. "What's going on here?"

"Get out of that chair, please," Cruz said. "Hands away from your body."

The room went silent. A handsome sixtyish woman in a red dress was standing in a corner with arms crossed, watching. "Excuse me," she said. "What do you think Professor Sinclair has done?"

"Get up, Sinclair," I said. "Hands out."

Sinclair stayed seated, hands wide to his sides. The woman crossed the room to stand before us. "I repeat," she said. "What has Dr Sinclair done?"

"Who are you?" I asked, maybe not as politely as I might.

"My name is Dorothy Balfours. I'm a director of the center. And who are you?"

I heard Cruz's whisper at my ear, so close I could feel its warmth. "Miz Balfours has big money and big friends, Carson. Be nice."

"I'm Detective Carson Ryder, Ms Balfours," I said, switching to a more civil tone. "We're here because it seems the professor has very ugly thoughts about women."

"Bullshit," Balfours said. "I've known Dr Sinclair for over thirty years. He's the driving force behind the creation of the women's center: his idea, my money."

I removed the pages supplied by Krupnik from my briefcase and held them toward her. Sinclair saw the screed against women. "Oh shit," he said, slumping. "That thing."

Balfours donned reading glasses, took the sheaf and studied for a three-count before handing it back.

"I know this work," she said. "I edited it."

"What?" Cruz said.

"It was my small way of helping Dr Sinclair with his magnum opus."

It seemed the world had gone mad. "Magnum opus?" I croaked.

Sinclair sighed from his chair, crossed one leg over the other. "I'm currently researching and writing a history of misogyny."

"This?" I said, waving the sheaf of hateful pages.

"Of course not that," Sinclair said, rolling his eyes. "What you're holding is bait."

"Can someone help me understand what's going on?" Cruz said.

"I'd like that, too," Sinclair echoed.

The loft of an elegant eyebrow said Ms Balfours would be appreciative of same.

We studied one another like visitors from different planets.

58

"This horror is inside the system *now*?" Sinclair said after my three-minute synopsis of events. "Christ." He shook his head in disbelief. "It's for real."

"What's for real?" Cruz asked.

"A destructive action against women. I've been hearing about it for months."

"How about you start at the beginning?" I said.

"The real beginning starts forty years ago."

"Edit tight."

Sinclair paced the room as he spoke, hands in pockets. He looked like a hulking pirate someone had mistakenly dressed in tweed and corduroy.

"My father died when I was eight. My mother remarried when I was ten, an angry and domineering military man who called me Sissy, Nancy-boy, Faggot . . . If I challenged him I'd regain consciousness five minutes later.

It was horrific is all I'll say. When she'd gotten me safely off to college my mother walked out. My stepfather found and killed her."

Faces dropped in the audience, intakes of breath. Murmurs of consolation. Judging by the faces, only Miz Balfours had known of Sinclair's history. Sinclair continued.

"I finally felt I could deal with my history from an intellectual point of view by writing a book. I researched misogynist websites but needed a more personal interaction with these . . . people. I learned the language of hate and joined in secretive chat rooms using the idiotic handle of Promale. I joined extreme sites and met all manner of women-haters, most of whom were notable only in their insecurities. Some, however . . ." He raised a dark eyebrow.

"Were flat-out scary," I finished.

"One of the most disturbing entities went by HP Drifter. He was intelligent – very well spoken when not ranting – yet brimming with hatred. I yearned to get closer, to find the genesis of his hatred. But I was just one more angry newcomer to that world."

"It's hard to gain acceptance," I said. "The paranoia effect." I'd done research on the Aryan movement, knew newbies were automatically suspected of being plants.

A wry smile from Sinclair. "I engineered a break-through, Detective: I revealed to Drifter that a fellow chat-room member named Raisehell was a spy."

"Excuse me, Doc," Cruz said. "But how could you know that?"

Sinclair set his hands like a pianist spanning five octaves. "Two computers. My right hand played Promale, my left played Raisehell. I built suspicious little aspects into Raisehell. Promale detected them, snitched to HP Drifter."

"Creating a bonding experience with HP Drifter," I said, impressed.

"It allowed me to tout an anti-feminist essay I'd written. Such screeds abound, but Dorothy and I engineered mine to push every button –"

"Academic and insane in equal measure," Balfours said.

"These people love pseudo-intellectual justifications of their pathology,' Sinclair said. 'Drifter was excited by my screed, ready to appoint me philosopher of his movement. He implied it was about to enter a new phase, something big was about to happen. But in that nasty little world . . ."

"Everyone's planning something," I finished.

"Still, something in Drifter felt sinister. I was trying to get closer to him with the screed. Then something amazing happened: I found out who he is . . ." Sinclair clapped his big hands. "Bang! Just like that."

"You know who Drifter is?" Cruz said.

Sinclair pulled pages from his briefcase and a pen from his pocket and began underlining. "Copies of a recent chat-room conversation," he said.

I peered over his shoulder at the underlined text:

PROMALE: I've got to get away for a while. Somewhere beyond the whining and mewling of
women.
HPDRIFTER: I go to the forest to escape the
castrating whores. There are mountains near. I
sit in silence and plan the destruction of the
Femisluticunt cabal.
PROMALE: Solitude!
HPDRIFTER: Yes. I love smelling pinesap and
hearing streams tumbling down ravines like
surprised by their joy.
PROMALE: Beautiful words, Drifter. You have
poetry in your soul.
HPDRIFTER: I take my handle from the Clint Eastwood movie, High Plains Drifter. Sometimes I
think I'm a solitary rider alone with the wind as
it hisses through the pines and the moonlight
snow is covered with the tracks of mule deer
and rabbits.
PROMALE: Thank you for sharing. I have to go,
Drifter, things to do.

"I'm missing something," I said.

"Just hours before this conversation occurred, I'd
spoken with a minor character in my department, an
undergrad working – slowly and poorly – on a degree
in sociological statistics. While waiting for him to make
some copies, it occurred to me that I'd been a bit hard

on the pathetic sap. So I took a few moments to talk to him, a meaningless chat about loving the outdoors."

"And?"

Sinclair took the pages and snicked them with a finger. "The underlined words in the chat-room conversation are virtually identical to things I said to the undergrad . . . a boring little fellow named Robert Trotman."

59

Her captor seemed to move in and out of the cavern for no particular reason, Rein noted from the floor of the cave, her eyes riveted on the rock above. Sometimes he crossed at the edge of the room, sometimes making a point of stepping over her. It seemed ritualistic, as if he needed to demonstrate the territory was his. There was something childlike in his motions.

"I have to pee," Rein said on his fourth repetition. "Plus the other."

Robert Trotman stared. She said, "You do them, too, I expect."

He left the chamber without saying a word. Rein heard the scrape of a shovel. He returned ten minutes later with a coil of lariat in his hand.

"Sit up and lean your head forward."

Taking a deep breath, Rein did as told. The man swung

a noose-like coil in front of her. "Put your head in there," he said.

"Can't I just –"

"PUT YOUR FUCKING HEAD THERE, YOU LITTLE PUNK!"

Rein shot a glance at her captor. He seemed to be looking through her with eyes like stones. She held up her hands in acquiescence and slipped her head through the circle of rope. He pulled tight and Rein's hands went to her neck. "Y-you're choking me," she gasped. His eyes flickered as if awakening from a reverie. He fed rope through his palm, loosening the coil, and walked her like an upright dog down a lantern-lit tunnel, Rein moving in six-inch steps, all her leg-hobble allowed.

He pointed to a fresh hole in the ground and pulled a wad of tissues from his pocket, tossing them to the floor. Rein lowered her jeans and panties and positioned herself over the hole. He backed up a few feet, feeding out rope. Finished, she wiped with the tissue. A dark stain caught her eye, blood.

She'd started her period.

Rein turned away and secured her jeans. The man stood across the room, shovel in one hand, and rope in the other. Rein thought a moment, stepped back from the hole, stared at her captor as if waiting for him to perform a task.

"What?" Trotman said.

"Cover it up so we don't have to smell it." She put a

whisper of demand in her voice. He frowned and started forward, stopped himself.

"Cover your own shit," he said, throwing the shovel to the floor. Rein picked up the implement and began slowly scraping puffs of dirt over her excretion, feeling the shovel's weight and balance.

"Enough," he ordered. "Set the shovel down."

Rein judged the distance to her captor at a dozen feet. He had his end of the rope wrapping a wrist.

"Just another little bit," she said.

Her captor tugged the rope, pulling Rein off balance. "Put the shovel down, whore!"

Again, she thought. *Do that again, harder.* She started to scrape another puff of dirt into the hole. He yanked hard, the rope pulling Rein toward him. She launched, bound legs jumping twice, halving the distance, quartering it. Rein swung the shovel like an ax, the blade slicing toward his head. He threw up his arm in wide-eyed defense, ducking. The shovel slammed his shoulder and swooped over his head. He dove back, tightening the rope, a flaming wire around Rein's neck.

She tumbled to the floor.

"YOU WHORE!" Trotman screamed, his words echoing down the rock corridors. He put his foot on her chest and pulled the rope tighter, cutting deep into her flesh. Rein felt her face swelling, saw the rock walls begin to swim in a lazy circle. Her eyes felt like they were about to explode. Rein's captor moved his foot to her throat as he leaned low, sniffing the air above Rein like a rare wine.

His nostrils flared. "You went ripe," he said. "I smell it."

He went to the corner, opened a trunk and produced a rag and a metal bottle.

Cruz and I sent everyone from the room except for Sinclair. I tried to keep the incredulity from my voice as I studied the professor. "You're saying the hardcore misogynist in the chat room – HPDrifter – is some guy in your own department?"

"I couldn't believe my eyes," Sinclair said. "There was no doubt Trotman was HPDrifter. The asshole I'd been trying to dissect for weeks was just down the hall from me. I was pretty sure Drifter worked in a university setting. He was always ragging on college women and intellectuals. And he referred to my in-process diatribe as a manuscript, the proper academic term."

"What'd you do when you found out?" Cruz asked. "With Trotman?"

"We were alone in the office yesterday. I tried to bond with him, pretending to be half screwy, affecting some anti-women attitudes. He was scared and pleased in equal measure, not knowing the best way to please Daddy. I made sure to pat his skinny butt, a little homoerotic behavior is catnip to these pinheads. I invited him to dinner this weekend."

"Why?"

"To pretend to buddy-bond for another week or so, find out what made him tick – part of my research – then chuck his ass out the door."

"That's too weird," Cruz said. "The guy you're after is a colleague."

"I started thinking about it," Sinclair said. "And it made perfect sense. If you're a misogynist statistics student who lives in this locale, getting into the Sociology department here would be a coup."

Cruz nodded. "The Women's Studies department is part of the Sociology department."

"The plan was, in its own nasty way, inspired," Sinclair continued. "Little Bobby Trotman doubtless saw himself as a master spy gathering information about the enemy. If you dream yourself as leading an uprising against women, where better to battle them than from behind enemy lines?"

"Unfortunately," I said, "Robert Trotman didn't just dream of leading an uprising, Professor. He was commanding one."

Cruz and I stepped outside and told the center folks they could return to the meeting room, and to hang loose. Liza Krupnik looked worn and I figured she was dreading telling her boss she'd grabbed his papers. We still had the issue of the security code given to Bromley, then to Bemis, who'd opened the system as if cracking a coconut. Cruz had some calls out. Her cell rang and she took it. I watched her face turn to puzzlement. She stepped to the curb and stared upwards with a confused frown. She ended her call with her head shaking.

"Campus security reports that Trotman's not in the Sociology building," she said.

"You got his address, right?" I said. "Where he lives?"

"We're already there, Carson," she said. "We're at his front door."

"What?"

She pointed to the apartment above the Beacon. "According to university records, Trotman's been living above the bar for one year and two months."

Robert Trotman's rooms had less personality than the waiting room at a muffler-repair shop. There was a chair in which to sit, a folding table from which to ingest food, a chest of drawers for the scant array of clothing. His bed was a mattress beside a shade-less lamp. The kitchen held only a stove, microwave and refrigerator, nothing in the latter save for a carton of apple juice and a dozen cheap frozen dinners. The bathroom held the basic personal-maintenance items. There was no television, no radio.

There was, however, a professional-grade camcorder set on a tripod and aimed across the street at the center. "I'll bet he records every second," Cruz said, checking the angle of the lens. "Who goes in and out, license plates. Everything."

"Cerberus," I said. "The dog that never sleeps."

We creaked across the age-warped floor, not covered by so much as a ratty rug. "It's like a shell in here," I said. "Not even a computer."

"He probably uses a laptop," Cruz said. "Boulder has free wifi everywhere."

I stood back and studied the sad and desolate digs. Something didn't add up, and I thought of obsessive people I'd dealt with in the past.

"Trotman doesn't live here," I said.

"What are you talking about, Carson?" Cruz said. "It's a shitty little life, from the looks of things, but –"

"He eats and sleeps and performs his ablutions here. But he doesn't *live* here."

"Ah. You mean he comes alive somewhere else."

"Where he lives the fantasy. Where he's not Robert Trotman, minor academic assistant in statistical analysis or whatever."

"Scary shit," Cruz said, checking a closet. I saw her start to close the door, pause, stick her head back inside. The next thing I knew she was on her hands and knees, leaning her head to the floor.

"Think the camera is something, Carson?" she said. "Come take a listen."

I dropped to hands and knees and listened between slats in the floor. I heard the jukebox in the bar, an old Green Day piece. I listened closer.

"*. . . maybe we should contact other centers and . . .*" Madrone.

"*. . . hold on until the detectives find out something that . . .*" Balfours.

"*. . . you found and copied my little piece of fiction, Liza? . . .*" Sinclair. Laughing, thankfully.

"We're directly above the meeting room," I said. "You can hear every word."

Cruz shook her head. "Didn't Madrone say they had meetings and training sessions down there? Talking about everything from procedures to passwords?"

"Answers that question," I said.

60

We figured Bromley and Trotman were in league, having met over the net or via one of Bromley's trips to the law firm's Colorado escape in Aspen. Trotman had wormed into the university job and taken up residence above the bar. His spying provided the password to the center's computer. Then Bromley put Bemis on the job and they gained all the access they needed.

When a woman boarded the train, Trotman positioned himself to intercept her. We figured he was probably watching as Lainie Krebbs emerged into the Boulder night, hoping she was free. He followed her, found out where she was living, passed the word to Bromley, who discovered the woman's husband was a fellow Mobilian. He reeled the ridiculous Krebbs into his net like a panfish.

I relayed the bizarre story to the center's people.

Sinclair pulled me aside. "You don't think my piece, my false work in any way helped them . . ."

"This madness started before you put out your bait, Dr Sinclair," I said. "You did nothing but draw interest."

"How long have they been killing?"

"We're uncertain. One woman from Mobile was found in Denver. A woman found in Utah. They abducted a woman in Florida and held her until her boyfriend could come from Boise to kill her. Plus we have Butterfly Lady: a woman found in the Mobile dump who's never been identified."

Sinclair frowned. "Butterfly?"

"She had a tiny tattoo on her back, a butterfly."

I saw Sinclair waver as if about to faint. I grabbed his arm.

"What's wrong, Professor?"

"Dr Bramwell, our head of Gender Studies, has a tattoo like that."

"Is she Hispanic, athletic?"

He nodded. "Her father's from the US, but her mother's from Ecuador. She's a bicycle fanatic and a skier."

I guided Sinclair to a bench outside the Beacon where he sat with his head in his hands. Traffic whizzed by, oblivious to the drama a dozen feet away.

"Trotman begged Dr Bramwell to let him into the department," he said softly. "She took pity on the guy because he seemed so lost. She had him doing statistical analyses of women's salary histories in various fields. She was getting suspicious of his conclusions, thought him a bit sloppy." Sinclair looked at me. "Jesus, Detective, what if she confronted him about it?"

I looked into the stream of cars and bicyclists moving past, considering the ease with which Trotman could have waylaid the woman. No eavesdropping, no computer passwords, simply arrive shortly before Bramwell was due to leave the country. Trotman had likely taken her to some offsite lair, kept her for a week or so, and called his buddy Nathaniel Bromley.

"Can you run up to a place in Missouri, brother? I'll have a package for you."

We thought Butterfly Lady a runner in the system, but in all likelihood she was a woman who had performed a kindness for Robert Trotman, paying the ultimate price for her compassion.

The day had been long and wearing, a mix of luck and coincidence, despair and hope. The next step was finding Robert Trotman, which would take manpower and a blizzard of *Be On the LookOuts*. Cruz's people worked while we grabbed snippets of sleep, starting afresh in the morning. It turned out that Robert Trotman had grown up in a tiny desert community between Boulder and Denver. The local cops had been canvassing the old digs, and we headed over there, finding a rough outskirts neighborhood of desolate trailer courts and tight streets with bungalows falling into rotting disrepair. Everything seemed the color of desperation.

The sun still low in the desert-wide eastern sky, Cruz

conferred with a young guy in uniform, nodded, walked back to the car. "We've got something," she said, pulling from the curb. "Miz Emily Adams, school nurse at Bellville Elementary School. Been there twenty-one years. She became agitated when asked about Robert Trotman."

The principal led us to the office of the school nurse, walls dressed with colorful children's drawings. Nurse Adams was a small and round woman in her fifties, brown hair going gray, her eyes dark and piercing over the tops of her half-glasses.

"I recall little Bobby from the fifth and sixth grades. Some children stay with you, but so do nightmares."

"Nightmares?" Cruz said.

"It was a dysfunctional family. Abuse. As bad as I've ever seen."

"You met them, then?"

"I went to the house to talk to the mother once. Robert had head lice and I wanted to explain treatment and prevention."

"The father wouldn't let you in?" I said.

"The mother. She was a big woman, drunk. Unwashed. She bellowed at me to get off her property and never come back. Her breath was the worst thing I ever smelled, and I'm a nurse."

I looked to Cruz. "Doesn't sound like the kind of woman who'd take much abuse."

"Not the mother," Adams said. "She ruled that house like the Queen of Crazy."

"Mother was the abuser?" Cruz said.

"The husband was handicapped, a leg gone up high, one arm missing at the elbow. I heard from another teacher she'd push over his wheelchair on the porch, kick him around, call him every name in the book while he tried to crawl back to his wheels. If that was in public, I can't imagine behind closed doors." Adams's face wrinkled as if smelling Trotman's mother's breath. "There was no morality in that house. Nothing was normal."

"How do you know that?" I asked.

Adams lowered her voice. "The school psychologist told me. She wanted me to understand why Robert was put in foster care later that year."

We thanked Nurse Adams for her help and were walking out the door when she spoke. "Detectives?"

We turned. Nurse Adams swallowed hard. "When I was checking Robert for the lice, he had a foul odor coming from him. I asked him what that smell was."

"What did he say?" I asked.

"He said it was Mommy."

"We've got a hit, Harry," Sally Hargreaves said from the chair on Nautilus's front porch, calling over her shoulder and into the house. "A patrol car just made the ID."

The door opened. "Bromley?"

"He's back. His big bright car is parked a half-block down the street from the women's center."

"Then lawyer-boy still doesn't know Krebbs is at the Prosecutor's office singing his lungs out."

Hargreaves grinned as she stood. "Sometimes staying incommunicado can be a bitch."

"Tell the cops to detain Bromley if he tries to leave the area, Sally, but otherwise they're to stay out of sight."

Hargreaves relayed the message as they strapped on their weapons and moved the operation to the cruiser in Nautilus's drive.

61

We stood outside the school as Cruz checked with her people, busily tearing apart the box Robert Trotman had placed around his life. "No one's found a single friend," Cruz said as we turned toward the car. "What Trotman does have is permits for four weapons, and those are probably just the ones on the books."

"Gimme the news."

"A Ruger Bearcat .22 revolver, a Colt .45 six-shooter with a ten-inch barrel, a 30-30 Winchester Model 1894 . . ."

"Cowboy-style guns," I said.

Cruz laughed without mirth. "You haven't heard the best. Trotman has a Henry .45 magnum lever-action rifle. Guess what the model is called."

I shrugged. "The Ranger?"

"The Big Boy."

"Jesus," I said. "HP Drifter has his Big Boy loaded."

We climbed into the cruiser. Cruz said, "Seems the only real people this loser ever associated with were in the department. They were as close as he ever came to human interaction, and he killed one of them."

We went to the Sociology department of the university. Sinclair's office was relatively spacious, the walls taken up with books stacked on end, on sides, on tops of one another. "I've been reading every online communication with Trotman–Drifter," he said. "Trying to see into him."

"Trotman couldn't have given away much," Cruz said. "He spent fifteen hours a week down the hall and you never noticed."

"But now that I know, places and actions make more sense." Sinclair said. "Drifter mentions hiking from Stegosaurus ridge toward the notch."

Cruz thought for a second. "From the Flatiron Mountains to Saddle Rock."

Sinclair nodded and turned back to his printouts. Cruz and I went down the hall to Liza Krupnik. She was curled in a chair. Her eyes were red from crying.

"He really killed Dr Bramwell?"

"I'm sorry, but it doesn't look good," Cruz said.

Krupnik suppressed a shiver. "There were times we were alone together."

"He was probably happily using you. He knew you worked at the women's center?"

"Of course. He always seemed interested in what we did. Now I know why."

"Did you tell him when you had meetings and such?"

Krupnik nodded to her wall. "All he had to do was check my calendar. It's all there."

I studied the wall. Another mystery solved. Trotman knew whenever the center folks gathered to discuss business, changes in procedures, passwords and so forth. He'd be a few feet above with his ear to the floor. Trotman may have been subject to several pathologies, but he was a hell of a planner. Obsession can do that.

"Trotman was your friend?" Cruz asked Krupnik.

"I felt sorry for him because he seemed so afraid. Especially of Dr Sinclair. Robert practically ran when he saw the professor coming."

"Odd," Cruz said.

"Not really," I said. "Sinclair is big, strong and outdoorsy. Assertive. Unabashedly masculine. Sinclair's everything Trotman wishes to be, consciously or subconsciously. It's probably less fear of Sinclair than awe."

We heard the big voice of Sinclair boom down the hall.

"DETECTIVES! Come here!"

We jogged back to find Sinclair waving a page of print. "A sentence from a month back. I asked, or rather, Promale asked, 'Where is your favorite place to escape the whores, Drifter? Where do you go when it all gets too much?' He replies, 'Neverland.' Another online character asks, 'Like Peter Pan? LOL'. Drifter says, 'My Neverland is a world of its own. I am king of Neverland, the Guy whose day is about to come.' I thought it seemed odd at the time, but Drifter had flights of weirdness. I never made a connection until thinking regionally."

"I'm not getting it," I said.

"I sure as hell am," Cruz said. "Nederland."

"What?"

"Nederland is a small town fifteen miles west of here, famous for Frozen Dead Guy Days – a festival where there's actually a frozen dead man on display."

"Trotman's making word play?" I said. "The live guy in Neverland?"

"Or the dead man about to be awakened," Sinclair suggested. "There are metaphors aplenty."

Cruz said, "I'll get the Trotster's pic sent to the local constabulary."

We waited for two hours, Sinclair continuing to pore over his messages, finding other allusions: "*There are no bleeding whores in Neverland.*" "*When I am in Neverland I am at True Home.*" Sinclair read passages from the Trotman/Drifter chat rooms. Sometimes Drifter sounded like a commando on steroids, sometimes a whiney child.

Cruz's phone rang, one of her colleagues who had been in Nederland for ninety minutes, checking computer records. She spoke, looked at me with a thumbs-up, rang off.

"Robert Trotman owns eight acres of land southwest of Mud Lake. Purchased eleven months back. His piece of Neverland."

"Where the Lost Boys never grow up," Sinclair said, recalling the Barrie tale about Peter Pan.

Harry Nautilus and Sally Hargreaves were one hundred feet behind the bumper of Nathaniel Bromley's Benz, bent low in the seats and watching. Bromley had exited the car, strutting down the block twenty paces before returning, his eyes always on the building, as if measuring something.

"Ready?" Nautilus said.

Hargreaves nodded. They pulled past the lawyer, who didn't notice. The pair exited the car, walking quietly to the man's back. "Getting ready for the big show, Mr Bromley?" Nautilus asked. "Figuring out the camera angles?"

Bromley spun, frowned. "Our stalwart detectives. Are you following me? Do I have to call your chief?"

"I was simply checking on the center, Mr Bromley," Hargreaves said. "I have friends there."

The man's frown turned to a grin. "No doubt. You seem the type."

"What type is that, sir?"

Bromley grinned and ignored the question, turning to the center and giving the detectives his back. He bounced on his heels, a contented man. "You mentioned camera angles, Detective. I'm thinking the TV people could grab an establishing shot of the logo, pan to me for a close-up. Sound good?"

"When do the fire trucks come in?" Hargreaves asked.

"Fire trucks?"

"You're about to burn down a crucial service that women's centers offer."

"Just the ones that engage in brainwashing. It's been going on far too long."

Nautilus stepped into Bromley's view. "How about your buddy Larry Krebbs? He gonna be part of things?"

"Larry's our plaintiff. He has a story to tell."

"*Our* plaintiff? You're representing some kind of group? Like a class-action suit?"

Bromley paused. "A figure of speech. *The* plaintiff."

"Playing the part of the man who lost his wife to the women's underground railroad?" Hargreaves said, stepping forward. "That sisterhood of death?"

"Come watch the show, hon," Bromley winked. "Or stay home. It'll be on all the channels."

"How about your wife, Nate?" Nautilus asked. "Will she be here to balance the story?" He watched as Bromley's smile flickered. It was less than a microbeat before the teeth returned. The man did a credible perplexed, Nautilus thought.

"I'm not married. What do you mean, balance?"

"The woman who escaped her scumbucket abuser and made it to safety," Hargreaves said. "I hear she's a happy woman these days."

"Who the hell are you talking about?"

"Your wife, Nate," Nautilus said. "You and Larry sure are forgetful about women."

"I just told you, I'm not –"

"How about the company party?" Hargreaves interrupted. "Dribbling your date's head on the desk like a basketball? That still in the ol' memory box?"

Bromley spun to Hargreaves. "There are laws against slander, girly. You better be damn ready to prove what you say. And it sounds to me like you've got nothing more than a big leaky pail of hearsay."

Nautilus crowded closer. "We know about the woman in Pensacola, Nate. And Utah. We know about Boulder and Trotman."

Bromley cocked his head, seemingly amused. "Is there a reason you're reciting a list of names and locales that have no meaning to me? I've already said I'm a frequent visitor to Colorado. I've met dozens, no hundreds, of folks up there. In bars, restaurants, on the ski slopes. So many I can't begin to remember them all, much less what we may or may not have talked about. Are you trying to gin up some kind of circumstantial evidence? Good luck. I eat that kind of thing for breakfast."

"Your buddy Trotman's holding a woman," Nautilus said, tiring of the game. "We need you to tell us where to find him."

"What is a Trotman?" Bromley sneered. "Does it have to do with horses?"

"Trotman's the guy who brought you and Larry Krebbs a woman in Missouri, remember? Wrapped in a tarp. Her name was Judith Bramwell, a professor at the University of Colorado. She died in your trunk in Vicksburg while you and Larry were having lunch."

"Tarps? Vicksburg? Lunch? What are you babbling about?"

"Your good brother Larry confessed to everything, Nate," Nautilus said quietly. "It seems he's having *you* for lunch."

Bromley froze for a millisecond, then shook his head and flicked a piece of lint from his lapel. Nautilus knew the lawyer's mind was moving at warp speed, weighing the angles. "Larry Krebbs is a loser's loser and a congenital liar, Detective. Whatever he's lying about has nothing to do with me. The man's sick in the head."

Hargreaves looked up the street and waved her hand in the air. A block distant a big Jerr-Dan car carrier roared from the curb toward the center, stopping in front of a gleaming black Mercedes.

"What's that for?" Bromley demanded.

"We're gonna haul your pretty car to our forensics bureau, Nate," Nautilus said. "Go through your trunk with a microscope."

Hargreaves stepped to Bromley, false concern dripping in her voice. "Did you clean the trunk real good after you got rid of Dr Bramwell, Nate? Or did you do a half-ass job, thinking a day like this could never come?"

She winked. Beads of sweat formed on the lawyer's brow as the carrier operator flipped a switch and the Mercedes rolled on to the transport platform.

"You better talk to me now, Nate," Nautilus said, pulling out the cuffs. "Otherwise it won't mean a thing."

"I . . . might have heard of a Bob Trotman," Bromley

said, his voice a dry rasp. "I think he works at the University of Colorado."

"We know that," Nautilus said. "Where is Trotman right now?"

The lawyer could only shake his head, *No idea.*

62

Cruz and I raced to Nederland at a hundred miles an hour, a State Police vehicle leading the way. It occurred to me that this was how everything started: racing to the morgue as Rein cleared the path.

"Bromley didn't know anything?" Cruz asked.

"Not about Trotman's whereabouts. At least, that's what he claims. I figure it's right."

"Have you got enough to hold him?"

"The current charge is conspiracy to commit murder. The judge took a look at the evidence and denied bail."

"A hotshot like Bromley got remanded to custody?"

"It seems the first thing the forensics people saw when they popped his trunk was a smear of blood beneath the carpet. Human blood that's now being tested for DNA."

"He didn't clean up? He had that much ego?"

"Whom the gods wish to destroy, they first exalt," I said. "What's the plan?"

Cruz shot a glance at her watch. "Strather's got his team moving, gonna direct the operation from above, says we're welcome to fly along."

"Nice of him to offer," I said.

"I think he's doing it to keep you in sight," she said. "Given how you started freelancing at Flood's place."

Rein opened her eyes to see a rectangular cavern, large, perhaps ten paces by eight. There was a table, a chair and ottoman, three lamps hung from beams, the light low and amber. Heat poured from a kerosene heater in a corner. Strips of plastic covered one end of the room, keeping the heat from escaping.

Living in a big cave, Rein thought. Like the fucking Flintstones.

There was a bookcase. A cedar chest. Atop a table in a corner sat a bowl and pitcher like in antique stores. But it was the décor that pulled Rein's awakening eyes: a huge poster from the movie *High Plains Drifter* centered the far wall, Clint Eastwood under a fiery sky, gun in one hand, whip in the other. Freakier were the half-dozen posters from the movie *300,* bands of rock-bodied Spartans with weapons drawn.

"I see you," said a voice from the far side of the strips. He entered with a collapsible sawhorse in one hand, a pair of boards in the other, spaghetti-strand muscles laboring against the weight.

"Your stench is about to make me puke," he said, setting up the sawhorses and laying boards between them. He left the room, returning a minute later with a cloth tool bag, setting it on the table at his back. "If you try to hurt me again I will shoot you in your guts and piss on you while you squirm. You will lay on this table and do exactly what I say."

He pulled the knife and sliced the tape. Rein felt blood flow back into her hands and feet.

"Take off your clothes. Don't look at me like that. DO IT!"

Rein stood naked before her captor. He stared with disgust. "Don't stand with your feet apart. Keep them tight."

Rein shuffled her feet together. "Lay on the board," he commanded, opening the tool bag and producing a roll of duct tape, binding Rein's ankles to the board. She expected her hands to be next and wondered if she could get her nails to his eyes. Instead, he produced a square of black oilcloth the size of a bandana. He set the cloth and tape on her belly.

"Tape the cloth to your stomach so the cloth goes over your thing."

Rein looked down at herself. "I don't understand."

"TAPE THE CLOTH OVER YOUR FILTHY CUNT, YOU STUPID COW!"

Dr Kavanaugh was right, Rein thought, stripping off a length of tape, her mind pushing free of the chloroform and thinking from a dozen directions at once. *He's*

408

terrified of my vagina. She laid the swatch of plastic over her groin, taped it down. Trotman produced a length of rope, snapping it between his hands. He reached into the bag and found a spoon, its edges polished bright, sharpened.

The rope will tie my torso down, Rein realized. *The spoon will remove my eyes.*

Rein's mind remembered something Carson had said about psychopaths: *When all else fails, and there's nothing between you and death, fuck with them.*

"Did you ever get that espresso machine?" she asked, fighting to keep the fright from her voice.

"What?"

"You were Astra," Rein said. "I see it now. You had me convinced you were a woman."

"I did what was necessary," Trotman grunted, pulling a bottle of alcohol from the bag.

"I'll bet you like being a woman. Wearing a big wig, putting on the make-up. It's fun, isn't it?"

"Shut up."

"You sure talked about sex a lot. Tantric sex with men? A transgendered partner? You ever get confused about just what –"

Trotman snarled and punched her face. "Wearing a wig," Rein continued, shaking off the blow. "A dress. Make-up. You liked being a woman, you freak. But you're a lousy woman and a worse man."

He hit her again, his fist bouncing off Rein's forehead. She saw stars.

"Eunuch," she spat. "Ball-less little scumba—"

Trotman roared and kicked at her head. The impromptu table tipped over, spilling Rein to the floor, feet bound to the wood. "LOOK WHAT YOU DID!" he screamed. "YOUR SICKNESS IS ALL OVER!"

Rein looked down. Her menstrual release was in full flow, blood running down the board from beneath her, smeared by her buttocks. The plastic was askew, her pubic hair in view.

"COVER YOURSELF!" he yelled, waving the gun. "COVER IT!"

Was it a fear of female genitalia? Rein wondered. *Or was it the menses?* She ran her hands across her labia, felt the wetness in her palms as he crouched and checked her bindings. Rein sprung forward, her gymnastics-trained body pushing the limits. She reached out, her hands wiping across his face and hair.

Trotman stumbled back grabbing at his face. He saw Rein's blood on his fingers. "I'M GOING TO DIG YOUR HEART OUT THROUGH YOUR EYES," he screamed, beginning to gag, running to the pitcher in the corner and pouring the bowl full, dunking his head in the water as if his face were on fire.

63

The helicopter skimmed the treetops, the snow-covered peaks of the high Rockies in the distance. We were heading toward Trotman's Neverland, Cruz and I in back, Strather and the pilot up front. The SWAT team was racing in from below, a couple miles behind us, moving along dirt roads.

"It looks like the middle of nowhere," Cruz yelled over the roar of the engine. "But it's twenty minutes to downtown Boulder."

Strather alternately studied the map in his hands and looked out the window through massive binoculars. "ETA is four minutes," he said, frowning down at the verdant ridge top. "I'm not seeing a place to set down."

Her captor gagging and splashing water over himself in the far corner of the room, Rein's eyes frantically searched the dirt. She saw the upended bottle of alcohol, the roll of tape . . .

Where is it?

There! In the dust at her feet. Rein snatched the sharpened silver spoon from the dirt. It took two strokes to cleave the tape from her ankles. The man was hunched over the bowl splashing soap and water across his face.

"This FILTH is ALL OVER ME!"

Rein considered attacking with the spoon, but he had a gun. He lifted the bowl in both hands, pouring water over his head. She slipped between the plastic slats, bolted down the tunnel, lit by lamps hung every dozen or so feet. And then, to the side, another plastic-slatted opening. She poked her head through the plastic, looking for a way out.

His bedroom: a mattress on a log frame, a stump for a bedside table. Another fucking Eastwood poster. Two more *300* posters. An elk head above the bed. The kerosene heater. In the corner, a gun safe, sized for at least a dozen long guns. Rein dashed to the metal box. *Please*, she implored, *be open.*

The safe was locked. She spun back toward the tunnel. Saw a bottle of Hoppe's solvent beside the low bed, a box of barrel patches. Had he been cleaning . . .? A pistol! A .22 revolver on the floor, magazine snapped open. Rein grabbed it and ran. A howl of rage echoed through the mine. The bowl shattering, thrown.

"GET BACK HERE," the man screamed.

Rein vaulted back into the tunnel. The floor elevated

to her right, angling up. She ran like wolves were on her heels.

"The property is around here somewhere," Strather said, the chopper hovering three hundred feet above fir and aspen and jagged outcroppings of gray rock. My heart was as loud as the roar of the engine.

"When will the team catch up?" I yelled, two feet from Strather.

"Ten minutes," Strather said. "But I don't see any dwellings."

I looked down. The trees were evenly and thinly distributed. There weren't many places a cabin could be built.

"Over there," I said, catching a line through the green. "Is that a road?"

Strather lifted the binocs. "Good eyes," he said, giving a thumbs-up. "Not much more than a trail." He gestured for the pilot to track the road below and radioed directions to the on-racing team of warriors and medics.

Rein saw a pile of beams. A dead-end? She dashed to the pile of rotting wood, not a dead-end, but a subterranean crossroads. Darkness in both directions. Rein listened into the space at her back.

Nothing. What was he doing?

Rock chips exploded from the wall, stinging her face, the rifle shot cutting through the mine like a sonic knife. The man had visited his gun locker. Her captor loosed another shot and Rein heard the ugly *tup* as the slug

413

sizzled past her ear. She dove to the ground as a half-dozen more rounds clattered through the tunnel.

Then quiet. Reloading?

Rein had two directions she could go. She started to the left, stopped as the echoes of the gunshots faded. Was that the sound of a helicopter? No way. Still, she zigged to the right, shots starting again. He was running after her. The tunnel veered, almost black now. In her path lay a wall of boulders the size of appliances. Rein patted until finding an opening, pushed through. Rounds screamed into the rocks. But there, up ahead, was that light?

And dammit, that *was* a helicopter.

64

We followed the road, the pilot ascending to avoid a pillar of rock jutting past the trees. Strather was leaning forward, the lenses tight to his face. I saw his hand point before his voice spoke. "A vehicle, two o'clock, about five hundred yards. Looks like an Explorer. Black."

"What Trotman drives," Cruz confirmed.

The pilot banked and we were there in seconds, Strather sucking in detail, barking into his helmet mic, relaying the info to his team leader: ". . . road veers past creek bed, small ravine, cut to north another quarter mile. Truck against outcropping, west side. No subjects visible."

"It's mining country," Cruz said. "The ground is probably like a honeycomb."

"I've been after people up here before," Strather said. "If a mine opening's small and remote enough, you can hide it with deadfalls."

"We've got to get down there," I said.

"No LZ," the pilot said. "Not for miles."

"ETA on the team?" Cruz asked.

"Still ten minutes, Detective."

The pilot settled into a hover, waiting on further instructions. I saw him lift his sunglasses as if unsure of his eyes.

"Down there. What the hell's that?"

"What?" Strather said.

"Just popped out from under that cliff, look left."

Strather aimed the binocs. His mouth fell open. "Christ almighty," he said. "It's a naked woman tearing through the brush."

"I'm on it," the pilot said, nudging the controls as the chopper tumbled sideways. I could see her now, a blur of motion beneath the trees. I watched her stumble down an incline.

"It's Rein," I yelled.

"What's she running from?" Strather said as the upper windscreen shattered.

"We're taking fire!" the pilot yelled, instinctually rolling the chopper. Another round punched through the skin. "I see the shooter," the pilot called. "Nine o'clock, moving low and fast toward the woman. Rifle in hand, another over his shoulder."

"Trotman," I yelled. "Go after him."

"This ain't an Apache, Detective," he said. "It's a search-and-rescue craft. He can shoot this thing down."

As if knowing a point was to be made, another round

whanged off the craft. "Extra glasses?" I yelled to Strather, fingers indicating circles around my eyes. He reached to the pack at his feet and jammed binoculars into my hand as the pilot retreated to safer air. I searched the ground frantically, saw Rein running toward the jutting peak we'd just skirted, a solid wall of rock.

"NO!" I yelled. "OTHER WAY!

"Shit," Strather whispered, watching.

"What's going on?" Cruz said, her voice dry with fear.

"Rein's out of room," I said. "She's trapped."

"Come on!" Strather yelled into the microphone.

"How soon?" I said.

"Three minutes."

The helicopter was still in the air, Rein saw, but hanging in the distance, as if barred by an invisible shield from getting closer. The man had stopped running; he was moving towards her at a leisurely pace, an afternoon walk. Now and then he'd fire a shot, laugh. Rein's feet were bloody from running over shards of broken rock, her breath ragged gasps.

She ducked behind a tree and studied the path ahead, seeing why her pursuer was amused: a plate of gray rock rising into the sky, nowhere to hide. The man had only to walk up and shoot her.

Bang. Just like that.

Rein looked at the gun in her hand, five rounds in the chamber, 22-caliber, about as effective here as the plastic guns she'd carried as a child, pulling her badge and announcing she was Harriet Nautilus, Girl Cop. A slug whumped into the Douglas fir shielding her, telling her he knew where she was. Another laugh. He was a hundred feet away, Rein figured.

She looked up the rock wall ahead of her, a looming gray gravestone. Rein glanced around the tree, saw him closing in with a lever-action rifle in hand. He was wearing a goddamn cowboy hat.

"This what it takes to make you feel like a man?" she called. "Hunting a defenseless woman?"

"What's the best thing about a blow job?" he yelled back. "Ten minutes of silence."

"Who fucked you up most, sonny?" Rein called. "Mommy or Daddy?"

He growled something incomprehensible and fired into the tree. Rein held her breath, scrambled to another tree eight feet back. She was almost to the cliff.

He kept moving forward.

Down to this, Rein thought. She listened into her head, heard Carson's words from the long night at the range: *What I do is lock my shoulders, elbows and wrists into a solid unit and roll with my . . .*

"Step out here, Mama," the man said, two dozen feet away. She heard him cock the rifle. "I got more important things to do."

Rein dove out from behind the tree, hitting the ground and rolling. The man jacked his rifle to his shoulder . . .

* * *

418

"Did you see that?" Strather said, glasses to his eyes. "Jesus!"

"Is . . . am I seeing right?" I croaked, my heart so high in my throat I could barely speak.

"What is it?" Cruz said, shaking my arm. "What's going on?"

"I . . . think . . ." I couldn't speak. I could only shake.

"The shooter is down," Strather barked into his mic. "I repeat, The shooter is down. Approach with extreme caution."

"Carson?" Cruz said. But I could only open and close my mouth like a fish out of water. Cruz looked to Strather, his own glasses to his eyes.

"Your officer is on the move again," he grinned. "Looking safe and uninjured. Our people will have her in one minute."

65

The punch I made for the party at my place used rum and tequila and vodka and I called it Tubman's Delight, because three cups would put you underground. It seemed funny when I thought it up.

Everyone who'd worked close on the case attended except for Cruz, who said she had "more paperwork to do than there probably is in the world". But she was going to take a break next month, flying down to visit Casa Carson for at least a week, so the future was bright.

Rein was the star of the event. She wore a University of Colorado ski cap to hide her shiny pate, but everyone had to kiss the smooth terrain. She said you could make a wish and it would come true, called it baldhead voo-doo. People thought that was a lot funnier than Tubman's Delight.

About halfway through I was at the railing looking

out over the water. The moon was a new sliver, a "hopeful moon" Rein called it. She sashayed up to me, shot a glance behind her, Harry in a deck chair, Sally beside him. They looked good.

"How you doing, girl?" I asked.

"Trying to get the hate gang out of my head. It helps to realize a lot more women might have been killed if we hadn't dug Trotman out of the woodwork."

I nodded. "Little Bobby spent a lot of time cork-screwing himself into the university, a helluva plan. His only bad luck came when the head of his department started writing a history of misogyny. Even when Sinclair discovered Trotman, he had no idea the squirmy little monster was a killer." I grinned. "Nailing Trotman was your doing, Officer Early."

Rein turned to study the moon, her elbows on the railing. She stole another glance behind her, saw Harry wandering into the kitchen for a refill.

"Do you think Harry'll ever come to grips with me being a cop?" she asked, her voice low. "Stop worrying?"

"Fully? No. It's the way he is, Rein."

She sighed. "I'm re-thinking law school, Carson."

"For you, or for Harry?"

"I shouldn't put him through this any more. It's not fair to –" Rein's cell phone buzzed from her belt. She started to shut it off, saw the caller was Treeka Flood, now somewhere in Florida, Tommy Flood headed for federal prison.

I backed away and left Rein with her call. It was the

first Rein had heard from Treeka since the rescue and I could pretty much figure what Miz Flood had to say. The conversation took three minutes and when Rein returned to me her eyes glistened with tears.

"Treeka said . . . she said I gave her a chance to have, to have . . ."

"Yeah," I said. "Sometimes it happens like that."

Harry wandered up with a fresh drink and started to say something. He frowned at Rein. "What's wrong, girl? You look sad."

Rein wiped a tear from her cheek and downed the rest of her punch. She grinned and poked Harry in his belly.

Said, "Bet I can make detective faster than you did."

Killer Reads.com

The one-stop shop for the best in crime and thriller fiction

Be the first to get your hands on the **latest releases**, **exclusive interviews** and **sneak previews** from your favourite authors.

Browse the site and sign up to the newsletter for our pick of the **hottest** articles as well as a chance to **win** our monthly competition!

Writing so good it's criminal